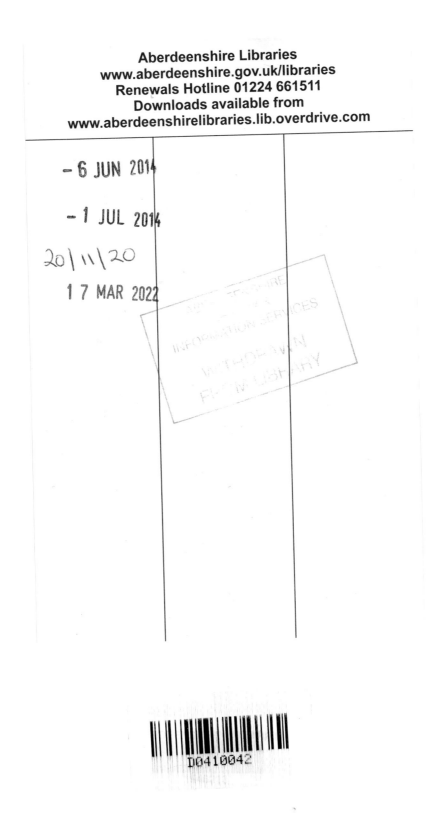

Mrs Caldicot's Knickerbocker Glory

Complete Guide To Sex (1993)
How to Conquer Backache (1993)
How to Conquer Arthritis (1993)
Betrayal of Trust (1994)
Know Your Drugs (1994, 1997)
Food for Thought (1994, 2000)
The Traditional Home Doctor (1994)
I Hope Your Penis Shrivels Up (1994)
People Watching (1995)
Relief from IBS (1995)
The Parent's Handbook (1995)
Oral Sex: Bad Taste And Hard To Swallow? (1995)
Why Is Pubic Hair Curly? (1995)
Men in Dresses (1996)
Power over Cancer (1996)
Crossdressing (1996)
How to Conquer Arthritis (1996)
High Blood Pressure (1996)
How To Stop Your Doctor Killing You (1996)
Fighting For Animals (1996)
Alice and Other Friends (1996)
Spiritpower (1997)
Other People's Problems (1998)
How To Publish Your Own Book (1999)
How To Relax and Overcome Stress (1999)
Animal Rights – Human Wrongs (1999)
Superbody (1999)
The 101 Sexiest, Craziest, Most Outrageous Agony Column
    Questions (and Answers) of All Time (1999)
Strange But True (2000)
Daily Inspirations (2000)
Stomach Problems: Relief At Last (2001)
How To Overcome Guilt (2001)
How To Live Longer (2001)
Sex (2001)
How To Make Money While Watching TV (2001)
We Love Cats (2002)
England Our England (2002)

novels
The Village Cricket Tour (1990)
The Bilbury Chronicles (1992)
Bilbury Grange (1993)
Mrs Caldicot's Cabbage War (1993)
Bilbury Revels (1994)
Deadline (1994)
The Man Who Inherited a Golf Course (1995)
Bilbury Country (1996)
Second Innings (1999)
Around the Wicket (2000)
It's Never Too Late (2001)
Paris In My Springtime (2002)
Mrs Caldicot's Knickerbocker Glory (2003)

short stories
Bilbury Pie (1995)

on cricket
Thomas Winsden's Cricketing Almanack (1983)
Diary Of A Cricket Lover (1984)

as Edward Vernon
Practice Makes Perfect (1977)
Practise What You Preach (1978)
Getting Into Practice (1979)
Aphrodisiacs – An Owner's Manual (1983)
The Complete Guide To Life (1984)

as Marc Charbonnier
Tunnel (novel 1980)

with Alice
Alice's Diary (1989)
Alice's Adventures (1992)

with Dr Alan C Turin
No More Headaches (1981)

Mrs Caldicot's Knickerbocker Glory

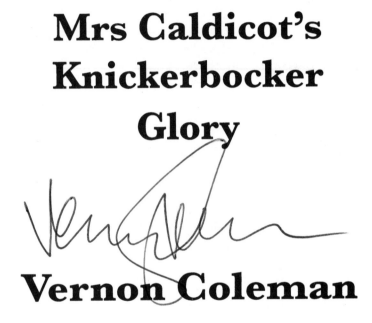

Vernon Coleman

Chilton Designs

Published by Chilton Designs, Publishing House, Trinity Place, Barnstaple, Devon EX32 9HJ, England

ISBN: 1 898146 60 8

A catalogue record for this book is available from the British Library.

FT

Printed by J.W. Arrowsmith Limited, Bristol

Dedication

To Donna Antoinette, my Welsh Princess, with my love

CHAPTER ONE

Anyone old-fashioned enough, and optimistic enough, to expect the calendar to give some guidance on temperature and weather might have expected a warm, sunny day; a few, small, fluffy white clouds scattered artistically across a perfectly sky-blue sky, jolly birds happily singing their little hearts out in a vain attempt to drown out the sound of suburban lawnmowers, and gardens everywhere a blaze of sunlit summer colour.

Such optimism would not have been well rewarded. It had been raining heavily for hours. In the traditional way things happen in a country where it rains for 300 days a year, downpipes were gurgling, drains were failing to cope with the flood of water and deep puddles were forming everywhere. In modern Britain a leaf or two on the lines will halt the heaviest and most majestic of trains; tons of highly crafted metal brought to a standstill by a modest flutter of nature's arboreal offcasts. A flake or two of snow will close motorways and send cars sliding and slithering out of control. And a few hours steady but unspectacular rain always seems to result in flooding.

There was, as usual, a huge puddle outside the front entrance to The Twilight Years Rest Home (prop. Thelma Caldicot, No Cabbages Allowed) and as the two ambulancemen carefully carried the occupied wheelchair in through the front door they found themselves splashing through water which reached well over the tops of their shoes.

'Oh, bugger!' cursed the younger of the two; a florid faced man, rather too overweight to be an advertisement for good health. He paused and looked down. 'My socks are soaked.'

'Stop moaning, keep moving and lift your end up,' retorted the older man, balding, thinner, altogether leaner and fitter looking.

The third figure in this moving tableau, the occupant of the wheelchair, said nothing. Since he seemed to be either asleep or drugged, this was not particularly surprising. He took no more interest in his surroundings than he would have done if he had been a sack of potatoes.

Earlier in its long life the building which was now known as the Twilight Years Rest Home had been the imposing residence of an important local Victorian entrepreneur called Baldcock.

Mr Baldcock had made a substantial fortune out of the manufacture of sewage pipes and, anxious to obtain a social status above and beyond that which the manufacturer of such an unappetising product might expect, had spared no expense to give his family a substantial and worthy home. The hall and landing windows were made of stained glass, the drainpipes and gutters were decorated with cast iron gargoyles and the stonework above the bay windows was more than amply decorated with numerous stony representations of well fed cherubs. And, naturally, the front door was protected from the elements by a large open fronted porch with a tiled floor. Six stone steps led from the puddled driveway to the porch and the two ambulancemen climbed these steps at commendable speed. The porch was so large that even two ambulancemen and a wheelchair did not overcrowd it.

'Funny looking place,' said the younger of the two ambulancemen, a youth who was known to his mother and girlfriend as Cyril and to everyone else as 'Chips' (a nickname which accurately reflected his dietary taste).

'Don't take any notice of the building,' said Bertie, his colleague. 'This is Mrs Caldicot's place.'

'Mrs Caldicot?'

'You've not heard of her?'

Chips shook his head.

'Her relatives put her into a nursing home. She couldn't stand the smell of cabbage so she led a revolution. Took all the other residents with her to stay in a hotel. Then went back and took over the whole place.'

'Bloody hell,' said Chips, surprised and impressed. 'Che Guevera in two-way stretch elastic stockings.'

'There was a book written about it. Called 'Mrs Caldicot's Cabbage War,' the older ambulanceman told him. 'You could probably borrow a copy from the library.'

'I don't read books,' said Chips.

'Then watch the movie.'

'There's a movie?'

'Based on the book.'

'What's it called?'

'Mrs Caldicot's Cabbage War. The same as the book.'

'With that woman in it? Mrs Caldicot?'

'No, you plonker! An actress called Pauline Collins plays Mrs Caldicot. I heard Mrs Caldicot say she thought she was wonderful. She was on the radio.'

Chips grinned, pleased with himself. 'Oh, I've heard of Pauline Collins,' he said. 'She's married to that John Alderton.'

Chips put down his end of the wheelchair and was about to press the doorbell when the front door swung open and a woman dressed in a lemon-coloured jumper, bright red trousers and a multicoloured woolly hat appeared. She was pushing a silver coloured metal scooter. At first the ambulancemen thought that she was a teenager. Only when they looked closely did they realise that she had almost certainly already celebrated her seventieth birthday.

'Hello!' she cried, beaming. 'What a lovely day!'

The two ambulancemen looked at one another and then out at the rain beating down outside, the puddles and the over-flowing gutters. It was, to them, a dark, damp and desperately dismal day. The woman with the silver scooter paused and looked around. She saw the same day, the same rain, the same puddles and the same overflowing gutters but to her eyes the day seemed exciting. With a wave she started to bounce her scooter down the stone steps. She was halfway down the steps when a pretty, plump, black woman in a smart nurse's uniform appeared in the doorway. She had a name badge pinned to her chest. The single name 'Mrs Roberts' was the only printing on the badge. She looked to be in her mid forties and was holding a large yellow plastic cape and a yellow plastic rain hat. She had an easy-going manner and a smile which Mrs Caldicot often described as being that of an angel. She was a loyal friend and employee.

'Miss Nightingale,' called the nurse waving the two items in one hand. 'You forgot your cape!'

The woman with the scooter stopped, turned and came back up the steps. 'Silly me!' she said. She rolled her eyes as though to say 'What a silly woman!' and gently slapped her own wrist. She leant her scooter against the wall, held her hands up above her head and let the nurse slip the cape over her upstretched arms and her head. The nurse then added the hat and tied two pieces of cord into a neat bow underneath the old lady's chin. 'Don't be long,' the nurse warned. She smiled and added: 'And have a nice time.'

Miss Nightingale nodded, her eyes sparkling and full of life, and rushed off into the rain with her silver scooter.

'We've got a new resident for you,' said the older ambulanceman, nodding towards the man asleep in the wheelchair. He pulled a crumpled piece of paper out of his pocket and examined it. 'Mr Williams,' he read from the paper.

The nurse bent down and examined the man. She touched his hand and then gently shook his shoulder. She seemed cross. 'Has he been sedated?' she demanded.

'I expect so,' replied Bertie. 'Where he came from everyone who isn't dead or on the staff is sedated.' He paused. 'And if the rumours are right most of the nurses and doctors are sedated too,' he added.

Behind the ambulance a small grubby estate car skidded to a halt on the gravel. A short, balding, overweight man got out of the car, clutching a bulging black briefcase. Stooped in the rain he fumbled with his key, eventually managing to lock the car door. Neither the ambulancemen nor the nurse took any notice of his arrival.

'Would you bring him in, please,' said the nurse. She stepped into the hallway and nudged the door open as wide as it would go so that the two ambulancemen could push the wheelchair through the door more easily.

'We've got to take the chair back,' said the younger ambulanceman. 'It belongs to the hospital. It's signed out as a temporary loan.'

'Would you do me a favour and carry the patient upstairs?' asked the nurse. 'Mrs Caldicot, the proprietor is busy locked in her office with the cook.'

'No problem, love,' said the older ambulanceman. 'I'll take him.' He bent down, picked the sleeping patient up out of his wheelchair as though he was a small child, and carried him upstairs. 'I'll get his luggage,' said Chips, picking up the wheelchair and taking it back to the ambulance.

CHAPTER TWO

'I'm here to examine your extractor fan statutory warning notice,' announced the fat man with the black plastic briefcase. He had run less than twenty yards, and climbed a short flight of stone steps, but even in the cold and the rain the exercise had made him red-faced and breathless. Despite the weather he was sweating profusely. He took a plastic wallet from his inner jacket pocket and held it under Mrs Roberts's nose.

'Oh, right,' said Mrs Roberts. 'The extractor fan? Well I'm sure we have one. But I don't know where it is.'

'This is a random spot check authorised under sub-law 872c of the 1999 Act,' said the short man. 'You are obliged by law to cooperate with my enquiries. Failure to do so will be reported to my superiors and regarded as a breach of your legislative responsibilities. I suggest that you notify the registered proprietor without delay.'

'Mrs Caldicot is in her office with the cook,' repeated Mrs

Roberts. 'If we do have an extractor fan I expect it will be in the kitchen. I suspect that would be the ideal place for it. Perhaps your notice will be there too.'

'And where's the kitchen?' demanded the short visitor.

'Straight ahead down the corridor,' said Mrs Roberts. 'The door is open. Just help yourself.'

The short man hurried past her and down the corridor. Mrs Roberts, with more important things on her mind, hurriedly climbed the stairs.

CHAPTER THREE

Mrs Caldicot was coming to the end of her tête-à-tête with the cook. It had not, she would afterwards confirm, been one of the happiest encounters of her life.

'I have not been entirely happy with your work,' Mrs Caldicot had begun, tactfully. She had been rehearsing her opening line for two days.

The cook, a mountainous woman in her mid forties, said nothing but just glowered at Mrs Caldicot. Her white overall was, Mrs Caldicot noticed, heavily stained. The cook herself had lank, greasy black hair and did not appear to have washed for some time. Though she smelt strongly of peppermint there were other, less pleasant, underlying odours fighting for attention.

'When you came for your interview you told me that you had plenty of experience in this area of catering,' continued Mrs Caldicot. It was difficult to accept that this malodorous creature was the same person as the rather shy, eager to please applicant who had arrived for her interview a few months earlier.

The cook remained silent and threatening.

'I don't wish to dispute your previous claims,' lied Mrs Caldicot. 'But several aspects of your work here seem to suggest to me, and, indeed, to others, that you may not have quite the extent of experience which you indicated.'

The cook frowned as though she was having to struggle to understand what Mrs Caldicot was saying; her huge, hairy eyebrows, already dark and unkempt, swooped inwards and joined together for support. 'Are you implying that I lied?' she demanded.

'Oh no, no,' said Mrs Caldicot hastily. 'Of course not.' She instantly felt ashamed of herself. That was exactly what she had intended to imply.

'Good,' said the cook, leaning back in her chair. She took a packet of French cigarettes from one pocket and a box of matches from another.

'It's just that some of the meals you've prepared have been not quite adequate for the number of people involved,' said Mrs Caldicot.

The cook shook one of the cigarettes out of the packet, put it between her lips and lit it. Mrs Caldicot wanted to tell her that she didn't like people smoking in her office but felt intimidated and didn't have the courage.

'I don't know what you're talking about,' said the cook, having blown a lungful of smoke all over Mrs Caldicot.

'Well, I've got one or two examples here,' said Mrs Caldicot. She looked down at the thick folder in front of her and opened it. 'For example,' she began, 'last Wednesday you served jam sandwiches to the residents for their evening meal.'

'Lots of the old dears don't have their own teeth,' explained the cook. 'Jam sandwiches are easy to chew.'

'But you served just four rounds of bread,' continued Mrs Caldicot. 'There weren't enough sandwiches to go round.'

'Most of them are overweight,' said the cook. 'It's my job to look after their dietary health. I decided they needed to diet.' Mrs Caldicot suddenly realised what the smell of peppermint was hiding. Alcohol.

'That was very noble of you,' said Mrs Caldicot. Looking at the cook's immense bulk, words such as 'glass houses', 'stones' and 'throw' sprang to mind but she decided not to explore that particular avenue. She picked up a butcher's bill from the folder. 'What also puzzles me is the fact that although the residents were not served any meat in that particular week – they were served sandwiches on nine separate occasions – you nevertheless author-ised payment of several hundred pounds for steaks, bacon, chops and so on.'

'There wasn't room to put them in the freezer,' said the cook. 'The meat went off so I threw it all away. Would you rather I served the residents bad meat?'

'No, of course not.'

'Because I wouldn't do it anyway,' said the cook. She straight-ened her shoulders and pulled herself to her full height. 'I've got my standards and I'm not going to endanger the lives of those lovely old people just to please you.' She turned her head and looked out of the window.

'I didn't...' began Mrs Caldicot, wondering how she had suddenly found herself on the defensive.

'Hrmph!' snorted the cook, seemingly exhausted by the modest physical effort she had just made, and relaxing and slump-ing back in her chair.

'Is it true that you're related to the butcher?' asked Mrs Caldicot.

'He's my brother,' said the cook. 'Are you saying it's a crime to give business to my brother?' She scowled. 'I'll have you know that he gives me a very special discount on account of the fact that I'm family. And we get the best cuts he's got.'

'That's very good of him,' said Mrs Caldicot, now woefully aware that she had lost control of what she had intended to be a final interview with the cook. 'Very good of him.'

There was a long silence while Mrs Caldicot decided on a new line of attack.

'Can I just go back to your original application form?' asked Mrs Caldicot.

'If you like.' The cook looked at the clock. 'Lunch will be late. But it will be your fault.'

Mrs Caldicot looked up. 'Lunch has been late nearly every day since you've been here,' she said. 'On the rare occasions when it wasn't at least an hour late it was over two hours early.'

The cook pulled a face. 'I had to go out. I didn't want them to go without their lunch. It didn't seem right that they should be inconvenienced on account of me having to go and see the doctor.'

'You served lunch at 9.30 am,' said Mrs Caldicot. 'And you told the residents that they had to be finished by 9.45 am.'

'It doesn't do them good to sit around,' said the cook. 'I thought I was doing the right thing.'

'On your original application form you said that you'd had many years of experience in hotels and institutions throughout the country,' said Mrs Caldicot.

The cook didn't say anything.

'You said, for example, that you had experience at the Imperial Hotel in Carmarthen.'

'Yes.'

'When I belatedly rang them yesterday they told me that they had no record of ever employing anyone of your name.'

'I didn't say I was employed there.'

Mrs Caldicot looked at her, raised an eyebrow and waited.

'I stayed there with my mum and dad when I was a kid.'

'You stayed there?'

'Yes. With my mum and dad. For a week.'

'I don't think many people would regard that as relevant employment history.'

The cook shrugged.

'And Holloway Prison?'

'It was only three months.'

Mrs Caldicot waited.

'It was a set-up,' said the cook. She sounded very defensive.

Mrs Caldicot didn't speak. She looked down at her sleeping cat, Kitty, lying peacefully on the carpet at her feet. Just looking at Kitty always helped to bring her blood pressure down.

'Anyway, everyone does it.'

'Does what?'

'A bit of shoplifting. The shops expect it. They allow for it in their costs.'

'Ah,' said Mrs Caldicot. 'So, you didn't actually work at Holloway Prison either?'

'Oh, yes I did,' insisted the cook. 'In the kitchen.'

'But not actually on the staff?'

'Not properly what you'd call on the staff. No, not in that way. But I did work in the kitchen.'

'Peeling potatoes?' guessed Mrs Caldicot.

'And chopping them. I was in charge of the chips.'

'What about the qualifications you listed on your application form?'

'I'm going to get them,' said the cook. 'It's just that I haven't had the time. What with one thing and another...' She paused to tap more cigarette ash onto Mrs Caldicot's carpet. 'I could get them easily,' she insisted.

'Let me move onto breakages,' said Mrs Caldicot.

'What breakages?' demanded the cook cockily.

'Well,' said Mrs Caldicot, extracting another piece of paper from her folder, 'since you've been in charge of the kitchen we have had to buy 76 replacement plates, 39 cups, 49 bowls, 64 saucers and 23 serving dishes.'

'If you'd bought decent stuff in the first place it wouldn't keep breaking,' said the cook. 'And if I had more help in the kitchen there probably wouldn't be so many breakages.'

'And we seem to have a lot of trouble with disappearing cutlery,' said Mrs Caldicot. She took another sheet of paper from the cook's folder. 'We've had to replace 124 missing teaspoons, 124 missing forks, 124 missing dessertspoons, 124 missing soup spoons and 124 missing knives.'

'They get lost,' said the cook with a shrug.

'Doesn't it strike you as odd that we've lost exactly the same number of spoons, forks and knives?'

The cook thought about this for a moment. 'No,' she said. She shrugged. 'Probably just a coincidence.'

'In your experience would you say that those sort of losses are normal?' asked Mrs Caldicot.

The cook nodded. 'Normal,' she confirmed. 'Everywhere I've ever worked cutlery has gone missing. It's just a fact of life.' She shrugged. 'A spoon here. A fork there. They get lost behind the fridge.' Another shrug. She looked around for an ashtray, couldn't see one, so continued to tap the ash from her cigarette onto Mrs Caldicot's carpet.

Mrs Caldicot opened the drawer in her desk and took out a fork. 'Do you recognise this fork?'

'It looks like one of ours.'

'It is one of ours,' said Mrs Caldicot. 'But it is one of the new forks which arrived yesterday afternoon. It hasn't been used yet.' She handed the fork across the desk to the cook.

'It looks like one of our forks,' said the cook.

'Would you be kind enough to turn it over,' said Mrs Caldicot.

The cook turned the fork over.

'If you look on the back of the handle you will see two initials scratched into the metal.'

The cook examined the handle.

'The initials are D.L.,' said Mrs Caldicot. 'They stand for 'David Livingstone.''

'Wasn't he an explorer?'

'He was. But I'm not interested in that one,' said Mrs Caldicot. 'Our Mr David Livingstone has been a resident here since we opened. He has a strange habit of scratching his initials onto the back of his cutlery. Then he likes to use the same pieces of cutlery at every meal.'

The cook didn't say anything.

'Mr Livingstone lost his fork a week ago,' said Mrs Caldicot. 'And now, curiously, a brand new fork arrives with his initials scratched on the back.'

'That's really odd,' said the cook.

'Can you tell me where the new cutlery came from?' asked Mrs Caldicot.

'A shop,' replied the cook.

'What sort of shop?'

'Oh a sort of second-hand shop,' said the cook. 'I thought it would be cheaper to buy the cutlery from a second-hand shop. Especially since we lose so many pieces.'

'How did he manage to sell us back a fork that we lost a week ago?' asked Mrs Caldicot, smiling sweetly.

The cook said nothing, scowled, and stood up. She stubbed

out her cigarette on Mrs Caldicot's desk and left. Mrs Caldicot reached down and tickled a sleeping Kitty behind the ear. Kitty, awake, looked up, spotted an empty lap and filled it.

Twenty five minutes later the cook left the nursing home and was never seen again. She took with her six towels, a plastic bag filled with assorted cutlery and three bottles of sherry.

Chapter Four

'Thanks a lot,' said Mrs Roberts to the ambulancemen, finding that the new patient had already been put into an armchair in a small but neat and nicely furnished bedroom.

'These come with him,' said the ambulance man known as 'Chips'. He had followed his colleague up the stairs, struggling with three brown leather suitcases. Breathing heavily, and clearly out of condition, he put the suitcases down and then pulled a plastic bag out of his jacket pocket and handed it to the nurse. 'His pills,' he explained.

'Is there a letter?' asked the nurse.

'No,' replied Chips. 'But the nurse at the hospital said that the instructions for the drugs are on the bottles. And his GP is Dr Snoot.'

Mrs Roberts shook her head, both disappointed and disgusted. 'We'd better be off then,' said the older ambulanceman.

'Watch out for Miss Nightingale,' warned Mrs Roberts. 'She was going to the paper shop to buy a magazine but she might still be playing in the drive.'

'Is that the nutty old bat with the scooter?' asked Chips.

Mrs Roberts glowered at him.

'Don't take any notice of him,' said the older ambulanceman, who instantly sensed Mrs Roberts's disapproval. 'He's too thick to know any better.' He clipped his younger colleague around the head and then led him to the stairs and back down, out of the rest home.

Mrs Roberts opened the plastic bag containing the new resident's drugs and, one by one, put eleven bottles side by side onto the top of the dressing table. She examined the bottles as she did so, and shook her head disapprovingly at each one. When she'd finished she glanced out of the window. Resplendent in her yellow cape, Miss Nightingale, who had been racing through the puddles on her scooter, had stopped to wave goodbye to the ambulancemen as their vehicle was driven out of the driveway. Two arms appeared, one from each side of the vehicle, as the two ambulancemen waved goodbye to her.

Mrs Roberts did not even notice that the small grubby estate car, and its driver, the short man with the black plastic brief-case had both disappeared. Smiling at Miss Nightingale's activities, she turned away from the window, took another look at the still sleeping newcomer, and hurried out of the room and down the stairs.

CHAPTER FIVE

Mrs Caldicot and Mrs Roberts were sitting in the office.

'I've had to sort of fire the cook,' confessed Mrs Caldicot. 'I feel terrible about it. I've never had to fire anyone before.'

'How do you sort of fire someone?' asked Mrs Roberts.

Mrs Caldicot explained. 'Actually she left,' she said. 'Before I had to fire her.'

'Thank heavens for that!' said Mrs Roberts.

'You don't think I was too harsh?' asked Mrs Caldicot.

'You should have fired her weeks ago,' Mrs Roberts assured her. 'I would have got rid of her.'

'Would you really?' asked Mrs Caldicot, clearly delighted to know that her colleague would have acted in the same way.

'She was a terrible cook, she was always in a foul temper, she was a drunk, she never produced meals on time and she broke more dishes every day than the average person breaks in a lifetime,' said Mrs Roberts, counting these criticisms off on the fingers and thumb of one hand. 'She used to steal food, she was the untidiest person in the entire history of the world – with the possible exception of my sister Beryl, but that's another story and at least she's clean. And dirty! She was the most unhygienic person I ever saw working in a kitchen and if one of those inspectors from the council had seen her at work he would have closed us down in seconds...' Mrs Roberts was busy counting these criticisms off on her other hand.

Mrs Caldicot started laughing. 'OK!' she said, holding up a hand. 'You've made me feel better.'

'I could go on,' said Mrs Roberts. 'If I take off my tights I've got ten toes too...'

'No, you've convinced me I did the right thing,' said Mrs Caldicot. She sighed. 'It was just, well, difficult. I've never had to do anything like it before.'

'You had to do it,' said Mrs Roberts, putting great emphasis on the second word. 'Apart from anything else she would have probably poisoned us all if you hadn't!'

'OK. So I had to fire the cook,' said Mrs Caldicot, sounding relieved. 'But now we have to find a replacement.'

'Listen,' said Mrs Roberts, quite seriously. 'If I have to do the cooking myself we'll eat better meals than we did when she was here. And with the amount of food she wasted we'll be better off sending out for 'takeaway' meals! Have you seen the food bills?'

Mrs Caldicot rummaged around on her desk. 'I know,' she agreed. 'They're awfully high aren't they.'

'She must have been stealing from you,' said Mrs Roberts. She picked up one of the bills at random. '£69 for one week's milk bill!' she said. 'And how could we possibly spend £132 in one week on bread?'

'I should have kept an eye on things,' said Mrs Caldicot. 'It's my fault. I trusted her.'

Just then they heard a crash.

'What on earth was that?' asked Mrs Caldicot.

'I don't know,' Mrs Roberts replied. 'But I think it came from upstairs. It may have been the new resident – Mr Williams.

He was sedated when he arrived. Perhaps he's woken up.'

They ran up the stairs together, Mrs Roberts leading and Mrs Caldicot following, and met the new resident staggering out of his room. He was holding onto the door frame and looked very unsteady.

'Who are you?' demanded the man. 'Where am I?'

'My name is Mrs Roberts. I'm a nurse. You've been admitted to the Twilight Years Rest Home. And this is Mrs Caldicot; she's in charge.' Mrs Roberts turned to Mrs Caldicot. 'He was sedated by the hospital staff,' she explained. 'I expect his sedation is wearing off.'

'So now we know who you are and where I am,' said the stranger. 'That just leaves one question.'

Mrs Roberts looked at him, and waited.

'Who the hell am I?' he demanded. 'And what in blazes am I doing in an old folks' home?'

'That's two questions,' said Mrs Caldicot. She took his arm and led him back into his room and helped him to sit down in the same chair in which the ambulanceman had deposited him not long before.

'Is it?'

'You're Henry Williams and you're here because the hospital needed your bed and you're not well enough to go home. They asked us to find you a bed and a room.'

'Who said I'm not well enough to go home?'

'The doctors at the hospital.'

'Bloody idiots. What do they know about anything?' muttered Mr Williams. He licked his lips. 'I've got a dry head, my mouth is as stinking as a birdcage and I could drink a horse.'

'I expect that will be the drugs,' explained Mrs Roberts. 'Do you mean that you're hungry or thirsty?'

'Thirsty, of course,' said Henry Williams, impatient with what he saw as the nurse's stupidity. 'I could drink a horse.'

'Would you like a cup of tea?' asked Mrs Caldicot.

Mr Williams's eyes lit up. 'I'd kiss for a cup of tea.'

'Don't you mean 'kill'?' asked Mrs Roberts.

'Mr Williams frowned, clearly puzzled. 'Why would I want

to kill anyone for a cup of tea?' he asked. 'I'd kiss you, though.'

'You stay there,' said Mrs Roberts. 'I'll go and get you a cup of tea. Don't you go anywhere!'

'I'm not going anywhere,' said Mr Williams. 'Especially if you're going to bring me a cup of tea if I stay here.' He paused. 'Besides where would I go?' he asked. He thought for a moment. 'Have I got anywhere to go?' he asked.

Mrs Roberts and Mrs Caldicot turned and headed back for the landing. The door to Mr Williams's room was packed with faces. 'Is he all right?' demanded Mrs Torridge, a sprightly woman in a pink cardigan and a blue dress with a floral pattern.

'He needs a cup of tea,' said Mrs Roberts.

'I'll put the kettle on,' said Mrs Torridge. She hurried off down the stairs, followed back down the stairs by the half a dozen other residents who had accompanied her up the stairs.

As they all trooped down, there was a shout and a crash at the top of the stairs. Henry Williams had wandered out of his bedroom again. This time he had knocked over a small table and a large vase of flowers. Mrs Roberts and Mrs Caldicot rushed up the stairs. Mr Williams fell to his knees and started to cry. 'I think I ought to call his doctor,' said Mrs Caldicot.

'You call the doctor,' said Mrs Roberts, bending down and helping Mr Williams to his feet. 'I'll help Mr Williams back into his room and stay with him.'

CHAPTER SIX

Most of the residents at the Twilight Years Rest Home had arrived with Mrs Caldicot. But, like Mr Williams, there were a few new-comers. There was, for example, an elderly married couple called Maurice and Maple Merivale.

The Merivales arrived at the nursing home the day before Henry Williams had been delivered by ambulance. They stood on the doorstep, a pile of luggage stacked neatly beside them, and politely asked if they could speak to Mrs Caldicot. Mrs Merivale, stout but tall, wore a thick, dark green coat and a pair of light green ankle boots. Mr Merivale, slightly taller and slightly less stout, had sallow features and an impressive thatch of jet black hair.

'We're pleased to meet you,' said Mrs Merivale, when Mrs Caldicot hurried to the door, wiping her hands on a towel. 'We've heard a lot about you.'

'Won't you come inside?' asked Mrs Caldicot, who was, as always, slightly embarrassed that anyone should recognise her.

'Oh no thank you, Mrs Caldicot,' replied Mrs Merivale. 'Not yet. We've just come to ask you if you have a room.'

'You want to stay here?'

'If it's possible,' said Mrs Merivale, with a nod. 'We'd very much like to make this our home.'

'Both of you?'

'Oh yes, both of us. Both of us are looking for a new home,' replied Mrs Merivale. 'That's just the point, you see. We would like to share a room. We've slept together for 58 years now. We haven't spent a night apart in all that time.'

'You're looking for a double room?'

'Exactly,' nodded Mrs Merivale. 'A double room is just what we want. For tonight if possible.'

'Where are you living at the moment?' asked Mrs Caldicot, puzzled.

'Well, we aren't actually living anywhere at the moment,' answered Mrs Merivale. She leant forward and lowered her voice. 'Until this morning we were living at a nursing home in Pallborough Avenue?'

'I know the one,' said Mrs Caldicot.

'It was taken over by a new company,' said Mrs Merivale. She pulled a face to show that this was not a development of which she approved. 'And they told us at breakfast today that we couldn't have a double room together.' She looked at her husband, standing silently beside her, and took his hand in her own. 'We've always been together,' she told Mrs Caldicot.

'Why did they want to split you up?' asked Mrs Caldicot, horrified.

'They said it was cheaper for us to be in separate homes,' explained Mrs Merivale. 'They assessed us and decided that although my husband needs Category 3 care I only need Category 4 care.'

'That's terrible!' said Mrs Caldicot.

'They said it would save them money,' said Mrs Merivale. 'But it would have broken our hearts.'

'Did you protest?'

'We said we weren't happy about it,' said Mrs Merivale. 'But they didn't seem interested. So, on balance we thought it best to leave.' She leant forward, conspiratorially, 'We don't like to stay where we aren't wanted. Besides, I've never liked making a fuss,' she added. She leant forward and whispered. 'In fact one of the nurses once told me off for being too self-effacing.'

'She told you off for being self-effacing?'

'Yes. She was quite firm about it.'

'How did you get here?' asked Mrs Caldicot, looking at the couple's luggage, spread around and behind them.

'Oh, we walked,' said Mrs Merivale.

'South along Pallborough Avenue for four hundred yards,' said Mr Merivale. Mrs Caldicot looked at him. It was the first time he'd spoken. 'Then we took the first left after the school, went for two hundred yards down Beech Drive and then took the first left after the postbox into Steeple Road.'

'Ah,' said Mrs Caldicot, nodding and understanding.

'We went down Steeple Road for five hundred yards and then turned left into Maple Avenue.' Mr Merivale smiled. 'And as soon as we reached Maple Avenue we could see your nursing home.'

'Thank you,' said Mrs Caldicot.

'Of course, we were lucky,' said Mr Merivale. 'If there had been road works in Steeple Road and they'd dug the pavement up, which they sometimes do, we would have had to go down Dartington Avenue and that would have added another ten minutes to the journey.'

'Of course,' agreed Mrs Caldicot, impressed. 'But how did your luggage get here?'

'We carried it,' explained Mrs Merivale, with a shrug. She

sighed, looked at her husband and squeezed his hand. 'So do you have a room we can share?'

When Mrs Caldicot said she had a room they could have Mrs Merivale started to cry. 'Thank you,' she said. 'That's wonderful.' She turned to her husband and kissed him full on the mouth. He looked surprised but pleased. Then Mrs Merivale leant forward and kissed Mrs Caldicot on the cheek. 'Thank you,' she said. There were tears flowing down her cheeks.

Mrs Caldicot took Mr and Mrs Merivale upstairs to show them their new room. She helped them carry their luggage. The suitcase she carried seemed to have been filled with bricks.

'I'm afraid there isn't much space in here,' said Mrs Caldicot, dropping the suitcase and looking around. She rubbed her aching arm.

'Oh, that doesn't matter, Mrs Caldicot,' said Mrs Merivale. 'That doesn't matter at all. The important thing is that Mr Merivale and I can be together. In the same home. In the same room.'

'There's one other thing,' said Mrs Caldicot, feeling rather uncomfortable and embarrassed. 'I hate bringing this up but, as you can probably imagine, we have quite a lot of bills and I naturally have to ask residents to make a contribution; to help pay the expenses of running the nursing home. We don't have any formal arrangements. People just contribute what they can afford.'

'Oh quite right too,' said Mrs Merivale. She opened a huge, old-fashioned, battered black leather handbag and rummaged around inside until she found her purse. She took out her purse, opened it and peered inside. After a moment she took out a single five pound note which she handed to Mrs Caldicot with much ceremony. Without the five pound note the purse was empty.

'Here you are, dear,' she said, as though handing over a shovelful of gold sovereigns. 'You let us know when this has run out.'

'Thank you,' said Mrs Caldicot, accepting the note graciously.

'Is there anything we can to do to help you?' asked Mrs Merivale.

Mrs Caldicot looked at her.

'Mr Merivale and I like to keep busy,' explained Mrs Merivale. 'Cleaning, cooking, tidying up. We've always been busy. If you've got something we can do to keep ourselves busy we'd be very grateful.' She paused, put her head to one side and smiled. 'It'll keep us out of mischief,' she said, as though if she and her husband were not kept busy they might set fire to the garden shed or start hurling Brussels sprouts at the postman. When she put her head to one side Mrs Caldicot thought she looked rather like a rather large sparrow.

'Well, if you're sure that would be wonderful...' said Mrs Caldicot. 'We need some help in the kitchen.'

'As long as we're not getting in anyone's way,' said Mrs Merivale. She lowered her voice, looked first to the left and then to the right as though concerned lest someone hear her, and then whispered. 'I know some cooks are a bit funny about having outsiders helping in their kitchen.'

'That isn't really a problem at the moment,' said Mrs Caldicot. She felt rather embarrassed to have to admit this to her newest resident. 'I'm afraid we don't have a cook,' she said.

'No cook?'

Mrs Caldicot shook her head.

'No cook at all?

Another shake of the head.

'Well, that's wonderful!' said Mrs Merivale. 'Mr Merivale and I will be happy to do the cooking for you.'

'That's very kind of you,' said Mrs Caldicot, rather uncertainly. 'Do you have any experience of cooking for large numbers of people?'

'Oh bless you, yes,' said Mrs Merivale. 'I used to be in catering when I was younger.'

'That would be marvellous,' said Mrs Caldicot. 'Marvellous. What sort of remuneration would you be looking for?'

Mrs Merivale looked at Mrs Caldicot as though she had spoken to her in a foreign language.

'Pay,' explained Mrs Caldicot. 'Wages.'

'Oh good heavens don't you be silly,' said Mrs Merivale, clearly rather shocked. 'We won't want any payment. It'll be a pleasure. A real joy. And you won't have to worry about hiring any assistants. I know how difficult it can be to find good kitchen maids. Mr Merivale loves to put on a pinny and help me out in the kitchen.'

'That's wonderful,' said Mrs Caldicot, genuinely delighted. 'I'll help you clean out the kitchen ... it's a bit grubby at the moment ... and then it will be all yours.'

CHAPTER SEVEN

Three and a half miles away from The Twilight Years Rest Home, two well-dressed men in their fifties were standing in an expensively furnished living room in an expensive detached house looking out at the gardens through the French windows. Both men had grey hair, both men looked distinguished and it was clear that both men had money.

'It's embarrassing to see him out there in this weather,' said the shorter and stouter of the two men. The man he was talking about, his father, a wiry, elderly looking fellow, was standing in an ornamental pond dragging out weeds with his bare hands. He wore waders, old grey trousers and an old plastic fertilizer sack which had three holes cut in it – one for his head and one for each arm. On his head he wore an old brown trilby. The men looking at him both knew that he wore nothing at all underneath the fertilizer sack and that his trousers, which had been purchased from a charity shop, were several sizes too big for him and were held up with the aid of a piece of orange baler twine.

'He's a wonderful gardener,' said the second man, the owner of the house in which they were standing, the owner of the garden they were looking at, and the employer of the man they were talking about. 'I inherited him, you know. When we bought the house. That must have been, oh, eighteen, nineteen years ago. I don't know how long the previous owners had him. At least fifteen years I should think. Probably longer.'

'He's been working here for fifty years,' said the first man.

'Half a century of pulling up weeds. He was eighty last year. He should be tucked up somewhere nice and warm. Watching the TV. Playing a bit of bowls when the weather is nice. Playing whist in the evenings.'

'I've never known anyone with such a wonderful touch in the garden. Whatever he plants seems to come up. Flowers, vegetables, shrubs, trees – they all seem to bloom for him.'

'When he was younger I offered him a job in my office. We needed a cleaner. Someone to help tidy up in the evenings. No one would have seen him or known about it. But he wouldn't take it. I mean, what's the difference between mowing someone's lawn and doing a bit of cleaning and polishing? No difference at all is there really?'

'Do you know when he was ill a couple of years ago nearly everything in the garden died. I watered and weeded and did what I thought I was supposed to do. I think the plants missed him. When he came back everything perked up again. It was amazing.'

'He was off because he had a liver infection. He should have stopped work then. I asked him to. But he wouldn't, of course. Stubborn as a mule.'

'Why don't you let him work on for another summer? He enjoys it you know. I'll have a word with him if you like and try to persuade him to stay in the potting shed when the weather is bad. I'll still pay him, of course. He can always get on with cleaning the tools, that sort of thing. I don't know where I'll find anyone else like him. Totally trustworthy, you know. But then of course you would know that.'

'I really don't think so. Not now that I've been made senior partner. It really isn't on, you know. Having my father work as a gardener. It would be so humiliating for my wife and I if it got out.'

'Well, at least let's leave it to him. I mean it's his life, his job. Why not just let him decide? I'll happily stand by whatever his decision might be.'

'I don't think so. We both know what his decision will be. And that really isn't what I want at all.' The gardener's son paused and cleared his throat. 'I think that perhaps you ought to be aware of your own rather delicate position,' he said. 'My father is over eighty. He is frail and rather vulnerable. He isn't as steady as he used to be. I would hate to hear that he'd stabbed himself in the foot with a fork or fainted and drowned in your pond. You would be liable, of course. Have you checked your employer's liability policy? You do have one of course?'

'Er, I'm not, er...'

'Many of these policies, and I do hope for your sake that you have one, have exclusion clauses which rule out cover for older employees. So you could find yourself totally exposed. I can't tell what sort of damages we would be looking for if anything happened. And, of course, my being a leading local lawyer would mean that we wouldn't have to worry about finding the very best representation.'

'No. I see.'

The gardener's son turned round and walked back into the room. 'I see that you are a collector of old photographs.'

'Yes, I have one or two.'

'Very interesting stuff,' said the gardener's son. 'I'm a collector too. This is a Brassai isn't it?'

'Yes.'

'I thought so.'

'And a Cartier-Bresson. And isn't that an early Henry Williams?'

'Yes. I'm impressed. You know a good deal about photography.'

'I've had one or two clients who were keen. I was executor for one fellow. We had to get an expert up from London to look at his collection. I was surprised to see what they fetched. Just old snaps, you know. He had an early Williams. Very similar subject to yours. I was very impressed with what it fetched at auction. I started collecting similar stuff after that.'

'So, if you collect early Williams you presumably collect old photographs of Paris?'

'Yes. That's something of a speciality of mine.' The gardener's son looked around. There were around thirty framed photographs on the walls. All the photographs were in black and white. 'I suspect you'd rather hate to have to part with any of these.'

'Absolutely. I wouldn't part with them for anything.'

'Except perhaps a costly legal action, eh?' The gardener's son looked at his father's employer meaningfully.

The gardener's employer, the owner of the house, the garden and the collection of photographs, said nothing.

'So what are we going to do about my father then?'

The employer licked his lips. 'I'll have a word with him this afternoon.' He spoke quietly, as though rather ashamed of what he was saying.

'And tell him that you no longer require his services?'

'Yes. I suppose so.' He spoke in what was now a whisper.

'No need to be brutal about it. Just explain that you're going to look for someone a bit younger. Someone a bit fitter and stronger.'

'Yes. Quite.'

'Nice to have met you at last. After all these years. Don't bother to see me out.'

Chapter Eight

'How did it go?' asked the woman in the front passenger seat of the Jaguar. She was blonde, and although there was no visible evidence to lead a casual observer to question what they saw, those who had known her longer, back in days now rather further away in time than she might willingly acknowledge, were well aware that blonde had not been the colour of her hair when she had first appeared on the world's stage.

She was wearing a fur coat which was unfastened. Underneath the fur she wore a short green dress which was several sizes too small for her. She wore a huge diamond ring on the third finger of her left hand and enough additional jewellery to look noticeably over-dressed. Her husband, the gardener's son, had on several occasions tried to persuade her to dress a little less ostentatiously but her motto was 'if you've got it, flaunt it' and so, since she had it, she invariably flaunted it.

The gardener's son was looking pleased with himself. 'He'll fire my father today,' he said. 'He was scared witless when I pointed out to him just how vulnerable he was. Are there any more?'

His wife opened the small green, leather bound notebook which lay on her lap and studied it for a moment. 'No,' she said. 'That was the last one. Four employers.' She half turned and smiled in admiration at her husband. 'And all four have agreed to fire your father.'

'Splendid. Do you fancy a spot of lunch?' He turned to look at his wife. 'Shall we go to the Connaught Arms?'

'That would be nice, dear. But let's get a table by the door. I hate it when they put us in a corner where no one can see us.'

CHAPTER NINE

While Mr Roxdale Jr was celebrating having arranged for his father to be sacked, Mr Caldicot Jr was paying his first visit to his mother's new home.

'Well, mother,' said Derek, looking around him. 'I have to hand it to you. It's a fine looking building.' He said this as though with regret rather than admiration. He was not a generous boy and he even found it difficult to part with compliments. He took after his father in that respect.

Derek, his wife Veronica and their son Jason had come to visit Mrs Caldicot for the first time since she had re-opened the nursing home. It had been a long time since she and they had met. 'I'm amazed. You've done a pretty good job of this place,' said Derek at last; managing to spoil the compliment by making it sound patronising.

'Thank you,' said Mrs Caldicot, accepting the compliment

for what it was. It was, she thought rather sadly, probably the most generous thing he'd ever said to her.

'Of course,' he continued, looking around and lowering his voice just enough to make it clear that he was conscious that anyone who overheard him might be offended but not quite low enough to make sure that no one did overhear him, 'the big question is: 'Are you making a profit?''

'That's not *the* big question,' thought Mrs Caldicot. 'It's *your* big question.'

'That's not why I opened the home,' Mrs Caldicot told him.

'But if you don't make a profit you'll have to close down,' Derek pointed out.

'Yes,' agreed Mrs Caldicot. 'But that doesn't mean that making a profit is the main reason why the home is open. Making a profit is merely a means to an end, not an end in itself.'

Derek thought about this and looked rather confused. He had never done anything in his life where making a profit had not been the prime driving force.

'Do you have a freezer?' asked Jason.

'Yes. Quite a big one,' Mrs Caldicot told him proudly.

'Does it have ice cream in it?'

'I think so.'

'I want one. Have you got pistachio?'

'I'm not sure,' answered Mrs Caldicot, trying to remember what was in the freezer. 'I'm pretty sure we've got chocolate, coffee and strawberry. Oh, and vanilla, of course.'

'Oh, those are all boring,' sneered Jason.

'They're the flavours the residents prefer,' said Mrs Caldicot.

Jason screwed up his nose in disgust. His mother comforted him.

Mrs Caldicot took Derek upstairs to look around.

'Good heavens,' said Derek. 'The rooms are huge. But there's only one bed in most of them.'

'That's right,' said Mrs Caldicot. 'I made sure that everyone had their own room – unless they wanted to share, of course. Mrs Peterborough and Miss Nightingale would hate to be parted so they share one of the biggest rooms on the front.'

'But you'll never make any money that way,' said Derek, in despair. 'My firm has a retirement home division so I know about these things. The profitability of a nursing home venture depends entirely on bed occupation. You have to cram in as many beds as you can and you have to make sure that they're constantly occupied. If someone dies in the middle of the night you need to get them into the morgue straight away and have a fresh body getting out of the bed at breakfast time.'

Mrs Caldicot stared at him and, not for the first time, wondered whether the nurses at the maternity home could possibly have got her baby mixed up with someone else's.

'You're not listening to me mother,' said Derek. 'What are you thinking?'

'I was just thinking how much you remind me of your father,' said Mrs Caldicot.

Derek took this as a compliment.

'If you don't mind, dear, I'd rather just carry on as I am,' said Mrs Caldicot.

'Oh, I give up with you,' snapped Derek. 'Sometimes you are just so damned stubborn these days. I really don't know what's come over you since father died. You were never like this before.'

'No, dear,' said Mrs Caldicot sweetly. 'I wasn't, was I?'

'I've had enough of you and all this,' snapped Derek. He turned to his wife and son. 'Come on,' he said brusquely. 'We're going.' He turned back to his mother. 'And don't you come crying to me when this all goes pear shaped,' he warned her, wagging a finger. 'As far as I'm concerned you can do what you like. I want nothing more to do with you or this place.'

And with that Derek, Veronica and Jason stalked out of the nursing home and Mrs Caldicot's life.

Mrs Caldicot was neither surprised nor upset.

Chapter Ten

The Merivales were still unpacking and settling into their room and Mrs Caldicot was in the kitchen washing dishes. She was furious and was taking out her anger on the crockery. She had already broken two plates and a cup but felt no shame or sorrow. There were soap suds everywhere. Mrs Caldicot was angry because she had spent twenty minutes unsuccessfully trying to get hold of Mr Williams's doctor.

After four calls she had finally spoken to a very bored sounding receptionist who had announced that Dr Mr Snoot and Dr Mrs Snoot were both unavailable.

'Dr Mr Snoot and Dr Mrs Snoot?' thought Mrs Caldicot. 'They sound like a pair of characters in a children's cartoon series.' They would, she thought to herself, have to be the baddies.

'Is it an emergency?' the receptionist had enquired, managing to make the question both patronising and disdainful.

'Well, not really an emergency,' admitted Mrs Caldicot. 'No one's bleeding to death if that's what you mean.'

'Then call back later,' said the receptionist, for whom the word 'charm' was more likely to be associated with the word 'bracelet' than the phrase 'human relations'. And then 'click' – the phone had gone dead.

Mrs Caldicot, still furious, angrily thrust her dish mop to the bottom of a large green mug and then blinked as soapy water splashed onto her face and into her eyes.

'There's a gentleman here for you,' said Miss Nightingale, suddenly appearing behind Mrs Caldicot. Miss Nightingale lowered her voice and spoke in what she clearly seemed to think was a whisper. 'It's your nice fancy man, Mrs Caldicot.'

Startled, Mrs Caldicot turned from the sink; as she moved soapy bubbles dripped onto the floor from her wrists and forearms.

A smartly dressed man in his late fifties was standing in the doorway. Mrs Caldicot instantly recognised the visitor and blushed.

Jenkins, tall, broad-shouldered and slightly balding, was a

senior editor on a national newspaper. What hair he had he wore collar length. He had a commanding presence. When, just a few months earlier, Mrs Caldicot had led a walk-out of the residents of the Twilight Years Rest Home it had been Jenkins who had published her life story in The Sunday Globe newspaper. It had been a cheque from The Sunday Globe which had helped rescue her from potential bankruptcy and enabled her to find a deposit to buy and reopen the nursing home. Mrs Caldicot knew that without Jenkins's help and encouragement she would not have been able to cope with the media storm her 'cabbage war' had aroused. Nor would she have been able to buy the nursing home and find a home for her eccentric band of friends and followers. It was not surprising that she felt genuinely grateful to Jenkins.

But gratefulness wasn't the only, or the most powerful, emotion she felt towards him. It wasn't gratefulness that made her blush and made her knees weaken when he suddenly appeared in her kitchen. It wasn't gratefulness that made her feel as coy and as nervous as a schoolgirl.

Miss Nightingale, her eyes twinkling, curtsied, rather clumsily, giggled and disappeared. Mrs Caldicot and Jenkins could hear her laughing gaily as she skipped off down the corridor.

'I met Miss Nightingale in the driveway,' explained Jenkins. 'Actually she nearly ran me over with her scooter. She insisted on bringing me in.' The visitor was wearing a navy blue suit with a white chalk stripe, a pale blue shirt and a perfectly tied dark blue tie. There wasn't an inappropriate crease anywhere. He would not have looked out of place in the shop window of a superior men's outfitters.

'I'm sorry...' said Mrs Caldicot, still blushing. She waved a hand and sent a flurry of soap bubbles cascading around her. '...about that silly fancy man remark.' A few strands of hair fell across her face. 'I don't know where she got that idea from.' She reached up and brushed them away, leaving a trail of soap bubbles across her forehead and into her hair. She realised that she was blushing and, feeling embarrassed by that, blushed a still deeper shade of red.

'Please don't apologise,' insisted Jenkins, with a grin.

'Actually, I confess I'm delighted that at least one person thinks of me as your fancy man.'

'Well, whatever...' said Mrs Caldicot, not bothering to hide her pleasure at this mildly flirtatious remark. The late and rather unlamented Mr Caldicot had never been in the slightest bit flirtatious. Much to her surprise she liked being flirted with. It made her feel rather naughty, but she definitely liked it. She felt forty years younger. She smiled. 'It's lovely to see you,' she said, meaning it. 'Your moustache has gone,' she said, suddenly noticing.

' I shaved it off,' said Jenkins, pleased that she had noticed.

'You look younger without it.'

'I'm sure I must look a terrible sight,' said Mrs Caldicot. 'It's been hectic here, as usual.' She patted her cheeks, as though this might cool them. 'I'm blushing like a schoolgirl,' she apologised, aware, as she said it, that the very admission was making her blush even more. Looking down she noticed the bubbles on her hands and wiped them both on her pinafore. 'And babbling like one, too.' She wondered how red she had become.

'It's very warm in here,' said Jenkins gallantly. 'I'm feeling a little hot myself.'

Mrs Caldicot smiled at him, gratefully. Mr Caldicot had never been gallant either. Not, at least, with her.

'The residents seem to have settled in well,' Jenkins said. 'When I passed by the door into the lounge I noticed that they were having a very energetic game of something involving a cushion and a row of chairs piled onto a table.'

'Volleyball,' explained Mrs Caldicot. 'They're all very keen on volleyball at the moment. They've worked out a schedule of matches and they're playing the World Cup. I think Argentina are playing France this morning.'

'It seemed a pretty energetic game.'

'It usually is. They do get very involved.'

There was a silence.

'I was just passing,' lied Jenkins. 'I thought I'd drop in to see if I could buy you lunch. But if it's inconvenient ... if you'd rather make it another day...' He left the sentence unfinished.

'Oh, no,' said Mrs Caldicot, perhaps, she thought, a trifle

too hastily. 'Oh, no. Lunch would be wonderful.'

'You're sure?' asked Jenkins.

'Absolutely!' said Mrs Caldicot. She flushed and smiled. She glanced at the clock on the wall and then down at her pinafore. The clock showed that it was five minutes to twelve. She hurriedly dried her hands on her pinafore.

The back door swung open. 'Pickering!' cried an unexpected voice which neither of them recognised.

Mrs Caldicot and Jenkins both turned. A large, red-faced man stood in the kitchen doorway. He wore a worn leather gilet, a red and black lumberjack shirt, a pair of brown corduroy trousers and a pair of muddy army boots.

'Pickering Organics!' repeated the untimely intruder. 'Your organic veg delivery.' He looked around. 'Where's Enid?'

'Oh right, good,' said Mrs Caldicot. 'That's wonderful. Thank you. Enid left I'm afraid. Could you bring everything into the kitchen please?'

The delivery man did nothing to hide his disappointment, though there was no way to tell whether it was inspired by the absence of Enid, by the discovery that he was expected to bring in the fruit and vegetables by himself or by a mixture of both these factors. 'Haven't you got someone who could give me a hand?' he moaned. 'I've got my bad back to think of.'

'I'm afraid there isn't anyone available to help you,' said Mrs Caldicot. 'And could you hurry please? I'm going out to lunch.'

Jenkins looked down at his unblemished and impeccably tailored suit and his perfectly polished shoes. 'I'd be glad to help but I'm afraid I'm not really dressed for humping boxes of vegetables.'

The delivery man looked Jenkins up and down and sniffed contemptuously. 'You wouldn't be no good anyway,' he complained before disappearing. He looked at Mrs Caldicot. 'Don't I know you from somewhere?' he demanded. 'Are you famous?'

'If you've heard of me then I am,' replied Mrs Caldicot. 'But if you haven't then I don't suppose I am.'

'What's your name?'

'Caldicot. Thelma Caldicot,' replied Mrs Caldicot.

'I think I may have heard of you,' said the delivery man, screwing up his nose and giving a rather poor impression of a man lost in thought. 'Perhaps you used to be someone famous?' he suggested at last.

'Perhaps I did,' said Mrs Caldicot. 'You'll be famous too if I bash your head in with a saucepan,' she thought.

The delivery man left.

'Do you get a lot of that?' asked Jenkins, with a slight smile.

'A little,' confessed Mrs Caldicot.

'You handled it very well,' said Jenkins. 'You seem very confident these days.'

'Thank you,' murmured Mrs Caldicot. 'But 'seem' is the operative word. I've just got better at faking it.'

'Who was Enid?' asked Jenkins.

'Oh don't ask!' said Mrs Caldicot, holding up both hands and pulling a face. She sighed and then answered the question anyway. 'Enid used to be our cook. I hired her in something of a rush when I first opened the nursing home. But I discovered that she was secretly ordering a crate of sherry a week and drinking it all by herself. I had to let her go. It was my own fault. I should have spotted there was something wrong when she served pilchards four days running.'

'I quite like pilchards,' said Jenkins. 'Under-estimated delicacy. Nothing wrong with serving pilchards. Full of vitamins and fish oils.'

'But she served them for pudding,' said Mrs Caldicot. 'With custard.'

'Ah,' said Jenkins, pulling a face. 'Possibly not such a terribly good idea.'

'I should have realised then that there was something not quite right,' said Mrs Caldicot. 'But it wasn't until I got the bill from the grocers' and saw how much sherry we'd been getting through...'

'Then you fired her,' said Jenkins, with a slight smile. 'Good for you.'

Mrs Caldicot held up a hand and shivered involuntarily. 'Oh, please don't use the 'f' word,' she said. 'It makes me go all funny inside. Being able to let people go makes me sound too much like a boss.'

They were interrupted by the arrival of Mrs Roberts, Mrs Caldicot's senior nurse and right hand. Mrs Roberts appeared in the doorway which led into the hall and the body of the nursing home, looking flustered, as though she'd been hurrying. She was not built for hurrying. There was a large, damp stain on the front of her blue uniform. 'I'm sorry to bother you, Mrs Caldicot,' she apologised. She lowered her voice and spoke in a whisper. 'But it's Mr Williams. Henry Williams. The new resident. It's just a teeny, weeny bit of an emergency.'

'What's the trouble?' asked Mrs Caldicot anxiously.

'He wants to leave,' explained Mrs Roberts. 'I'm afraid he's being rather aggressive.' She plucked at her damp uniform. She leant forward and whispered. 'He attacked me with a vase of flowers.'

'You weren't hurt?' asked Mrs Caldicot, concerned.

'Oh no,' replied Mrs Roberts. 'Fortunately, he didn't let go of the vase. Freesias aren't very heavy and water's just damp isn't it?'

'Oh dear me,' said Mrs Caldicot.

'I think it's probably just the pills he's been taking,' explained Mrs Roberts.

Mrs Caldicot turned to Jenkins. 'I'm sorry,' she said. 'I'd...'

Jenkins interrupted her. 'You go and sort out Mr Williams,' he said. 'Would you like me to come with you?'

'Oh no, thank you,' replied Mrs Caldicot. 'But if you could stay here and keep an eye on the delivery man....'

'I'll count in the carrots,' promised Jenkins, as Mrs Caldicot, followed by Mrs Roberts, left the kitchen and headed for the stairs.

CHAPTER ELEVEN

By the time Mrs Caldicot and Mrs Roberts got upstairs Henry Williams had collapsed back onto his bed and was staring rather morosely at his slippered feet.

'Is he all right?' Mrs Roberts asked Ruth, a plump young girl who had been hired to clean, tidy and generally help out once or twice a week. Eighteen-year-old Ruth was a naturally calm, peaceful, seemingly unflappable girl who had taken to her work with gusto. She was a big girl, who had weighed her age for as long as she could remember. She had weighed ten stones at the age of ten, twelve stones at the age of twelve and fourteen stones at the age of fourteen. Following this simple pattern she now weighed eighteen stones and, with a birthday coming up in three months, was eating with an enthusiasm pretty well guaranteed to ensure that she did not disappoint anyone who might be plotting her age and weight and hoping to continue their chart with a neat line.

Ruth, who was sitting in an easy chair watching Mr Williams staring at his feet, turned and nodded before noticing Mrs Caldicot. She jumped to her feet as quickly and as daintily as an eighteen stone teenager can do and curtsied. This was something Mrs Caldicot had, unsuccessfully, tried to persuade her to stop. No one had ever curtsied to her before and still not being entirely sure of the appropriate response she simply smiled and said 'hello' and quietly and tactfully suggested to the girl that she should pick up the small table which she had inadvertently and unknowingly knocked to the floor during the execution of the curtsey.

'Maybe we'd better call Dr Snoot again,' Mrs Caldicot said to Mrs Roberts.

'I telephoned them,' said Mrs Roberts. 'I got Dr Mrs Snoot. She said that after she'd finished her lunch, she would be busy in a meeting with social workers and told me to give him another tranquilliser. To be honest I don't think she had the faintest idea who he is.'

'You didn't give her any more details about him?'

'No.'

'Probably just as well. Don't want to burden her with too much information. Sounds like she's a busy woman.'

CHAPTER TWELVE

Downstairs, in the kitchen, the bad-tempered delivery man had finished bringing in the boxes of vegetables and fruit. The boxes were now stacked neatly in three piles just inside the back door.

'That's the last one,' said the huge, sweating, red-faced man, dropping a box full of carrots down onto the last remaining square of spare kitchen table. There were already boxes of potatoes, cauliflower, turnips, beans, broccoli and other vegetables on the table. There were boxes of apples, oranges and bananas too.

'Sign here, mate,' said the sullen delivery man, pulling a piece of pink paper out of his gilet pocket and thrusting it under Jenkins's nose. Jenkins unfolded the paper, and studied it carefully for a few moments. The top, pink, sheet had a copy attached to its underside. The delivery man arched his back and gave it a meaningful rub.

'What happened to the radishes?' Jenkins asked.

'Out of radishes.'

'I'll cross them off the list then, shall I?' said Jenkins. He took a slim, gold ballpoint pen out of his inside jacket pocket and drew a neat black line through the word 'radishes'. He then made an appropriate amendment to the total at the bottom of the page and signed his name. He checked that the amendments and his signature had passed through to the second copy. 'Do I keep the top or bottom copy?' he asked.

'Bottom.'

Jenkins kept the bottom copy and handed the top copy back to the delivery man who took it, and hesitated. There was clearly something on his mind.

'Tell Mrs Caldicot that she don't get no more veg until I get paid,' He folded his arms, held his head back and put on the look he always gave people when they owed him money. He had once been told that it made him look hard. When he had been younger and slighter this may well have been an accurate observation. But it is difficult for an overweight man with thinning ginger hair, an overhanging paunch and ill-fitting false teeth to look menacing.

'Right,' said Jenkins. 'I'll tell her.'

'She's a few weeks over,' explained the man.

'Right,' said Jenkins. 'I'm sure it's an oversight. I'll tell her.'

'Can I ask you something?' asked the delivery man, allowing his hard-man look to fade away.

'Of course,' agreed Jenkins. 'Ask away.'

'Why does she never have no cabbage?' he asked.

'I beg your pardon?' said Jenkins.

'The woman who makes up the order,' explained the delivery man. 'She never puts cabbage on the list.' He paused, clearly puzzled. 'What's wrong with cabbage?'

'I don't think she likes cabbage,' explained Jenkins. 'It's a long story.' He slipped the greengrocer's invoice into his jacket pocket.

CHAPTER THIRTEEN

Mrs Caldicot entered the kitchen at speed.

'Doctors!' she cried. 'They make me so angry!'

'What's the matter?' asked Jenkins.

Mrs Caldicot told him of the trouble she'd had trying to get hold of Mr Williams's general practitioner. As she talked she stroked Kitty, who was sleeping on her rug on top of the boiler. Stroking Kitty always helped calm her down.

'Ring again,' suggested Jenkins.

'I will!' said Mrs Caldicot. She looked at the clock. 'But later,' she added, with a slightly coquettish smile. 'Are you still willing to take me out to lunch?'

'The minute you're ready,' answered Jenkins.

'Give me two minutes to brush my hair and freshen my make-up,' said Mrs Caldicot. 'Why don't you wait in the lounge? You should be safe enough. The volleyball players are having their lunch.'

Jenkins, puzzled, looked around. 'I was wondering about

that,' he admitted. 'Who made their lunch?'

'The chef at the pizza parlour,' replied Mrs Caldicot. 'I said that as a treat while Mr and Mrs Merivale get settled in they could have a take-away for lunch. I gave them a choice between Chinese food, Indian food and pizzas but told them they all had to have the same because we get a discount on bulk orders.'

'And they chose pizzas?'

'Well, actually, no, they didn't. Half of them wanted Chinese and half of them wanted Indian and neither half would give in so they compromised on pizzas which none of them actually wanted.'

'Sounds like a good, sound democratic solution,' nodded Jenkins. Mrs Caldicot hurried off to do things to her hair and make-up. In the hallway she met Mrs Roberts, her arms full of towels.

'Where did you meet him?' whispered Mrs Roberts. 'He's gorgeous!'

'Who?' asked Mrs Caldicot, pretending not to understand.

'You know who. The gorgeous hunk in the kitchen. The one who's taking you out to lunch.'

'Oh, that's Jenkins,' explained Mrs Caldicot, trying to sound dismissive and unconcerned. 'He's a newspaper editor. We met when I left the nursing home and had that very public battle with Muller-Hawksmoor.'

'Well, he's very dishy,' whispered Mrs Roberts. 'If people say I'm looking a funny colour today it's because I'm green with envy.' She turned, hurrying on her way with her towels. A few feet down the corridor she half turned. 'You take as long as you like over lunch,' she said, over her shoulder. She grinned and winked. 'You enjoy yourself. We can cope without you for a few hours.'

Meanwhile, Jenkins used his mobile phone to call the restaurant where he had already booked a table, to warn them that he and his guest would be late and to ensure that they would hold the table and the booking, and then wandered out of the kitchen and headed towards the lounge. As he passed the dining room he was distracted by a conversation between two female voices he recognised.

'So, what sort of morning have you had?' asked the first woman, who sounded like Miss Nightingale.

'Terrible,' answered the second woman. 'Our entire computer system was down for two hours. I don't know why we have so many IT consultants. They're useless. More problems with the new software too. My desktop froze up so often I ended up working on my laptop. Our supplier in Frankfurt has let us down again, the air conditioning has packed up, Trent from head office has been promoted over me when everyone knows he can't tie his shoelaces without help, the contract from Brussels didn't arrive, my secretary is leaving to have another baby and, to top it all, by the time she got to me the tea lady didn't have any Jammy Dodgers left. What sort of day did you have?'

'Awful. Simply awful,' said the voice which sounded as though it belonged to Miss Nightingale. 'The washing machine got stuck on programme five so all your white shirts are now bright pink and two sizes too small, the postman left next door's mail for the third time this week, the dishwasher overflowed all over the kitchen floor, two Jehovah's Witnesses called and I couldn't get rid of them for half an hour, a man from the garage rang and said that my car is unroadworthy because the ashtrays are full and there's a spider in the garage twice the size of King Kong.'

'Oh dear,' said the second woman. 'You poor thing. Mr Hopping in accounts came in to see me. He says that I can't claim for the cup of tea I had when I went to Newcastle on the train a week last Wednesday. He says that the board has decided that cups of tea are no longer to be considered necessary expenses. Worst of all, there's a rumour that Miss Onions in the typing pool is pregnant though I don't know how that could be because I'd heard that she was on the pill. Oh, and I may be an hour or two late tonight. Mr Farthing wants me to go over the Global Moulding account with him.'

Jenkins, extremely puzzled by what he was hearing, was beginning to feel guilty for eavesdropping (even newspaper editors have scruples) when one of the residents came out of the dining room and nearly ran into him.

'Hello, Mr Jenkins!' cried Mr Livingstone. 'Won't you come

and join us? Have a slice of pizza? There's plenty.' He waved an empty bottle. 'I'm just off to get more wine.'

Jenkins was thanking him and explaining that he had already made arrangements for his lunch when Mrs Caldicot came skipping down the stairs.

'I'm sorry,' said Mrs Caldicot, rather breathlessly. Jenkins looked at her. In less than fifteen minutes she had somehow succeeded in transforming herself. She looked beautiful and radiant. He told her.

'Don't be silly,' she said, blushing and giggling, though secretly she herself was quite pleased with the way she now looked. After tidying up her hair and her make-up and slipping into something a little slinkier than she normally wore she had caught sight of herself in the bathroom mirror. For a brief moment she had almost failed to recognise herself.

'I'm serious,' insisted Jenkins as they left.

In the car Jenkins turned to Mrs Caldicot. 'Can you explain something for me?' he asked. 'When I was in the hall I distinctly heard two women talking about the sort of morning they'd both had at work. I didn't think any of your residents had jobs.'

'Oh that would have been Miss Nightingale and Mrs Torridge!' laughed Mrs Caldicot. 'They just pretend. It's a little game they play at meal-times. They're quite good at it.'

For a moment Jenkins felt rather foolish. Then he saw the funny side of it. 'They were very convincing,' he smiled.

'Mrs Torridge is an amazing woman,' said Mrs Caldicot. 'She always keeps all her clocks and watches at different times. She says she's done it since she was 20 and that it completely eliminates boredom from her life.'

Jenkins laughed.

'You'd like her,' said Mrs Caldicot. 'She's a terrible hypochondriac but great fun. She is the sort of woman who never has a cold but always has the flu. But you'll like her! I've forgotten how old she is because she always lies about her age. The other day I heard her tell someone that she is 92.'

'Why on earth does she do that? I thought women usually liked to pretend they are younger than they really are.'

'Not after a certain age,' explained Mrs Caldicot. 'Mrs Torridge reckons that if people think she's ten years older than she really is they'll always tell her how good she looks. It works too. People are always paying her amazing compliments. The others have started doing it too. Miss Nightingale now always lies about her age. Mrs Peterborough simply can't remember hers.' Mrs Caldicot sighed. 'All our residents are wonderful. The other day Mr Hewitt told me that he had only ever wanted the simple things in life. When I asked him to define what he meant by the simple things, do you know what he said?'

'No,' laughed Jenkins. 'Tell me.'

'Love, money, power and immortality,' laughed Mrs Caldicot. She had laughed more with Jenkins than she'd ever laughed with the late Mr Caldicot. She suddenly realised how happy and content she felt when she was in his company. And safe too. In the months since her husband had died she'd had to grow a great deal. But underneath the tough exterior there was still a very soft inside. She wondered if Jenkins asked her out because he wanted to or simply because he thought he ought to keep in touch with her. She very much wanted it to be the former but was worried that it might be the latter. It had been a long, long time since she'd felt like this. She felt slightly bewildered and embarrassed and could sense that she was blushing again.

'I like the new building,' said Jenkins. 'It looks very elegant.'

'I was sad that we had to move,' said Mrs Caldicot. 'But some of the residents just couldn't settle in at the old place and we needed somewhere a bit bigger.' She paused. 'Besides...' she began and suddenly wished she hadn't.

'Go on,' encouraged Jenkins, as he accelerated past a bus.

'It's silly,' said Mrs Caldicot. 'You'll laugh.'

'No I won't,' said Jenkins. 'And what does it matter if I do. You think it's silly anyway.'

She looked at him. He was so kind. He always managed to make her feel good about herself. 'I had the old place painted and we moved out all the furniture and the carpets and the curtains.' It did seem silly. She couldn't help herself. She grinned. 'But we just couldn't get rid of the smell of cabbage.'

He laughed. But it wasn't a nasty laugh. He wasn't laughing at her. He was laughing with her.

'That's a pretty good reason for moving,' he told her.

'I spent far too much on moving,' admitted Mrs Caldicot. 'I'd like to have really nice furniture, carpets and curtains so that it will look more like a hotel than a rest home. The place we're in now must have been wonderful when it was last decorated but I seriously suspect that was probably a century ago!'

'It looks wonderful,' said Jenkins. 'You bought all the furniture with the new place, didn't you?'

Mrs Caldicot nodded. 'The place had been in the same family for generations,' she said. 'They hadn't done anything to it. When the old man who'd been living there died he left it to his children. But they didn't want anything to do with it. They just wanted the place sold quickly so that they could split up the proceeds.'

'I don't know anything about furnishings or furniture but it looks very grand,' said Jenkins. 'Some of that furniture looks quite valuable to me. If I were you I wouldn't change a thing. And there's no smell of cabbage. Do you have nothing now to remind you of that chap who used to run the Twilight Years ... what was he called? Muller-something wasn't it?'

'There's a vase in the lounge that used to stand on the hall table. Miss Nightingale rescued it and brought it with us.' She paused. 'Actually, I wish she hadn't,' she said. 'It annoys me because it's the only reminder of the past.'

'I shouldn't worry too much about it,' said Jenkins. 'The way your residents chase around it won't last long.'

'No,' agreed Mrs Caldicot. 'I suspect that you're right.'

CHAPTER FOURTEEN

'Would you order for me, please?' said Mrs Caldicot quietly, folding her menu and putting it down on the immaculate, white linen tablecloth. 'I honestly don't understand any of this,' she said, tapping the closed menu with a forefinger. 'It's all in French.' She had also been slightly bewildered by the fact that her menu hadn't contained any prices.

'Do you like salmon?'

'Oh yes, very much.' Mrs Caldicot lowered her voice still further. 'But isn't it terribly expensive?'

'Not at all,' Jenkins assured her.

'How can you possibly know?' asked Mrs Caldicot, looking around anxiously. 'There aren't any prices on the menu.'

'There are on mine,' Jenkins assured her. 'They gave you a menu without prices so that you wouldn't know how much of a cheapskate I am.' He smiled.

Mrs Caldicot smiled back. She found the newspaperman irresistible.

'Are you sure the rest home will be OK while you're away?' Jenkins asked. 'Everything seemed so hectic that I feel a little guilty taking you out.'

'Everything will be fine,' replied Mrs Caldicot. 'Mrs Roberts is in charge. She's marvellous.'

Jenkins frowned. 'Mrs Roberts? I don't know her do I?'

'You saw her briefly,' said Mrs Caldicot. 'Gina Roberts. She's plumpish, mid forties, black and she has the smile of an angel. She's always laughing. I sometimes think that everyone who knows her regards her as their very best friend.'

'I remember.'

'When I re-opened the Twilight Years Rest Home I had to hire all sorts of staff. I'd never done anything like it before and to be honest I wasn't very good at it. For example, the cook we've just lost was one of my first appointments.'

'The sherry enthusiast?'

'That's the one,' said Mrs Caldicot, with a roll of her eyes. 'My oh my, she was a mistake. Not that she was the only mistake. I hired a housekeeper who stole from the petty cash and two young men who were supposed to do the heavy work but who spent all their time picking up local girls and bringing them back to their rooms. Mrs Roberts has more than made up for all the mistakes I made. She's a real gem. She's one of those people who always seems to get so much more out of giving than receiving. She always wants to do things for people but gets very embarrassed if anyone does anything for her. She used to work as a nurse at the Twilight Years Rest Home back in Muller-Hawksmoor's days and I remembered her from my brief stay there. She's wonderfully kind and sympathetic. She'd just got divorced and was living in a tiny flat so she moved in with us. The Twilight Years Rest Home is now her life – just as it is mine. She cares about people so much that I sometimes think that if the unions found out about her they'd have her hung, drawn and quartered. Now, she's our Matron and I honestly don't know how I'd cope without her.'

'Matron?'

'Yes. It's a wonderfully old-fashioned word, isn't it? But it sounds much nicer than 'head nurse', don't you think? Mrs Roberts tells me that in hospitals these days the senior nurses never actually see any patients. They have numbers and spend all their days either shuffling bits of paper around or attending meetings. Most of them have long since forgotten how to bandage someone. They go around telling young nurses off if they're seen sitting on the beds, comforting the sick and the needy. Mrs Roberts is a proper nurse. She doesn't mind getting her hands dirty. And she's old-fashioned enough to believe that comforting the sick and the needy is what a nurse is there for.'

'It sounds as if you're lucky to have her.'

'Oh, I am,' agreed Mrs Caldicot.

'Now, what shall we have after the salmon? A raspberry sorbet? And then how about beef and Yorkshire pudding?'

'That sounds wonderful,' agreed Mrs Caldicot. She laughed. 'It sounds absolutely marvellous.'

Jenkins smiled. 'I love to hear you laugh,' he told her. He closed his menu and, moments later, murmured the order to the waiter who had miraculously appeared at his shoulder.

'Excellent choice, sir,' murmured the waiter. Mrs Caldicot couldn't help wondering why this choice deserved a compliment and what horrors they had avoided by not choosing the spring lamb chop or the braised liver.

'Would you like some wine?' Jenkins asked Mrs Caldicot.

'Oh no, I don't think so,' said Mrs Caldicot. 'Not at lunch-time. I'll fall asleep.'

'We could just have a glass of champagne with our salmon and then half a bottle of a nice red between us with our main course,' suggested Jenkins. 'I've got to drive so I won't drink more than one glass.'

'You're leading me astray!' laughed Mrs Caldicot. She paused, looked at him and remembered. 'But then you've always been very good at that.'

'I'll ask the wine waiter to come over,' murmured the waiter, before picking up the two menus and shimmying away silently.

'I think you deserve a little leading astray,' said Jenkins, when the waiter had gone. He leant across the table a little. 'And, if someone's going to do it, I'm very happy to apply for the job.'

Mrs Caldicot, blushing, looked down and played with her cutlery.

'I have a confession to make,' said Jenkins suddenly.

Mrs Caldicot looked across at him, surprised.

'I didn't turn up at the home by accident,' he told her.

'Oh.'

'I came quite deliberately. To see you.'

'Oh.'

'I've been trying to pluck up the courage to come and see you for ages.'

'Why on earth would you need courage to come and see me?' asked Mrs Caldicot.

'I don't know,' admitted Jenkins. 'Perhaps because I was frightened that you might say 'no' if I invited you out. And being able to hang on to the thought that you might say 'yes' was more acceptable than the possibility of finding out that you might say 'no'.'

Mrs Caldicot couldn't think of any suitable reply to this and so she said nothing for a while. Since Jenkins was hoping that Mrs Caldicot might say something encouraging he too stayed silent. He had been astonished to find just how delighted he had been to see her and just how much he had missed her.

'Why do they do that?' she asked at last, very quietly.

'Do what?'

'Congratulate you on what you've ordered. If I'd ordered the steak and kidney pie would he have leant down and quietly told me that I'd made a terrible decision because it's rancid?'

Jenkins laughed. It was a long time since he'd met a woman with Mrs Caldicot's uniquely honest approach to life. He very much enjoyed being with her.

'I don't know,' he said. 'And I'm not going to ask. I have very few rules,' he continued. 'But one of them is never to argue with or embarrass a waiter before I eat a meal at the restaurant where he works. It is a simple, unambitious rule but it is, I believe, one which has helped to protect me from food poisoning on four continents.'

A young girl, dressed in a black skirt and a white blouse, appeared at their table carrying a basket full of bread rolls. Jenkins chose a white roll covered in a thick sprinkling of sesame seeds. Mrs Caldicot selected a small brown roll, baked in the shape of a small Hovis loaf.

Jenkins had booked a table at the best local hotel he could find. He had been abroad on a lengthy assignment for the proprietor of the newspaper for which he worked and he had missed Mrs Caldicot very much. He had never before become emotionally involved with the subject of a story but had thought about her often while he'd been away. Several times he'd picked up the telephone, intending to call her. But on each occasion he had put the telephone back down without making the call. He knew why he had wanted to call. But up until now he hadn't been at all sure why he hadn't gone through with it. Now he knew. He had been frightened that he was getting too closely involved. He had been frightened by the intensity of his own feelings. Now, it was too late.

'How has life been for you personally?' Jenkins asked, breaking his bread into several pieces. 'I know how things have been for the Rest Home. You have done amazing things. But what about you?'

Mrs Caldicot thought for a long moment before answering. 'My biggest surprise was that I found dealing with my husband's death harder than I thought I would,' she confessed. 'Everything happened so quickly that I never really had chance to come to terms with what had happened. I neither asked for, nor expected, anything from my husband and so I was never disappointed. But you get used to people, nevertheless, and with all the drama and the excitement I didn't get a chance to mourn him properly. If 'mourn' is the right word.' Following her dining companion's example Mrs Caldicot picked up and broke her own bread roll.

'My GP arranged for me to see a bereavement counsellor,' continued Mrs Caldicot. 'Though before he died I never knew such people existed.'

'I didn't know they existed within the NHS,' commented Jenkins, whose view of the Britain's state organised health service was poor.

'They don't,' said Mrs Caldicot. 'I had to pay this one £90 an hour.'

'Was he any good?'

'To be perfectly honest my hairdresser gave me better support and much better advice,' laughed Mrs Caldicot. 'And he did my hair too.'

Jenkins, buttered the two halves of his bread roll. Mrs Caldicot continued to break hers into smaller and smaller pieces. 'He calls himself Luigi but I happen to know he comes from Southport,' said Mrs Caldicot. 'He did once go to Calais on one of those cheap wine and cigarettes shopping expeditions but he's never been to Italy.'

Jenkins took a bite of bread roll and chewed for a moment before he said anything. 'Luigi was the hairdresser?'

Mrs Caldicot laughed. 'Oh yes. The bereavement counsellor was called Ms Cook. I don't know her first name. Isn't that odd? I don't know the hairdresser's second name and I don't know her first name. I think she said her parents came from Sydney but I'm pretty sure she said she was born in Dudley.'

'Did she help at all?' asked Jenkins, just before taking another bite of bread roll.

'I was asked to describe Mr Caldicot's virtues at the bereavement counselling,' she said. 'The only thing I could think of was tidiness. He was always a very tidy man. He always put his dirty washing straight into the raffia work washing skip at the top of the landing. But it's not a lot to say of someone is it? That you remember them because they were 'tidy'?' She paused and looked down and there was a silence for a few moments. 'I didn't really need to mourn him,' she said, reflecting. 'I didn't miss him in a spiritual sort of way. It was more that I just needed to get used to him not being there. I missed not having to cook for two and I missed not having to wash and iron his shirts. But those aren't really things that you miss, are they?'

'Would you like another roll?' Jenkins asked Mrs Caldicot. She looked down. The roll with which she had been playing was now nothing but a pile of crumbs on her plate.

'Oh dear,' she said, looking down and staring aghast at her plate. 'Did I really do that?' She picked her handbag up off the floor, brought it underneath the table and opened it. She then tipped the crumbs from the plate into her handbag.

'I think the bereavement counsellor would probably call it 'anger displacement', and charge you another £90,' said Jenkins.

Another waiter brought their two glasses of champagne. Jenkins asked him to bring Mrs Caldicot a fresh roll. When he had gone Jenkins lifted his glass. 'To health, love and money and time to enjoy them all,' he said.

Mrs Caldicot lifted her glass, repeated the toast, touched her glass against Jenkins's and took a sip.

'Mmmm,' she said. 'This is very good.'

Two waiters brought two plates upon which silver domes hid the food. The waiters placed the plates on the tablecloth, paused and then, in unison, lifted the domes to reveal their salmon – the first course.

'Doesn't it look wonderful?' said Mrs Caldicot, her face as excited as a child's at Christmas.

They ate in silence for a while.

'Do you have all the residents who used to live at Mr Muller-Hawksmoor's establishment?' Jenkins asked.

'Oh no,' replied Mrs Caldicot. 'A few were so upset by

everything that had happened that they went back to live with their families or in rest homes or sheltered accommodation nearer to relatives. Two are currently in hospital, and, of course, poor old Mrs Davies – whom I don't think you ever met – died.'

'Is Mrs Peterborough still with you?'

'She's with me. She's as dotty as ever but just as adorable. She still repeats everything Miss Nightingale says. And we've got Mrs Torridge, of course, who has her little quirks too. Do you know she wakes up sometimes and decides she's really someone else. One day last week she decided that she was Harold Wilson. She borrowed an old pipe and went around making speeches all day long. Her family turn up occasionally and want to have her committed to a mental institution but she's very happy with us. If she was richer people would just think her rather eccentric.'

'And Mr Livingstone is still with you, isn't he? I saw him.'

'Oh yes. And dear old Mr Hewitt. Actually, it's a good job we don't have as many residents as there were before because Muller-Hawksmoor had his residents sharing two or three to a room and now everyone has their own room – except Mrs Peterborough and Miss Nightingale who can't abide the thought of being separated and who insisted on sharing a room – and Mr and Mrs Merivale too, of course.'

'Mr and Mrs Merivale?' said Jenkins, thoughtfully. 'I don't think I remember them.'

'No, they're new,' agreed Mrs Caldicot. 'Maple and Maurice Merivale. They're a lovely couple. Of course, we don't have as many rooms as there used to be. We knocked down some of the partitions, to make the rooms bigger and airier. It didn't take much work. Some of the partitions were so thin that if you put one nail in you could hang pictures on both sides.'

'And who is the latest patient – the one whose doctor you were trying to contact?'

'That's a gentleman called Mr Williams. He came because the hospital needed his bed. We've only got two empty rooms now.'

'I don't wish to sound horribly mercenary,' said Jenkins. 'But can Mr Williams afford to pay anything for his board and lodging?'

'I've no idea,' admitted Mrs Caldicot.

'And you didn't ask?'

'Good heavens, no,' said Mrs Caldicot.

'No,' sighed Jenkins, a slight smile creeping onto his lips. 'I suppose not.'

CHAPTER FIFTEEN

'I've been very lucky,' said Mrs Caldicot, as she tackled her salmon. 'We don't have much income but all the residents help out when they can.' She paused. 'They're brilliant,' she said. 'All we need now is someone to do the roof.'

'It's leaking?'

'Only when it rains,' said Mrs Caldicot. Realising what she'd said she laughed at herself. 'I'm looking for a roofer who will overcharge and do a shoddy job. At least then I'll know that I won't be disappointed as well.'

'But, apart from the roof, it's all working out OK?' asked Jenkins.

'We all do our best,' said Mrs Caldicot. 'The only real problem is that instead of doing what they can to make things easier the authorities bend over backwards to make things difficult. All I want to do is run a little home for a few friends – provide them with a roof and so on. It doesn't seem a lot to ask, does it?'

Jenkins, who sometimes thought he knew far too much about the way the world works, said nothing and smiled at her.

'I sometimes wake up not really sure what happened to me. One minute I'm a slightly dotty old lady whose relatives decide she needs to be put into a home. The next minute I'm still a slightly dotty old lady but now I'm in charge of the home. Phrases like 'putting the lunatics in charge of the asylum' spring to mind. But then I just get on with life and try not to worry too much. Though I confess I do often ask myself whether doing the right things for the wrong reasons is worse or better than doing the wrong things for the right reasons.'

'I'd rather leave the metaphysics to our philosophy editor, if you don't mind,' said Jenkins.

'Have you really got one? A philosophy editor?'

'Good heavens, no,' laughed Jenkins, clearing his plate and laying down his knife and fork. 'I'm a great fan of yours and really admire what you've done. I like the way you did it your way – just one woman up against the system. It's something a lot of people dream about but it doesn't happen often. The story we ran about you struck a real chord with our older readers,' Jenkins told her. 'There's a lot of resentment among older people at the moment.' He stopped, and thought for a moment. 'No,' he said, correcting himself. 'Resentment is too strong a word – though to be honest I personally don't think it would be inappropriate or out of place. A lot of old people just feel rather sad and abandoned. They feel that the elderly are no longer respected.'

'I'm not surprised,' agreed Mrs Caldicot. 'They are abandoned and they certainly aren't respected. Millions of elderly people are now officially living in poverty. They've worked hard all their lives but they can't even get decent health care now. They're pushed around, bullied, ignored and treated as though they're just a nuisance.'

'I spend quite a lot of time on what used to be called the Continent,' said Jenkins. He finished his champagne. 'And I have to say that they treat their elderly relatives quite differently over there.'

'Really?' said Mrs Caldicot.

'Absolutely,' said Jenkins. 'The French, the Italians, the Spanish and so on all treat their elderly relatives with great respect and love. The eccentricity of the old isn't regarded as a cause of embarrassment as it is in Britain. They don't think that a bit of forgetfulness has to be covered up with sedatives and anti-psychotic drugs. In cafés all across mainland Europe the best café seats, the seats near to the window in the summer, or near to the stove in the winter, are reserved by popular consent, for the elderly. Old grannies are given a chair in the grocery store so that they can sit and chat with their friends. Benches are put out in the village squares so that the old men can sit around, admire the young women parading by for the benefit of the young men on their motorbikes, reminisce about their own greatest conquests, share a bottle of wine and a packet of cigarettes and keep track of all the essential comings and goings. They have the place of honour at meal-times and they sleep in their own beds, in their own rooms, with their families.'

'Golly,' said Mrs Caldicot. 'Are you sure that's not heaven you're describing?'

Jenkins smiled. 'In a village I know well in France, the waiter at the café where I usually take my evening glass of wine fetches two of his elderly and frail patrons from their homes every morning at eleven. They spend all day in the café, buying an occasional glass of wine or cup of coffee, and maybe a small meal, and then, at the end of the day, when he is about to close up his café, he takes them back home again. It seems to me to be a considerably more decent life than the sort of life we offer our elderly folk. Given a choice between a café and a day centre furnished with plastic chairs, over-loud television and a succession of patronising volunteers I know which I would choose.'

'From what you say it seems that everyone seems to have much more patience with the elderly than they have in this country,' said Mrs Caldicot. 'Here the notion of the extended family – going back three or four or five generations – is now merely something you read about in history books. We have our relatives 'put away' when they become a burden. We're too busy for family loyalties; too obsessed with our ambitions to be concerned with what happens to our old people. We make more fuss over the deaths of complete strangers – murder victims, members of the royal family – than we do about the deaths of our own relatives. How many of the thousands who went to London to lay flowers outside Kensington Palace after Diana died would have made the same trip to lay flowers on their own grandparents' graves? Most people over 60 have had to learn to accept the inevitability of systematic and continuous disappointment. Just when the commitments and responsibilities have gone, just when you no longer have to be nice to bosses and partners and customers whom you can't stand the sight of, and have a right to be able to look forward to a bit of fun

– look what happens! The only thing doctors and nurses in our hospitals will do for you is give you a metaphorical bang on the head and knock you out with some disgusting cocktail of sedatives. I wouldn't do that to my worst enemy.' Mrs Caldicot paused and thought for a moment. 'Well, I could, of course probably be persuaded,' she added. Jenkins smiled. 'The thing is that today if you're over 50,' Mrs Caldicot continued, 'the nurses don't really care whether you live or die as long as you have your bowels opened regularly. Appallingly, it's now perfectly legal for doctors and nurses to drug the elderly – just to keep them quiet and to stop them from complaining.'

'It's a scandal,' agreed Jenkins.

'I read somewhere – I think it might have been in your paper – that the increase in the prescribing of anti-psychotic drugs for the elderly is going up 70 per cent a year. In some so-called 'care' homes half or even all the patients are permanently zonked out with pills they don't need. And the government has now made it legal for the nurses and doctors to do it.' Mrs Caldicot was getting into her stride. 'The old are expected to be grateful for every little favour, thankful for their pensions. They're almost expected to give thanks for being allowed to stay alive. Doesn't anyone ever stop to think that the elderly have earned their pensions and that they are entitled to more from life than the chance to sit quietly and watch the dross on daytime television. Our old people deserve better.'

'Stop! Stop!' cried Jenkins, laughing. 'You don't have to convince me. I'm on your side. We really should get you onto the television to talk about this.'

Mrs Caldicot held up a hand. 'Oh, no, thank you,' she said. 'I think my television career is over.'

'That's a great pity,' said Jenkins. 'You were a breath of fresh air. You'd bring a lot of sense to TV discussion programmes. You could become a standard bearer for the elderly.'

'Oh I do hate that word!' said Mrs Caldicot.

'Which word?'

'Elderly. It has all sorts of unpleasant connotations. It always makes me think of geriatric wards, nasty smells and Zimmer frames.'

Jenkins smiled. 'There you are, you see!' he said. 'Always defying convention and making people think.'

'You're the one who should be on the television,' said Mrs Caldicot. 'I've never known anyone with such a sweet tongue,' She looked at her companion. 'I've told you far too much about me,' she said. 'What about you? Are you happy? Content? At peace?'

'Good heavens!' said Jenkins with a laugh. 'When you ask questions you don't mess around, do you?'

'No,' admitted Mrs Caldicot, enjoying the change of roles. 'How are you enjoying life?'

For a moment Jenkins didn't answer.

'I'm sorry,' said Mrs Caldicot quietly. 'Have I said something I shouldn't have done?'

'No, no,' said Jenkins. 'Just touched a nerve I suppose.' He sighed. 'I've been getting more and more disillusioned with what I do and the people I do it with. I'm fed up with the world and I'm fed up with newspapers. I can hardly bring myself to read the papers any more. Every day fills me with frustration. I live in a constant state of rage at the levels of corruption in almost every aspect of public and corporate life. The Government survives on the apathy of the masses. There are only two reasons to read newspapers: for pleasure and for information. I no longer get any pleasure out of reading the papers. And I have more than enough information to last me a lifetime.'

Two waiters bought their next course.

'I thought you loved newspapers!' said Mrs Caldicot, dipping a spoon into her raspberry sorbet.

'I used to love newspapers,' said Jenkins, emphasising the second word. 'But these days the newspaper industry – like everything else – is run by bean counters. Mean-spirited men and women in expensive suits who know the price of everything and the value of nothing.'

'That's very nicely put,' said Mrs Caldicot.

'It's not original, I'm afraid,' confessed Jenkins. 'Oscar Wilde said it first, in *Lady Windermere's Fan*; though knowing his reputation he probably pinched it off someone else. It was his definition of a cynic.'

'I'm sorry,' said Mrs Caldicot. She felt embarrassed. 'I don't know much about literature. I'm very ignorant.' She brightened. 'But it is an area of my ignorance I've always wanted to remedy.'

'I didn't mean to sound patronising,' said Jenkins. He finished his sorbet. 'But never one to pass up an opportunity ... if you'd like to come to the theatre with me one evening I would love to take you.'

'I'd love that,' said Mrs Caldicot. 'Very much. But don't change the subject.'

'The bean counters have changed everything,' said Jenkins. 'There's no fun, no passion and very little sense of right and wrong in newspapers these days. I think I'm the oldest senior member of staff on my paper – and probably one of the oldest on any national newspaper. Most of the young fellows around these days are in it for money and power rather than because they're interested in finding out and exposing the truth.'

The waiters arrived to collect their empty sorbet dishes. Moments later they brought the main course. The wine waiter followed with half a bottle of claret.

'Let's get back to your life,' said Mrs Caldicot firmly. 'Wasn't there some journalist who once said that a journalist should treat politicians in the same way that dogs treat lampposts?'

Jenkins grinned broadly. 'Exactly!' he said. 'It was a chap called H.L. Mencken and he was absolutely right. These days most of the young guys in suits have probably never heard of Mencken. And they certainly wouldn't dream of treating a politician disrespectfully. Most of them suck up to politicians so that their bosses can get their deals pushed through and so that they can get their knighthoods and their well-paid positions on influential quangos.'

'You sound as if you consider yourself a bit prehistoric!' said Mrs Caldicot.

'I am!' said Jenkins. 'I'm an anachronism. I've always considered myself to be fairly tough and hardy – and even cynical – but the new editors I work with are ruthless. They're hard rather than hardy. They never let their emotions govern the way they treat a story.'

Jenkins picked up a spoon and started to play with it. 'I had lunch with my editor two days ago,' he said. 'At the Savoy in London. He ordered steak and chips, as he always does, and when it came he poked at it rather half-heartedly with his knife and immediately told the waiter that the steak wasn't cooked as he'd ordered it. The waiter was rather taken aback. He apologised and offered to take the steak back to the kitchen to be replaced. 'No. I haven't got time,' said the editor. And he dismissed the waiter with a wave of his hand. When the poor guy had gone he looked at me. 'Nothing wrong with the steak,' he told me coldly. 'Just thought I'd keep the guy on his toes and let him know who's in charge."

Neither Jenkins nor Mrs Caldicot said a word for a moment. 'I don't think I like your world very much,' said Mrs Caldicot.

'That's exactly my problem,' said Jenkins. 'I don't like it very much either. The modern corporate man operates on fear,' he said. 'He is frightened that without the fear his power will simply disappear. The editor's appreciation of his own power is confirmed every day by the fact that journalists shiver and jump when he approaches. If they stop shivering and jumping he won't know that he has the power. Of course, the poor fellow is driven by fear too. The power goes with the job. Without the job he will have no power.'

Mrs Caldicot looked at him, reached across the table and touched his hand. 'I am sorry,' she said. 'I think I always thought that your life was just all roses.'

Jenkins shook his head sadly. 'What a pointless and rather pathetic use of power,' he said. 'I find it frightening to realise that a man like that is running a national newspaper,' he said. 'He humiliated a perfectly decent human being just to show me how ruthless he is and to underline the gulf that exists between the two of them. It was also a message to me, to let me know he's the boss.' He looked across at Mrs Caldicot. 'I've got to get out,' he said. 'I'm terrified that I'll be contaminated by all this; that it will infect my soul. I'm already beginning to assume there is a hidden agenda behind everything people do.' He sighed. 'I've got to get away from it.'

'Perhaps you need a holiday,' suggested Mrs Caldicot.

'No, no. A holiday is no good I'm afraid. I won't be able to forget the sort of world I now work in. If I get too soft then when I get back I'll be massacred. I need to get out of it for good.'

The waiter arrived, waited for them to acknowledge his presence and then recited an impressive list of puddings.

'What would you like?' asked Jenkins, brightening up. 'No more of this misery, I promise you. I didn't bring you here to bore you silly with my complaints.'

'You didn't bore me,' insisted Mrs Caldicot.

'Choose a pudding,' said Jenkins, smiling. 'Something stuffed with calories.'

'You'll laugh,' said Mrs Caldicot, folding her menu and putting it down.

'No, I won't!' promised Jenkins.

'I'd like a Knickerbocker Glory,' said Mrs Caldicot.

'Why should I laugh at that?'

'It seems, sort of, childish, I suppose.'

'It seems wonderful,' said Jenkins. He turned to the waiter and ordered one Knickerbocker Glory.

'Of course, sir,' smiled the waiter. He turned to Jenkins. 'And for you, sir?'

'Just coffee for me, please.'

'You tricked me!' protested Mrs Caldicot. 'I thought you were having a pudding.'

'I'll get far more pleasure out of watching you eat yours,' said Jenkins. 'Do you want coffee?'

'No thanks,' said Mrs Caldicot. 'I haven't had a Knickerbocker Glory for years,' she confessed. 'Not since I was a girl. I don't know what gave me the idea.' She hesitated. 'Yes, I do,' she corrected herself. 'I don't think I've enjoyed a meal as much since I was a child. It sort of reminded me of happy times...'

'I'm pleased,' said Jenkins, who clearly meant it.

'So, what are you going to do about your life?' asked Mrs Caldicot. 'Do you have something planned?'

For a moment or two Jenkins didn't reply. He picked up his wine glass, inspected it as though looking for marks, stared at it as though he had seen it before but couldn't quite remember where, drank a little wine from it and gently put it down. 'I've been offered a new job,' he said at last. 'Abroad.'

Mrs Caldicot felt cold. She didn't know exactly why. 'That's wonderful!' she lied. She tried hard to sound enthusiastic but as she spoke she knew that she did not sound convincing.

Jenkins picked up the salt cellar and rolled it between his fingers. He stared at it, weighed it in his hand and then put it down again.

'Is it a good job?' asked Mrs Caldicot.

'It's a very good job,' replied Jenkins, without hesitation. 'It's in New York.'

'New York?' said Mrs Caldicot, trying hard to keep the shock and the sadness out of her voice.

'New York.'

'In America?'

'I think that's where they still keep it.'

Now it was Mrs Caldicot's turn to play with the cruet. She picked up the pepper pot and played with it. A few grains of pepper fell out onto the white damask tablecloth.

'Oh dear,' she said. 'Is pepper like salt? Do you have to throw a pinch of it over your left shoulder if you spill some?'

Jenkins looked up. He shook his head. 'I don't think so,' he replied.

'What sort of job is it? Are you terribly excited? Are you going to take it? When do you have to go?'

Jenkins looked at Mrs Caldicot, smiled and held up a hand. 'One at a time!' he said. 'You sound like a one woman press conference.'

'I'm sorry,' said Mrs Caldicot. She looked down. She wanted to run away; to hide. She could feel tears in her eyes. She should feel pleased for her friend. But she didn't. All she could think about was herself. She felt deeply ashamed. But she couldn't do anything about it.

'The proprietor of the Sunday Globe wants me to go to New York and edit a new tabloid he's bought there,' said Jenkins. He looked down at the tablecloth. 'Editing my own paper has always been my main ambition,' he told her. 'When I was a young reporter it was something I dreamt of. Loads of reporters dream of writing novels or screenplays. I've known some who wanted to be rock stars or sports stars – one or two actually made it. Some want to be businessmen – running their own operation. Some want to run pubs.' He sighed. 'I always wanted to be an editor.' He shrugged. 'That was it.'

Mrs Caldicot reached across the table and took hold of Jenkins's hand. 'I'm very pleased for you,' she said. 'You really deserve it. I'm very proud of you. And I know you'll make a wonderful editor.'

Jenkins looked at her, and put his free hand on top of the hand she had placed on his. 'Thank you,' he said. 'That means a lot to me.' But it wasn't at all what he'd wanted to hear. He had wanted her to burst into tears, to tell him that she didn't want him to go, to tell him that she wanted to see more of him, to ask him to stay. He knew she would never leave the Twilight Years Rest Home. He would never expect her to do that; not to abandon the people who depended upon her. But he had hoped that she might want him to stay and become part of her life.

'When do you have to go?' Mrs Caldicot asked him.

'Next month,' said Jenkins. 'If I say 'yes'.' He reached across the table with his free hand and took Mrs Caldicot's free hand.

'Are you going to take the job?' she asked.

'I don't know,' said Jenkins. 'I really don't know.'

Mrs Caldicot didn't say anything, mainly because she was frightened that if she spoke she would cry. She didn't want to cry. She was used to Jenkins being strong and giving her support. Now, curiously, imperceptibly, their roles seemed to have been reversed.

The waiter brought her Knickerbocker Glory and the inspired and colourful confection dominated the conversation for the next few minutes.

'Did it live up to expectations?' asked Jenkins, when Mrs Caldicot had finished.

'It was better!' she said, putting down her spoon, with a sigh.

'That's some going,' said Jenkins. 'Matching a childhood memory is usually nigh on impossible.'

'That really was better than I remembered,' Mrs Caldicot assured him, with a big smile. 'Thank you.' She looked at Jenkins. There was love in her heart and suddenly there were tears in her eyes after all.

'Why are you crying?' he asked her.

'Oh I'm just a silly, sentimental old thing,' she said, dismissively. 'Don't take any notice of me.'

CHAPTER SIXTEEN

When she returned to the nursing home Mrs Caldicot telephoned Henry Williams's general practitioner twice. She did so from her office while Jenkins sat opposite her.

The first time Mrs Caldicot telephoned she was told that the doctor couldn't come because she had to pick up her children from school. The excuse the second time was that she was halfway through an aerobics class. She spoke to the doctor herself. The doctor, wheezing and breathless, took the call on a mobile telephone.

'Well, perhaps you could call in afterwards?' suggested Mrs Caldicot, trying to sound sweeter than she felt.

'No, I don't think so,' wheezed the out of breath doctor. 'Can't you bring him along to the surgery in the morning?'

'I really don't think that would be a very good idea,' said Mrs Caldicot. 'He's just come out of hospital; he's very old, very confused and very sleepy.'

'He probably just needs another tranquilliser,' replied the doctor, now starting to get her breath back. 'The hospital wouldn't have sent him out if they hadn't been sure that all was well.'

'I hope you don't mind my saying so but I'm not sure that giving him another tranquilliser is a terribly good idea,' said Mrs Caldicot. 'I think the tablets are making his confusion worse.'

'I didn't know you had medical training,' said the doctor, sharply.

'I don't,' said Mrs Caldicot. 'But...'

'I didn't think you had. I think it would probably be better if you left medical work to those of us who are properly trained,' said the doctor, patronisingly. 'And I have to warn you, Mrs Caldicot, that if you keep interrupting me I will have to ask you to find another doctor to look after Mr Williams.'

'Well, since you refuse to come out and see him, do you mind if I ask our own doctor to visit?' demanded Mrs Caldicot coldly.

'You do as you feel fit,' said the doctor, coldly, breaking the connection.

'No luck?' said Jenkins, who had listened to Mrs Caldicot's end of the telephone call.

'Whatever happened to doctors who cared?' asked Mrs Caldicot.

'They went the way of policemen who would tell you the time,' replied Jenkins.

Mrs Caldicot picked up a bundle of unopened letters from the old-fashioned blotting pad on her desk.

'Afternoon post?' asked Jenkins.

'Bills,' replied Mrs Caldicot, flicking through the envelopes. 'Some of these shops charge like white rhinos. Their bills are massive and unstoppable.'

'Oh, I'm afraid I forgot,' said Jenkins. 'I hate to do this but I've got another one for you.' He took the organic grocer's bill out of his pocket and held it up.

'Just drop it on the pile,' said Mrs Caldicot, nodding towards a wire tray that was overflowing with pieces of paper.

'Those are all outstanding bills?'

'I'm afraid so.'

'Are you coping?'

Mrs Caldicot looked around. 'I don't like admitting this,' she said. 'But running a nursing home is harder than I thought it would be.'

'But you haven't been doing it for long,' Jenkins reminded her. 'It's bound to get easier with time.'

'I hope so,' said Mrs Caldicot.

CHAPTER SEVENTEEN

At 89, Doctor Bence-Jones was older than some of the residents in the nursing home. He dressed smartly in an elderly but still serviceable Harris tweed suit. The jacket had two rear vents, huge patch pockets with button down flaps, a capacious inner pocket (big enough for a stethoscope or a partridge) and button back cuffs. The trousers were plus twos and the whole ensemble (including a matching waistcoat) was always worn with long, olive green socks and elderly brown brogues which had been repaired so many times that virtually nothing of the originals now remained.

Dr Bence-Jones had been forced to retire from the NHS several decades earlier. A group of bland administrators had met and taken just seven minutes to bring an end to a career that had lasted four months shy of half a century. They claimed that they were retiring Dr Bence-Jones both for his own safety and security and for that of his patients.

'It is absurd that such an elderly doctor should still be expected to work within the NHS,' announced a pompous, self-important 24-year-old social worker who had somehow acquired authority over such things. 'And it is equally improper that customers should be exposed to such an elderly practitioner,' he added. He seemed to be as unaware of the fact that Dr Bence-Jones was happy to carry on working as he was of the fact that Dr Bence-Jones's patients were happy to carry on being looked after by him.

The real reason for Dr Bence-Jones's expulsion from the NHS (for that is what it was) was that administrators and social workers found his old-fashioned attitude rather difficult to accept.

When Dr Bence-Jones had first started his practice, back in the late 1930s, there had been no National Health Service. Theoretically, Dr Bence-Jones used to charge a nominal five shillings for a home visit and three shillings and six pence for a surgery consultation but, in practice, hardly anyone paid these sums. Instead, while Dr Bence-Jones charged his rich patients 10 shillings, or even £1, for a consultation he charged the poor patients nothing at all. This Robin Hood approach worked very well. It was much better than the then unborn but soon to become universally awful NHS which would eventually drag everyone down to the same gloomy level of incompetence.

Despite having been forced to retire from the NHS, Dr Bence-Jones still had a small private practice which he ran from his home, a huge, detached Victorian house which was situated conveniently close to the Twilight Years Rest Home, and which was outside the remit of the statutory authorities.

Dr Bence-Jones's name had been recommended to Mrs Caldicot by several of the patients now in her charge and she had very quickly acquired great faith in him, both as a friend and as a doctor. He may not have been entirely up-to-date with all the latest theories (Mrs Caldicot had not been quite sure whether or not he had been joking when he had handed over a prescription for penicillin with the remark 'let's see what this new fangled wonder drug can do for you') but his ignorance of the latest pharmaceutical wonders (not necessarily a bad thing in itself, thought Mrs Caldicot) was more than made up for by his extensive experience and his extraordinarily well-developed sense of intuition.

Most important of all, perhaps, was the fact that neither old age nor many years contact with NHS administrators had taken from him his love of his profession and his genuine love, and sense of compassion for, his patients.

Dr Bence-Jones would have no more thought of referring to his patients as 'customers' as he would have thought of cheering for Australia in an Ashes Test Match. Dr Bence-Jones was an old-fashioned Englishman, with an old-fashioned Englishman's sense of history, priorities and responsibilities.

Dr Bence-Jones drove himself to his calls in a pale blue 1958 S1 Bentley which had been left to him by a grateful patient. She had been the original 'one careful owner' and when she had passed on the Bentley had only just been run in.

Before he had acquired the Bentley the good doctor had done three quarters of his visits on an elderly bicycle with a wicker basket attached to the front handlebars. The remaining quarter he had done in a 30-year-old black Morris which had bald tyres, broken springs and a black canvas roof that had never fitted properly. The arrival of the Bentley had coincided nicely with the onset of arthritis in his knees and hips.

The good doctor had welcomed the gift of the Bentley with enthusiasm but had never really mastered the art of driving a car which seemed to him to be as long and as wide as a small county. Other motorists were never quite sure which side of the road he was driving on and when he parked the car he usually did so in such a way that it became a temporary traffic island.

Apart from his peculiar parking arrangements his other most noticeable motoring idiosyncrasy was his habit of leaving the car unlocked. An officious social worker had once reprimanded him for this, drawing his attention to the fact that doctors are, by law, required to ensure that their medicine bag is kept properly protected; locked away at all times. 'If you can get my bag out of my car then I'll lock the car when I leave it,' Dr Bence-Jones had promised. The social worker had marched straight over to the Bentley and opened the nearside passenger door. She had fled without bothering to close the door when Dr Bence-Jones's elderly Dobermann, which had been snoozing in the rear passenger footwell, had made its presence known to her. Dr Bence-Jones still left his car unlocked.

Once or twice, in the early days, he had tried driving the Bentley into the driveway in front of the nursing home. But these days he usually chose to park in the road outside. A series of minor collisions with the stone gates had done neither the stonework nor the Bentley's huge chrome bumpers a great deal of good.

'I called you because we're having a few problems with a new patient,' explained Mrs Caldicot, as she led the way down the hall. Dr Bence-Jones had to stop for a rest every couple of steps so it was a slow journey. 'That's disappointing,' replied the doctor, breathing heavily. 'I thought that p'raps you'd called me round 'cus you'd got a pretty young new nurse who needed a full medical.'

Mrs Caldicot laughed. 'No, I'm afraid not.'

'I never get any perks these days,' muttered the doctor, shaking his head in mock misery.

As they walked down the hall Dr Bence-Jones poked his head into the lounge. The residents were playing cricket. Mr Hewitt, using a well-strapped piece of willow which had been his most treasured possession for nearly three quarters of a century, was batting in front of a set of stumps which had been created with the aid of an umbrella stand, two walking sticks and a very neatly furled black umbrella with a silver handle. Using a pair of very neatly rolled-up thick woollen green socks as a ball Miss Nightingale was bowling.

'Aha!' said Dr Bence-Jones. 'Cricket!' He peered into the room. 'I say, the ball is the wrong colour,' he said, rather indignantly. 'I mean, I don't think there's anything in the rules against using rolled-up socks for indoor cricket but darn it if you're going to use socks they should surely be red.'

'Mrs Caldicot confiscated our only cricket ball,' said Mr Hewitt, glumly. 'And I haven't got any red socks.'

'I had to confiscate it,' said Mrs Caldicot to Dr Bence-Jones. 'I really don't like interfering and I honestly didn't much mind about the furniture or the ornaments, though I think Mrs Roberts was a little sad to see the one-legged fairy lose her remaining lower limb albeit to what I understand was a perfectly executed straight drive, but both Mrs Peterborough and Miss Nightingale had terrible black eyes and we had to take Mr Hewitt to the hospital with a suspected fractured tibia.'

'Pshaw!' said Mr Hewitt, shaking his head. 'Just a bit of a bang on the shin.'

'Mr Hewitt, two doctors spent three quarters of an hour studying your X-rays,' Mrs Caldicot reminded him. 'And if I remember correctly you had a bruise the size of a football that lasted for two weeks.'

'Rugger ball,' muttered Mr Hewitt. 'Size of a rugger ball. Can't stand soccer. Damned game for poofters and nancy boys. Always was. These days it's just got worse. No self-respecting heterosexual would dare get down into the scrum these days.' He snorted derisively.

In the corner of the room Mrs Merivale was watching a repeat of a television chat show. A distinguished British actor was telling bright and jolly anecdotes in order to drum up business for his latest film.

'Who's that?' demanded Dr Bence-Jones, his attention drawn from the game of cricket, where there was at the time no discernible action, and towards the television screen where there was plenty of activity going on. He pointed at the screen. 'I'm sure I know the name but I can't think of the face.'

'It's Sean Connery!' said Mrs Merivale. 'He sends Mr Merivale and me a Christmas card every year.'

'Does he?' said the doctor. 'That's very nice, dear.'

Mrs Merivale nodded contentedly to herself as she watched Mr Connery finish a long anecdote with a perfectly timed punchline.

'Isn't he just wonderful?' she purred. 'Lots of the stars send us cards,' she told the doctor.

Mrs Caldicot introduced the doctor to the Merivales and the Merivales to the doctor.

'You look in good condition, young man,' said the doctor to Mr Merivale.

'Oh, it's all a false front,' said Mr Merivale. 'Don't believe it. My wife makes me dye my hair so I don't look too old. She's very conscious of the fact that I'm five months older than her.'

'Ah,' nodded Dr Bence-Jones, who had been in practice far too long to be surprised by anything he heard.

'I tell her, let people think I'm your sugar daddy,' said Mr Merivale.

'I don't want people thinking I'm some cheap bimbo just with you for your money,' said Mrs Merivale.

'I haven't got any money!' Mr Merivale pointed out.

'That makes it even worse!' Mrs Merivale pointed out.

The doctor, sensing a modest marital disagreement, tactfully withdrew.

'Are you chaps playing or talking?' demanded Mr Livingstone, who was both acting as umpire and fielding at short-extra-sofa and who knew nothing about the cinema or the television.

'Bowl away, Miss Nightingale,' said Mr Hewitt, responding to this enquiry by waving his bat around in the air. 'I'm ready when you are.'

Miss Nightingale bowled (for the record, it was a right arm over the wicket donkey drop) and Mr Hewitt, who, despite his brave bluster, had not been in the slightest bit ready, and whose bat had still been pointing up towards the ceiling, watched in horror as the neatly rolled-up green socks sped precisely between the sides of the umbrella stand and clattered into the neatly arranged walking sticks and umbrella, disrupting them so comprehensively that it was difficult to entertain any hope that he might survive the umpire's inevitable decision.

'Out!' cried Mr Livingstone, holding aloft the index finger of his right hand.

'That was clearly a no ball!' protested Mr Hewitt, who was in all other aspects of life a fair and decent fellow but who had never been a good loser when it came to cricket. In a career stretching back the better part of a century Mr Hewitt had been dismissed several hundred times but he would happily argue that on no more than a handful of those occasions had the umpire's decision been sound or reasonable. On this particular occasion he had a powerful weapon in his favour: the bat was his and, as anyone who has ever played cricket in such circumstances will undoubtedly confirm, ownership of the bat invariably trumps the decision making power of an umpire.

'Shall we go?' Mrs Caldicot quietly suggested to Dr Bence-Jones. 'These technical discussions can sometimes go on for some time.'

'Very wise, Mrs Caldicot,' muttered Dr Bence-Jones. They left, quietly closing the door behind them, and headed for the stairs.

Chapter Eighteen

'I wish you'd have a lift installed,' the doctor wheezed, clasping the bannister with both hands, and looking up at the stairs above him and down at the stairs behind him. 'I'm getting a little old for mountaineering.' Mrs Caldicot was carrying the doctor's old-fashioned black Gladstone bag. She had never seen him open it and had no idea what it contained.

'A lift is definitely on my list,' Mrs Caldicot assured him. 'Or perhaps a chairlift?'

'One of those things that whizzes up down the stairs on a rail?'

'Yes.'

'Yes that might be fun. I fancy myself on one of those.'

'Well, I'll put both on the list. Of course, it may be a year or two before we can afford them.'

'I'll try and hang on,' said Dr Bence-Jones. 'And, anyway, hire the pretty young nurse first. I'd rather examine a pretty young nurse than ride up the stairs.'

'You're incorrigible!' laughed Mrs Caldicot.

'I hope so,' replied the doctor. 'Just keep encouraging me!'

They arrived at last at Mr Williams's room. The new patient was looking much better and calmer than he had looked the previous night. Mrs Caldicot introduced the two old men to one another.

'You're the doctor!' said Mr Williams, clearly astonished. He turned to Mrs Caldicot. 'It's a long time since I saw a doctor who was older than me.' He paused and screwed up his eyes. 'You aren't really as old as you look are you? Tell me that you're 33 but you've lived a very debauched life.'

'Shut up, young man,' said Dr Bence-Jones. 'Don't be cheeky or I'll have you sent to bed without any supper.'

'Big deal,' said Mr Williams. 'I'm already in bed. And I haven't had any supper.'

Dr Bence-Jones snorted.

'I'm already on Mrs Caldicot's starvation diet,' moaned Mr Williams. 'Now I suppose you've come to stick needles in me.'

'If you don't watch your mouth I'll have you on twice daily laxatives and hourly injections in your bum,' retorted Dr Bence-Jones. 'Now shut up before you deafen me,' he added. He had one end of his stethoscope connected to his ears and the other end placed on Mr Williams's chest.

It took the doctor less than five minutes to declare Mr Williams perfectly fit. 'He's healthy enough to hang,' he announced. 'Did you manage to get hold of his doctor.'

'Yes,' said Mrs Caldicot. 'But she won't come. The last time I called she told me that she always has lunch with drug company representatives on weekdays and that it will be at least ten days before she can get here. Until I described him she couldn't even remember Mr Williams and had no idea what drugs he is on. She told me to give him a tranquilliser. And she told me to make sure that he keeps taking his arthritis drugs because they're part of a trial she's conducting for a drug company.'

Dr Bence-Jones strode across to where Mr Williams's pills were lined up on the dressing table and picked the bottles up one by one. 'This one is for arthritis,' he said. He turned back to Mr Williams. 'Do you have arthritis young man?'

'Not particularly,' replied Mr Williams.

'Your GP does lots of tests for drug companies,' Dr Bence-Jones said. 'However, they already know that the stuff causes stomach problems.' He picked up the second bottle. 'So he takes this one. Which is supposed to cure stomach ulcers but which causes diarrhoea.' He picked up the third bottle. 'So he takes this one to control the diarrhoea. But it can cause depression.' He picked up the fourth bottle. 'So he takes this one which is an anti-depressant but causes anxiety and sleeplessness for which he takes this one,' he picked up another bottle, 'and this one,' he picked up the next one in line, 'and this one.'

'Three for anxiety?'

'Three for anxiety,' agreed Dr Bence-Jones. 'And one of the drugs he takes for anxiety causes asthma. So he takes those blue capsules to prevent his asthma. And because the asthma drug causes headaches he takes these red pills which are painkillers which can cause blood clotting. So he takes these white tablets to stop his blood clotting. They can cause high blood pressure so he takes these green ones to keep his blood pressure under control. And these green ones can cause potassium loss so he takes these fawn coloured things for that.'

'There's one left,' said Mrs Caldicot.

'This violet one,' agreed the doctor. 'It's another drug to stop him feeling anxious.'

'Doesn't it cause any side effects?'

'I think so,' said the doctor. 'But nothing he isn't already taking something for.'

'Does he really need all these?'

'I don't think so,' said Dr Bence-Jones. 'If he stopped the pills to stop the arthritis he probably hasn't got he probably wouldn't need any of the others.'

'What about the drugs for his anxiety?'

'If I was taking this many pills I'd be anxious,' said Dr Bence-Jones. 'Wouldn't you?'

'Yes, I suppose I would,' admitted Mrs Caldicot. 'So what are you going to do?'

'Give the sewer rats a treat,' replied Dr Bence-Jones. He scooped up all Mr Williams's pill bottles and carried them into the bathroom. A minute or so later Mrs Caldicot heard the sound of the lavatory being flushed. She got up and rushed into the bathroom, just in time to see a variety of coloured tablets and capsules disappearing down into the sewers.

'Should you have done that?' she asked.

'Oh absolutely,' replied Dr Bence-Jones. 'Oh definitely. Don't you think so?'

'But couldn't you get into trouble?'

'What sort of trouble?'

'I don't know. Aren't there any rules about throwing away someone else's tablets?'

'What tablets?'

'What about if he falls ill because he's not taking his tablets?'

'Then I've no doubt that some kind doctor will give him some more,' replied Dr Bence-Jones. 'Meanwhile, there is, I hope, a chance that without his tablets he will wake up, remember who he is and be able to walk around without falling over.'

'One of these days you're going to get into trouble,' said Mrs Caldicot.

'I'm sure you're right,' said Dr Bence-Jones. 'But I'm very

old and I don't care. If they put me in prison I will, with any luck, be put in a cell with a nice bank robber who will teach me how to open safes.'

Chapter Nineteen

'Do you need to see the other residents,' asked Mrs Caldicot when they got back down into the hall.

Dr Bence-Jones answered by poking his head into the lounge again. A cushion missed him by inches. He pulled his head back. 'What the hell is going on in there now?' he demanded.

Mrs Caldicot looked at her watch. 'I expect someone is practising for the next indoor volleyball match,' explained Mrs Caldicot. 'It's China versus the USA. It's something of a grudge match.'

'They all look fine to me,' said the doctor. 'Does anyone need a sick note? Prescription? Passport application form signed?'

'No, thank you,' said Mrs Caldicot. 'I think we're OK for today. I just wanted you to check over Mr Williams. But he does seem a lot calmer today.'

Dr Bence-Jones poked his head into the lounge again, this time to say goodbye. As he opened the door a rolled up pair of socks headed straight for him. Instinctively he put his hands up to protect his face and caught the socks.

'Howzat?' cried Miss Nightingale.

'Couldn't possibly be out,' protested Mr Hewitt. 'The man's a spectator not a player. You can't have batsmen given out because they've been caught by a spectator. That was a six!'

Mrs Merivale, who was still watching the television, had now been joined by Mrs Peterborough.

'There's just been a fashion expert on the television,' she told Mrs Caldicot. 'He says that the wrinkled look is in this season.'

'For people or clothes?' asked Mrs Caldicot.

'Oh for clothes, I think,' replied Mrs Merivale. 'But it means

I no longer have to iron Mr Merivale's shirts. If I leave the creases and wrinkles in them he'll be fashionable.'

'Why do they decide that now?' asked Mrs Caldicot, who had spent too many years of her life ironing sharp creases into the late Mr Caldicot's shirts and under-clothing. Her late husband had even insisted on having his socks ironed.

'Oh, it's just fashion,' said Mrs Merivale. 'Next week they'll decide that we have to put concertina pleat creases into everything.'

'I'm just waiting for some fashion guru to arrange for ink and chocolate stains to become fashionable,' said Mr Livingstone. 'Overnight I'll become the most fashionable man in Europe.'

CHAPTER TWENTY

When the doctor had left, Mrs Caldicot went back upstairs to Mr Williams's room.

'Would you like me to help you unpack?' she asked, nodding towards his still unopened suitcases.

'Thanks,' said Mr Williams. 'Can I stay here?'

'Of course you can,' said Mrs Caldicot.

'As long as I like?'

'Of course?'

'In this room?'

'Yes.'

'I don't have to share with anyone?'

'Not unless you want to.'

'I used to have a small flat,' he told her. 'I bought it after my wife died. We'd been together for sixty years. I wasn't very good at living by myself. I've always been a bit of a loner. My wife was the only friend I had or needed. I didn't have a 'first footer' until May last year. And then it was a man who came to read the gas meter.'

'So, that was 'home' until you came here?'

'I suppose so,' agreed Mr Williams. He looked around. 'But

I could be at home here. I've always believed that home is where you are – not where you come from.' He paused and cleared his throat. 'What are the fees?'

Mrs Caldicot felt uncomfortable. She didn't like talking about money. It was, she knew, one of her failings as the proprietor of a nursing home. 'We don't really have 'fees',' she said. 'Pay whatever you think is appropriate,' she said. 'What you can afford.'

Mr Williams levered himself off the bed, half walked, half lurched across the room and put one of the suitcases flat on the floor. 'I haven't got many clothes,' he said, unfastening the case's twin catches. The suitcase was crammed with black and white photographs, some in folders, some simply packed loosely into the case.

'My word!' said Mrs Caldicot. 'You're obviously keen on photography.'

'Yes,' said Mr Williams. He took out a photograph of some children playing in a street. It was a night scene, lit by a street lamp and the moon. Mrs Caldicot recognised the church in the background. 'Isn't that the famous church in Montmartre in Paris?' she asked. 'The white one that always reminds me of weddings?'

'Sacre Coeur,' said Mr Williams.

'That's the one. Do you still take photographs?'

'No. I sort of gave it up. For the last two decades I've specialised in losing and finding. I've spent half my life losing things and the other half of my life looking for them.'

Mrs Caldicot laughed. 'I know what you mean.'

Mr Williams handed the print of Sacre Coeur to Mrs Caldicot. 'Take it and sell it,' he said. 'I'll give you another one in a month or two.'

He nodded towards the suitcase. 'And don't worry. When I run out I've got the negatives somewhere.'

Mrs Caldicot looked at the photograph. It looked vaguely familiar. But she felt embarrassed. She really would have to try to run the nursing home in a more professional way.

'I'll sign it on the back,' said Mr Williams, taking the print back off Mrs Caldicot. 'Have you got a pen?'

She handed him a pen. He scrawled his signature, and added

the date, before handing the pen and the photograph back to her.

'Thank you,' said Mrs Caldicot. She was touched by Mr Williams's gift but couldn't help wondering how it was going to help her pay the growing collection of overdue bills on her desk. She couldn't see the electricity company being too thrilled if she tried to pay their bill with an old snap.

Downstairs the other residents were still playing the world volleyball championships. When Mrs Caldicot put her head around the door someone told her that China was beating the USA three nil, and admitted that a badly directed cushion from one of the American players had broken a china model of a spotted dog.

CHAPTER TWENTY ONE

A few miles away, on the fourth floor of an ugly, nondescript concrete, glass and plastic tower block occupied exclusively by employees of the local council, an assorted variety of nondescript professional busy bodies were fully occupied thinking of ways to interfere in the normal, contented lives of unsuspecting, innocent, hard-working local citizens. It was their collective and diseased mission to bring chaos to order and to add confusion, bewilderment and a real sense of injustice to those whose lives were merely harassed by too much work and too little time.

At one corner of the fourth floor, in a spacious office tucked in between the emergency staircase and the men's lavatories, the eleven senior members of the local authority's Rest Home Supervisory Unit (rather grandly and self-consciously they liked to refer to themselves as Supervising Outreach Coordinators) were holding a meeting.

This was not an unusual occurrence. The Supervising Outreach Coordinators held a lot of meetings – at least one a day – though there were those (especially those hard-working members of the public who were trying to run rest homes which fell within the remit of this dreary bunch of bureaucrats) who felt that the

Supervising Outreach Coordinators did not hold anywhere near enough meetings and that if they were to organise more meetings and to go out less, write fewer letters and generally speaking keep themselves to themselves and interfere less with those trying to a do a real job of work outside, then the world would be a far, far happier, more contented and less troublesome place. The eleven officials were all petty-minded people whose own otherwise dull, grey and miserable days were made acceptable by the fact that their work gave them regular opportunities to patronise those whom they encountered in their professional capacity.

These simple daily pleasures were augmented by the fact that at regular intervals they also had a chance to humiliate their victims – rather than merely to make their lives miserable. Naturally, as cowards, they usually picked on the weakest and most vulnerable, invariably becoming servile and sycophantic when faced with more robust, self-confident individuals.

'I had a splendid visit to a rest home in Buckberrington Street yesterday,' said an apparently elderly grey man with seemingly elderly grey hair. He wore an elderly grey suit, had elderly grey eyes and even those who knew him well would probably be surprised to know that he was still not out of his thirties. The man, called Hiscock, had copious amounts of grey dandruff on the shoulders of his grey jacket. He cultivated the dandruff look and deliberately did everything he could to encourage the stuff. He felt that dandruff on his shoulders gave him a suitably solid, reliable image and marked him out as a man who was not likely to be impressed by ordinary, everyday standards or expectations.

The others looked up from the copious quantities of paper which lay spread out on the table in front of each of them. If there was one thing these eleven purveyors of dissatisfaction liked even more than meetings it was paperwork. If their first mission in life was to bring frustration and chaos to the lives of ordinary, hard-working citizens their second mission was to turn the world's forests into filing cabinet fodder.

'I've never been able to find anything wrong before,' Hiscock said, ruefully. 'The proprietor has run the place quite adequately.' Those other members of the unit who had been unfortunate enough to visit this establishment nodded to show that they understood; they had shared their colleagues' gloom and understood that the phrase 'quite adequately' was code for 'he hasn't done anything wrong and has never put so much as a finger out of place'.

'But yesterday,' he announced, his voice rising in triumph, 'I asked to see the new Extractor Fan Unit warning notice which, in accordance with the appropriate EU notification I had demanded, in an official communication, be placed in position beneath the fan.'

There would have been a buzz of excitement from his colleagues if they had been the sort of people who ever allowed themselves to get excited. As it was they contented themselves with raising their heads. The nine who were doodling stopped their pens so that they could give their colleague their total concentration.

'When I measured the notice I found that it was just 17.9 cm wide.' There was a pause while the rest of the team digested this piece of news. They could not have been more shocked (nor more excited) if they had discovered that Himmler was running a nursing home in their locality, with Dr Josef Mengele living in and providing the patients with his own unique brand of medical care.

The grey man looked around his audience. 'As you all know,' he said, 'Regulation 282/gh12 states quite clearly that such notices must be 18.0 cm wide. The proprietor claimed that the sign company had measured the item inadvertently in old-fashioned imperial units and that there had been an error in translating the illegal imperial units into proper metric units. He claimed that it was, therefore, their responsibility.'

'Naturally, however, I told him that it was his responsibility and that I would consequently be giving him a formal, written warning. I gave him formal notice, as required by the legislation, that if he received another warning within three years his Rest Home licence would be withdrawn.' The grey, but now proud, Hiscock looked around the table and came as close to looking contented as he had ever looked. He paused before delivering the coupe de grace. 'The proprietor then burst into tears,' he announced, with great pride.

The other council employees sitting around the table would have started applauding if they had been the sort of people who applauded things. Instead they all nodded and congratulated their colleague. To find a Rest Home proprietor at fault was a joy. To see a Rest Home proprietor in tears was a high point – a moment that made the job worth doing, a moment to be cherished and remembered; a memory to ease the tedium of long days of retirement.

'I am revisiting this afternoon,' said Hiscock. 'I have high hopes that at that time I will be in a position to issue an official closure notice.'

Breath was drawn in sharply around the table. A closure notice was something they all dreamt of. But closure notices came far too infrequently.

'When I visited last time, I noticed that the front doormat was not the requisite size,' continued the grey man. 'I did not mention this at the time, of course. But when I go back today I will measure it. And if it is the wrong size – and I am quietly confident that I will find it at least three centimetres too wide – I will immediately issue the appropriate 14 day closure notice.'

This time his colleagues simply could not restrain themselves.

'This is precisely why I joined this department,' said a bent, weedy looking man with poor complexion and greasy hair.

'Well done,' said a young black woman called Ms Jones BA. She wore a green anorak and had several dozen coloured folders spread around on the table in front of her.

'I think it is worth pointing out that this particular institution has been operating apparently blamelessly for nearly thirty years..,' said a fat, florid faced woman who wore a black T-shirt and a pair of black jeans.

'...twenty seven years to be precise, Chair,' interrupted Hiscock.

'...for twenty seven years,' continued the fat woman, known as 'Chair'. 'And this will, to the best of my knowledge, be the first time that we have managed to serve a closure notice on the proprietor.'

'That is correct!' confirmed another grey man. 'We got close eight years ago but it turned out that although our regulations limited the minimum width of garden paths there was, at that time, no limit to the maximum width of garden paths. Therefore, although the proprietor had built paths which were twenty two centimetres wider than the permitted minimum there was nothing we could do about it. It is good to feel vindicated at last. And it will send a warning bell to other facilities – letting them know that our vigilance will be maintained and that should we fail to obtain a closure notice we will be back.'

'So, there we are! A splendid piece of work!' said the woman in black. 'Congratulations to Mr Muldoon.'

Mr Muldoon, the young grey man, would have purred if he had been a cat.

'We will, of course, instigate an enquiry into just how long the faulty notice and over-sized doormat have been in situ,' said the woman in black, who clearly had some sort of management role. 'It may be possible for us to add a hefty fine to the closure notice, particularly since, with two offences in such a short space of time, it will clearly be easy for the department to argue that the man is a recidivist and clearly unfit for any sort of position in the caring and welfare community.' She paused, as a thought wandered into her unwilling mind. 'Let us hope that these are new faults,' she murmured, now specifically addressing her remarks to the young, grey man, 'and that we will not find ourselves laid open to a charge of negligence in having missed these items on previous inspections.'

'There is no risk of that,' said the young grey man. 'Both these items are brand new – I am confident that they were introduced onto the premises subsequent to our last visit. I have added a file note confirming that observation.'

The woman in black smiled and nodded. She looked comforted and relieved. 'Is that all for this session?' she asked, looking at the clock. 'We've been going for nearly thirty minutes. Shall we adjourn for an extended refreshment opportunity?'

'There's just one small item which I think we could perhaps usefully squeeze through in this session,' said a short, round, woman whose sari might have suggested that she (or her ancestors) could at some stage have travelled from the Indian continent but which was, in fact, simply her way of expressing solidarity with her colleagues from that continent (all of whom, it has to be said, were happily wearing Western clothes).

'We have a new establishment to monitor,' she said. She examined some papers in front of her; frowned, shuffled them a little more. 'One of our sub-inspectors visited the Twilight Years Rest Home, which has recently come under new management, to check on the extractor fan statutory warning notice and although the notice was in position he reported that he did not feel that his visit was treated with the appropriate level of solemnity or respect.'

A small, dapper man with an arrogant air coughed to attract attention. He wore a grey suit with, underneath it, a grey cardigan. He also wore a pair of half-moon spectacles with tortoiseshell frames. He wore these because he had once been told that half-moon spectacles put up the wearer's IQ by 15 points and turned a meek person into someone quite intimidating. 'Do we have details of the new management?' he asked.

'It's a Mrs Thelma Caldicot,' said the woman in the sari, studying the paperwork in front of her.

The small dapper man sat up, as suddenly and as conspicuously as if someone had put a firework up his bottom and lit the fuse. None of his colleagues noticed anything unusual. They were not a particularly observant bunch.

'I haven't heard of her myself,' continued the woman in the sari, 'but a colleague told me that she has appeared in the media, though I'm not sure in what context.' She smiled sweetly and looked around the room. 'I don't think I've read anything about her in Social Work Weekly,' she said. 'And if she has appeared in the pages of The Guardian I missed it.' Heads were bowed, as though in silent but respectful prayer, when she mentioned The Guardian. She paused. 'Naturally I don't watch the television.'

A murmuring of 'naturally's ran clockwise around the table.

'I'd like to take on responsibility for assessing the Twilight Years Rest Home,' said the small man. 'I do have some professional knowledge of the proprietor's activities,' he said. He didn't bother to mention that he hated Mrs Caldicot with a vengeance. She had publicly humiliated him, and forced him to close the nursing home he'd been running. She'd arrived at his nursing home as a resident and had led the residents in a mass walk out. 'Perhaps I can use my specialist information for the benefit of the department.'

'I think that would be a splendid idea,' said the woman in black known as 'the chair'. 'We were all very impressed with your last investigation Mr Muller-Hawksmoor. To manage to close down two Rest Homes within a week of their opening shows diligence and determination. The department could do with more like you. I suggest that perhaps you take Ms Jones BA with you as co-investigating officer.'

'Splendid,' said the small, dapper man.

Ms Jones BA, clearly unhappy about this, started to protest.

'I think you'll complement one another perfectly,' the woman in black told them. She looked at the clock. 'And now I really do feel that we need our break!' She paused, and glanced at the clock again. 'Otherwise, I fear that we will be breaking our working condition guidelines.'

As the others dragged themselves to their feet and started to leave the room, Mr Muller-Hawksmoor walked over to where Ms Jones BA was still sitting, gathering up her papers and fitting them neatly into a black plastic attaché case. 'Would you like a coffee or tea?' he asked. 'So that we can get to know one another a little better?'

She looked up. 'Yes,' she said. 'I suppose that might be useful.'

'Coffee?' asked Mr Muller-Hawksmoor, walking across to the coffee machine.

'Yes,' said Ms Jones BA who regarded the word 'please' as politically incorrect.

'Black or white?' asked Mr Muller-Hawksmoor.

Ms Jones BA glowered at him. 'I regard that as a racially offensive remark,' she said icily. 'If you repeat it at any time in the future I will make a formal complaint about you.'

'Er ... I'm sorry. Would you like it with or without milk?' asked Mr Muller-Hawksmoor, who felt that he was going to enjoy working with Ms Jones BA.

CHAPTER TWENTY TWO

Mr Roxdale lived in a small, terraced house in an old part of the town. He had lived there since his marriage. When he and his young wife, Matilda, had first moved in there had been no electricity and no gas. The only mains services were water and sewage.

For several decades Mr Roxdale and his wife had held out against progress; steadfastly refusing to allow their landlord to instal either electricity or gas. The landlord, who owned the houses either side, had arranged for the pipes and the wiring to be brought into the house but he had been unable to persuade either Mr Roxdale or Matilda to have the house fitted with pipes, wiring or appliances. Mr Roxdale would have agreed. He didn't like to see anyone disappointed. But his wife was a nervous woman and she didn't want her home to be fitted out with these modern services. She didn't trust them. 'We've survived very well without them,' she argued. 'Why do we need them now?' She was worried that the gas, or the electricity, or both, would blow them to smithereens. The precise nature of her concern really didn't matter. All that concerned Mr Roxdale was that his wife didn't want electricity or gas in their home. If she had wanted it he would have done everything he could to get it for her. If she didn't want it then they wouldn't have it. Simple.

After Matilda had died Mr Roxdale had succumbed. He didn't much care then. And he didn't have a great deal of choice. His general practitioner, worried about Mr Roxdale's heart, asked a consultant to visit Mr Roxdale at home. (In those far off days hospital specialists used to do such things quite often.) Wanting to plug in his portable electrocardiograph machine the consultant had been shocked to discover that there was no mains electricity in the house. He'd been even more shocked to discover that Mr Roxdale cooked on a wood stove and lit his home with paraffin lamps. Social workers had been called. And that was the end of Mr Roxdale's seemingly eccentric stand against progress. Mr Roxdale was just pleased that it had all happened after his dear, beloved wife had passed on. She would have been terribly upset by it all. He wouldn't have liked to have seen her upset. It would have broken his heart.

Mr Roxdale was sitting in his tiny parlour, consoling himself with a cup of strong tea and a ginger biscuit.

'Hello Dad!' cried Nigel, his son, opening the front door and walking straight along the narrow passageway and into the parlour. There was no door between the passageway and the parlour; just a length of heavy brown velour hanging from a brass rail. The curtain was too long and the bottom two feet of the velour sat in thick folds on the carpet.

Mr Roxdale turned and greeted his son.

He was proud of what Nigel had achieved. Apart from his growing legal practice Nigel also owned a good deal of property in the area. Several years earlier, for example, he had bought the entire terrace of houses which included Mr Roxdale's home. But, although he was proud, Mr Roxdale didn't particularly like his son. And, sadly, he knew him well enough to know that he could not be trusted.

'How are you today?' asked Nigel.

'Not so bad,' answered Mr Roxdale. He always answered that question in the same way. He would have used the identical words if he had been dying.

'How's the gardening business these days?' asked Nigel.

'Not so bad,' answered Mr Roxdale, who might have been a little slow in his movements but was not slow in his thinking. He knew it was no coincidence that he had been fired by every one of his employers in the same week. He would have known that Nigel was involved even if he had not seen his son's conspicuous Jaguar parked outside at least two of the houses where he had worked.

'I've heard there's something of a recession developing in the service industry,' said Nigel.

'I heard that too,' agreed Mr Roxdale, nibbling at his ginger biscuit. 'Would you like a cup of tea?'

'No thanks,' said Nigel. 'Fenella doesn't like me drinking tea.'

'Ginger biscuit?'

'No thanks. Fenella has got me on a diet.'

They sat in silence for a while. Mr Roxdale drank his tea and nibbled at his ginger biscuit. Nigel fiddled with his watch strap and listened with increasing impatience and irritation to the tick tock of the clock on the mantlepiece. The ticks and the tocks seemed to get louder and louder.

At last Nigel could bear the silence no longer. He cleared his throat. 'I can tell there is something wrong,' he lied. He leant forward. 'Tell me about it, Dad,' he said. 'Have you had some trouble with the gardening business?'

His father didn't answer.

'There's no shame in losing a job,' said Nigel. 'It happens all the time these days.' He swallowed hard and shuffled uneasily in his chair. 'You've lost your jobs, haven't you?' He was usually a very good liar. Deception was his stock in trade. He was a lawyer and property developer. He lied at least fifty times a day. He was a professional. But for some reason he still found it difficult to deceive his father. He always felt that his father knew the truth. Not that he could. He couldn't possibly, of course. There was no way that he could know the truth. No way.

Mr Roxdale said nothing but reached for the packet of ginger biscuits. He was not a man driven by hedonism but he felt reckless. He plucked a second biscuit from the packet. He stared at it for a moment. A terrible idea had occurred to him.

'If you think about it sensibly it's probably all for the best,' said Nigel. 'You're not getting any younger. And being out in the rain and the snow isn't good for a man of your age.' He paused. 'It isn't good for a man my age.' He sort of laughed. It was an unpleasant sound. Nigel didn't laugh often. He'd pretty much forgotten how to do it. 'I don't know how you did it,' he said. 'Gardening for all those years.' He sat back. 'Still. All that's behind you now. And so now you've got to look forward. You've got a great future ahead of you.' And then he spoilt it. 'I have to tell you that I'm not sorry,' he said. 'I don't think you've ever realised it but your being a jobbing gardener has been a considerable embarrassment to myself and Fenella. We have a position in this town and your being a gardener hasn't exactly been a help you know.'

Mr Roxdale hadn't heard a word of this. He was still staring at his biscuit and wondering if he should. He'd heard of people doing it. He'd seen people do it. But he'd never done it himself.

'The first thing we've got to do is to get you out of this place,' said Nigel. He looked around. 'It worries me to think of you here, all by yourself.'

Mr Roxdale decided to do it. He pulled his cup of tea towards him and, without any further hesitation, dunked his ginger biscuit. He took it out again so quickly that the biscuit was hardly even damp.

'If there was an emergency you could, of course, always ring Fenella and myself day or night,' said Nigel. 'But I've been saying to Fenella – and I have to say that she has been totally supportive of me on this, utterly regardless of the expense – that I would be happier if you were living somewhere where you could have some 24 hour a day support.'

The second time would, Mr Roxdale thought, probably be easier. It was. He pulled the ginger biscuit out of the tea just seconds before it broke up. It felt deliciously decadent.

'So, in preparation for this moment, I've been looking around,' said Nigel. 'Actually, and I know you've not always seen eye to eye with her, much of the spadework has been done by Fenella. And she's found a wonderful little place. Just opened. It's being run by a woman called Thelma Caldicot. Have you heard of her?'

Mr Roxdale looked up, thought for a moment and shook his head.

'She was on the TV and in all the papers just a while ago,' said Nigel. 'She was a resident in an old people's home. She didn't like the way the place was being run and so she led all the other residents out on strike. They moved into a hotel. The papers called it 'Mrs Caldicot's Cabbage War' – I think that one of the things she was complaining about was the fact that the whole place smelt of over-cooked cabbage. Are you sure you haven't heard of her?'

Mr Roxdale shook his head. He didn't own a television set or a wireless and he never read newspapers. If it didn't happen in his living room or in one of the gardens he was looking after then he probably hadn't heard of it. He tried to keep busy so that he didn't notice what they were doing to the world. 'I used to read the papers. Forty years ago. But I had to stop. Now I try to keep myself busy. If I had time to read the newspapers and to worry about what the politicians and industrialists are doing to our world I would become suicidal,' he once told a neighbour. He could tell you the exact date when the roses would be in bloom and when the peas would be ready to pick. But he had no idea of the name of the Foreign Secretary or the singer at the top of the hit parade. He looked out of the window at his own small garden. It was only a few feet wide and, perhaps, a hundred feet long, but it was packed with life. The first third of the garden was all flowers. The rest of it was devoted to vegetables and fruit: there was an asparagus bed, a strawberry bed, raspberry canes, radishes, lettuces, marrows and herbs galore.

'I've spoken to Mrs Caldicot and she has a couple of spare rooms,' said Nigel. 'Single rooms, beautifully furnished. You can mix in with the other residents if you want to. But you don't have to. It's entirely up to you. You'll get your meals, you'll get your laundry done and you'll get medical attention when you need it.'

Mr Roxdale, stopped looking out of his window and put the rest of his soggy biscuit into his mouth.

'So what do you think?' asked Nigel.

Mr Roxdale looked at him. 'Pretty good,' he said. He closed his eyes and chewed. 'I'm still not sure though.'

'Well, take your time. Do you want to think it over?'

'No,' drawled Mr Roxdale. 'Not really. No.' He thought hard. 'I'm pretty sure.' He closed his eyes. 'I really do think I like them best undunked.'

Nigel frowned. He leant forward. 'What are you talking about, Dad?'

Mr Roxdale looked at his son. 'Biscuits,' he said. 'Dunked or not. I think they're better undunked. I like to drink my tea and to eat my biscuit separately.'

Nigel paused, waited and swallowed hard. 'But what about the residential home?' he asked. 'What do you think about moving into Mrs Caldicot's old people's home?'

'What's a 'residential home'?' asked Mr Roxdale, looking puzzled. 'I always thought all homes were residential.'

'Well, I suppose they are,' agreed Nigel, in a bit of a huff. 'It doesn't really matter what you call it.'

'I don't mind much either way,' said Mr Roxdale. 'But I don't have any savings. Maybe £200 in the Building Society. I put that aside for emergencies. If it costs more than the rent I pay you then I won't be able to afford it.' He paused, suddenly remembering that his income had suddenly stopped. 'Actually, son, I'm not sure I can still pay you the rent.'

'Don't worry about money, Dad. I'll take care of the financial side of things.'

Mr Roxdale looked at him. 'I can't let you do that.'

'Of course you can, Dad,' said Nigel. 'It'll be a real pleasure for me to be able to do something tangible for you.'

'But aren't these homes very expensive?'

'You're not to worry about any of it,' insisted Nigel. 'You let me worry about the money. All you have to do is pack your bags. Take your clothes and any knick-knacks you want to have with you.'

Mr Roxdale looked around. He was surrounded by objects which were, together, the essence of his home. Most of them had been part of his life with Matilda.

'When do you want me to move?' he asked his son. 'It's your house so you call the shots.'

'Well, if you're going to do it you might as well do it now,' said Nigel. 'Waiting and thinking about it won't make it any easier.'

Mr Roxdale nodded.

'So, why don't I pick you up in the early afternoon tomorrow? Say two fifteen?'

'Tomorrow?'

'Is that too soon for you, Dad? We can make it the day after tomorrow if you like.'

'No. Tomorrow is fine,' said Mr Roxdale. 'I can be packed by then. We might as well get it over with.' He looked around again. Suddenly the furniture and the pictures looked old and tired. As old and as tired as he felt. 'What about all this stuff?' he asked.

'Do you want to leave that to me?' asked Nigel. 'I could ask Fenella to get an auctioneer in. One of the house clearance specialists.'

'Whatever you think, son. Whatever you think best.'

Mr Roxdale seemed very old and very tired. But he wasn't particularly old or tired. He was, however, bored by his son and happy to agree to anything to get rid of him.

Chapter Twenty Three

Outside, in the car, Nigel wanted to telephone his wife. He wanted to tell her what had happened. Her approval would help eradicate the guilt he felt. But he also desperately wanted a drink and so he didn't stop to make the call.

Nigel lived less than four miles away from his father's terraced house. He drove home as quickly as he could. As soon as he had put the car in the garage, hung up his coat, changed his shoes for his slippers, washed his hands and exchanged his jacket for a cardigan he sat down in his usual armchair.

'It's all fixed,' he told Fenella, taking from her the gin and tonic which she had fixed. 'I'm picking Dad up and taking him round to the nursing home tomorrow afternoon after lunch.'

'Was he difficult about it?'

'No. Not at all really.'

'There you are. I told you he'd just give in quietly.' Fenella was sitting on the arm of Nigel's chair. She put her arm around his neck and kissed his ear. 'You're brilliant, darling,' she told him.

'I'll ring the builders in the morning,' Nigel told her.

'How soon can they start?'

'Monday,' said Nigel. 'They've got all the materials they need – new doors, new bath, partitions, paint – that sort of stuff. They should be finished in less than a month. And the estate agents have already found someone desperate to rent it. I got a call from Tony this morning.'

'How much are they paying?'

Nigel sipped at his drink, turned his head, grinned and told her. 'It's amazing what these old places fetch these days. They'll be paying eight times what Dad was paying in rent.'

'And that chap you know at the council has approved the payment of your Dad's nursing home fees?'

'Absolutely. No problem at all. Dad doesn't own the house, he hasn't got any capital. They don't have any option. They're obliged to pay the fees.'

'He'll be much, much happier in a nursing home than he ever was in that funny little house,' said Fenella.

'Oh absolutely,' agreed Nigel. 'I wouldn't dream of doing it if it wasn't the right thing for him. Oh, I nearly forgot there is some old junk in the house. Old furniture. Nothing valuable. Nothing decent. It's nearly all stuff that he and mother bought when they first started out. Would you give the chap at the auction rooms a call? Robbie isn't it?'

'Ronnie.'

'Ask him to take a van round there and clear out everything they can move.'

'Do you want them to give you a price first? Do you want me to get a quote?'

'No. Don't bother. Just ask them to take the stuff away. If there's money left over after they've covered their costs get them to let you have it in cash. I can take it round to Dad when I visit him.'

'What about our costs?'

'Oh, I think it would be fair to just take 17.5 per cent of the gross,' said Nigel. 'Take it out of the cash. I'd rather keep it all as a cash transaction.'

'No one can say you haven't been a wonderful son,' said Fenella.

'I'll be a lot happier knowing that he's being well looked after and not standing out in the rain,' said Nigel.

Fenella shuddered. 'I'm so glad his gardening days are over. I don't mind admitting that I was terrified people would find out. I hate to think what the Mertons would have said if they'd found out your father was working as a jobbing gardener.'

Nigel shivered. 'Let's not even think about that,' he said. 'It's all over now.' He emptied his glass.

'Would you like another one, dear?'

'Why not?' asked Nigel. 'I think we can afford to celebrate a bit tonight.' He squeezed Fenella's left buttock as she got up off the arm of his chair.

Fenella giggled, coquettishly. 'Oh dear me,' she said. 'I think I'd better get out my sexy nightie.' She smiled at him and then hurried off to the kitchen to get him another drink.

Nigel fiddled with the buttons on his cardigan, closed his eyes and relaxed. He was very pleased with himself and, indeed, with life in general. The day had gone much better than he had dared to hope.

CHAPTER TWENTY FOUR

'There's a new resident in the hallway,' whispered Mrs Roberts.

Mrs Caldicot, sitting at her desk and staring glumly at a thick pile of bills, looked up.

'Our new resident, Mr Roxdale, looks lovely, but there's a very pompous fellow with him who says he's a lawyer and Mr Roxdale's son. I don't like him at all.'

Mrs Caldicot hurried out into the hall.

'Mrs Caldicot?' asked the lawyer.

Mrs Caldicot confirmed her identity.

'This is my father, Mr Roxdale,' said the lawyer. 'Have you got someone who can help with his bags?'

'Er...' began Mrs Caldicot, looking around rather helplessly.

'I can get them,' said Mr Roxdale.

'You stay here,' said his son. 'They'll have someone to do that sort of thing.'

Mr Roxdale didn't seem sure what to do.

'I'll go,' said Mrs Roberts quickly. 'Are they in the car?'

'There are two cases in the boot,' explained the lawyer. 'And,

I'm afraid, a variety of garden tools poking out through the near-side rear window. Mr Roxdale simply wouldn't be parted from them. They have sentimental value. I'll help you with those in a minute. There's another case to bring. I couldn't fit it in the car today. I'll bring it over tomorrow morning.'

'OK,' said Mrs Roberts.

'The car is open. Just make sure you mind the paintwork,' said the lawyer. 'It's an expensive car.'

Behind his back Mrs Caldicot and Mrs Roberts pulled faces. The older Mr Roxdale looked embarrassed.

Suddenly there was a scream of laughter from the lounge.

'What on earth was that?' demanded the lawyer.

'Oh, just some of the residents having a little fun, I expect,' explained Mrs Caldicot. 'We're one big happy family here.'

There was a shout and the sound of crashing furniture.

'It rather sounds to me as though someone is fighting,' said the lawyer, disapprovingly.

Mrs Caldicot walked across the hall to the lounge and gingerly pushed open the door. Miss Nightingale was sitting on the floor, looking rather dazed. None of the other residents were identifiable. They were a mess of arms, legs, heads and torsos; apparently joined together as a huge many limbed monster.'

'What's going on?' asked Mrs Caldicot, in a whisper.

'We're playing Twister,' explained Miss Nightingale.

Mrs Caldicot shut the door and turned back to the lawyer. 'Nothing at all to worry about,' she reassured him. 'A few of the residents are playing a rather heated game of bridge.' There was a crash from within the lounge. It sounded as though a large piece of furniture had been knocked over.

'Someone has gone no trumps, I expect,' said Mrs Caldicot.

The lawyer frowned. He didn't approve of card games. He remembered students playing the game thirty years earlier when he had been at University. He hadn't approved of bridge then. 'Is that entirely appropriate for people of mature years? I would have thought that a more dignified pursuit might be more suitable. I trust there isn't any money changing hands?'

'Oh no,' Mrs Caldicot assured him. 'I'm absolutely sure that there is no money changing hands.' She paused. 'Our Miss Nightingale is very keen on embroidery,' said Mrs Caldicot. 'And another one of our residents is an enthusiastic philatelist with, I'm told, a very fine collection of French Colonials.' She swallowed hard. 'Naturally, we would not expect your father to take part in any activity which he felt inappropriate. Shall we go and take a look at Mr Roxdale's room?' She headed for the stairs and then, halfway up, stopped and turned when she realised that although Mr Roxdale senior was following her Mr Roxdale junior wasn't. He was standing in the hallway staring at the wallpaper.

'We're going to have the whole place redecorated,' said Mrs Caldicot, apologetically. 'I'm afraid we just haven't had time.' The truth was that it was money rather than time that they were short of. But she didn't like to mention that.

'No, no, I don't think that's necessary,' said Mr Roxdale. 'I was just admiring the pattern. Very unusual.'

'I don't think they make it any more,' said Mrs Caldicot. 'I tried to get a roll at the local hardware shop to repair some scuffed spots. But they didn't have anything like it.'

'No,' said Mr Roxdale, thoughtfully. 'No. I don't suppose they did.' He moved, apparently reluctantly, away from his study of the wallpaper, stopped for a few moments to examine a piece of furniture at the bottom of the stairs, and only then did he start up the stairs.

'You've got a lot of grass,' said Mr Roxdale the elder, peering out of the window at the back garden.

'Oh, yes,' said Mrs Caldicot. 'It costs a fortune to keep it all cut. But in the summer one or two of the more active residents like to totter out for a quiet game of croquet.'

'Splendid!' said Mr Roxdale junior.

'It must take a day and a half a week to cut all that grass,' said the older Mr Roxdale. 'Including the lawn at the front,' he added.

'I think you're probably right,' said Mrs Caldicot, who did not like being reminded of the gardener. He had that morning told Mrs Caldicot that he would not be returning until his bill had been paid in full. 'What do you think of your room?' she asked the older Mr Roxdale.

'I liked my old place,' said Mr Roxdale senior. 'I had a nice little garden.'

'If you feel the urge to get out there in the garden you'll be very welcome. I'm sure our own gardener won't mind.'

'I don't think my father really wants to get his fingers dirty any more,' said young Mr Roxdale. He spoke, Mrs Caldicot thought, as though he had several plums in his mouth. 'He's a bit old for physical work now.'

Mrs Caldicot sensed animosity. She looked first at the old man and then at his son. The elder Mr Roxdale looked rather sad. Mrs Caldicot looked at him, smiled and winked. Surprised, he grinned and winked back.

Mrs Caldicot and the two Roxdales went downstairs. Mrs Roberts had brought in the older Mr Roxdale's suitcases. She took them upstairs and offered to help the new resident unpack. Meanwhile, Mr Roxdale junior removed his father's garden tools from the Jaguar, taking great care not to chip the car's paint, and tossed them unceremoniously onto the ground beside a shed at the side of the house. He was glad to be rid of them. He was glad to be rid of his father too.

CHAPTER TWENTY FIVE

It was dusk. From inside the brightly lit clubhouse the 18th green seemed pitch black. It was difficult to believe that anyone could see to play golf. Outside on the green, where the final two players of the day were completing their round, things did not look anywhere near as black. The clubhouse, lit up and silhouetted against the skyline, looked like a liner quietly cruising in some calm Caribbean waters. Nigel Roxdale slipped his putter into his bag, took hold of the handle on his trolley and headed back for the clubhouse.

'Are you popping in for a quick one?' he asked his playing

partner, a short thick-set man who, although it hadn't rained all day, was cocooned in bulky waterproofs and had a multi-coloured woolly hat pulled down over his ears.

The man wearing the woolly hat pulled back his jacket sleeve and studied his watch. 'Better not, old man,' he replied, rather mournfully. 'Beryl will be furious if I'm late for dinner.' He held out a hand. 'But thanks for the game.' The two men shook hands.

At the top of the path leading to the clubhouse the players parted company. The man with the woolly hat turned right and headed for the club car park. Within less than five minutes he would have packed his bag and trolley into the boot of his car, exchanged his spiked golf shoes for a pair of black loafers and started the short journey home.

Nigel Roxdale, the other golfer, turned left and headed for the clubhouse. He parked his trolley, complete with clubs, in a small space created for that purpose, entered the clubhouse and headed for the locker room. He changed his shoes, socks and trousers, swapped his Pringle sweater for a sports jacket, put on a tie, combed his hair and headed straight for the bar, confident that although the bar would be quiet there would be someone there whom he knew. His confidence was, as usual, entirely justified.

He was ordering himself a gin at the bar when he heard a voice he knew well call his name. He turned, smiled and waved back at a small man sitting in a huge, brown leather easy chair next to a raging log fire. This was the quietest time of the day for the bar. Most of the members who had been playing golf had gone home for their dinner. At about eight the bar would start to fill up again as members brought their wives for a drink, a game of bridge and a gossip. During the daytime the clubhouse was full of insurance salesmen doing deals. During the evening it was full of women with unlikely hair-dos mumbling four no trumps and spitting out catty remarks about one another.

'Can I get you a drink?' Nigel called across.

'Another gin, thank you!' replied the small member, holding up his almost empty glass.

Nigel carried the two gins across to the fireplace, handed one to Mr Muller-Hawksmoor, put the second down on a low oak table and then slumped down into the other chair, a twin to the one in which Mr Muller-Hawksmoor was settled.

They talked for a while about golf.

'Another one?' asked Nigel Roxdale after fifteen minutes. 'Thanks!' said Mr Muller-Hawksmoor. Suddenly he sat up. 'My round,' he remembered. He started to lever himself out of the chair.

'No, my treat,' insisted Nigel. He turned, caught the barman's eye, held up his glass and pointed to Mr Muller-Hawksmoor. The barman nodded. 'I've had a good day,' sighed Nigel, replete with self-satisfaction. 'I managed to persuade my father to retire and go into a retirement home.'

Mr Muller-Hawksmoor looked at him and gently raised an enquiring eyebrow. He couldn't quite see why this was good news but he knew Nigel Roxdale well enough to guess that this hadn't been an entirely altruistic manoeuvre.

'He's been living alone for years,' said Nigel. 'Far too old, of course. He needs looking after. Better to get him used to the idea now rather than wait until he's senile. I've heard that when old folk get senile they find it more difficult to settle.' He paused. 'Of course,' he said, 'that's your line of work isn't it?'

'You did the right thing,' said Mr Muller-Hawksmoor.

The barman, a wiry, weary looking man in his late sixties, appeared with their drinks. He put the full glasses down on the table, picked up the empties and put them onto his tray. He had a slight tremor. This didn't much matter when he was picking up empty glasses but it meant he always spilt something when he was moving a full glass. The members tolerated this only because it gave them an excuse not to tip him. The barman waited while Nigel rummaged in his back pocket for the right change. As usual the barman did not expect a tip and, since his expectation was fulfilled, he was not disappointed in this.

'The odd thing was that the place where I took him turned out to be a damned treasure trove,' said Nigel quietly. He looked around to make sure no one could overhear him. There was no one within twenty feet.

'I spotted William Morris sunflower wallpaper in two rooms

and William Morris trellis wallpaper in the lounge. Unbelievable! There are silk oak pattern curtains in the lounge too – I checked with a dealer I know who told me that when Morris's company sold that material in 1910, it cost 45 shillings a yard. And I spotted at least four genuine pieces of William Morris furniture including two high-backed chairs and several pieces of furniture which were, I'm sure, produced at Morris's Red Lion Square workshop.'

'And they don't realise what they've got?' said Muller-Hawksmoor who knew only vaguely who William Morris was but who nevertheless recognised the commercial value of Nigel Roxdale's discovery. He was far too vain to confess his ignorance.

'I'm sure they don't have the slightest idea!' said Nigel. 'No idea at all. The daft woman running the place actually apologised to me for the state of the curtains and wallpaper. Said she was going to have the place redecorated when she had time.'

'How valuable are they – these things?' asked Mr Muller-Hawksmoor.

'Couldn't put a price on them,' said Nigel, emphatically. 'I did hear of a house in Somerset where they found a room covered with William Morris wallpaper. Some guys came down from London and spent a month peeling it off so they could use it to decorate an apartment in Knightsbridge.'

'Really?' said Mr Muller-Hawksmoor, impressed.

'You could take the stuff out and sell it of course, but by far the best thing to do would be to buy the place and open it up as an exclusive hotel,' said Nigel. 'Small, exquisitely furnished, private hotels are all the rage these days. And one with genuine William Morris stuff on the walls and real William Morris furniture...' he paused. 'You could charge what you liked for a weekend.' He sipped at his drink. 'Of course, I wouldn't bother opening a hotel myself. I'd just sell the place on to one of these chains specialising in small, private hotels.'

'What's the name of the place?' asked Mr Muller-Hawksmoor. 'I probably know it.'

'The Twilight Years Rest Home,' replied Nigel Roxdale. 'Run by a slightly dotty old woman ... I've forgotten her damned name ... Calders ... something like that ...'

'Caldicot?' suggested Mr Muller-Hawksmoor, who had gone very pale. He took a large swig from his glass.

'That's it! You know her?'

'I've got to visit the place tomorrow,' said Mr Muller-Hawksmoor, ignoring the question. He emptied his glass. 'Routine sort of check. Make sure they're obeying all the regulations.'

Nigel thought for a moment. 'What happens if a nursing home proprietor doesn't obey all the rules?' he asked. 'What sort of disciplinary powers do you lot have?'

'Oh vast,' said Mr Muller-Hawksmoor. 'We can close a place down in a flash.'

'You can actually close it down?'

'Oh yes.'

'You can really do that?' asked Nigel. 'By yourself?'

'Oh yes. If there's a breach of regulations. And there are a lot of regulations we can enforce.'

'Really,' said Nigel. 'That's very interesting. Let's have another drink, shall we?'

CHAPTER TWENTY SIX

Mrs Caldicot lived in a room on the top floor of the nursing home. It was no bigger and no smaller than anyone else's. Like each resident, she had a small private bathroom and in her bedroom there were two fitted wardrobes and a dressing table which also served as a desk. She also had an easy chair and a small table. Mrs Roberts also had her own room on the top floor. The other staff members lived out.

Mrs Caldicot woke, as she always did, at seven thirty sharp. As usual Kitty, her cat, was curled up next to her. Moving gently, so that she would not wake Kitty, Mrs Caldicot swung her legs out of bed, stood up, found her slippers and, as was her habit, padded across the bedroom floor to draw back the curtains and find out what sort of day it was.

Mrs Caldicot was a deep sleeper who was accustomed to getting the full benefit out of her eight hours and she didn't realise that she had noticed anything unusual until, two minutes later, she was bent over her washbasin with her face covered in soap. She quickly rinsed off the soap, grabbed a towel and padded back into her bedroom. She looked out of the window again.

At first Mrs Caldicot thought that perhaps she was imagining things. So she blinked and rubbed at her eyes and then looked back again. This time it was clear that she wasn't dreaming. There was a man out in the garden digging up the lawn. Judging by the amount of turf he had already moved he had clearly been out there for some time. But who on earth was it?

Not bothering to get dressed Mrs Caldicot headed for the door still wearing only her nightie. And then, as things so often do, it came to her in an unexpected flash. 'Mr Roxdale'. Her new paying guest. The elderly man who had been brought in by the middle-aged lawyer in the Jaguar.

She hurried along to Mrs Roberts's room. There she banged on the door. Mrs Roberts came to the door holding a huge white bath towel around her.

'What's up?' Mrs Roberts demanded, anxiously. She was not accustomed to getting visits at this time of the morning and Mrs Caldicot's unexpected knock on her door had alarmed her.

'Mr Roxdale is in the garden,' said Mrs Caldicot. 'He's out there digging up the lawn.'

'Mr Roxdale? The new resident?'

'Yes,' said Mrs Caldicot.

'Why?'

'Perhaps he's trying to find oil. Maybe he just hates grass. I don't know. But we've got to stop him. I'm going out to see what's going on,' said Mrs Caldicot.

'I'll come with you,' said Mrs Roberts, dropping her towel and quickly grabbing a dressing gown from a hook behind the door.

The two women hurried off down the stairs, through the kitchen and into the garden. The rest of the home was quiet. In the lounge Miss Nightingale was watching television and in the kitchen Mr and Mrs Merivale were making toast and coffee. They both looked up, said 'good morning' first to Mrs Caldicot and then to Mrs Roberts and then stared out of the window as the two women marched out of the back door and into the garden. Mr and Mrs Merivale looked at one another for a moment, shrugged and then went back to their chores.

'Good morning!' called Mrs Caldicot to Mr Roxdale as soon as she was in earshot.

The gardener, who had his foot on his spade and was about to remove another piece of turf from the already decimated lawn, stopped what he was doing, turned and grinned, first at Mrs Caldicot and then at Mrs Roberts, hurrying up in her wake.

'What on earth are you doing?' Mrs Caldicot asked. She regretted the banality of her question the moment the words had left her mouth.

'Digging,' replied Mr Roxdale.

'Yes, I can see that,' said Mrs Caldicot, conscious of the fact that the answer she had received was no more stupid than the question she had asked. 'But why?'

'I thought you'd like some flowers and some vegetables instead of all this grass,' said Mr Roxdale, waving an arm around. 'Don't get me wrong, I'm not completely against grass. In the right place a little lawn can look very nice indeed – especially if it's well tended – but you've just got too much lawn here.'

'Where did you get the tools from?'

'They're mine,' explained Mr Roxdale. 'The ones I brought with me.' Mrs Caldicot remembered the tools that Mr Roxdale's son had extracted from the Jaguar. He leant on his spade and waved towards a neat pile of turves. 'None of this need cost you a penny,' he said. 'I even know a man who'll buy this turf from you,' he told her.

Mrs Caldicot stared at him. 'You know a man who'll buy clumps of grass?'

'Oh yes. There's always a demand for good, clean grass. You've got good stuff here. Just the thing for making lawns.'

'It is a lawn,' pointed out Mrs Caldicot.

'That's what makes it valuable,' explained Mr Roxdale. 'And

you can use the money you get from the turf to buy seeds,' explained Mr Roxdale. 'So, you see, you can start your garden without it costing you a penny.'

Mrs Caldicot had started out from her bedroom intending to tell Mr Roxdale to put back all the turf. But now she wasn't so sure. She looked around. There was too much grass. It was boring. And she had to admit that the residents hardly ever came out into the garden at all.

'If we put in some fast growing crops there's still time to get quite a decent return this year,' said Mr Roxdale. 'We want high productivity crops that will produce a good return in a short space of time. And, if you're looking to save money the best bet would be to plant the sort of things that are cheap to grow but which take a little bit of knowledge and a bit of effort to harvest.'

'You could organise all this for us?' asked Mrs Caldicot.

'Oh yes,' said Mr Roxdale. 'Shall I carry on?'

Mrs Caldicot looked at Mrs Roberts. Mrs Roberts shrugged. 'Well, yes, I suppose so,' said Mrs Caldicot. 'Yes. I think that would be a splendid idea.' She paused. 'As long as you don't grow chrysanthemums.' The late Mr Caldicot had been keen on chrysanthemums. Mrs Caldicot could now not bear the flowers.

'OK,' said Mr Roxdale, unquestioningly. 'That's fine. No chrysanthemums.'

Mrs Caldicot turned to head back towards the house. 'Do you always start work this early in the morning?'

'No,' said Mr Roxdale. 'Not this early.'

'So why did you start this early today?'

'I thought that if I asked you if I could dig up the garden you probably wouldn't listen but would just say 'No',' explained Mr Roxdale. 'But I reckoned that if I'd already started you'd want to know why − and you'd listen to me.'

Mrs Caldicot looked at him and smiled. It was the sort of thing she would have done herself. 'Have you had any breakfast?' she asked.

Mr Roxdale shook his head.

'Then for heaven's sake come in and have something to

eat,' she told him. 'I can't bear to see a man work on an empty stomach.'

Mr Roxdale stuck his spade into the turf and followed Mrs Caldicot and Mrs Roberts back to the kitchen.

CHAPTER TWENTY SEVEN

Mr Roxdale was sitting in the dining room finishing off a huge plateful of bacon and eggs. Thelma Caldicot and Mrs Roberts, now both dressed and decent, were sitting in Mrs Caldicot's office sharing a rack of toast and a pot of coffee. Mrs Caldicot was wearing a bright blue suit, a white blouse and a pair of hold-up stockings which had a pretty pattern running down the back of each leg and which made her feel young, feminine and delightfully and surprisingly reckless. Although the knowledge no longer worried her she was well aware that her former husband, the late Mr Caldicot, would have had an apoplectic fit if he could have seen her dressed in such a way. He believed that a woman's clothes should be designed solely to maintain warmth and dignity. Mrs Roberts was wearing her nurse's uniform and looked very crisp and professional.

'We'll save a fortune,' said Mrs Roberts. 'If Mr Roxdale digs up enough of the garden we won't have to pay anyone to come and cut the grass. And we'll save a fortune on greengrocery bills.'

'I suppose so,' said Mrs Caldicot, smearing thick-cut marmalade onto her third slice of toast.

'Plus we get genuine organic food,' said Mrs Roberts. 'That's got to be a good thing. I'm always a bit suspicious of some of these organic farmers. You never know whether or not they've crept out in the middle of the night with a bag of chemical fertiliser or weed-killer.'

Mrs Caldicot, her mouth now full of toast and marmalade, nodded her approval.

'So, what's worrying you?' asked Mrs Roberts, who was, as usual, on a diet and had already passed her self-imposed limit of two slices of toast.

There was a pause while Mrs Caldicot finished the mouthful of toast she was eating. 'Oh, I don't know,' she sighed. She thought for a while. 'Yes, I do,' she confessed. 'I'm not really cut out for running an old people's home.'

'Of course you are!' cried Mrs Roberts. 'What on earth makes you say that?'

'It's the finance side of things that I can't manage,' said Mrs Caldicot. 'I know that everyone chips in with whatever they can afford but we're accumulating debts at a frightening rate. I simply didn't have the heart to ask Mr Williams for a cheque. He doesn't seem to have anything except a couple of suitcases of old photographs.'

They sat in glum silence for a few moments. Mrs Roberts, absorbing some of Mrs Caldicot's depression, reached out for another slice of toast.

'Did I tell you he gave me one of his old snaps in lieu of payment,' said Mrs Caldicot. She rummaged around on her desk, found the photograph, wiped a little marmalade off it and handed it to Mrs Roberts. 'It's quite nice,' said Mrs Roberts.

'It's very nice,' agreed Mrs Caldicot. 'But I can't see the water company or the electricity company accepting a photograph instead of a cheque, can you?'

'I suppose not,' agreed Mrs Roberts.

They both jumped when they heard the front doorbell.

'Oh damn,' said Mrs Caldicot. 'Who can that be.'

'Let's just leave it,' said Mrs Roberts. 'My old auntie never answers her front doorbell. She says that people who ring her doorbell always want something from her. And she's right. When was the last time you opened the front door and had a nice surprise? When was the last time you opened the door and found someone standing there waiting to make your life better?'

The bell rang again.

'Oh I suppose I'd better go,' said Mrs Caldicot.

'I'll go,' laughed Mrs Roberts, who was nearer the door.

'You finish off that last piece of toast.'

Mrs Caldicot, ignoring the demands of her figure and succumbing to temptation, had smeared marmalade on the last piece of toast and just taken a sizeable bite when Mrs Roberts entered the office again. 'It's Mr Roxdale's son,' she whispered. 'He's brought another suitcase and he wants to see you.'

'Qnhell snhow hchim hin,' spluttered Mrs Caldicot, hurriedly finishing the mouthful of toast, and hiding the remains of her breakfast under a pile of bills.

Mrs Roberts turned round to fetch Mr Roxdale but he had followed her and was already in the room.

'Has my father settled in?' he asked.

'Oh yes, I think so,' said Mrs Caldicot, rising. 'Would you like to see him?'

'Oh no, no, no. Don't disturb him,' said Nigel. 'I just called in with another suitcase of his.' He looked at Mrs Caldicot's desk.

'Please excuse the mess,' said Mrs Caldicot, rather embarrassed. 'I was just having a bit of a tidy up.'

'That's an interesting looking photograph you've got there,' said Nigel. He reached out, his fingers hovering above the photograph. 'May I?'

'Of course,' said Mrs Caldicot, with a wave of her hand.

Nigel picked up the photograph, carefully blew away some toast crumbs, and then turned the photograph over. He blanched noticeably when he saw the signature on the back. 'Where on earth did you get this?' he asked.

Mrs Caldicot started to explain that a resident had given it to her. But something, she did not know what, warned her not to tell the whole truth.

'Oh, it's just something I was given,' she said.

'I'm a bit of a collector of old photographs,' said Nigel, trying to remain calm. 'Do you happen to know if the signature is real?'

'Oh yes,' said Mrs Caldicot. 'It's real.'

'It looks authentic,' said Nigel, examining it closely. 'Yes, I'm sure it is.' He looked across at Mrs Caldicot. 'Would you be prepared to sell this to me?'

'I don't know,' said Mrs Caldicot. 'I hadn't really thought about selling it.'

'You know who the photographer is, of course?'

'Yes,' said Mrs Caldicot hesitantly.

'I mean, you know who he is,' repeated Nigel. He suspected that if Mrs Caldicot had known the photograph's true value it would not have been lying on her desk half covered in crumbs.

Mrs Caldicot, confused, shook her head.

'This is, I'm pretty sure, an original print of a photograph by Mr Henry Williams.'

'Yes,' said Mrs Caldicot, surprised. 'Mr Henry Williams. That's the name.'

'Do you know who Mr Henry Williams is?'

Mrs Caldicot suppressed the temptation to say that Mr Henry Williams was a rather confused old man whom she had last seen attacking scrambled eggs on toast in the dining room. Instead, she simply looked puzzled.

'Mr Henry Williams is a legendary English photographer who worked in Paris with Cartier-Bresson. He's one of the best and most collected English photographers.' Nigel scratched his nose. 'I don't even know whether or not he's still alive,' he admitted. 'The last I heard he had left France and come back to England. But for the last thirty years he's been a bit of a recluse.'

'What's it worth?' asked Mrs Caldicot, trying not to sound excited.

'I'll give you £500 for it,' said Nigel. He thought for a moment. 'No,' he said. 'That's not fair. The print is signed and the signature looks genuine. I'll pay you £1,000 for it.'

Mrs Caldicot swallowed hard. 'Do you mind if I talk to one of my colleagues?' she said in a voice she hardly recognised. She got up and headed for the door and then turned back, smiled at Nigel, took the photograph from the desk in front of him and left.

She found Mr Williams upstairs in his room.

'Are you the Mr Henry Williams?' she demanded.

'I'm Mr Henry Williams,' said Mr Williams, rather defensively. 'But I don't expect I'm the only Mr Henry Williams.'

'But you're the photographer Mr Henry Williams?'

'Yes.'

Mrs Caldicot held out the photograph he had given her. 'There's a man downstairs who's just offered me £1,000 for this!' she said.

'Don't take it,' said Mr Williams firmly.

'Don't take it?'

'No. He's ripping you off.'

'You mean it's worth more than £1,000?'

'The last print of that photograph went for £5,000 plus 17.5 per cent auctioneer fees,' said Mr Williams. 'And it wasn't signed.'

Mrs Caldicot sat down on Mr Williams's bed. 'So what is this one worth?' she asked.

'It should fetch between £7,500 and £10,000 at auction,' said Mr Williams. 'Maybe more. Who knows.'

'I can't take this,' said Mrs Caldicot, putting the photograph down on the bed. She looked at it as though it was likely to bite her.

'Why on earth not?' asked Mr Williams. 'I've got a suitcase full of them. And I can always print more if I run out.'

Mrs Caldicot looked at Mr Williams's suitcase and went cold. 'Don't you think those should be in a bank?' she asked.

'Oh no,' said Mr Williams. 'These are only prints. The negatives are in a box in the bank.'

'Anyway I can't take that,' said Mrs Caldicot. 'It's worth far too much.'

'How much did you think it was worth when I gave it to you?' Mr Williams asked her.

Mrs Caldicot looked embarrassed.

'You just thought it was an old man's snap – worthless – didn't you?'

Mrs Caldicot felt herself blushing.

'But you took the photograph, you didn't say anything and you didn't throw me out?'

'No ... but ...'

'I like you,' said Mr Williams, beaming. 'I like you very much. You're kind. I don't meet many kind people these days. Keep the photograph and sell it at auction. You'll get the best price for it that way. And I'll give you another one next month.'

'No, no!' said Mrs Caldicot, jumping up off the bed. 'You can't do that!'

'They're my photographs,' Mr Williams pointed out. 'I can do what I like with them. What else am I going to do with my money? For years now it's been my plan to leave nothing when I die. Except debts to the lawyer and the undertaker.'

'Nothing at all for your family?'

'Why should I leave money to my family?' asked Mr Williams, seemingly quite genuinely puzzled. 'I started out this life with nothing and I intend to finish my journey in the same state. Most people think that accumulating money is like a game,' said Mr Williams. 'They want to be in a good position in the game when they die. My hero is the Count of Paris,' he went on. 'He was the heir to the French throne and in 1940 he inherited the equivalent of £200 million. In 1999 he died, leaving 6 monogrammed handkerchiefs to be divided between his 11 children. What a man! What a way to go. There was a man who timed his life and his death to perfection.' He sighed, knowing that unless he destroyed his life's work, his negatives and his photographs, he had no chance whatsoever of emulating his hero. He grinned at Mrs Caldicot. 'I told you,' he said to her. 'I admire what you did. I was talking to Miss Nightingale at breakfast. I wish I'd been there to record it all with a camera.' He chuckled.

Mrs Caldicot got up, now even more embarrassed.

Mr Williams picked up the photograph and held it as though about to rip it in half. 'Please take it,' he said. 'If you don't I'll rip it in half.'

'You can't do that!' said Mrs Caldicot, horrified. 'That would be terrible.'

'So, what's it to be? Are you going to take the photograph or am I going to rip it up?'

Mrs Caldicot looked at Mr Williams and smiled. 'Thank you,' she said, quietly. 'I will accept this one photograph. It's very generous of you and it will get us out of a very big hole. But I can't let you keep bailing us out. So, no more photographs, please.'

'But ...' began Mr Williams.

'No buts!' insisted Mrs Caldicot, firmly.

Mr Williams sighed. 'OK,' he said. 'But can I ask you one favour? If you've got a collector downstairs please don't tell him where you got the photograph. I don't want a queue of collectors at the front door – all wanting their photographs signing.'

'I won't,' said Mrs Caldicot. 'I promise.' She left Mr Williams's room and met Mrs Roberts on the landing.

'Mrs Roberts,' she said, handing her the photograph. 'Put this into an envelope and hide it somewhere safe.'

'Why?' asked Mrs Roberts. 'Is it valuable?'

'It's worth between £7,500 and £10,000,' Mrs Caldicot told her.

Mrs Roberts stared at her disbelievingly.

'I know,' said Mrs Caldicot. 'You could have knocked me down with a bus when I found out. But it's true. Mr Roxdale's father just offered me £1,000 for it.'

Mrs Roberts, suddenly white, took the photograph as though it was made of delicate porcelain and walked slowly away with it.

Mrs Caldicot went back downstairs to tell Nigel that although she very much appreciated his kind offer she had to tell him that for the moment the picture wasn't for sale.

Nigel offered £2,000.

Mrs Caldicot smiled very sweetly and said 'No, thank you.'

When Nigel had gone she went looking for Mr Roxdale, to tell him that his other suitcase had arrived.

'He's back in the garden,' Mrs Merivale told Mrs Caldicot. 'Still digging up the lawn.'

Mr Roxdale was in the garden but he was not alone. Mr Hewitt, Mr Livingstone and Mrs Caldicot's cat, Kitty, were all helping him. Mr Hewitt who was, like Mr Roxdale, a former gardener, was delighted to be getting his hands dirty again.

CHAPTER TWENTY EIGHT

Later that day, while an exhausted Kitty slept on her rug on top of the boiler, Mrs Caldicot, Mrs Roberts and the Merivales cleaned the kitchen. This was an extensive task, for the cook who had recently left had not regarded cleanliness as a priority or, indeed, as much of a virtue at all.

Mrs Caldicot was on her hands and knees in front of the oven, scrubbing at stains which had clearly been accumulating for some time. Mrs Roberts, also on her hands and knees, had undone the pipe-work underneath the kitchen sink and was struggling to deal with a blockage by extracting rotting vegetable remains. Mrs Merivale was sitting at the kitchen table folding and refolding a duster so it would look neat when she started work. Her husband, who did not like to be far from her, was cleaning out the fridge.

Mr and Mrs Merivale were by now well settled into the kitchen at the Twilight Years Rest Home.

Some people enjoy a retirement which allows them to potter around, avoiding responsibilities and commitments, getting up when they want, going to bed when they want and doing whatever they fancy in between.

Others prefer to keep busy. They like knowing that they are making a difference to someone else's lives. They need to know that they are needed.

Mrs Merivale was one of those others. And Mr Merivale, who had never had to deal with such twentieth century tortures as ambition and drive, was extremely happy doing whatever kept his wife happy. For him a pile of dirty dishes and a bowlful of soapy water was a promise of an hour or two of fulfilment, the comforting knowledge that there would be a warm glow of satisfaction when the dirty dishes had been washed, wiped and stacked away and, above all, the knowledge that what he was doing would elicit a smile and a hug from Maple Merivale, the only woman he had ever loved, ever wanted to love or ever seen any reason to want to love.

Although they had only been working in the kitchen for a short time, Mr and Mrs Merivale had already earned the respect, affection and gratitude of everyone else in the Twilight Years Rest Home. Mrs Merivale ran a neat and efficient kitchen and produced her meals on time. But it was Mr Roxdale who best summed up what the others liked best about Mrs Merivale when he said: 'She cooks wonderful food and serves generous portions.'

The fashionable television chefs may come and go, parading their skills with rare and barely edible Pategonian vegetables, decorating their plates as though preparing them for an exhibition at the Tate Gallery, and spending hours turning tomato skins into roses, but in the long run cooking is about one thing, and one thing only: satisfying appetites with tasty, wholesome, nutritious food. And Mrs Merivale was better at doing that than any fancy television chef. She knew what her diners wanted and she made sure that she gave it to them – in good portions.

CHAPTER TWENTY NINE

In order to make the time pass more pleasantly Mrs Caldicot was telling them all about her most recent lunch with Jenkins and had just reached the end of the meal ('while Jenkins finished his coffee, this hunky bloke brought this tray full of gorgeous petits fours – I hate to think what it all cost') when their peace was interrupted by the familiar sound of the front doorbell.

'Darn it,' said Mrs Caldicot, stopping in mid-scrub, turning her head and banging it against the side of the oven. 'Can you go, Mrs Roberts?'

'I've got my hand halfway down the drain,' said Mrs Roberts, gouging another glop of unrecognisable black goo from the waste pipe. 'By the time I've made myself presentable whoever is ringing the bell will have forgotten why they ever called.'

'Perhaps one of the residents will answer it,' suggested Mrs Caldicot. They waited. The doorbell rang again. And again.

'I think the residents are all too busy having a good time,' said Mrs Roberts.

'What are they all doing this morning?' asked Mrs Caldicot.

'They were playing 'musical chairs' when I last looked,' replied Mrs Roberts. 'Mr Hewitt was sitting on the sideboard claiming that it counted as a chair because he could sit on it. They wanted me to act as referee but I declined and left quickly.'

'Very sensible,' said Mrs Caldicot who still remembered and regretted having agreed to act as referee in a very hectic game of Twister. The bell rang again. The caller was clearly not going to give up. 'Mrs Merivale, would you be kind enough to pop and answer the door for us?' asked Mrs Caldicot.

'Oh!' said Mrs Merivale, slightly startled and flustered. 'Are you sure it will be all right for me to do that?'

'Just open the door and see who's there,' said Mrs Caldicot. 'Ask them what they want and then come and tell me.'

'Oh. Right. I think I can probably manage that,' said Mrs Merivale. 'I'll just pop and get my hat.'

Mrs Merivale had stood up and taken just two paces towards the door when Mrs Caldicot and Mrs Roberts stopped what they were doing, looked first at one another and then at Mrs Merivale and finally spoke together. 'Why do you need a hat to open the door?'

Mrs Merivale stopped and turned. 'I always wear a hat when I open the door,' she told them.

'Yes,' said Mrs Caldicot. 'But why?'

'My mother always did it,' replied Mrs Merivale. 'She would never answer the door unless she was wearing a hat.'

'Yes,' repeated Mrs Caldicot. 'But why?'

'So that if she didn't want to see the visitor who was standing on the step she could tell them that she was just going out,' said Mrs Merivale. 'They would see the hat on her head and think she was telling the truth.'

'And if it was someone she wanted to see?'

'She'd still tell them she was just going out but would remove her hat and say that her errand could wait. That would make them feel wanted and important.'

'And you've always done this?'

'Oh yes. Without fail.'

'That's brilliant!' said Mrs Caldicot, in awe.

'It's simple but so clever!' agreed Mrs Roberts.

'We will keep a hatstand in the hall,' said Mrs Caldicot. 'In future I will never answer the door unless I'm wearing a hat.'

'Nor will I,' said Mrs Roberts.

'Shall I pop and get my hat, then?' asked Mrs Merivale.

'Most definitely,' said Mrs Caldicot.

She left the kitchen. Mr Merivale followed close behind.

CHAPTER THIRTY

A minute or two later Mrs Merivale returned to the kitchen. She was wearing a neat little hat with a feather in it. 'I'm sorry,' she said to Mrs Caldicot. 'You'll have to come. They want to see you and they won't even tell me who they are or what they want.'

Mrs Caldicot got up and walked to the front door. There were two people, a man and a woman, standing in the porch outside (Mrs Merivale hadn't invited them in since they had refused to tell her who they were). Both were carrying clipboards.

The woman was probably in her thirties, though it was difficult to tell with any accuracy. She wore grey, mannish trousers which had huge patch pockets on the thighs and a heavy green anorak with lots of pockets. She had lank, greasy hair which would not have looked out of place on the head of a down-on-his-luck heavy metal fan who was sleeping rough. She had black skin, wore no make-up and had small, rodent-like eyes. She looked as if she needed a good bath. She had the stony-faced, heartless look of a professional social worker about her. Mrs Caldicot had seen that look before, and it made her feel cold inside.

But it was the man, not the woman, who made leaden-footed butterflies in Mrs Caldicot's stomach start jumping cartwheels. It was a face that Mrs Caldicot knew very well. It was a face she had hoped she would never see again.

When her husband had died, Mrs Caldicot's son and daughter-in-law had decided that Mrs Caldicot wasn't capable of looking after herself at home alone. They had booked her into an old people's home called The Twilight Years Rest Home, run by a cruel, heartless man called Muller-Hawksmoor. Within days an irate Mrs Caldicot, angry at being told that she could no longer keep her cat Kitty with her, and fed up of the smell and taste of over-cooked cabbage, had summoned up courage she never knew she had, and walked out of the rest home – followed by many of the other residents. Mrs Caldicot's astonishing 'escape' had made national news and Mr Muller-Hawksmoor had ended up losing his nursing home.

It was a smirking Muller-Hawskmoor, the very same Muller-Hawksmoor, who was now standing on the step of the nursing home. The smug, self-satisfied former rest home owner looked extremely pleased with himself.

For a brief moment Mrs Caldicot just stared at him.

'Mrs Caldicot?' he asked.

'Of course it is. What do you want?' said Mrs Caldicot. 'You're not welcome here.' She did not even try to disguise her hostility.

'My name is Muller-Hawksmoor...'

'I know who you are.'

'...and this is my colleague Ms Jones.'

'Ms Jones BA,' the woman caller corrected him. She glowered at Mrs Caldicot. 'In addition to attending as Mr Muller-Hawksmoor's Associate I have to tell you that I am appointed by the council as the statutory lesbian feminist advocate liaison representative for your staff and residents.'

'That's very nice, dear,' said Mrs Caldicot. 'But I'm afraid you're not welcome here, either of you.' She attempted to close the door but found that Muller-Hawksmoor had put a suede clad foot in the way.

'We're from the local council,' said Muller-Hawksmoor, 'and this is official. My colleague, Ms Jones BA, and I represent the council's Rest Home Supervisory Unit. It is our Unit's broader responsibility to examine all the residential institutions in this area which are offering accommodation, nursing services or other facilities for the elderly.' He paused, and the smirk grew wider. 'Ms Jones BA and I have statutory authority,' he told Mrs Caldicot. 'You are legally obliged to allow us free access to your facilities at any time convenient to us. If you refuse to comply with our requests we are entitled to serve you with a closure notice, which will give you a limited time to find alternative accommodation for your residents and then immediately close down your facility.'

'Do you have any official identification?' Mrs Caldicot asked him.

'Of course,' said Mr Muller-Hawksmoor, as smooth and unruffled as a kitchen salesman. He slipped a hand into his inside jacket pocket and brought out a wallet. From the wallet he took a plastic identity card which carried his photograph, official status and various identifying details. By the time Mrs Caldicot had studied Mr Muller-Hawksmoor's identity card, and handed it back, Ms Jones had taken her own identity card out of one of the many pockets in her anorak. She held it a few inches away from Mrs Caldicot's nose; so close to her face that Mrs Caldicot had to move her head back an inch or so in order to read it. The photograph made Ms Jones look like the subject of a 'wanted' poster. 'Statutory Lesbian Feminist Advocate Liaison Representative' screamed red capital letters underneath her photograph.

'I have been married three times,' said Ms Jones BA.

Mrs Caldicot looked at her, slightly puzzled. 'Congratulations!' she said, not sure of the relevance of this but not sure what else to say.

'That was before I decided to convert to fundamental lesbianism,' continued Ms Jones BA.

'Of course,' agreed Mrs Caldicot.

'Men are very weak,' said Ms Jones BA. 'All my husbands committed suicide.'

'Oh good heavens,' said Mrs Caldicot. 'How, er distressing.' Suddenly she brightened. 'I only had the one,' she said. 'I could never quite persuade him to take the plunge. You'd better come in.' She opened the front door wide and stood back so that they could enter. She would have been more enthusiastic about allowing a pair of pythons, or a pair of psychopathic mass murderers into her rest home. But she realised that she had no alternative. When a man in a cheap suit flashes a plastic identity card establishing him as a council employee every castle must lower its drawbridge.

'What do you want to see?' she asked them.

'This is just a preliminary reconnaissance,' said Mr Muller-Hawksmoor. 'Just an initial visit for us to get some basic details. To begin with we need an up-to-date inventory of your residents.'

'We don't keep an inventory of our residents,' said Mrs Caldicot sharply. She was holding her head high and trying not to show how nervous she felt. 'The residents at this rest home are regarded as guests, not listed on a computer programme alongside the towels and bits and pieces of furniture.'

'Very noble,' said Ms Jones BA, who, Mrs Caldicot thought, had all the charm of a hungry scorpion. 'But you presumably have some idea of the names of your clients.' She spoke with ill-disguised contempt and managed to make the word 'clients' sound like an insult. 'And let's get on with it, shall we? I don't want to do this any more than you do. I would much rather be doing something socially significant.'

'What sort of thing would you consider socially significant?' asked Mrs Caldicot.

'It is my intention to set up a lesbian mothers' unit,' said Ms Jones BA.

'You don't consider working with the elderly to be socially significant?'

'No, of course not,' answered Ms Jones BA. 'The elderly haven't been oppressed for countless generations.'

'It's people like you who've turned us into the ignored majority,' said Mrs Caldicot. 'Just because our oppression is relatively new doesn't excuse it.'

'I have no interest in the elderly,' said Ms Jones BA.

'That's a very ageist remark,' said Mrs Caldicot. 'I'm surprised the council approves of your attitude.'

'Let's get on with it, shall we?' said Mr Muller-Hawksmoor. 'We have some confidential enquiries to make,' sniffed Ms Jones BA. 'We will need to talk to your staff and to your clients.' She looked at Mrs Caldicot contemptuously. 'You can go now,' she said. 'We will let you know when we need you.'

'I'll just tell my residents that you will be wandering about asking questions,' said Mrs Caldicot, walking ahead of them. 'I don't want any of them being upset.' She opened the lounge door and entered, closely followed by Mr Muller-Hawksmoor and Ms Jones BA. The lounge was empty. Utterly deserted.

'Ah,' said Muller-Hawksmoor, walking across the room and stopping in front of a bookcase on top of which stood the vase which Miss Nightingale had found in the kitchen. 'I'm pleased to see that you've still got my old vase on display.'

Mrs Caldicot looked at the vase he was examining. 'Oh yes,' she said. 'One of our residents found it in a kitchen cupboard.'

'I always rather liked that vase,' said Muller-Hawksmoor.

'I hope you haven't mislaid your guests,' sneered Ms Jones BA, who had little time for idle chitter-chatter. 'We usually expect proprietors of care establishments within our jurisdiction to have some idea of the whereabouts of their people.'

'I haven't mislaid them,' said Mrs Caldicot, frostily. 'And they're not 'my people'. It's a nice day so perhaps they are outside, in the garden.' She opened the door to the kitchen and poked her head inside. Mrs Roberts was still on her knees, doing unspeakable things to the drains.

'Who is it?' whispered Mrs Roberts.

'Inspectors from the council,' replied Mrs Caldicot. 'They want to speak to everyone.' She paused, and lowered her voice still more. 'One of the inspectors is Muller-Hawksmoor!'

Mrs Roberts knew far more than she wanted to know about Muller-Hawksmoor. Her dropped jaw was, however, far more eloquent than any words would have been. She would have been more cheerful about this invasion if Mrs Caldicot had told her that they were being inspected by a troupe of hungry cannibals looking for something to cook. 'That's crazy!' she said at last.

'It's like putting Herod in charge of the maternity ward!' whispered Mrs Caldicot. 'Do you know where everyone is?'

'I think they're all out in the garden, helping Mr Roxdale,' replied Mrs Roberts. 'Mr Williams had some more spades and forks delivered so that they'd have one each.'

'Then let's take the Gestapo outside,' said Mrs Caldicot. 'Let's hope Mr Williams has got enough extra spades for them to help too.'

CHAPTER THIRTY ONE

Out in the garden Mr Roxdale and his small army of helpers were digging up the remains of the lawn with surprising speed. The lawn looked as though a very large, incompetent golfer had been practising.

'This is the best fun I've ever had,' said Miss Nightingale, stabbing her spade into the ground and, after a struggle, managing to dig out a small divot.

'This is the best fun I've ever had,' said Mrs Peterborough, whose habit of repeating things had not diminished with time. Trying to copy Miss Nightingale she thrust her spade into the ground and then wrestled with it in a vain attempt to dig out a piece of turf. She managed to produce a tiny divot that a baby rabbit might have been proud of. It was clear that, despite their enthusiasm, if Miss Nightingale and Mrs Peterborough were to take leading roles in converting the lawn into a productive garden the task would probably outlive them all.

'I'm sorry to bother you,' said Mrs Caldicot, speaking loudly to attract their attention. 'But we are being inspected by two representatives of the local council. This is not something over which I have any authority. The council's representatives tell me that they have the authority to question us all,' she said, 'and I understand that they may want to ask you all questions.' She turned her head and waved a hand to indicate the two visitors who were standing behind her. 'Some of you may remember Mr Muller-Hawksmoor,' she said. 'He was formerly proprietor of the Twilight Years Rest Home but is now an employee of the local council.'

There was much muttering at the announcement of the name Muller-Hawksmoor.

'Can't stand the man. Nasty piece of work,' said Mr Livingstone, glowering in Muller-Hawksmoor's direction. 'I always thought he was a socialist.'

'He's a socialist, is he?' said Mr Hewitt. 'Ha! That explains a lot. I always wondered about him.'

'Who is this fellow?' Mr Roxdale asked Mr Hewitt.

'He's the most obnoxious, cruel, horrid, wicked, heartless...' Mr Hewitt began to run dry.

'Disreputable, crooked, mean...' continued Mr Livingstone, helping him out.

'Put him top of your hate list,' Mr Hewitt told Mr Roxdale.

'No room at the moment I'm afraid,' said Mr Roxdale. 'I try to limit myself to being annoyed by about 100 things at a time. I find that I can't cope with more than that.'

'He's worth a spot right near the top,' Mr Hewitt assured him.

'OK,' said Mr Roxdale, generously. 'But he'll have to jump the queue. I already have a fairly long waiting list of things to get cross about.'

'Mrs Caldicot and this fellow had a terrible row,' Mr Hewitt said. 'They loathe one another.'

'In that case I think he can jump the waiting list and go straight into the top five,' said Mr Roxdale.

'If he comes near me I'll brain him with my spade,' added Mr Livingstone.

'Don't be silly,' said Mrs Caldicot, who had overheard and who was slightly worried that things might get out of hand. 'You mustn't do that.' She tried to make her disapproval sound convincing, though this wasn't easy.

'No, don't do that,' said Mr Roxdale, stopping digging and placing a restraining hand on Mr Livingstone's hand. 'These spades have good edges. If you use one to brain a council employee you'll probably wreck the cutting edge,' he explained. 'Council employees all have rocks inside their skulls,' he added. Mr Roxdale had had enough experience of council workers to know that he did not like them.

'I rang the council once,' said Miss Nightingale. 'I was surprised to discover that it is a very civilised place. Did you know that they have a man there who has a piano in his office and just sits and plays the piano all day long?'

Everyone looked at her.

'What makes you say that, Miss Nightingale?' asked Mr Livingstone, not wishing to display the mild scepticism which he felt but hoping that a single question might clear up the confusion.

'A very busy lady told me to hold on and then she put me through to someone who was playing the piano,' said Miss Nightingale. 'He – and I don't know why but I've always assumed it was a 'he', possibly because of the rather enthusiastic way he threw himself at the keys – didn't say anything at all but just rattled along obviously enjoying himself very much. I like piano music so I didn't mind. It was something by Mozart I think. I listened to him for twenty minutes or so, said 'thank you' very quietly, so as not to disturb him, and put the telephone receiver down. I had by then completely forgotten why I had telephoned in the first place.' She stopped and thought for a moment. 'Of course,' she said, 'If you had an urgent enquiry you might not be so pleased to know that council employees were enjoying themselves playing the piano, rather than getting on with collecting rubbish and replacing burnt-out street lamps.'

'I'll have you know that I'm not just a council employee. I'm also a qualified social worker,' cried Ms Jones BA, worried that things were getting away from her and interrupting Miss Nightingale's account of her personal interface with the council.

'Do you have a piano?' Miss Nightingale asked her.

'I have a BA,' shouted Ms Jones BA. 'I most certainly do not have a piano.'

'Never mind, dear,' said Miss Nightingale. 'Perhaps when

you get promoted and become a little more senior.'

Ms Jones BA glowered. 'I am a fully-qualified social worker,' she shouted. 'I have a BA.'

Mr Roxdale liked social workers even less than he liked council workers. 'I don't care if you're Ms Jones LUFTHANSA, QUANTAS and AIR LINGUS, love,' he told her. 'As far as I'm concerned you're still just a bloody social worker.'

Ms Jones BA might have been (just) able to cope with the fact that her degree (with an added diploma in social history – which she, naturally, preferred to describe as social hertory) did not immediately win her the respect which she regarded as her right, and she might (just) have been able to cope with being called 'love'. But both at once was just too much for her. She opened her mouth and tried to say something but failed. There was simply too much indignation crowding her brain for the words that wanted to get out to get sorted into any sort of order, let alone passed on down the relevant pathways for vocalisation to take place. She made some dry, guttural sounds but that was all.

'Oooh,' said Miss Nightingale, looking up from her endeavours with the spade and spotting that the other visitor had oozed closer. She pulled a face. 'It's Mr Fuller-Mawkhoor. Boo hiss.'

'Boo hiss,' said Mrs Peterborough, not bothering to look up, but merely following her good friend's example. 'It's Mr Huller-Hawkhoor. Boo hiss.'

'We need to know all your identities,' said Mr Muller-Hawksmoor, struggling to ignore these votes of no confidence and trying hard to retain his composure and sense of authority. He was not concerned by the fact that he did not seem to be universally popular among the residents (universal popularity had never been his ambition) but he was a vain and self-important man and he did not like having his authority undermined. 'Ms Jones BA and I will come among you with our clipboards so that you can answer our questions.'

CHAPTER THIRTY TWO

Mr Muller-Hawksmoor and Ms Jones BA were not getting on very well.

They had, perhaps, made a mistake in starting their search for information by questioning Mr Roxdale.

'What's your name?' Ms Jones BA had demanded, pen poised over her clipboard.

'Naff off,' replied Mr Roxdale. 'Why should I tell you anything?'

'I am an accredited representative of the local council,' replied Ms Jones BA.

'Well tell the council they can all naff off,' said Mr Roxdale. 'I wrote to them twice about the trees they were chopping down in Sittercombe Park. Old oaks they were. Beautiful trees. Chopping them down for car parking. I wrote twice but didn't get back a single reply. They don't take any notice of me so why should I take any notice of them?'

'You have to reply to my questions,' said Ms Jones BA. 'These are official forms.' She tapped her clipboard with the top of her pen.

'How many forms have you got there?' asked Mr Roxdale. He looked at her clipboard. 'There's only one form. But there are three copies of it. Why on earth do you need to have your forms in triplicate?' he demanded. 'It's a waste of good trees.'

If she had been an honest woman Ms Jones BA would have replied that she and her fellow employees always took three copies because their filing system was so poor that they usually lost one copy within hours and a second within days. Having three copies meant that there was a slightly better than evens chance that they would still have a copy in a month's time.

'We've dramatically improved our procedures this year,' replied Ms Jones BA. 'We used to have five copies of every form.'

'Well I'm not interested in filling in any of your damned silly forms,' said Mr Roxdale.

'You are obliged by law to assist me in my enquiries,' lied Ms Jones BA.

'Calamity Brown,' said Mr Roxdale, instantly.

Ms Jones BA stared at him. The name seemed vaguely familiar but she didn't know why. Her BA had been acquired in the study of something called 'Social Administrative Studies', an academic discipline which was built upon the asking of questions rather than the providing of solutions, and no amount of stretching of the imagination could allow anyone to describe her as being either well or widely educated.

Mr Roxdale repeated the name. Ms Jones BA asked him how to spell it and then, reluctantly, (for she was not entirely convinced that Mr Roxdale was telling her the truth) carefully wrote the name down on the top form on her clipboard. She wrote slowly and deliberately, somehow managing to put her free hand around what she was writing to prevent anyone else from copying, and sticking out her tongue as she wrote.

'How long have you been living here, Calamity?'

'I don't know,' said Mr Roxdale, with a sigh. 'I suffer from intermittent Alzheimer's Disease. Sometimes I can remember things. But other times I can't remember why I got up. What's your Christian name?'

'I don't think that's any of your business,' snapped Ms Jones BA.

'In that case please address me as Mr Brown if you speak to me again,' said Mr Roxdale.

Ms Jones BA glowered at him, wrote something on her clipboard, and turned to Miss Nightingale. 'Name?' she demanded gruffly.

'Gertrude Jekyll,' replied Miss Nightingale, without any hesitation.

'Gertrude Jekyll,' said Mrs Peterborough, without waiting to be asked. As usual Mrs Peterborough was standing next to her friend Miss Nightingale.

'I'll come to you in a minute,' snapped Ms Jones BA.

'I'll come to you in a minute,' Mrs Peterborough snapped back.

'Her real name is Mrs Peterborough,' said Miss Nightingale, not wanting her friend to get into trouble. 'She sometimes just says what other people say but she never means any harm.'

'Her real name is Mrs Peterborough,' said Mrs Peterborough solely because her friend Miss Nightingale had said it. 'She sometimes just says what other people say but she never means any harm.'

Ms Jones BA glowered again and looked across at her colleague, Mr Muller-Hawksmoor.

'It seems to me that this person is mentally impaired,' she said. 'I think we should arrange for her to be moved to more suitable accommodation.'

'Oh yes, I remember this one,' said Mr Muller-Hawksmoor, glowering at Mrs Peterborough. 'As nutty as a pound of peanut brittle. I'll get the official psychiatrist to come round and make the necessary arrangements.'

'You're not moving her anywhere,' insisted Miss Nightingale. 'She stays with me.'

'She needs proper care,' insisted Ms Jones BA.

'She gets all the care she needs here,' said Miss Nightingale. 'She'll become confused if you make her go somewhere else.'

'I think we'll leave that to the psychiatrist, shall we?' said Ms Jones BA. 'Now, how old are you Miss Jekyll?'

'I'm 79 years old,' said Miss Nightingale who wasn't but who now followed Mrs Torridge's example and always lied about her age as a matter of principle.

Ms Jones BA wrote this down on the form attached to her clipboard, making sure that the entry appeared on the copies beneath it.

'Today,' said Miss Nightingale, 'is my birthday.'

'Congratulations,' said Ms Jones BA.

'What for?' demanded Miss Nightingale. 'I found getting old remarkably easy. It took virtually no skill at all.' She held her head to one side and looked at Ms Jones BA. 'Even you will probably be able do it,' she suggested.

'I am neither amused nor impressed by any of this,' said Mr Muller-Hawksmoor, who had clearly had enough. 'Ms Jones BA and I will return shortly to continue our investigations.' He turned to Mrs Caldicot. 'When we return we will expect you to have a full list of your residents – with names, former addresses and dates of birth. Meanwhile, what sort of exercise programme do you run for your residents?'

Mrs Caldicot stared at him as though not sure that she'd heard properly.

'Low Impact Aerobics? Non-Competitive Athletics? Late 18th Century Polish Folk Dance? Martial arts and self-defence?'

'I ... er ... we don't ... er ... actually ... er ... have a formal exercise programme,' Mrs Caldicot stuttered.

Mr Muller-Hawksmoor tutted and shook his head. Ms Jones BA, who regarded herself as something of an individualist and liked to plough her own furrow, shook her head and tutted.

Mr Muller-Hawksmoor fiddled with his clipboard and slid a piece of paper from the back. He handed the sheet to Mrs Caldicot. 'On this sheet you will find a list of fully approved and accredited trainers,' he told her. 'You are quite at liberty to select the discipline of your choice but you must select one of these disciplines and accredited trainers immediately and within five days of this formal notification you must offer your resident clients an approved exercise programme. If you select a discipline and trainer now we will arrange for your classes to start.'

Mrs Caldicot looked down the list which she had been handed. 'Oh dear,' she said. 'I really don't know.' She showed the list to the small crowd which had gathered around her. There was much shaking of heads.

'Do I have to pick one?' asked Mrs Caldicot.

'You do.'

'Then we'll have this one,' said Mrs Caldicot, blindly stabbing a finger at the sheet and thrusting both sheet and attached finger under Mr Muller-Hawksmoor's nose.

'Martial arts and self-defence,' said Mr Muller-Hawksmoor. 'With Dirk.' He looked at her, then at the seemingly frail group standing around her and frowned. 'Are you sure? That is a Grade IV Class.'

'Oh yes, thank you,' said Mrs Caldicot, now thoroughly flustered and confused. 'We'll definitely have the Martial Dirk and Self with Arts and Defence.' She had acquired the habit of becoming particularly firm and committed whenever she was flustered and confused.

'Sign here,' said Muller-Hawksmoor, thrusting his clipboard underneath Mrs Caldicot's nose.

Mrs Caldicot signed there.

Mr Muller-Hawksmoor and Ms Jones BA exchanged meaningful glances but neither spoke until a few minutes later when they were fastening their seat belts in Ms Jones BA's second-hand Ford Fiasco GTX.

'I'd like to see that lot of sad old crumblies struggle to cope with one of Dirk's classes,' sniggered Mr Muller-Hawksmoor. 'We'd better have a couple of ambulances on stand-by for his first class.'

'Well, it's all that silly woman Caldicot's responsibility,' said Ms Jones BA. 'We've got her signature on form ETY 292.' She turned, gave Mr Muller-Hawksmoor something that she thought was a smile and then put the Fiasco GTX into a gear. Unfortunately the gear was not a particularly suitable one for starting off and Mr Muller-Hawksmoor had to grip the dashboard as the car jumped and hopped down the drive and onto the road. He managed to snatch a glance at his watch. 'On the way back to the office would you like to pop into the pub?' he asked. 'I'm told that they do a very nice ploughperson's lunch at the Black Ferret.'

'I would like that very much, Mr Muller-Hawksmoor,' said Ms Jones BA. She swerved to avoid a pothole and bounced off the kerb. Driving was not her strong point. 'I would just like to say that I was extremely distressed by the way the residents of that home treated you.'

'Oh it was just their little way of having fun, I suppose,' murmured Mr Muller-Hawksmoor weakly.

'It wasn't right, it wasn't good enough and it wasn't acceptable,' said Ms Jones BA firmly. 'I think we should keep a very close eye on that establishment.' She braked hard to avoid a parked car which had suddenly appeared directly in front of her.

Mr Muller-Hawksmoor, who now had one hand gripping the dashboard and the other clutching his seatbelt, smiled and sat back. He felt almost happy.

Back at the home Mrs Caldicot and Mrs Roberts had watched them disappear.

'It's not fair,' said Mrs Roberts.

'Of course it isn't, dear,' agreed Mrs Caldicot.

'It's not supposed to be like this,' said Mrs Roberts.

'It's not supposed to be like anything,' said Mrs Caldicot, now far older and wiser than she'd ever wanted to be, putting an arm around the younger woman's shoulders and giving her a hug.

Mr Roxdale appeared by their side. 'Let's go and feed the birds,' he said.

Mrs Caldicot and Mrs Roberts both looked at him.

'I've got some rice and sunflower seeds in my pocket,' he whispered.

He slowly set off for a quiet corner of the garden and they followed him.

A few minutes later the three of them were standing underneath a large chestnut tree feeding grains of rice and sunflower seeds to a motley crew of assorted birds.

'Forget the idiots from the council,' advised Mr Roxdale softly. 'This is what life is all about.' He paused for a moment, crouched down and allowed a robin to jump onto the palm of his hand. Calm, unflustered, and seemingly fearless the robin took the rice grains that were offered and ate them. Then he looked around before flying off.

'Feeding the birds is the nearest you and I can ever get to being God,' said Mr Roxdale.

'Closer than sowing seeds and watching them grow?' asked Mrs Roberts.

'Oh yes,' said Mr Roxdale. 'When I sow seeds I'm just acting as a labourer for God. It's his garden. His skill that brings the rain and the sunshine. But when I feed the birds I'm giving them something they may need to live; something they perhaps can't get anywhere else. Those few grains of rice I scatter may mean the difference between life and death. For a few moments I'm a God in their world.'

Both Mrs Roberts and Mrs Caldicot knew what he meant. Temporarily, at least, the two busybodies from the council, now plotting away in the snug at the Black Ferret public house with two halves of lager shandy, two slices of processed cheese, four slices of white bread and two small, slightly bruised tomatoes in front of them, seemed very insignificant indeed.

CHAPTER THIRTY THREE

A tall, arrogant and bored looking young man wearing a black martial arts costume stood in the bay window of the lounge. He'd had all the furniture moved to the sides of the room so that there was a large, clear space in the middle. He had an olive complexion and jet black hair tied in a long ponytail. He wore no shoes or socks and when Mrs Peterborough had drawn attention to this fact, wondering aloud whether they should club together to help him buy a pair of shoes and a pair of socks, Miss Nightingale took the opportunity to point out to her friend that the sockless visitor's feet weren't quite as clean as they might have been. 'You'd have thought he would have had a good bath, wouldn't you?' she whispered. 'He may not be able to afford shoes but it doesn't cost much to keep your feet clean.' Unfortunately, Miss Nightingale wasn't getting any younger and her hearing wasn't getting any sharper. Her idea of a whisper was most people's idea of a full-throated bellow. 'His feet are filthy,' she added.

Mrs Peterborough repeated her friend's rhetorical question and simple observation, also pretty much at full volume.

The young man with the ponytail, Dirk, looked up and glared. Most people who knew him were afraid of his glare and he was accustomed to seeing people wither when they received one of his cold stares. But Miss Nightingale was no witherer and anyway she was staring at Dirk's feet rather than his face. Not even Dirk had managed to master the art of making his slightly grubby feet look menacing.

'A good scrubbing,' said Miss Nightingale, in another of her whispers. 'That's what he needs.'

Mrs Peterborough repeated this, for the unintentional benefit and amusement of those members of the audience who hadn't heard it the first time. Even Mrs Caldicot sometimes found this curious facility of use. If she ever missed something said by Miss Nightingale all she had to do was wait for the instant repeat from Mrs Peterborough.

'This is supposed to be an advanced Grade IV class,' began Dirk. 'How many of you have martial arts experience?'

There was a long silence.

'The former Mrs Livingstone and I were going to watch a Bruce Lee movie once,' said Mr Livingstone. 'But I couldn't find anywhere to park and so we went for a curry instead.'

'Have any of you studied karate?' asked Dirk, rather exasperated.

'I got as far as Calcutta in the war,' said Mr Roxdale. 'But I don't think we ever went to Karachi.' He stopped and scratched his nose. 'Was it called Karachi then?' He looked around. No one had the foggiest idea what he was talking about. 'They keep changing the names of places,' he explained.

'If there was no such place as Karachi then where did all the people who live there now think they were living?' asked Mr Livingstone. 'They can't have just been sitting around waiting for someone to give their town a name.'

'Oh they probably could,' said Mr Roxdale. 'If their council was anything like ours.'

'That's true,' agreed Mr Livingstone.

Dirk raised his voice. 'Has anyone studied self-defence?' he demanded. He was losing his temper and he knew that he shouldn't. His hands and feet were trained to kill. He made a powerful effort to remain calm.

Everyone stared at him. No one said anything. The silence was deafening. Mrs Caldicot, who was standing near the door leant towards Mrs Roberts. 'I'm beginning to feel sorry for him,' she said. 'I expect he thinks he's good-looking.'

'Too young, too good-looking and too full of himself,' said Mrs Roberts. 'His sort run off and break your heart. I prefer the more mature man myself.'

'He thinks he can do what he likes with our lot,' said Mrs Caldicot. 'I really ought to tell him not to be so cocky.'

'He's no match for them,' agreed Mrs Roberts.

'It'll end in tears,' said Mrs Caldicot. 'You mark my words.'

Dirk, who had not heard any of this exchange, sighed wearily. He only ran these classes to try and raise the money to go to Japan to study under the great masters. He wondered if any of them had ever had to go through this sort of humiliation. He was bored.

'Then I'll assume no one knows anything and we'll start from the beginning,' he said. He looked around to see if anyone objected to this. No one did. Either everyone thought that starting at the beginning was a wise move or else no one gave a damn where he started.

'The secret of self-defence is to think quickly, to act decisively and to use whatever weapons are to hand,' he said. 'When it comes to self-defence there are no rules – you are allowed to use reasonable force to protect yourself and your property. Never forget that your primary objective is merely to stop your assailant doing you harm.'

'I don't know how he can stand there without any socks on,' Mr Roxdale said to Mr Williams. 'My feet would be cold.'

'Mine too,' agreed Mr Williams. 'I feel the cold a lot these days.' The two men looked at one another. Both were wearing thick worsted suits, woollen shirts, knitted waistcoats and ties.

'Do you remember when we were young laughing at the old men who always used to wear knitted waistcoats, and thick jackets even when it was boiling hot?' Mr Roxdale asked Mr Williams.

'Of course,' said Mr Williams. He leant back against a large cupboard and a vase on the cupboard toppled forward. Dirk, spotting the falling object, leapt forwards and caught the vase neatly.

'That was very impressive,' said Mrs Roberts. 'He's certainly got good reactions.'

'Damned him,' muttered Mrs Caldicot. 'I hate that vase. I wish it had smashed.'

'We've become those old men,' said Mr Roxdale.

'Do you mind?' asked Mr Williams.

Mr Roxdale thought about this for a while. 'No. At least I now know that I won't die at 17 in a motorbike accident. I like being old. I know I've had my fair share of life. I'm 76 I think. From here on in, every day is a bonus. I enjoy every day like I've won it in the lottery.'

Dirk was beginning to wish he'd stayed in bed. His girlfriend hadn't wanted him to go. She's asked him to ring the council and tell them he was ill. But he didn't think that saying he was ill was a very good idea for someone who was supposed to be young, healthy and super fit. 'I need a volunteer,' he said.

'I think it's time we toddled off,' said Mrs Caldicot. 'I can see what's coming and I don't think I can bear to watch. He seems quite a nice boy in a simple sort of way and I don't want to see what is going to happen.' She and Mrs Roberts oozed away quietly.

'I'm not volunteering for anything,' said Miss Nightingale. She paused and added. 'I don't like the look of those feet.'

'I won't hurt anyone,' Dirk assured them all, in quiet desperation. 'I just need someone to volunteer so that I can demonstrate what I'm talking about.' He'd never had trouble like this before. He had taught teenagers at the roughest school in town and things hadn't been this bad. The PE teachers had asked him to let two of them stay in the gym in case things turned nasty. But he'd turned the offer down. The kids had been like putty. He'd shown them how to take a knife away from someone and they'd followed his every move with eyes eager for learning. Students who never listened when being taught history or maths had given him their whole attention. He'd taught policemen and young mothers too; his classes had always gone down well.

'Why didn't he bring his own volunteer?' asked Mr Livingstone of no one in particular. 'He's getting paid for this isn't he?'

'I'll volunteer,' said Maple Merivale, unexpectedly rescuing Dirk from the embarrassment of having to demonstrate his deathly skills on an embroidered cushion.

'Right. Splendid,' said Dirk, immensely relieved. 'I'm going to mug you and I want you to stop me. Remember: you do whatever you can to try and protect yourself. I will then show you where you've gone wrong and how you should do it.'

'Why did you do that?' asked Mrs Merivale's startled husband.

'Because I felt sorry for him,' Mrs Merivale replied. 'He looked so sad.'

'Come here then, dear,' said Dirk. This immediately annoyed Mr Merivale who did not like to hear his wife ordered about. He had, in any case, already taken a strong dislike to Dirk, whom he regarded as a jumped-up little twerp. He was an ex-army man who had spent much of the Second World War crouching in soggy bits of jungle being hunted by Japanese soldiers. In addition, he did not have much affection for men who wore ponytails.

Gingerly, Mrs Merivale stepped forwards until she was standing right in the middle of the room. Dirk stepped forward too, so that they were standing just a couple of feet apart.

'Now. Imagine that I'm a mugger,' he told her.

Mrs Merivale stared at him but did not move. She was, to be honest, rather confused. She had thought they were having a class in flower arranging.

'Give me your purse!' said the instructor, advancing upon Mrs Merivale with his arm upraised, as though he was holding a knife. He paused, and waited, hoping that Mrs Merivale would make a lunge at him. His teaching programme could not go forward until she made a move.

'No!' said the old woman, most indignantly. She was now feeling rather aggrieved. For one thing she did not understand how the lecturer in flower arranging thought he could get away with stealing her purse in front of all her friends. For another thing her purse was in their bedroom on the first floor.

Mr Roxdale awoke suddenly from a pleasant doze in which he had dreamt of a field of sunflowers. 'What's happening?' he asked Mr Williams.

'Dunno,' said Mr Williams, who wasn't wearing his spectacles and couldn't see much of anything without them. He turned to Mr Merivale, who was standing next to him. 'What's happening?'

'The sissy bloke with the ponytail seems to have gone stark raving bonkers,' explained Mr Merivale, rather excited. 'I think he's got a knife. He's trying to mug my wife! He's wants her purse.'

'Oh I say,' said Mr Roxdale. 'We can't have that, can we?' He stood up. 'I must say I'm surprised that Mrs Caldicot let him in,' he said. He made a fist and stuck out his chin, ready to defend his friend's wife.

'Oh no, it's all right,' said Mr Merivale. 'She's sorted him out.'

'Good for her!' said Mr Roxdale. 'Great stuff.'

'No one messes with my wife,' said Mr Merivale proudly.

Chapter Thirty Four

Mrs Caldicot and Mrs Roberts were in the office, having a nice cup of tea and working their way through a new packet of Garibaldi biscuits when they heard a commotion in the lounge. There was a yell, a crash, a scream, another crash and then, in the comparative silence that followed, the sound of someone crying.

'Did you hear that?' asked Mrs Roberts.

'I did,' admitted Mrs Caldicot. She took another biscuit out of the packet and slipped it, whole, into her mouth.

'I hope they haven't hurt him too badly.'

'We'd better go and have a look,' said Mrs Caldicot.

They found Dirk in the middle of the lounge. He was kneeling on the floor, holding his groin with his left hand and his head with his right hand. He was as pale as snow and clearly in pain.

'Oh dear,' said Mrs Caldicot, stooping down beside him. 'Are you all right, love?'

'No!' complained Dirk, in between sobs. 'They attacked me.'

'Who did?'

'I don't know,' confessed Dirk, miserably. 'It was all over too quickly. It wasn't fair.'

The class stood around Dirk and there was clearly little sympathy for the wounded young man.

'What happened?' asked Mrs Caldicot sternly.

'He tried to mug my wife,' said Mr Merivale.

'I think he had some sort of fit,' explained Mr Roxdale. 'We had to subdue him.'

'It was only a demonstration!' sobbed Dirk. 'I wasn't going to hurt her. I was only pretending.'

'You had a knife!' said Mr Williams. 'And it looked very realistic to me.'

'I only pretended to have a pretend knife,' protested Dirk. He started to sob again. Most of the residents, feeling embarrassed, looked away. Mr Roxdale took out his penknife and started to carve at his fingernails.

'The police shoot people who have pretend guns,' Mr Williams pointed out.

'But I didn't even have a pretend knife,' insisted Dirk, tears rolling down his cheeks. 'It was only an imaginary knife.'

'Well I do think that if you're going to have a pretend knife it should be a real pretend knife,' said Mr Roxdale. 'An imaginary pretend knife is a bit confusing. At least, with a pretend knife we might have had an opportunity to realise that it was a fake.'

'What happened?' asked Mrs Caldicot, with a sigh.

'I kicked him in the goalmouth,' said Mrs Merivale. 'I think that's what it's called.'

'I think you probably mean you kicked him in the goolies,' Mrs Caldicot corrected her.

'I hit him on the head with a vase,' said Miss Nightingale. 'I've seen people do that on the television,' she added, rather proudly. 'It was quite satisfying, though I'm afraid the vase broke,' she added, looking apologetically at Mrs Caldicot.

'That's all right, Miss Nightingale,' said Mrs Caldicot reassuringly.

'We were going to save her but they were too quick for us,' claimed Mr Roxdale, slightly aggrieved. 'Mr Williams and I. And Mr Merivale.' He pointed at Dirk with a trembling finger. 'He was attacking Mrs Merivale.'

'He told us that if we are attacked we should use whatever we can to protect ourselves,' explained Mr Williams.

'Those quick-thinking ladies probably saved his life,' said

Mr Merivale. 'I was going to hit him.' He moved his arm back but the years had not been kind to him and the joint was stiff. It took him a long time to move his fist just a few inches. He would, in truth, have had difficulty in hitting a statue. 'It's an old jousting injury,' explained Mrs Merivale to Mr Roxdale. Mr Roxdale thought this odd but Mrs Merivale was being quite accurate.

'I think I'm dying,' complained Dirk, still pale and still on his hands and knees. 'They've killed me. Call the council, a lawyer, the police, and an ambulance.' Mrs Caldicot bent down and examined his skull. She bent further, as though to examine the other injured area. Dirk pushed her hand away and glowered at her.

'Not too bad, then,' said Mrs Caldicot. She stood up. 'I'm glad you're teaching them how to look after themselves so successfully,' she added. She was clearly not terribly impressed with his injuries. She swept past the kneeling man into the lounge and beamed when she saw bits of the vase she hated so much lying on the floor.

'Perhaps we can have it repaired,' said Miss Nightingale, who had trotted along behind her.

Mrs Caldicot looked at the vase, now in several hundred pieces. She thought it looked much better that way. 'Oh, I don't think so,' she said quickly.

'I'll get the dustpan and brush,' said Mrs Roberts.

'What about my ambulance?' demanded Dirk. 'And my lawyer. And the police.' He paused, gently rubbing his head and examining his hand occasionally to check for blood. He looked up, still not quite sure what had happened to him. 'And, whatever else it was I wanted,' he added, rather miserably. He looked around, his gaze settling finally on Mrs Caldicot. 'I'm going to sue you,' he threatened.

'Oh I don't think that would be a terribly good idea,' said Mrs Caldicot. She turned to Mrs Roberts. 'Can you imagine the headlines, Mrs Roberts?'

'Martial Arts Expert Flattened By Old Lady,' said Mrs Roberts instantly. She wrote the words in the air with a forefinger.

'Dirk Crushed By Pensioner,' suggested Mrs Caldicot.

'Frail Octogenarian Fells Karate Kid With One Blow,'

offered Mrs Roberts.

'If I were you I'd settle for a cup of tea,' said Mr Roxdale to Dirk.

Dirk held his head and began to cry again. 'I want to go home,' he said. 'I want my mum.'

Mrs Caldicot rang for a taxi and sent him home to his mother. They never saw him again.

CHAPTER THIRTY FIVE

After dinner that evening Mrs Caldicot and Mrs Roberts were sitting in the kitchen sorting through the thick pile of bills which had accumulated.

'Shall we sort them by date?' asked Mrs Roberts.

'Why?'

'Then we can pay the oldest ones first.'

'I suppose that sounds fair,' agreed Mrs Caldicot. 'But maybe we should pay the ones who are threatening to take us to court.'

'Oh no, I don't think we should let people bully us,' said Mrs Roberts. 'Just because we owe them money.'

'No, you're absolutely right,' agreed Mrs Caldicot. She sighed. 'I once met a woman who had a very sound approach to this business of paying bills. She had a very simple technique.'

'What was that?'

'She just didn't pay any. She said it saved her a fortune.'

'But they send you to prison if you don't pay your bills.'

'I know,' sighed Mrs Caldicot.

'You realise that you could very easily solve all your financial problems,' said Mrs Roberts.

Mrs Caldicot looked at her.

'By letting Mr Williams give you one or two of his photographs,' explained Mrs Roberts.

'I know,' sighed Mrs Caldicot. 'It is very tempting,' she admitted. 'But I can't. It isn't fair.'

'Mr Williams doesn't mind,' Mrs Roberts pointed out. 'He'll be happy to give you a handful of photographs. It wouldn't cost him anything at all and it would solve all our problems.'

'But it wouldn't be right,' insisted Mrs Caldicot. 'Taking photographs from Mr Williams would be like taking charity.'

'Lots of homes in our sort of position are charities!' Mrs Roberts pointed out.

'I know,' agreed Mrs Caldicot, with yet another sigh. She found it difficult to explain to Mrs Roberts or, indeed, to herself. 'You're absolutely right. But I can't avoid the thought that to let him solve all our financial problems would be sort of cheating. We wouldn't have solved anything permanently.'

'Nothing is permanent,' said Mrs Roberts. 'And a fistful of Mr Williams's photographs would be as damned near a permanent solution to our financial problems as we're likely to get.'

'But we wouldn't be doing it ourselves,' said Mrs Caldicot. 'When we first opened this place I felt really proud. It was the first time in my life that I'd ever done anything by myself. Mr Caldicot always used to tell me that I couldn't do anything – except perhaps help out in the local charity shop – and I believed him.'

'Then at least give yourself a chance by charging proper fees,' said Mrs Roberts. 'I don't think anyone staying here pays proper residential home fees. For example, how much do Mr and Mrs Merivale pay?'

Mrs Caldicot looked at her but didn't say anything.

'Come on, how much?' insisted Mrs Roberts.

'Mrs Merivale gave me £5 when they arrived,' admitted Mrs Caldicot sheepishly.

'For the two of them?'

Mrs Caldicot nodded.

Mrs Roberts smiled and shook her head.

'But they're helping out in the kitchen,' said Mrs Caldicot. 'And without Mrs Merivale we'd have to hire a cook.'

There was a loud crash from the hall outside.

'What on earth was that?' asked Mrs Roberts.

Mrs Caldicot shrugged.

There was another, equally loud crash.

'I suppose I'd better go and have a look,' said Mrs Caldicot. She got up, walked across the room and opened the door to the hallway. Miss Nightingale had a swede in her left hand and was clearly preparing to roll it at something. Mrs Caldicot looked down the hall. A row of seven large carrots were standing like skittles just inside the front door. Two carrots were lying on the mat. The carrots had all had their bottoms chopped off neatly so that they would stand up. Mr Roxdale seemed to be in charge of replacing fallen skittles.

'What on earth are you doing?' demanded Mrs Caldicot.

'We're playing skittles,' answered Miss Nightingale, as though surprised that Mrs Caldicot needed to ask. 'I have to roll this swede down the hallway and knock over as many carrots as I can. We have three goes each. And then it's someone else's turn.'

'Ah,' said Mrs Caldicot. She suddenly noticed that Mr Williams was standing facing the wall. He looked like a naughty schoolboy being punished.

'Hello, Mr Williams!' she said. 'It's good to see you up and about. How are you feeling?'

'Very well, thank you,' replied the photographer.

'Is everything ... er ... all right?' she asked him. 'Are you joining in ... not finding everything too boisterous?'

'No, no, everything is fine,' Mr Williams reassured her. 'I was just admiring your wallpaper.'

'I'm afraid it's rather old,' said Mrs Caldicot.

'Very old,' agreed Mr Williams. 'But very lovely. So are the curtains and, indeed, the furniture.'

'I like them very much, though I suspect that they're not everyone's cup of tea,' said Mrs Caldicot. 'The whole place needs redecorating. And we need some new furniture.' She shrugged. 'But that will all have to wait.' She looked around and then lowered her voice. 'And I have to admit that I do like this old stuff,' she confessed.

'I think you should leave it all alone,' said Mr Williams. 'I think the place is beautiful. In fact I've never seen anywhere quite so beautiful in my life. Promise me you won't have any of these things changed?'

Mrs Caldicot promised, smiled at him and headed back towards her office. Once inside she closed the door and went over to the chair behind her desk. Outside in the hall there was a thud.

'What are they doing?' asked Mrs Roberts.

'They're rolling a swede along the carpet and trying to knock down some carrots,' replied Mrs Caldicot.

'Oh,' said Mrs Roberts. 'Well, I suppose it keeps them out of mischief.'

'What exactly would you describe as mischief?' Mrs Caldicot asked her.

Mrs Roberts thought for a moment and then shrugged.

There was another crash.

'Do you find these bills as boring as I do?' asked Mrs Caldicot.

'I do.'

'The game they were playing looked quite good fun,' said Mrs Caldicot.

'This finance stuff is unspeakably dull,' said Mrs Roberts.

'I hate it,' agreed Mrs Caldicot.

There was another dull thud, then a crash, followed by whoops of joy.

'It does sound very good fun,' said Mrs Roberts.

'Come on, then,' said Mrs Caldicot. They got up and walked over to the door. Mrs Roberts opened it.

'Can you squeeze in another two players?' Mrs Caldicot asked.

The response was a huge cheer.

CHAPTER THIRTY SIX

It was raining again. The heavens seemed to have decided that they had surplus rain which they were anxious to get rid of before it passed its sell-by-date. The cast iron drainpipes and gutters at the Twilight Years Rest Home were gurgling greedily and the puddles in the front drive were filling up nicely.

At 7.30 pm sharp that evening a car splashed through the puddles and stopped at the bottom of the steps up to the front door. The driver adjusted the position of his car to make sure that his passenger would be able to enter the vehicle without getting too wet, then jumped out and bounded up the steps.

Mrs Roberts answered the door and smiled when she saw who it was. Jenkins had, she knew, called to take Mrs Caldicot out to dinner and the theatre.

'Hello, Jenkins,' she greeted him. 'Mrs Caldicot won't be a moment.'

Mrs Roberts liked Jenkins and very much approved of Mrs Caldicot's blooming romance. Technically, the two women were employer and employee but in reality they were more like two sisters. There was a more than twenty year age gap between the two women but neither of them was ever conscious of this.

'Would you like a cup of tea while you wait?' Mrs Roberts asked the visitor, closing the front door behind him and shutting out the storm. 'Or a coffee perhaps?' The Twilight Years Rest Home may have been a large building but it was, as always, warm and cosy inside.

Jenkins, who had been about to speak, stopped and dodged out of the way as a pair of rolled up socks bounced off the wall, just missed his head and landed on the carpet.

'Sorry about that!' apologised Mr Roxdale, rushing out of the lounge door, darting down the hall and picking up the ball of rolled up socks. 'Didn't know you were there.' He disappeared as suddenly as he had appeared.

'Cricket?' asked Jenkins, when Mr Roxdale had gone.

'Rounders, I think,' replied Mrs Roberts.

Jenkins looked slightly surprised. 'How long is she going to be?' he asked her.

'Oh not more than a few minutes,' promised Mrs Roberts. 'She was nearly ready when I last saw her.'

'I'm ready now,' said a voice halfway down the stairs. Mrs Roberts and Jenkins both turned. For a moment neither of them spoke.

'You look fantastic!' said Jenkins eventually, his voice soft but full of genuine affection and admiration. 'Absolutely fantastic.'

Mrs Caldicot continued her journey down the stairs. She was wearing a tight-fitting, low-cut scarlet silk dress and had a tiny black cape slung around her shoulders. She was carrying a small black clutch bag. She looked good.

'I think these shoes are a bit high for me,' she confessed, wobbling a little as she stepped down into the hall. Jenkins strode forwards and took her hand. 'But I decided, what the hell, I'd rather fall over trying to look stylish than stomp around safely in a pair of flat heels.'

'And besides, with my bum I'm not likely to hurt myself if I fall down am I?' Mrs Caldicot thought to herself. The late and unlamented Mr Caldicot would have said it and not even noticed her embarrassment, shame and sadness. The very much alive Jenkins would not, she firmly believed, even think such a thing.

'You look absolutely wonderful!' Mrs Roberts told her.

Mrs Caldicot smiled at her gratefully. Suddenly there was a commotion and Mr Roxdale shot out of the lounge, clearly having been pushed out into the hall by unseen hands.

'I'm sorry to bother you,' he said, addressing both Mrs Caldicot and Jenkins. 'But are you going into town?'

'We are,' answered Mrs Caldicot. 'Jenkins is very kindly taking me out to dinner.'

'The thing is,' started Mr Roxdale, clearly rather uncomfortable about what he was about to say, 'I wouldn't ask but it's a bit special, you see.'

'What's special?' asked Mrs Caldicot patiently and kindly.

'Mr Williams just noticed that the local cinema is having a Marx Brothers evening. They're showing both *Duck Soup* and *A Night At The Opera*. But it's a one night show – tonight only.'

'And you want to go?' said Mrs Caldicot.

'The problem is, you see, that if we try and get a taxi the first film will be half over by the time we get there. We wondered...'

'If we would take you?'

'Exactly!' said Mr Roxdale. 'We'll make our own way back, of course. There's a taxi rank right outside the cinema so getting back won't be a problem.'

Mrs Caldicot looked at Jenkins and raised an eyebrow.

'It's fine by me,' said Jenkins, with a slight shrug.

Mrs Caldicot took and squeezed Jenkins's hand before turning back to Mr Roxdale. 'How many of you are there?' Mrs Caldicot asked him.

'Mr Williams, Mrs Peterborough and Miss Nightingale,' replied Mr Roxdale, hoping that if he spoke quickly it would sound as though there were fewer of them than there were. 'And me, of course.'

'That's four of you!' said Mrs Caldicot, horrified. 'We can't possibly fit you all in.'

'We'll cram together in the back seat,' said Mr Roxdale. 'You won't even know we're there,' he promised. He grinned, unconvincingly.

Mrs Caldicot looked at Jenkins, who said nothing. 'Get your coats then,' said Mrs Caldicot with a sigh.

The front door was open and the six of them were all either on the steps or in the porch when a rather red-faced Mrs Merivale, huffing and puffing a little, appeared in the hallway.

'Mrs Caldicot!' she called. 'We're nearly out of toilet rolls. If by any chance you go past the supermarket would you pick some up, please?'

Chapter Thirty Seven

'Do you mind stopping here, for a moment?' asked Mrs Caldicot, as they approached a supermarket.

Jenkins, surprised, turned his head slightly, and looked at her quizzically.

'Loo rolls,' explained Mrs Caldicot. 'I need to buy some loo rolls.'

'I'm sure they'll have a supply at the restaurant,' said Jenkins. 'I really don't think they'll expect us to bring our own.'

'Mrs Merivale caught me just as I was coming out,' explained Mrs Caldicot. 'We're apparently running rather low.' She smiled at him and shrugged as though to say: 'This really isn't my fault but what can I do?'

'Right,' agreed Jenkins. He slowed, indicated and turned right into the supermarket car park. As he did so he noticed that an old man had built a rough, temporary shelter on the traffic island, using nothing more substantial than a large, old cardboard box over which he had draped several pieces of threadbare and clearly unwanted carpet. The box was almost invisible, half hidden between the bushes with which the local council's gardening department had chosen to decorate the island. Jenkins tried to get another look at the old man in his rear-view mirror but there were too many heads and bodies piled into the back seat of the car for him to see much through the back window.

The rain was now hammering down and the old man had been huddled inside his cardboard box. He had looked cold, weary and very, very lonely. No one else seemed to have noticed the cardboard box or the old man and Jenkins found himself wondering whether he had really seen the old man or whether the whole vision had not, perhaps, been nothing more than a mirage.

'What are we doing?' demanded a voice from the back seat. Mr Roxdale tried to move forward so that he could look through the windscreen. Unfortunately his success in completing this simple manoeuvre was limited by the presence of Mrs Peterborough, perched on his lap. 'Is this the way to the cinema?' he asked, looking around.

Mrs Caldicot explained about Mrs Merivale's request again. 'I'll only be a minute,' she added. 'At this time of night there will be hardly anyone in there.' She turned round. 'Do we need anything else, apart from loo rolls?'

Mrs Peterborough started to recite a list of things she thought Mrs Caldicot should buy. 'Broccoli, candles, sardines, paper napkins, treacle, tomatoes, chocolate-covered digestive biscuits...'

'Forget all that!' interrupted Mr Roxdale. 'We'll be here all night.' He paused for a moment, clearly reflecting on something Mrs Peterborough had said. 'Actually, it might be a rather good idea if you would just get the chocolate-covered digestive biscuits,' he said.

Jenkins parked the car just a few yards from the entrance.
'Shall I come with you?' he asked.

'No thanks,' replied Mrs Caldicot. 'I'll only be a moment.'
She picked up her handbag, climbed out of the car and hurried
into the supermarket.

'Did you see a man on that traffic island we just passed?'
asked Jenkins.

None of the others had.

Two minutes later Mrs Caldicot wheeled her trolley to an
empty check-out counter where a bored looking teenager was examining a chip in her nail varnish.

'I'd be grateful if you could process these for me fairly
quickly,' said Mrs Caldicot, piling twelve double packs of toilet
rolls and six packets of chocolate digestive biscuits onto the
black rubber conveyor belt.

The girl stared at the pile of toilet rolls with undisguised
astonishment.

'I've got a large family,' explained Mrs Caldicot. 'And we all
like curry.'

The girl just stared at her and then started waving each
item in front of the electronic scanner on her till.

A few moments later, pushing a laden trolley and carrying a
considerably lighter purse, Mrs Caldicot emerged back into the
early evening gloom and the rain. It now seemed pretty clear that
the rain had previously only been practising, for it was now
coming down so hard and so fast that it seemed inconceivable it
could continue at this pace for much longer.

Jenkins jumped out of the car, opened the boot and helped
Mrs Caldicot stack away her purchases. When she herself was
safely stowed beside him in the front passenger seat he fired up the
engine, increased the speed of the windscreen wipers and moved
gently away from the supermarket.

If Jenkins hadn't already spotted the old man and his cardboard box it is doubtful if any of them would have ever noticed
him now that the rain was even heavier. Jenkins and Mrs Caldicot
were both peering through the windscreen, trying to check the
road in front of them.

It was Jenkins who again saw the old man, and the youths who had appeared as though from nowhere and who were now surrounding him.

'Look!' he shouted, excitedly. Everyone looked.

'On the traffic island,' Jenkins told them.

The old man was still crouched inside his carpet-sheathed cardboard box. But he was no longer alone. A group of marauding youths, who clearly had been drinking, were dancing around the old man's temporary encampment. They all had shaved heads and, despite the weather, wore only dirty singlets and jeans. They were laughing and sneering and clearly having great fun kicking the old man's few possessions off the island and into the road. One of them found a plastic bag, filled with bits and pieces of a lonely, itinerant life, and spread the contents of the bag with a single kick. Another climbed up on top of the old man's fragile home and started to jump up and down. The box, weakened by the heavy and incessant rain, gave way instantly. As the box collapsed the other youths started kicking. When the old man tried to crawl out to safety they deliberately aimed their boots at his head, body and legs. He tried, in vain, to defend himself with his hands and arms.

The six in the car never agreed on the number of youths who were responsible for the attack. Jenkins, Mr Williams and Mrs Caldicot thought there were five. Mr Roxdale felt sure that there were six. Miss Nightingale and Mrs Peterborough were both quite insistent that there were at least fifteen. The old man who was the victim of the attack had absolutely no idea who his attackers were, or how many of them there might have been.

As soon as he saw what was happening Jenkins slowed right down and looked for somewhere to park. There wasn't anywhere suitable and so, after having driven twice around the traffic island, he simply drove up onto the grass and parked with his nearside wheels on the road and his offside wheels, and the bulk of the vehicle, on the island. Followed by the others, and not having the faintest idea what he was going to do, Jenkins leapt out of the car.

The youths were so intent on having their fun with the old man that it wasn't until Jenkins's car was parked on the traffic island that they even noticed its presence. The first youth to notice shouted out to call his mates's attention to the newcomers. They stopped what they were doing and just stared. They were clearly astonished; frozen not by fear but by puzzlement. They considered themselves to be hard men and they were used to seeing people run away from them. When they walked through town in broad daylight, it was their experience that everyone – old people, young people, women with prams, men in suits – would all cross the road to get out of their way and avoid confrontation and conflict. When they saw the ages of the people getting out of the car they were hardly able to believe their eyes.

To everyone's surprise it was Mrs Peterborough who struck the first blow. She was, as usual, carrying her handbag, a large, capacious and heavy item which weighed so much that Mr Livingstone had once hazarded the opinion the bag must, at the very least, contain half a dozen house bricks.

She walked straight across the grass, seemingly undeterred by fear, swung the bag by its handle and caught the nearest youth on the head. Knocked off balance, and screaming with both fear and rage, he fell into the nearest bush. His comrades were clearly both startled and disorganised by the viciousness of her attack.

While they were still staring, open-mouthed at Mrs Peterborough and her well swung handbag, the youths were subject to yet more unexpected attacks. First, Mr Williams knocked one of the youths flat with an extremely creditable right hook which seemed to come out of nowhere. This blow landed on its target with extraordinary accuracy and, for Mr Williams, a very satisfying 'crack'. Mr Roxdale completed the insult by walloping the fallen hooligan with a rubber traffic cone which he had found in the bushes. And then Jenkins incapacitated two of the aggressors by literally banging their heads together in the way of a schoolmaster dealing with two badly-behaved infants. The two youths whose skulls had been ill-served in this traditional but demeaning way, fell to the ground with astonishing grace and lay, temporarily unconscious, among several cotoneaster bushes.

Moments later the battle was over. The defeated bullies, whimpering and threatening to report the incident to their fathers and the constabulary, limped away into the darkness. Before they had disappeared from view Jenkins had taken out his mobile telephone and telephoned for the emergency services.

'Are you all right?' Mrs Caldicot asked, kneeling beside the terrified looking gentleman who had been the victim of the original, unprovoked attack.

'I'm not entirely sure,' confessed the stranger. To Mrs Caldicot's surprise he spoke with an educated accent. He crawled out of his cardboard box, looked around and then stood up. Not unsurprisingly, he looked slightly bewildered by what had happened. His head was bruised and he was bleeding from his nose and mouth. Mrs Caldicot stood up too, and brushed the mud and grass from her knees.

'I think we'd better get you to the hospital,' said Mrs Caldicot, taking a clean handkerchief out of her handbag and dabbing at the blood on the stranger's nose. 'Should you be standing? Do you think you've got any broken bones?'

'I'm afraid I really don't know,' the man admitted. He touched one arm with the other and winced, then he looked around again. 'Have they gone?' he asked, nervously. He spoke quietly, diffidently.

'Yes,' said Mrs Caldicot. 'You're safe now.' She introduced herself and explained that she and her friends had just been passing when they had spotted him being attacked. She looked round as Jenkins approached.

'I've telephoned for an ambulance,' said Jenkins, quietly. 'There should be one here in a few minutes. I asked for the police to come too.' He looked at the stranger. 'Why don't you get into the car?' he said. 'You'll be more comfortable there.' He walked across to his car and opened the front passenger door.

'Don't like to presume on your kindness yet more, but I don't suppose you have a blanket, do you?' asked the stranger.

'Are you cold?' asked Jenkins.

'No, no,' said the man. 'But as you can see I'm awfully grubby ... and I'm bleeding too. Your car...' he pointed to the smart, new upholstery of Jenkins's car. He wouldn't get into the car until Jenkins had found a rug from the boot and had draped it over the front passenger seat.

'Perhaps we should move away while we wait for the ambulance,' said Mrs Caldicot, when the man they'd rescued was settled in the car. She lowered her voice. 'Do you think those youths will come back?'

'No!' replied Jenkins without hesitation.

'But they might come back with their fathers – or the police,' said Mrs Caldicot. 'They said they would.'

Jenkins laughed. 'Don't worry,' he assured her. 'They're bullies. They'll be far too embarrassed to tell anyone that they've been beaten up by a bunch of old-age pensioners.'

Mrs Caldicot looked at him and slowly she smiled too. 'Do you know, I think you're right,' she said. She felt more comfortable then.

They waited on the traffic island for twenty minutes but neither ambulance nor police car came.

'This is daft,' said Jenkins at last. 'Where's the nearest hospital.'

'It's no more than five or ten minutes from here,' replied Mrs Caldicot.

'OK,' said Jenkins. 'Let's drive there. Can you all get into the back seat?'

They tried but even four people in the back had been a tight squeeze. It was impossible for five people to fit in.

'Why don't Mr Williams and I sit in the boot with the loo rolls?' asked Mr Roxdale. 'We'll leave the lid up and you drive slowly.'

And that is what they did.

CHAPTER THIRTY EIGHT

It took the hospital just four hours to find a doctor. It took another two hours for the doctor, who looked about sixteen and spoke some words of English quite well, to examine the battered tramp, clean him up and stitch up his wounds. He was aided in this by a grumpy nurse with baggy two-way stretch elastic stockings and by a deaf auxiliary with a facial tick. Jenkins, Mrs Caldicot and the rest of the party sat in the waiting area, soaking, dripping and steaming, and waited.

'Why don't you all go on to the cinema,' said Mrs Caldicot to Mr Roxdale, Mr Williams, Mrs Peterborough and Miss Nightingale. 'There's no need for us all to wait.' She looked around and sighed. The casualty department looked as though it had been built, painted and equipped a long, long time ago. The floor was covered with thin carpet tiles which were curling at the edges and heavily stained. The walls had been painted once but the paint had been peeling off for years. A false ceiling had been created with the aid of white polystyrene tiles but roughly a third of the tiles had fallen down, revealing dusty ceiling spaces and bits of weary looking wiring.

'There's no need for any of us to wait,' Mr Roxdale, pointed out, accurately.

'But we'd like to,' said Mr Williams. 'We want to know that he's OK.'

'We can give him moral support,' said Mr Roxdale. 'Spiritual comfort. When you're not well it's nice to know that you've got friends nearby.' He looked around and blushed, as though rather embarrassed by this confession.

'Besides,' said Miss Nightingale. 'It's very nice here. We're having a lovely time.'

Mrs Peterborough nodded. 'Very nice,' she agreed, looking around.

And so they all sat. And they waited.

It was well after midnight when a large, well-starched nurse walked up to their end of the casualty department. 'Are you Peter,' she looked down at her clipboard before continuing, 'Peter Twist?'

Everyone stared at her. No one spoke.

'Peter Twist?' she repeated, lowering her clipboard and looking sternly at them all, one at a time. Mrs Caldicot, who neither liked nor trusted people with clipboards, felt intimidated and shrank down and tried to disappear into her plastic seat. She was tired. It seemed to her that she spent all her life fighting nasty, cruel people. At that moment she felt that she'd had enough. She wanted to hide in a corner and cry.

'Are you asking us if any of us are called Peter Twist? Or are you asking us if that is the name of the gentleman we brought in?' asked Jenkins.

Mrs Caldicot turned and looked. She felt full of admiration for him.

The starched nurse turned her glare onto Jenkins. 'Peter Twist is the name of the tramp you brought in.'

'Right,' said Jenkins. 'Thank you. Good. We didn't know that.'

'You brought someone in but you don't know his name?' the nurse demanded, incredulous.

'That's right,' replied Jenkins.

The nurse snorted rather contemptuously.

'We found the poor fellow on a traffic island,' explained Jenkins. He spoke slowly and patiently, as though he was speaking to someone of rather limited intelligence. 'He was being attacked by a gang of youths. I'm afraid that there simply wasn't time for proper introductions.' He paused, reached into his pocket and took out his spectacle-case. He opened the case, took out his spectacles and put them on. He then peered over the top of them at the nurse. 'What's your name?' he demanded.

'So, if you just found him on a traffic island, why are you all sitting here waiting for him?' demanded the nurse, still suspicious but far less arrogant.

'We wanted to make sure that he was all right,' explained Jenkins. 'And your name is?' With his right hand he took a small green notebook from his outside jacket pocket. With his left hand he took a slim gold pen from his inside breast pocket.

The nurse snorted and stepped backwards, as though she felt under threat. She told him her name.

Jenkins opened his notebook and wrote in it. Holding the notebook and pen in his left hand he then used his other hand to reach into a trouser pocket and pull out his leather wallet. He opened the wallet, took out one of his visiting cards and handed it to the nurse.

'My name is Jenkins,' he said. 'As you will see from the card.'

The nurse examined the card, saw the name of the newspaper Jenkins represented, licked her lips and swallowed rather noisily.

'Anyway. Er ... we've finished with him. We've looked after him very well. You can take him now,' the nurse said.

'Take him where?' enquired Jenkins.

The nurse seemed puzzled by this. 'Wherever you like,' she replied. 'Back to the traffic island I suppose.'

Jenkins just stared at her over the top of his spectacles.

'We don't have any beds,' she explained. 'None at all.'

'It's all right,' whispered Mrs Caldicot to Jenkins. 'I can find him a bed.'

Jenkins turned to her. 'Are you sure?'

Mrs Caldicot nodded. 'I'd rather,' she said. 'We can look after him.' She looked around and shuddered. 'I wouldn't want to leave him here,' she whispered.

Jenkins turned his attention back to the nurse, who was standing waiting. 'What would you do with him if we hadn't waited?' he asked her. He looked around the waiting area and then around the remainder of the casualty department. 'I have to tell you that I think this hospital is a disgrace. It's filthy and quite disorganised. Even if you had a bed available I would be unhappy about Mr Twist staying here.'

The once pompous nurse now seemed thoroughly deflated as well as defeated. She appeared, Mrs Caldicot thought, to have shrunk several sizes while standing before them. The woman who had filled the room, her ego steam-rollering all before it, now stood before them looking more like a penitent child, anxious to know what was going to happen to her.

'I suppose we'd, er, arrange for him to be found a bed somewhere,' she admitted.

'Of course you would,' agreed Jenkins, calmly and appreciatively. 'You aren't complete barbarians, are you?'

'No,' said the nurse. 'Thank you. No, of course not.' Mrs Caldicot half expected her to curtsey. But she didn't.

'Well, as I said, I don't think I would be entirely happy about

Mr Twist staying here with you,' said Jenkins, examining the nurse over the top of his spectacles. 'And my dear friend Mrs Caldicot here has very generously offered to find Mr Twist a bed for the night.'

'Oh,' said the nurse. She sounded relieved. 'Are you sure?'

'Absolutely sure,' said Jenkins. 'But we will need an ambulance.'

'Of course,' said the nurse, too relieved to argue with this. 'That won't be a problem at all. I can arrange that.'

'And a wheelchair.'

'We can definitely lend you one of those,' said the nurse. 'Just, er, let us have it back when it's convenient to you ... there's no hurry.'

'Good,' said Jenkins, firmly. 'Then let's go and see Mr Twist, and take him home.'

They all stood up.

Mrs Caldicot wanted to cheer but she felt that Jenkins might consider this rather inappropriate so, instead, she simply gave a little silent whoop, smiled at all her friends, took Jenkins's hand and squeezed it. When he squeezed her hand back and turned and smiled at her she felt as though her life was complete.

As the nurse led them all to the cubicle where Mr Twist was waiting she felt strong again; strong enough to take on an army of clipboard carrying foot-soldiers.

'It's all very dirty, isn't it,' said Miss Nightingale.

'Very dirty,' said Mrs Peterborough.

The nurse, who was leading the way, turned round slightly and Mrs Caldicot could see that she was blushing with embarrassment. But she didn't say a word.

CHAPTER THIRTY NINE

'How are you feeling?' asked Mrs Caldicot. 'I've brought you a cup of tea.' She was carrying the tea in one hand and a pile of freshly ironed clothes on the other.

The man in the bed blinked and looked around as though not quite sure where he was.

'Am I dreaming?' Peter Twist asked.

Mrs Caldicot laughed. 'No,' she said. 'I don't think so.' She put the clothes down on the foot of the bed and put the cup of tea down on the bedside table. 'I hope you take milk?'

Mr Twist stared at her.

'In your tea.'

'Oh yes. Thank you.'

'There are some sugar cubes in the saucer,' added Mrs Caldicot.

'Is this your home?' Mr Twist asked her.

Mrs Caldicot laughed. 'Well it is in a way, I suppose,' she agreed. 'It's where I live so that makes it home. But it's what the authorities call 'a residential home for the elderly'.'

Mr Twist looked around the room he was in. 'It's very nice,' he told her. He looked down at himself. He was wearing freshly laundered striped pyjamas.

'I hope you don't mind,' said Mrs Caldicot. 'But I took the liberty of putting your clothes in the washing machine. There was some blood on them.'

Mr Twist seemed embarrassed and went rather red. 'I'm sorry you had all that trouble,' he said.

'Mr Roxdale and Mr Williams undressed you and put you to bed,' Mrs Caldicot explained. 'The hospital sent you out wearing one of their silly gowns. Mr Roxdale is about the same size as you so he lent you a pair of his pyjamas.'

'That was very kind of him,' said Mr Twist. He seemed very touched by this simple act of generosity. There were tears in his eyes.

'Are you all right?' Mrs Caldicot asked him.

'It's all a bit of a shock,' said Mr Twist quietly. 'To be honest, I'm not used to people doing things for me. Not kind things anyway.' He looked down again. 'I'm afraid I don't have any money,' he said. 'I can't pay you anything.'

'Golly!' said Mrs Caldicot. 'That's a bit of a disappointment. We only brought you here because we were convinced that you are a millionaire in disguise.'

Mr Twist looked at her uncertainly.

'A joke,' mouthed Mrs Caldicot, almost silently. She smiled at him. 'You can stay here until you feel fit enough to move on,' she said.

'I should be OK to travel later today,' said Mr Twist. He reached up and touched his head. His fingers found the stitches in his forehead and he winced.

'You won't be fit enough to travel today,' Mrs Caldicot insisted. 'I suggest you get accustomed to the fact that you're going to be here for at least a week.'

'But what about the people who run the place,' said Mr Twist, puzzled. 'Won't they be upset?'

'That won't be a problem at all,' promised Mrs Caldicot.

CHAPTER FORTY

'Is this an inconvenient moment?'

Mrs Caldicot, sat behind the desk in her office, looked up. The door to the office was open, as it often was, and a man was standing in the doorway.

'Hello, Mr Twist!' she said, genuinely pleased to see him. 'My word, you do look different!' He was wearing the same clothes that he had been wearing when he'd been attacked, but both they and he had been thoroughly washed and all parties had benefited from this experience.

'I feel a lot better,' said Mr Twist. 'I just wanted to thank you. And to say that I'm leaving now.'

There was a pause. 'Do you want to go?' asked Mrs Caldicot.

Mr Twist looked at her and then down at the floor. 'It's time I went,' he said.

'But why? Do you *want* to go?'

'No!' he said. His voice softened. 'No, of course I don't want to go.'

'You don't have to go,' said Mrs Caldicot. 'You can stay here for a while.'

'No,' said Mr Twist firmly. 'I'm already in your debt. There is no way I can repay your kindness.'

'You don't have to repay anything.'

'I don't want to be pitied or helped,' said Mr Twist.

'I don't pity you,' said Mrs Caldicot. She stood up. 'I'll very happily help you if you want me to. But I'm not going to force myself on you.' She sat down again, but this time on the corner of her desk. 'How did you end up living in a cardboard box?'

'Why do you want to know that?' asked Mr Twist.

'I want to know how and why a healthy, sane, educated man ends up living in a cardboard box on a traffic island.'

'Why should I bother to satisfy your curiosity?' demanded Mr Twist, suspiciously.

'Payment,' said Mrs Caldicot. 'You said yourself that you owe me for rescuing you. You can pay off the debt simply by talking. Tell me a little about yourself. Why do you live the way you do?'

'Those are the questions social workers always ask,' said Mr Twist. "How did I end up like this.' 'Why do I live this way.' Social workers and policemen. People like that. I never tell them. They wouldn't understand. They're a part of what I don't like – so how could they understand?'

'They probably ask you so that they can write you up properly in their reports,' said Mrs Caldicot. 'To them you're an interesting 'case'. I'm asking because I'm interested in you as a person.'

Mr Twist thought about this for a while. 'OK,' he said at last. 'I'll tell you if you answer me one question.'

Mrs Caldicot waited.

'You call everyone here by their surname,' said Mr Twist. 'You always address people as Mr this or Miss that.'

'Yes, of course,' said Mrs Caldicot.

'Why?' asked Mr Twist. 'Since I've been living rough no one has ever addressed me by my surname. Social workers and policemen always call me Peter. And it's been the same whenever I've been admitted to hospital.'

'Respect,' said Mrs Caldicot. 'That's all. It's just a sign of respect.' She nodded towards a chair. 'Why don't you sit down?'

Mr Twist nodded, but remained standing. 'It started with a little thing,' he said after a moment or two. 'Actually, I can tell you the moment when my life changed,' he began. He cleared his throat. 'I went into town one Wednesday to take a book back to the library. That's all. I parked in one of the Council car parks and discovered that they'd changed the machine they use to dispense tickets. In the past whenever I left the car park I'd always handed my ticket over to another motorist if I had some time left on it. If I bought a ticket for two hours and finished my errands in forty minutes I would just hand the ticket to someone driving into the car park. It always made me feel good and it always seemed to make them feel good too. They would smile and say 'thank you'. It was just a little thing. No one lost out because the space has been paid for. But on that Wednesday I found out that the Council had made it illegal to pass a ticket on to another motorist. And to make sure that we all obeyed their new anti-kindness law they'd installed machines – heaven knows how much they cost – into which you had to type your car registration number. The number you typed into the machine was then printed on your ticket and there was a notice saying that it was illegal to use that ticket on any other car.'

'I've seen those machines,' said Mrs Caldicot. 'The local Council has just introduced them here.'

'It made me both sad and angry,' said Mr Twist. 'I suppose the Council did it because they were desperate to grab every last penny they could but it seemed to me that what they were doing was stamping out any sense of public or community spirit in the town. They were stopping people being nice to one another.'

Mrs Caldicot nodded.

'It wasn't simply that, of course,' said Mr Twist. 'The car park machine was just the last straw. There were lots of things I didn't like about the society we've created. It seemed to me that when I walked down the street everyone was aggressive.' He looked down and then rubbed at his eyes with his coat sleeve.

'Take one of these,' said Mrs Caldicot, offering him the box of tissues which she kept on her desk.

Mr Twist took a tissue, murmured his thanks, wiped his eyes and held the tissue in his hands. 'Children coming home from school used to have fun and lark about. They don't lark about these days. They're young thugs; terrorising the weak and the elderly. Young mothers – most of whom seem hardly old enough to be out of school – use their prams as battering rams. People are all too aware of their rights and reluctant to accept their responsibilities. Corruption and deceit are spreading down from the top in politics and industry. Our towns are protected not by patrolling policemen but by cameras which merely record the violence rather than prevent it. A constantly prying Government has even turned road safety into a money making venture.'

'Teachers, desperate to win financial bonuses, help their students to cheat. Everyone in public service is there solely for the money. They want – and take – authority, but they don't want responsibility either. All our public services – our hospitals, our roads, our schools – are getting worse. Churches and libraries are closing. Police stations are shutting – leaving people to telephone helplines hundreds or thousands of miles away. Every year we pay far more in taxes and get considerably less in services. Nothing is as good as it was and yet everything costs more. Selfishness is the new mantra. Our freedom and privacy are disappearing fast – all in the false name of security. They say they have to take away our freedom in order to protect our freedom. What lunacy. The two things I see around me most often are fear and anger. Whatever happened to love and hope?'

Mrs Caldicot looked at Mr Twist. There was anger in his eyes but there were tears on his cheeks. She stood up, moved closer to him and took his hand.

'But the thing I like least,' continued Mr Twist, 'is the fact that we have created a society in which people are encouraged to be selfish; to think only of themselves. There is no sense of community any more.' He paused and wiped a tear from his cheek. He smiled at Mrs Caldicot and cleared his throat. His voice changed slightly. 'Do you know what appeals to me most about this place?'

Mrs Caldicot looked at him, thought for a moment, and then shook her head. 'No.'

'It's the sense of community you have created,' he told her. 'The way everyone here helps everyone else. You've created a sort of sixties commune. People here seem to be honest, decent and courteous to one another. You may not realise it but you're living in a spiritual oasis.'

'Without the long hair and free sex,' smiled Mrs Caldicot. 'Go on with your story,' she encouraged him.

Mr Twist blew his nose again and this time stuffed the tissue into his trouser pocket. 'I was incensed that the Council had made it illegal to help people. When I got back to my car I had an hour of time left on my ticket. I stood by the entrance and offered my ticket to other motorists driving in. A car park attendant saw me and told me that what I was doing was against the law. I said I didn't care. So he fetched a policeman. I was arrested and charged with something or other under the Public Order Act.'

'My wife wanted me to plead guilty and explain that I was upset because my father had died a few months earlier. My solicitor said that if I apologised I would get off with a fine. He said he might even be able to get me off without my having to plead guilty. He said that personally he agreed with me but that one couldn't change these things and that no one else really cared so there was no point in standing up and being a martyr.'

'But I insisted on pleading not guilty and taking on the system. I argued that the Council didn't have a right to outlaw kindness.' He shrugged and smiled thinly. 'Naturally, I lost. The prosecutor said people like me were a threat to the community. I was sentenced to two months in prison. It meant that I had a criminal record. The local paper ran the story on their front page.' He paused and swallowed as he remembered this final indignity. 'They made me look like a mass murderer. They didn't even say what the case was all about. I'd made this great speech in court about our community spirit being destroyed. I'd spent days preparing it. It really seemed important to me. But they didn't report any of that. All they were interested in was the fact that a tax inspector was going to prison.' He looked at Mrs Caldicot 'That was my job. I was a tax inspector.'

Mrs Caldicot didn't say anything.

'While I was in prison I found that my wife had left me. She started divorce proceedings within days of my being locked up. Her solicitor had effectively had me locked out of the house I'd bought for us. He convinced the divorce court that because I had a criminal record I was dangerous. Before I went to prison I'd had quite an important job at the Inland Revenue. But they fired me, of course. So I had no job, no wife and no home.'

'Didn't you have friends you could go to for help?'

'I didn't have any friends. I worked for the Inland Revenue.'

'So what happened?'

'I stayed in a hostel for three months. I applied for lots of jobs but I couldn't find anyone keen to employ a homeless 63-year-old man with a criminal record.'

'And so you ended up living in a cardboard box.'

'Several, actually,' he smiled. 'They don't last long when it rains. I used to get them from a local furniture shop. They had bigger, stronger boxes than anyone else.'

'Why on a traffic island?'

'Another tramp I met told me that you were less likely to be attacked or set on fire if you were on a traffic island.'

Mrs Caldicot, moved closer to him, put both her arms around him and hugged him. 'A few minutes ago I asked you if you really wanted to go,' said Mrs Caldicot. She let him go and looked at him.

Mr Twist nodded. There were tears rolling down his cheeks.

'I want to ask you the same question again.'

There was a long, long silence.

'No,' he said at last. He spoke so quietly that she could hardly hear him. 'Of course I don't.' He swallowed hard, took out his tissue and wiped his eyes. 'But I don't have any money, I can't pay your bills and I'm not a scrounger. I can imagine how much it must cost to run a place like this. It wouldn't be fair for me to stay any longer.' He paused. He seemed embarrassed. 'You've already been very kind to me.'

'If you stayed you could help us a good deal,' said Mrs Caldicot. 'You could more than earn your keep. You must stay here now.'

'I couldn't bear getting happy here and then having to move out in a few months time.'

'If you move in, you won't have to move out unless you want to,' said Mrs Caldicot.

Mr Twist looked at her eagerly. 'I would be happy to do anything you wanted me to do,' he said. 'I can wash dishes. Dig the garden.'

'Mr Merivale washes the dishes and Mr Roxdale has enough people helping him dig the garden,' said Mrs Caldicot. 'When you worked for the Inland Revenue did you learn how to do accounts?'

'Of course.' Mr Twist smiled at her. 'I always wanted to be an accountant,' he told her. 'When I was a boy it was my dream. But my parents and the careers teacher at school persuaded me to join the Inland Revenue.' He smiled thinly. 'They said that working for the Government was steadier and more respectable work.'

'I desperately need someone to help me with the accounts,' said Mrs Caldicot. She reached into one of the trays on her desk, took out a handful of letters and bills and handed them to Mr Twist. 'Could you sort these out for me?' she asked.

Mr Twist flicked through the papers. 'A lot of these are final reminders and demands,' he said.

'I know,' sighed Mrs Caldicot. 'One of the big problems is that I'm not very good at paperwork. My husband always used to deal with that sort of thing.'

'Do you have the money to pay these?'

'That's the other problem,' admitted Mrs Caldicot. 'We do have something of what I believe is called 'a cash flow problem'.'

'Ah,' said Mr Twist, understandingly.

'I need someone to sort these things out for me,' said Mrs Caldicot. 'And to hold the creditors at bay for a while.' She lowered her voice. 'I'd be grateful if you kept this to yourself,' said Mrs Caldicot.

'Of course,' said Mr Twist. As she had known he would, he felt more comfortable now that Mrs Caldicot had shared a secret of her own with him.

'I can do that for you,' said Mr Twist.

'Wonderful,' said Mrs Caldicot with a smile. 'Now, I'll take you to the lounge and introduce you to the guests you haven't met.'

'One other thing,' said Mr Twist, slightly apologetically. 'You won't tell anyone what I used to do for a living? People may be a little, well, unwelcoming, if they know I used to work for the Inland Revenue.'

'I won't tell anyone if you don't want me to,' Mrs Caldicot assured him. 'But what you used to do isn't anywhere near as important as who you are now.'

'Would it be terrible if I pretended to have been something else? Something a bit more exciting? Something a bit more acceptable?'

'What would you like to be known as?' asked Mrs Caldicot. 'Racing driver? Actor? Footballer?'

'An accountant would be nice,' said Mr Twist. 'I would be very happy if people thought of me as a former accountant.'

'A former accountant you shall be,' agreed Mrs Caldicot. She took his arm and led him to the lounge.

CHAPTER FORTY ONE

'This is my niece Daisy,' said Miss Nightingale, proudly. 'She's here on leave. She works as a nurse in Africa.'

The other residents, all kneeling on the floor, looked up.

'Hello Daisy,' said Mr Livingstone.

'Hello Daisy,' said Mr Roxdale.

'Hello Daisy,' said Mr Williams.

This continued until the only person remaining was Mrs Peterborough.

'Hello Daisy,' said Miss Nightingale.

Daisy looked a little surprised.

'Hello Daisy,' said Mrs Peterborough.

Daisy, a kind young woman in her thirties, understood. Her aunt had told her about Mrs Peterborough.

'Are you looking for something?' Daisy asked.

'We're playing tiddly-winks,' explained Mr Roxdale. 'I just tiddled a wink into the egg cup from three feet.' He looked around. 'Is it tiddling a wink or winking a tiddle?' he asked.

'I dunno what you call it, but it was a bloody fine shot,' said Mr Hewitt.

'Congratulations,' said Daisy.

'Daisy has been telling me that the hospital where she works is short of pills,' said Miss Nightingale. 'If any of you have any spare medicines she would be very grateful if you'd let her have them.'

'What sort of stuff do you want?' asked Mr Roxdale. 'I've got quite a good collection of stuff in my bathroom cabinet.'

'We're particularly short of antibiotics and painkillers,' said Daisy.

'I'm sure we can all find you something,' promised Mr Livingstone.

When Daisy left, an hour or so later, she was carrying bulging carrier bags full of pills. She was crying with joy.

'Will you come back and see us before you return to Africa?' asked Mr Livingstone.

'I certainly will,' said Daisy.

'I've got a little plan,' said Mr Livingstone, when she had gone. 'Listen...'

Chapter Forty Two

The golf club bar was packed. It was the club's evening for distributing prizes and cups. The bar was doing a roaring trade in gins and traditional ales and the two temporary members of bar staff were getting increasingly irritated as they struggled to keep up with the members' demands for alcohol. They wouldn't have minded being busy if they'd been picking up tips but the evening was well under way and neither of them had received a penny.

Two members of the golf club weren't in the bar, listening to the speeches and watching their fellow members feign modesty as they accepted assorted pieces of grotesquely ugly silverware. They were tucked away in the billiards room. They had started a game of snooker so that if anyone entered it would be clear that the room was occupied. But neither of the members were interested in the balls on the table. They were sitting, side by side, on a raised bench, each nursing a very large gin.

'You're sure this will work?' asked Nigel Roxdale.

'Oh yes,' replied Mr Muller-Hawksmoor confidently. 'I'm sure Mrs Caldicot doesn't have enough staff members. Being in breach of the required staff-patient ratio is a serious offence. I can close her down immediately.'

'And she won't be able to open up again?'

Mr Muller-Hawksmoor smiled. 'Oh, I don't think so,' he answered. 'This will be the last straw. And she knows that if she does open up again I'll be back. There are laws and regulations even I don't know about, and our good friends in Brussels are thinking up new ones every day.'

'She doesn't suspect anything? She doesn't realise why you want to close her down?'

'Oh good heavens no,' said Mr Muller-Hawksmoor, with a nasty looking smile. 'Mrs Caldicot and I go way back. She thinks I'm harassing her simply because I don't like her.' He shrugged and allowed the smile to broaden.

'Good. Keep it that way,' said Nigel Roxdale. He smiled and sipped a little gin. 'I've got a couple of backers lined up,' he said. 'Two clients of mine in the hotel trade who are looking for a new property. They're terribly excited about the whole thing. I've arranged for my bank to lend us the money to buy the place the minute it goes on the market. We then immediately sell it on to my backers.'

'And what do you think the profit will be?

'It all depends on just how cheap we can get it,' said Nigel. 'But we should be able to rely on at least £100,000 to split between us. After costs.'

'Fifty thousand!' said Mr Muller-Hawksmoor.

He couldn't believe his luck. He was closing down Mrs Caldicot's Rest Home and getting paid for it! Life had never been so joyful.

He drank some more gin, closed his eyes, settled back on the bench and smiled still more.

CHAPTER FORTY THREE

'Is this, er, the er...' the caller looked up and down and to the right and to the left as though looking for clues.

'What are you looking for?' enquired Mrs Caldicot gently.

It was raining again. The man who had rung the doorbell, and who was now sheltering in the porch, was probably in his mid fifties. He was short, round and bald and wore spectacles with glass so thick it looked as though it had been cut from the bottom of milk bottles. The lenses magnified his eyes and made him look almost comically fearsome. Standing on the top step he was a good foot shorter than Mrs Caldicot. He stared up at her and opened his mouth. 'Is this the old folks' home? I'm looking for er ... Mrs ... er...' he pulled a piece of paper out of his pocket and peered at it. 'Mrs Peterborough. I'm doctor ... er ... the psychiatrist.'

'This is the Twilight Years Rest Home,' confirmed Mrs Caldicot.

'Can I come in?'

Mrs Caldicot opened the door wide to let the psychiatrist enter. 'You're here to see Mrs Peterborough?' she asked him.

'I've got to certify the old biddy insane,' said the psychiatrist.

'If you would wait in here, I'll get Mrs Peterborough to come and see you,' said Mrs Caldicot pausing outside her office.

'There's no need to bring her in here,' said the psychiatrist. 'It's better to see the wild life in their natural surroundings than sitting in a zoo. Lead me to her. I hope she's not being a teapot today. The er ... council people told you I was coming?'

'They did,' confirmed Mrs Caldicot.

'I...er...don't suppose they told you my name, did they?'

'No,' said Mrs Caldicot.

'Never mind' said the psychiatrist, seemingly not in the slightest bit embarrassed by this example of memory loss. 'Doesn't matter. I sometimes wonder if I've got that disease. You know the one. I can't remember the damned name. Never mind, you seem to be the woman who runs the old folks' home and I'm pretty sure I'm the doctor. Lead me to her.'

CHAPTER FORTY FOUR

'Doctor, this is Mrs Peterborough,' said Mrs Caldicot, introducing Mrs Peterborough and the psychiatrist to one another. 'Mrs Peterborough, this is the psychiatrist. He's come to examine you.'

'So, you're my slice of fruitcake for today, are you?' said the doctor, staring rather aggressively at Mrs Peterborough.

Mrs Peterborough, confused by this, didn't say anything.

'You're a very rude man,' said Miss Nightingale.

'You're a very rude man,' repeated Mrs Peterborough.

The psychiatrist who didn't look in the slightest bit put out by this two-pronged attack, continued to stare at Mrs Peterborough. 'Ms ... er ... someone has asked me to ask you some questions,' he told her. He looked around, spotted a straight-backed chair, pulled it over and sat down on it. 'I'm going to ask you a question about current affairs.' He peered at Mrs Peterborough through his bottle-glass spectacles. 'What do you think of the situation in the Middle East?' he asked. He lowered his head and chewed at his bottom lip, deep in thought.

'Who is he? What's he want?' whispered Miss Nightingale to Mrs Caldicot.

'He's the psychiatrist sent by Ms Jones,' explained Mrs Caldicot in a whisper. 'He's here to decide if Mrs Peterborough is sane.' She and Miss Nightingale exchanged looks.

'And if he decides she isn't?'

'They'll insist on moving her somewhere else,' whispered Mrs Caldicot. 'To a hospital.'

'That would make her worse,' whispered Miss Nightingale, horrified.

'That would make her worse,' said Mrs Peterborough in what she thought was a whisper.

'I know,' whispered Mrs Caldicot.

'We must stop them,' whispered Miss Nightingale.

'But how?' whispered Mrs Caldicot. 'How are we going to do that?'

'Zzzz,' said the psychiatrist.

'We've got to convince him that she's sane,' whispered Miss Nightingale.

'Zzzz zzzz,' said the psychiatrist.

'Got to convince him that she's sane,' said Mrs Peterborough.

'How the hell are we going to do that?' demanded Mr Livingstone.

'Zzzzz zzzz zzzz zzzz,' said the psychiatrist.

'I think he's fallen asleep,' said Miss Nightingale.

'I think he's fallen asleep,' confirmed Mrs Peterborough.

They all looked at him. His head had fallen forwards onto his chest. A small dribble of saliva had escaped from his open lips and was heading down towards his tie in a long, sticky string.

'I love Mrs Peterborough very much, like a sister,' said Mr Livingstone. 'Actually more than my sister. Between you and me my sister is a mean bitch. Can't stand her. The most selfish, manipulative woman I've ever met. To be honest, I've never understood why my brother-in-law didn't bop her on the head and bury her in the garden years ago. But the problem,' he continued, 'and I say this very lovingly, is that Mrs Peterborough is, as we all know, a little bit different.'

'So we have to convince the psychiatrist that he's wrong about Mrs Peterborough,' said Miss Nightingale.

'So we have to convince...' began Mrs Peterborough. Having forgotten the rest of the sentence she faded out.

'That's more or less it,' said Mr Livingstone.
'How on earth do we do that?' asked Mrs Caldicot.

CHAPTER FORTY FIVE

The psychiatrist had been asleep for twenty minutes or so. There was now a large wet stain on his tie. Suddenly, he awoke with a start. He looked up, looked around and stared at everyone in turn. No one said anything.

'I suppose you all think I was asleep?' he said, accusingly.

'Oh no, not at all,' replied Mr Livingstone.

'It's a trick I often use,' said the psychiatrist, blinking. 'I trick patients into thinking I'm asleep. But all the time I'm listening to every word they are saying.' He glared at everyone in turn.

Mrs Caldicot looked at Mr Livingstone who looked at Miss Nightingale who looked at Mrs Merivale who looked at Mr Roxdale who looked at Mrs Roberts who, completing the cycle, looked at Mrs Caldicot.

'That's very clever of you,' said Mrs Caldicot. 'You pretend to be asleep but secretly you listen to what your patients are saying. That way you get to the truth much more quickly.'

'Exactly!' cried the psychiatrist. 'In a nut shell!'

'Did you find what Mrs Peterborough had to say interesting?' asked Mrs Caldicot.

'Oh, very much so,' nodded the psychiatrist.

'We were all fascinated by what she had to say,' said Mrs Caldicot. She looked around for support and confirmation. The others all nodded and murmured their agreement.

'Absolutely!' agreed the psychiatrist.

'I didn't realise she knew so much about the Middle East,' said Mr Roxdale. 'Very impressive. I learned a lot,' he added.

'Oh, yes,' said the psychiatrist. 'Very good indeed.'

'From what you've just heard I don't suppose you can be in any doubt about her mental state?'

'Er ... no, of course not,' confirmed the psychiatrist.

'I expect you're finished with her now?' said Mrs Caldicot. 'It's time for her physiotherapy so would you excuse her if Mrs Roberts takes her to her room?' Mrs Caldicot nodded to Mrs Roberts who got up and helped Mrs Peterborough to her feet. Miss Nightingale stood up too.

'Everything is fine,' said the psychiatrist. 'She can now go. I've finished with her.' He too stood up.

'It was nice to meet you, doctor,' said Miss Nightingale.

'It was nice to meet you, doctor,' said Mrs Peterborough.

Mrs Roberts and Miss Nightingale took one arm each and walked Mrs Peterborough to and through the door before the psychiatrist could ask her anything else.

'I'll show you out then, shall I?' said Mrs Caldicot to the psychiatrist.

'Er, thank you,' said the doctor. He seemed rather bewildered.

When he'd gone they celebrated.

Mrs Merivale cooked egg and chips for everyone and Mr Livingstone entertained them by playing a medley of favourite tunes on his trombone.

Chapter Forty Six

'I went for a walk to the paper shop this morning,' said Mr Williams. 'I've never seen so much traffic.'

'It is a busy road,' agreed Mr Roxdale.

'Loads of potential customers,' said Mr Williams.

Mr Roxdale, who didn't understand, looked at him quizzically.

'When the flowers and the vegetables we're growing are ready we could set up a stall by the roadside,' said Mr Williams. 'It would help bring in some money for Mrs Caldicot.'

'That's a brilliant idea!' said Mr Roxdale, as though no one had ever before thought of it. He had simple tastes and had never had a 'commercial' brain.

'It's a pity we have to wait for the darned things to grow,' said Mr Williams. 'It'll be months before there's anything to sell.'

'Does Mrs Caldicot need money now?' asked Mr Roxdale.

'I overheard her talking to Mrs Roberts,' said Mr Williams. 'Apparently they've got real financial problems. It costs a fortune to run a place this size and now the roof is apparently leaking.' He sighed. He had on several more occasions tried to give Mrs Caldicot a few photographs but she wouldn't accept them.

'We don't have to wait for the stuff in the garden to grow!' said Mr Roxdale, suddenly inspired.

Mr Williams looked at him. 'What do you suggest?' he asked.

'Selling grass-cuttings?' He paused and thought for a moment. 'I have to tell you that I'm a bit old for scrumping,' he said.

'No, no!' said Mr Roxdale. 'We can pop round to the garden at my old place. There's tons of stuff growing there. I don't think they've rented out the house yet.'

'Flowers?'

'Flowers and vegetables,' said Mr Roxdale. 'I haven't been looking after them but with any luck the birds will have left us some stuff we can sell.'

'How far is it?'

'We can walk it,' said Mr Roxdale. 'We'll take the wheel-barrow, fill it up and take it in turns to wheel it back.'

CHAPTER FORTY SEVEN

'I can just about still remember the enormous sense of relief I felt when I first discovered that I had become a shabby, dull, slightly podgy, old man,' said Mr Roxdale.

'I know exactly what you mean,' sighed Mr Williams. 'Same thing happened to me. Overnight. One day I went to bed a smart, young fellow, constantly worried about my hair and my figure. The next day I woke up fat and completely past it.' He paused, looked at his new friend, and grinned. 'What a wonderful relief. The last thirty years have been the best of my life.'

The two men were standing on the pavement outside the Twilight Years Rest Home. Every bucket they could find was filled with flowers. But business was not brisk and the two men had plenty of time to chat.

'Becoming old was the best thing I ever did,' agreed Mr Roxdale, with a nod. 'Best day's work I ever did. Best day of my life. I suddenly realised that I no longer had to bother. No one noticed me. I had become invisible. The joy! The freedom! I didn't have to iron my shirts or polish my shoes.'

'For me one of the great delights was the discovery that for the first time in my life young women were always happy to talk to me,' said Mr Williams.

'You know, exactly the same thing happened to me,' said Mr Roxdale.'

'They didn't feel threatened,' said Mr Williams.

'Absolutely,' agreed Mr Roxdale.

'I suddenly realised that young women were smiling at me not because they fancied me but because they rightly perceived me as a harmless old duffer – absolutely no threat to them,' said Mr Williams. 'Models, shop girls, girls in the bank, girls at parties. I could chat with them – even flirt with them without giving the slightest offence. They could smile at me, and talk to me without thinking that I could possibly imagine that they are flirting with me. At first I was disappointed but then I realised that I found it enormously liberating: it meant I got to talk to loads of young women without having to worry about whether or not I was going to pull, or whether I'd be able to perform. I didn't have to worry about anything any more. The flirting was the beginning, the middle and the end. Wonderful.'

'That's one of the good things about growing old,' agreed Mr Roxdale, with a nod. 'Marvellous.' He always enjoyed his visits to the corner shop to pay his paper bill. The twenty something girl who took his money always had a smile for him.

'You shouldn't flirt with that girl,' his daughter-in-law had told him more than once. 'You're too old. What will people think?'

'I'm too old to care what anyone thinks,' Mr Roxdale had replied. 'But not too old to flirt.'

They stood together in silence for a while, each possessed by his own happy thoughts. Mr Roxdale looked up. The sky was getting blacker.

'It's going to rain,' he said.

'They said on the weather forecast that it was going to be fine today,' said Mr Williams.

Mr Roxdale snorted. He did not have much respect for weather forecasters. 'I don't know how they get away with what they do,' he said. 'It's a big confidence trick. Other people have to be accurate or they get into trouble. But weather forecasters keep on getting it wrong and keep on getting away with it.'

They stood in silence for another few moments, both of them watching the blackening sky.

'Mind you, I'm not saying growing old is all wonderful,' said Mr Williams.

'No, it's not,' agreed Mr Roxdale.

'By the time I was seventy I'd lost most of my friends,' said Mr Williams. He didn't sound too sad about it. 'Never had many, mind you,' he added.

'Passed away, did they?' said Mr Roxdale, sympathetically.

'No, no!' said Mr Williams. 'Not really.' He thought about it for a moment. 'Well I suppose a few of them did drop off their perches. No, by and large, I gave them up. Stopped seeing them. We no longer had anything in common.' He shook his head sadly. 'D'you know most of 'em would only ever talk about what the doctor had said or what pills they were on.'

'It's raining,' said Mr Roxdale inconsequentially, but accurately.

Mr Williams looked up. A large drop of rain splashed on his face. 'It is,' he agreed.

'I had a chum who used to grow marvellous vegetables,' said Mr Roxdale. 'He grew marvellous runner beans. We used to meet in the pub three times a week. I stopped going. All he wanted to talk about was his new hearing aid and the trouble he was having with the pension people.'

Mr Williams nodded furiously. 'I had a pal who nearly drove me mad. If he wasn't telling me about his bowels he was giving me a detailed account of how his varicose veins were doing. He'd given me a word-by-word account of his latest visit to the doctor. 'Good morning, Doctor.' 'Good morning, Mr Blodget.' 'Chilly for the time of the year.' 'Very chilly, Mr Blodget.' That sort of thing. Then he'd get his new pills out. A blue one and a red one before getting out of bed. Then two white ones and a yellow one after shaving but before breakfast. On it went. Pills, pills, pills. He loved his pills. He lived for them.'

'I had a mate who always used to be great fun,' said Mr Roxdale. 'He used to be a traffic warden but he had a sense of humour nevertheless. Then his younger brother and two of his pals died and he went downhill rapidly. It really affected him. He stopped eating fatty foods, started going jogging and gave up the drink.'

'Completely?'

'Wouldn't touch a drop. He would sit there in his usual chair in the pub, nursing an orange juice, and bore your ears off with stories about his brother's last stay in hospital.' Mr Roxdale shuddered. 'Awful. I swore I would never let them get me into a hospital after that. Then he decided that the orange juice was giving him heartburn so he gave up that and started drinking plain water.'

'I never had much faith in doctors,' said Mr Williams. 'Bunch of murdering bastards.' He took out a large red handkerchief and blew his nose. 'They put me in a loony bin once, you know.'

'No I didn't know,' said Mr Roxdale.

'Doctor said I was depressed. Stupid prat. Only a bloody 110 per cent proof imbecile could go through life on this planet without being depressed. Anyone who isn't pretty well damned depressed should be locked up. Probably a psychopath.'

'They gave you pills, I suppose?'

'Buckets full of 'em. I never took the damned things though. Spat 'em out after they'd gone. Never took one. In the end I threatened to sue the bastards. Then they found out I'd got a bit of clout so they let me go. Most depressing time of my life. They put me in a ward with all these other depressed people. Dozens of em. All miserable as sin. We all sat around all day depressing each other. As soon as someone started to cheer up the others would drag him down again. Madness.'

'When I got home I decided to cure myself. I designed this sort of shock therapy. I invited round all my friends and acquaintances who had serious problems. Every miserable, pessimistic bastard I'd ever met. I gave them cheap booze and little vol-au-vents I'd bought in from a caterer and one by one invited them to talk endlessly about the awful things that had happened to them. I tell you it was fearsome stuff. I had to pop into the kitchen from time to time for a rest. At the end of the evening I threw 'em all out and never saw 'em again. I felt so much better. From that point on, I tried to surround myself with jolly folk.'

'I've never trusted doctors,' said Mr Roxdale.

'Never trusted doctors or any of those damned so-called experts,' said Mr Williams. 'When I was little I believed that one should always hire – and trust – experts. And so I hired an accountant. Who ended up costing me a fortune. I've had dentists who've nearly destroyed my teeth and doctors who've nearly killed me. I have hired lawyers who have cost me a fortune. I hired a pension company which totally screwed up the management of my pension. I have hired banks and investment companies which have lost money hand over fist. The list is endless. I have no faith in experts.'

They stood in silence for a moment as a young woman approached, pushing a pram. She was plump, blonde and pretty. She smiled at both men, in turn. Both smiled back. She stopped for a moment. 'Have you got the time?' she asked.

'Sorry, love,' said Mr Roxdale. 'I don't wear a watch.' He turned to his friend.

'No watch either, I'm afraid,' said Mr Williams.

'But it's morning,' said Mr Roxdale. 'If that's any help.' He handed her a pink rose.

The girl took the rose, smiled, thanked them and continued on her way.

'You see, thirty years ago I would have felt I had to say

something like 'I've got the time if you've got the inclination,' said Mr Williams. 'Then either she would have been offended or we'd have got involved in that courtship rigmarole.'

'Thirty years ago she wouldn't have asked us for the time,' said Mr Roxdale.

'Thirty years ago I could have told her,' said Mr Williams. 'I'd have been too scared of missing an appointment to go out without a watch.'

'I stopped wearing a watch when I was 62,' said Mr Roxdale. 'A pal of mine left work. I was invited to his leaving party. Do you know what they gave him?'

'A watch?'

'A watch and a clock. Why do they do that? What's the point? The last thing on this earth he wanted was a watch.'

'Or a clock.'

'It was like they were telling him that they knew he'd always have time on his hands. Cruel and thoughtless bastards. He died four days later. Four days of pension. Four days of retirement. He didn't get to enjoy any of it. Never even got time to find out if the bloody watch kept good time. Never even had to wind up the clock. Why do they do that? The one time in your life when you don't have to watch the time and they give you a watch.'

'Crazy, isn't it?'

'I took off my watch at his funeral and threw it into his grave. Never worn one since.' He turned slightly and watched the girl disappearing down the road. 'Nice-looking girl though,' said Mr Roxdale. 'Reminds me of my niece. She's divorced now. Works for an undertaker. I've told her I want her taking care of me when I've gone. Lovely soft hands.'

'When I turned fifty I bought an undertaker's place and turned it into a studio,' said Mr Williams. 'There was a mortuary at the back. Great big skylights. Beautiful natural light to work by. No one in my family would come to visit. They were all scared.'

'Really? What of?'

'They said that working in a place like that was asking for trouble. All those dead bodies, you see. They thought I'd be next on the slab.'

'What did you say?'

'I pointed out that no-one had ever actually died there,' said Mr Williams. 'Safest place in town from that point of view.' He stared down at the gutter and kicked at what looked like a cigar butt. 'Is that a cigar?'

Mr Roxdale lowered his head and stared at it. 'Dunno,' he said. 'I never pick up cigar butts these days. Too many small dogs around. And my eyesight isn't what it used to be.'

CHAPTER FORTY EIGHT

'How is it going?' asked a voice they both recognised. They turned and said hello to Mrs Caldicot.

'Not terribly well, I'm afraid,' admitted Mr Williams. 'There doesn't seem to be a great demand for flowers around here.'

'Taken just two pounds so far,' said Mr Roxdale, holding up the tin they had brought with them for their takings. 'And that was for the carnations we both bought.' He lifted his lapel to draw Mrs Caldicot's attention to the fine-looking carnation in his button-hole.

'What you really need is a bit of glamour,' said Mrs Caldicot with a laugh.

'So can you stay and help us?' asked Mr Roxdale gallantly.

Mrs Caldicot smiled and shook her head. 'I'm afraid not,' she said. 'But thank you for the compliment.' She headed back towards the house.

CHAPTER FORTY NINE

Mr Roxdale and Mr Williams had temporarily abandoned their attempts at flower selling. It had not been a huge success so far, but they had not yet given up. While Mr Williams wandered upstairs to his room to try to find a pair of gloves Mr Roxdale tottered into the lounge looking for his second best brown corduroy trousers. The trousers he had been wearing had been soaked when a bucket of water had tipped over them. He had had to take them off. Mrs Merivale had been mending his spare trousers the evening before and he had left them in her safe-keeping.

The television was on in the lounge. Half a dozen residents were watching a middle-aged man with orange skin and a far too perfect hairstyle interviewing a group of supposedly ordinary but surprisingly orange-skinned people. He spoke in a mid Western drawl. A caption on the screen told late coming viewers that the subject of the discussion was shyness. The man with orange skin held his microphone underneath the bulbous nose of a large woman who wore jeans and a bright red T-shirt as though they both had done something to upset her and needed to be punished. She too had orange skin.

'Mrs Merivale, do you know where my trousers are?' Mr Roxdale enquired.

Naturally, everyone turned to look.

'Nice legs,' said Mr Livingstone drily, nodding at Mr Roxdale's naked lower limbs. 'But if you're going to go out without stockings you should use some of that fake tanning lotion.'

'Could do with a shave, too,' said Mr Hewitt. 'Hairy legs are right out of fashion these days.'

'I'm President of The World Federation of Shy And Retiring People,' announced the large, orange-skinned woman dominating their television screen. 'A survey back home in Ohio, showed that for the last seven years I have been the shyest person in the whole wide world,' she concluded proudly. She folded her arms and glared around her, as though daring anyone to deny her this title. The orange-faced man, the presenter of the programme, nodded sagely, as though enormously impressed by this news. The large woman looked around beaming, when the audience, led by the presenter, applauded to show just how impressed they were.

'No, you're not! You're not!' screamed a woman in a bright yellow jumpsuit. She too had orange skin and she too sounded American. She jumped up out of her seat and pointed a podgy finger at the woman in the jeans and red T-shirt. 'She's a fraud!' she cried. 'She's not as shy as I am!'

'They're on the back of Mrs Torridge's chair,' Mrs Merivale told Mr Roxdale.

Mr Roxdale thanked Mrs Merivale, both for this information and for mending his trousers. With a smile and a wave of a hand Mrs Merivale dismissed the need for thanks and concentrated her attention on the television screen.

'Neither of them seem very shy to me,' muttered Mr Livingstone. He turned to Mrs Merivale, who was sitting next to him. 'Do you know any of these people?'

'I met the presenter once,' replied Mrs Merivale. 'He was born in Walsall. His real name is Sidney, he's married to a district nurse called Angela and he used to work as a postman in the daytime and as a sword swallower in the evenings.'

'He's not American?'

Mrs Merivale looked puzzled. 'Not unless the Americans colonised Walsall,' she said. 'But he was once arrested for sniffing coke,' she added, rather inconsequentially.

Mr Roxdale approached Mrs Torridge's chair and politely asked her to move forward a few inches so that he could retrieve his trousers. Mrs Torridge did as he requested and looked him up and down as though considering making an offer for the freehold. 'You look as though you're good with your hands,' she said, when she had finished her inspection. 'Will you tie me up, please?'

On the television the two Americans were now arguing vociferously.

'I've often wondered about sniffing coke,' said Mr Hewitt. 'Can you use anthracite? Or does it have to be coke?'

'I don't know,' confessed Mrs Merivale. 'Good question, though.'

'I beg your pardon?' said Mr Roxdale. He was not a man who was easily shocked but he felt sure that Mrs Torridge had asked him to tie her up.

'I've decided to be Harriet Houdini today,' said Mrs Torridge.

'Harriet Houdini?' said Mr Roxdale. 'Who on earth is she?'

'The famous escapologist,' said Mrs Torridge. 'Well she would have been famous,' she added. 'If her brother hadn't grabbed all the headlines.'

'Her brother?'

'Harry. Harry Houdini.'

'Of course. Have you got any rope? String? Strips of cloth?'

'I've got some rope,' said Mrs Torridge. She held out a length of what looked like carefully and neatly looped clothes line: Mr Roxdale took this from her before glancing at the television screen. The woman in yellow had flung herself on top of the woman in the red T-shirt. He watched, astonished, as they fell together onto the floor. The orange-skinned presenter smiled thinly but made no attempt to interfere in the fight. The camera zoomed in until the screen was filled with two clawing, screaming, sweating bodies.

'Where did you get this?' Mr Roxdale asked.

'I found it in the garden,' said Mrs Torridge, innocently.

'Did it by any chance have washing on it?' asked Mr Roxdale.

'Oh, yes. But the washing was dry so I took it off and put it into the laundry room. You'll need these as well,' added Mrs Torridge, handing Mr Roxdale a large pair of yellow, silk knickers.

'What on earth are these?' demanded the surprised recipient of this largesse, holding up the knickers and examining them as though they were the evidence and he the prosecuting counsel in an important trial.

'Bloomers.'

'I can see that. But what do I need these for?'

'To stuff in my mouth,' explained Mrs Torridge, patiently, as though talking to a rather dim-witted child.

Mr Roxdale, his confusion enhanced, stared at her.

'For a gag,' said Mrs Torridge.

'You want me to stuff these bloomers in your mouth for a joke?' asked Mr Roxdale, who had abandoned the hope of finding a reason and now simply wanted to be sure of what was expected of him.

'No. A gag,' explained Mrs Torridge, patiently. 'To stop me shouting for help.'

'Ah!' said Mr Roxdale, understanding at last. He glanced at

the television screen again and watched in horror as three huge, black men in black uniforms pulled the two women apart. The orange-skinned man was still watching and saying nothing.

'Strictly speaking we should use a freshly laundered linen handkerchief,' said Mrs Torridge. 'But everyone here uses paper handkerchiefs and a paper handkerchief wouldn't work. I'd be able to eat it. Or at least chew it up and spit it out. So since I don't have a proper handkerchief these will have to do.'

'Whose are they?' demanded Mr Roxdale, looking inside the bloomers as though expecting to see some sign of ownership, a neatly sewn name tag perhaps.

'Oh, they're mine,' said Mrs Torridge. 'And they're freshly laundered. I wouldn't want to have anyone else's knickers in my mouth even if they were clean.'

'No, quite,' agreed Mr Roxdale. 'I can understand that.'

Mrs Torridge held her wrists out in front of her. 'So,' she said, tiring of all these preliminaries, 'tie me up then.'

'Shall I tie you up first? Or gag you first?' asked Mr Roxdale.

Mrs Torridge didn't answer. She looked slightly worried by this question. It was clearly not a query she had expected.

'Tie her up first, silly,' said Mrs Merivale, who like the others had turned away from the television and was staring at Mrs Torridge. 'If you gag her first she won't be able to tell you whether or not the knots are tight enough.'

'No, I suppose not,' agreed Mr Roxdale. 'I hadn't thought of that.' He picked up the clothes line and tested it by holding it in both hands and giving it a good yank. He dimly remembered reading about people tying one another up in an illustrated magazine he had found in a potting shed belonging to one of his customers. He seemed to remember that black stockings had been used instead of a clothes line.

On balance he decided that he was pleased that Mrs Torridge had asked him to help her. He had long believed that one should be prepared to try anything once and he was well aware that, at his age, he was unlikely to be showered with requests to tie people up. Slowly and gently, but thoroughly, he began to tie Mrs Torridge's hands and wrists.

'Why did he sniff coke?' Mr Livingstone asked Mrs Merivale. She looked at him, slightly puzzled.

'You said he sniffed coke,' said Mr Livingstone, nodding towards the television. 'I've never heard of anyone doing that before.'

'They get high on it,' said Mrs Merivale. 'Everyone on television does it when they want to get up high.'

'Good heavens,' said Mr Livingstone. 'You learn something every day, don't you? And you can use anthracite if you don't have coke?'

'I suppose so,' agreed Mrs Merivale who wasn't really listening.

'Dunno why they don't just use a ladder like everyone else,' said Mr Hewitt.

Mr Williams, looking for his friend, poked his head round the door and spotted Mr Roxdale. 'Are you ready?' he called.

'I won't be long,' replied Mr Roxdale. 'I'm just tying up Mrs Torridge.'

'Do you need any help?' asked Mr Williams, who did not seem to be in the slightest bit surprised by this piece of news.

'No, I can manage thank you,' replied Mr Roxdale, busily wrapping the final few yards of clothes line around Mrs Torridge's ample form. 'I'll be finished in a couple of minutes.'

'OK,' replied Mr Williams. 'I'll get my hat and wait for you in the hall.'

On the television screen a huge black man was explaining to the orange-skinned presenter how shyness had affected his life. As he spoke he prodded the presenter with a podgy, heavily ringed finger and halfway through his monologue he started rapping, clicking his fingers and bouncing around as he continued his tale of woe in the sort of clumsy semi-rhyming format which such singers affect. Sadly, no one at the Twilight Years Rest Home was watching and his audience there was confined to a shabby sofa, half a dozen easy chairs, a coffee table and a bowl of fruit. None of these involuntary members of the audience seemed in the slightest bit interested in the shy black man's enthusiastic performance.

Mr Livingstone stood up and announced that he was popping out to the coal shed.

CHAPTER FIFTY

Mrs Caldicot was standing on the doorstep saying goodbye to Dr Bence-Jones when Jenkins arrived to take her out for lunch.

'You had a big surgery today,' she said to the doctor. She waved to Jenkins and smiled at him. She saw him most days now but the very sight of him always made her feel good.

'You've got a lot of sick people here,' the doctor told her.

'Really?' said Mrs Caldicot, surprised. 'They all seem all right to me.'

'I've never known such a lot of sick people,' the doctor told her. 'The ones that aren't crippled with pain have suddenly developed infections.'

'Good heavens,' said Mrs Caldicot.

'Cystitis, sore throats, earaches – you name it they've got it,' he said. 'I've done nothing but sign prescriptions today. Make sure you take a trailer when you trundle off to the pharmacy.' And with a cheery wave he shuffled off in the direction of his Bentley which was, as usual, parked in the road outside.

'He's a wonderful old chap, isn't he?' said Jenkins, climbing up the steps to where Mrs Caldicot was standing in the front porch. 'How old is he?' he asked, as the elderly doctor headed slowly for his car.

'He's nearly ninety,' replied Mrs Caldicot.

'He's amazing,' said Jenkins. 'He must be the oldest practising doctor in the country.'

'And one of the very few I trust,' said Mrs Caldicot.

'Are you ready for lunch?' asked Jenkins.

'I feel awful about this. I tried to ring you but you'd left,' said Mrs Caldicot. 'And your mobile phone was switched off.'

'I usually do turn it off when I'm driving,' admitted Jenkins. 'It's the only peace I get these days.'

'I'm sorry about this but I really don't think I can come out for lunch,' said Mrs Caldicot sadly. 'One of our new residents is a sort of accountant and he's been going through the books for me.' She sighed. 'We've got a bit of a crisis I'm afraid.'

'What's the matter?'

'Well, the main problem is that the council keeps bringing in more rules,' said Mrs Caldicot. 'As soon as we've dealt with one problem they find something else. Every time they introduce a new regulation it costs us money.'

'And your outgoings are greater than your income?'

'On yes, and by quite a long way. The council have now told us that we've got to completely redo the kitchen. I had a letter this morning telling me that we've got to rip everything out and rebuild it from scratch. It's all to satisfy some new rules and it's not going to make the kitchen better or safer but it is going to cost a fortune.'

'Do you think your wonderful Mrs Merivale would make us some of her splendid sandwiches?' asked Jenkins.

'I'm sure she would,' said Mrs Caldicot.

'Good. Then let's have lunch in. And while we eat we'll have a brainstorming session and try and work out how best we can raise some money to pay for all these alterations.'

CHAPTER FIFTY ONE

'I tried sniffing coke,' said Mr Livingstone, who had returned to the lounge. 'But it didn't do anything for me. I tried some anthracite too. Nothing. I never budged off the ground.'

Mrs Merivale looked at him. 'You've got a black splodge on your nose,' she told him.

Mr Livingstone wiped his nose with his handkerchief. 'I took precautions,' he told her. 'I tied myself to the coal shed door.'

Mrs Merivale looked at him, puzzled.

'To stop me going too high,' he explained.

CHAPTER FIFTY TWO

'I don't suppose you know any rich eccentrics?' asked Jenkins. 'Kindly millionaires who want to give their money to a good cause?'

'I'm afraid not,' said Mrs Caldicot, sadly.

'Pity,' said Jenkins. 'You could have turned the Twilight Years Rest Home into a charity.'

'There's Mr Williams, of course,' said Mrs Caldicot. 'But he's already helped us a great deal. And I really won't let him give us any more.'

'Mr Williams? Which Mr Williams?'

'Our Mr Williams,' explained Mrs Caldicot. She suddenly blushed. 'He doesn't want it widely known,' she said. 'But if you promise not to breathe a word to anyone...'

'I promise,' said Jenkins.

'Well our Mr Williams is Mr Henry Williams.'

Jenkins stared at her for a moment and then, slowly, shook his head. 'I don't know anyone called Henry Williams,' he confessed. 'Should I?' Suddenly he smiled. 'The only Henry Williams I knew of was the photographer.' He paused. 'But he must have died ten or fifteen years ago.'

'He's not dead. He's very much alive,' said Mrs Caldicot. 'The last time I saw him he was standing outside the gate with Mr Roxdale, trying to sell flowers.'

'Your Mr Williams is the Henry Williams?' Jenkins could not hide his astonishment.

'He gave me a photograph to sell when he first came here,' said Mrs Caldicot. 'I sent it to a dealer in London whom Mr Williams recommended. He then sent us a cheque for £7,250. It was a signed print.'

Jenkins just stared at Mrs Caldicot. 'How many photographs has he got?'

'Oh, he's got a suitcase full of them,' said Mrs Caldicot. 'But he's got the negatives in the bank.'

'It's a licence to print money,' said Jenkins. 'He worked with

Cartier-Bresson didn't he? His later photographs of Paris in the 1950s are classics.'

'I don't know very much about him,' admitted Mrs Caldicot. 'I keep meaning to go to the library but I haven't had the time.'

'He's the photographer who took that famous picture of two lovers feeding pigeons at the top of the Eiffel Tower. You see it on postcards and tea towels all over the place. He must have made a fortune out of that picture alone.'

'He wants to give me some more photographs,' said Mrs Caldicot. 'But it doesn't seem right.'

'But why?' asked Jenkins. 'The photographs in his suitcase alone are worth more than he could ever spend. And the negatives – well, I don't think anyone could put a price on those.'

Mrs Caldicot thought for a while and then shook her head. 'I can't let him,' she said eventually.

'OK,' said Jenkins, smiling. 'So we discount the easy solution. Let's try more difficult answers. What about a jumble sale?' he asked taking a huge bite out of a cheese, pickle and tomato sandwich.

Mrs Caldicot looked at him. 'Do people still have jumble sales?' she asked.

'I don't really know,' admitted Jenkins. 'They've probably been superseded by charity shops, car boot sales and garage sales. But I don't see why you shouldn't hold a jumble sale if you'd like one. That should help bring in some money.'

'Do you think there are any rules and regulations governing the storage, display and sale of jumble?' asked Mrs Caldicot. The regulations with which the council had recently bombarded her had induced a certain amount of nervousness.

'Almost certainly,' replied Jenkins. 'But in my experience the people who maintain these regulations are not quick workers. If you advertise your jumble sale no more than a week or ten days before the event the chances of the local authority's jumble sale department hearing of it and being able to take effective action will, I suspect, be rather slim.'

'We could have stalls,' said Mrs Caldicot, who was warming to the idea. 'Throwing tennis balls at old china, guessing how many peas there are in a bottle, throwing buckets of water over the vicar – that sort of thing.'

'That's more the sort of thing you find at a fête rather than a jumble sale,' pointed out Jenkins.

'So why don't we have a fête and a jumble sale?' asked Mrs Caldicot, who was never slow to adapt. 'If the weather is good we could hold the whole thing on the front lawn.'

'And if it's wet?'

'Oh, it won't be,' said Mrs Caldicot confidently. 'It'll be a gloriously sunny day. Just warm enough but not too hot. A lovely blue sky with a few fluffy little clouds scattered around.' She sighed and smiled at Jenkins. 'It will be a gorgeous day,' she said, not leaving any room for dissent.,

'And if it does rain?'

Mrs Caldicot glared at him. 'There you go,' she said. 'You're being pessimistic.'

'I'm being practical!' insisted Jenkins.

'If, against all the odds, it does rain then everyone will just have to bring umbrellas,' said Mrs Caldicot. 'And I'll ask Mrs Roberts to persuade the landlord at the pub down the road to lend us those huge umbrellas he has in his beer garden.'

'But he'll need the umbrellas himself if it's raining.'

'No he won't. No one sits out in a beer garden if it's raining. The umbrellas are only there to keep the sun off. And if there's sunshine we won't need the umbrellas.'

Jenkins found himself unable to counter this argument. 'Well, you'll have to abandon the 'throwing water over the vicar' stall if it rains,' was all he said. 'People will be able to just watch him getting wet anyway.'

'You come into the lounge and make yourself comfortable,' said Mrs Caldicot, laughing. 'I'll bring you a nice cup of tea and some chocolate biscuits and we'll talk about it some more.' She wandered into the lounge ahead of Jenkins to see who was there and what was going on. Apart from the Merivales, who were sitting on the sofa holding hands and watching an old Walter Matthau movie on television, the only person present was Mrs Torridge.

'Good morning, everyone,' said Mrs Caldicot.

The Merivales turned, waved and greeted Mrs Caldicot.

Mrs Caldicot nodded back and gave them a little wave.

'Gkeytsk bwnkh kehgl!' said Mrs Torridge.

'Good morning, Mrs Torridge,' said Mrs Caldicot gaily.

'Good heavens!' said Jenkins, who had followed Mrs Caldicot into the lounge and only spotted Mrs Torridge when he followed Mrs Caldicot's gaze. 'What on earth has happened to Mrs Torridge?' he asked Mrs Caldicot.

'I don't know,' said Mrs Caldicot. 'What has happened to Mrs Torridge?' she asked the Merivales.

'Mr Roxdale tied her up and gagged her,' explained Mrs Merivale.

'Oh fine, that's all right then,' said Mrs Caldicot. She turned to Jenkins. 'Mr Roxdale tied her up and gagged her,' she explained.

'I heard,' said Jenkins. He bent a little closer to Mrs Caldicot, so that he wouldn't be overheard. 'I don't wish to be a prude,' he said, but is, er, is that sort of thing allowed?' He looked around and lowered his voice still further, as though concerned that someone might overhear what he was about to say. 'I mean, what would the local authority have to say if they knew one of your male residents was going around tying up the female residents?'

'Oh I don't think he makes a habit of it. In fact I don't think he's done it before,' said Mrs Caldicot. She turned to Mrs Torridge. 'Are you all right?' she asked.

'Gkwhwgn kehaklh!' replied Mrs Torridge, nodding her head. Mr Roxdale had done a very good job with the clothes line and with the gag. The yellow bloomers were held firmly in place with Mr Roxdale's tie.

'I think perhaps you ought to see what she's saying,' said Jenkins.

'Do you really think I should?' asked Mrs Caldicot.

'I do,' insisted Jenkins, who could see the headlines. 'Elderly Woman Found Bound And Gagged In Nursing Home. Cabbage War Heroine Guilty Of Neglect.'

Mrs Caldicot, who had great respect for Jenkins's intuition, unfastened Mr Roxdale's tie and carefully removed the yellow bloomers from Mrs Torridge's mouth. As she did so Mrs Torridge became increasingly agitated.

'Put them back!' she cried, the moment her mouth was empty of underwear.

'Are you all right?' asked Jenkins.

'Of course I'm all right!' said Mrs Torridge, rather crossly. 'I'm an escapologist. Put the gag back!' She sighed, wearily. 'I bet Harriet Houdini didn't have people ripping out her gags.'

'Harriet Houdini?' said Jenkins, puzzled. 'Who on earth is Harriet Houdini?'

'Harry's sister,' explained Mrs Torridge. 'She would have been famous if it hadn't been for Harry. Put the gag back. I was just beginning to get it free. Now I'll have to start all over again.'

'Today you're an escapologist?'

'Of course.'

'And Mr Roxdale tied you up because you asked him to?'

Mrs Torridge stared at Mrs Caldicot as though she had gone off her head. 'Yes, of course, he did,' she replied, clearly running out of patience. 'Now, will you put the gag back, please.' Mrs Torridge opened her mouth wide and put her head back, waiting for the gag to be reinserted.

Gingerly, Mrs Caldicot put a tiny portion of the yellow bloomers back into Mrs Torridge's mouth. Crossly Mrs Torridge tugged at the bloomers with her teeth, pulling as much of the material as she could into her own mouth. Then, she looked down at Mr Roxdale's tie, which was lying on her lap.

When the tie had been tied around her head to her complete satisfaction Mrs Torridge nodded her thanks and began again to struggle to free herself from her gag and the heavily knotted clothes line.

'You made a good job of that,' said Jenkins. 'Are you sure you haven't done it before?'

Mrs Caldicot looked at him.

'Sorry!' apologised Jenkins.

'I'll go and make you a cup of tea,' said Mrs Caldicot. 'Then we can talk some more about the jumble sale and the fête.'

'Don't forget the chocolate biscuits,' Jenkins called after her.

CHAPTER FIFTY THREE

After Mrs Caldicot had disappeared Jenkins turned and, for the first time, noticed Mr and Mrs Merivale.

'Good movie?' he asked them.

'Wonderful,' replied Mr Merivale.

'One of the best,' added Mrs Merivale. '*Hopscotch*.'

'Starring Walter Matthau,' said Mr Merivale.

'And Glenda Jackson,' added Mrs Merivale.

'She was a great comedy actress,' Mr Merivale pointed out. 'She made a lovely film with George Segal.' He screwed up his eyes, clearly trying to think of the title. 'What was it called, dear?' He asked his wife.

'*A Touch Of Class*,' replied Mrs Merivale.

'That's the one,' agreed Mr Merivale. 'But I like this one better.'

'Matthau is very funny,' agreed Mrs Merivale. She turned her head. 'I knew him, you know,' she told Jenkins.

'And Jack Lemmon,' added Mr Merivale. 'We knew them both. Great stars.'

'Great stars,' agreed Mrs Merivale. 'I know her too,' she said, nodding to the screen where Glenda Jackson was coming out of a Post Office in a town which Jenkins thought looked distinctly Bavarian.

'Did I overhear Mrs Caldicot say we're going to have a jumble sale and a fête?' asked Mrs Merivale.

'I think that's the plan,' said Jenkins.

'She'll want someone famous to open it,' said Mr Merivale. 'We could help. If you like.'

'We know lots of famous people,' said Mrs Merivale.

'That would be wonderful,' said Jenkins. 'Who can you get?' he asked, thinking that he ought, perhaps, to humour them. 'Who would you like?' asked Mr Merivale.

'Michael Caine? Sean Connery? Roger Moore?' suggested Mrs Merivale.

'We could ask Glenda,' said Mr Merivale.

'She's retired now. She's got plenty of time,' said Mrs Merivale.

'She's a Labour MP,' said Jenkins.

'That's what I said,' insisted Mrs Merivale. 'She's retired now. Got plenty of time.'

'Do we know that other chap who played Bond?' Mr Merivale asked his wife.

'George Lazenby?'

'No. We don't know him.'

'Timothy Dalton?'

'That's him. Do we know him?'

'I do,' replied Mrs Merivale. 'I'm not sure about you.'

'And there's another one,' said Mr Merivale.

'Pierce Brosnan,' said Jenkins.

'Know him,' said Mr Merivale without hesitation. 'Lovely chap. Really nice.'

'And Judy Dench,' said Mrs Merivale.

'She's in the Bond films now,' said Mr Merivale. 'She plays M.'

'Any one of those would be marvellous,' said Jenkins. 'But I expect they'll be very difficult to get hold of. They're probably all very busy people.'

'It depends on who's in the country,' said Mrs Merivale. 'Just let us know the date. And try to give us as much notice as you can.'

'Here's your tea and biscuits,' said Mrs Caldicot, approaching Jenkins and the Merivales. She carried a tray containing a pot of tea, two cups, a jug of hot water, milk, lemon, sugar and a plateful of biscuits. 'Would you two like a cup of tea?' she asked the Merivales.

'Oh no, thank you Mrs Caldicot,' said Mrs Merivale. 'It's very kind of you but we've already got a pot,' she nodded towards the table in front of them on which stood a large green teapot and the usual extras.

'We were just talking about your jumble sale,' said Mr Merivale. 'We'll help you find someone to open it.'

Mrs Caldicot, slightly surprised, looked at Jenkins then

turned back to Mr Merivale. 'That would be very nice of you,' she said.

'Do you have a date yet?' she asked.

'I thought about having it a week on Saturday,' said Mrs Caldicot.

'That's a bit soon, isn't it?' said Jenkins.

'No,' said Mrs Caldicot firmly. 'We're not going to spend months planning this. Let's just do it. A week on Saturday it is. Rain or shine.'

'We'd better go and make a few phone calls,' said Mrs Merivale. 'Can I use your office Mrs Caldicot?'

'Of course you can,' she replied. When the Merivales had gone Mrs Caldicot turned to Jenkins and smiled. 'They mean well,' she said.

'I know,' said Jenkins.

'You must know all sorts of famous people,' said Mrs Caldicot. 'People you've interviewed and so on.'

Jenkins looked at her.

'I know,' said Mrs Caldicot. 'I'm sorry. But I'm desperate.'

Jenkins sighed. 'I'll see who I can come up with,' he promised her.

'You're a darling,' said Mrs Caldicot, and to her surprise as much as his she kissed him on the cheek.

CHAPTER FIFTY FOUR

When the doorbell rang, several of the residents, together with Mrs Caldicot and Mrs Roberts, were sitting in the lounge watching an old Marx Brothers film. Jenkins had had to go back to his office.

'What's that noise?' Mr Merivale asked his wife.

'It's the rain, dear,' answered Mrs Merivale.

'Don't be silly,' laughed Mr Merivale. 'I don't believe in Father Christmas, let alone all that stuff about Rudolf.'

'It's the doorbell,' Mrs Roberts told them. 'I'll answer it.'
She got up and left the room. Mrs Caldicot and the rest continued
to watch as Chico sold Groucho another thick form book for the
horse races.

Mr Merivale, who had clearly been puzzled by something,
spoke again. 'It's not really Christmas is it?' he asked his wife.

'Ssshhh!' she whispered, holding a finger across her own
lips. 'No, it's not Christmas,' she assured him.

Mrs Roberts came back into the room. 'It's that Mr Muller-
thingy again,' she told Mrs Caldicot.

'Oh damn. What does he want?' asked Mrs Caldicot. Mr
Muller-Hawksmoor and Ms Jones BA had become regular visitors
to The Twilight Years Rest Home; like smells from bad drains
they were both unwelcome and difficult to get rid of.

'I don't know,' said Mrs Roberts. She blushed. 'I forgot to
ask. But he's got that Ms Jones with him. And they've both got
clipboards.'

Mrs Caldicot took a deep breath and rolled her eyes heaven-
wards. 'I suppose we'd better find out what they want,' she said,
heading for the front door and apologising to Mr Livingstone and
Mr Hewitt who were enjoying a game of bowls on the hall carpet.

'Ah, Mrs Caldicot,' said Muller-Hawksmoor, smiling
oleaginously. 'May Ms Jones BA and I come in?' He put one foot
in the hallway and started to walk forwards.

'What do you want?' demanded Mrs Caldicot, frowning.

Mr Muller-Hawksmoor halted, as though playing 'statues'
and the smile disappeared instantly. 'I have to tell you, Mrs
Caldicot,' he said, assuming his most pompous tone, 'that Ms Jones
BA and I are here as official representatives of the local Council.
We are here to conduct a staff and customer census and you are
legally obliged to allow us unhindered and unfettered entrance to
your establishment. It is our belief that you have a mismatched
staff-customer quota and if our investigations confirm this then
Ms Jones BA and I have the authority here,' and at this point Mr
Muller-Hawksmoor pulled a piece of paper out of his breast pocket
and waved it in Mrs Caldicot's direction, 'to apply a closure order
to this establishment'.

Mrs Caldicot stared for a moment, first at Mr Muller-Hawksmoor and then at Ms Jones BA. Finally, she stepped back and opened the door wider. 'I wouldn't dream of hindering or fettering either of you,' she told them.

'Good!' said Mr Muller-Hawksmoor, striding into the hall-way. 'Very wise, Mrs Caldicot.' The smile had reappeared. It was about as honest and as long-lasting as a car salesman's promise. Ms Jones BA followed Mr Muller-Hawksmoor. She didn't bother to smile.

'What on earth did all that mean?' whispered Mrs Roberts.

'I think it meant that they think we don't have enough members of staff,' said Mrs Caldicot. 'If they can prove that they'll shut us down.'

Silent with horror, Mrs Roberts just stared.

'Please do be careful,' said Mrs Caldicot, as she closed the front door. 'Mr Livingstone and Mr Hewitt are playing bowls.' She pointed to an onion about a yard short of the front door. 'I think that's what they call the 'jack',' she explained.

'We are...' began Mr Muller-Hawksmoor.

'Ouch!' interrupted Ms Jones BA, leaping into the air, drop-ping her clipboard and grabbing her ankle. She swore loudly and impressively and started hopping around the hallway as though she had suddenly decided to play a solitary game of hopscotch.

'What on earth's the matter?' asked Mrs Caldicot.

Ms Jones BA, still hopping around, let go of her ankle and pointed to a large turnip which had rolled to a halt alongside a radiator pipe. 'I was attacked with that ... weapon!' she shouted.

'Excuse me,' said Mr Livingstone, with a polite smile. 'Can I have my ball back, please?' He squeezed between Mrs Caldicot and Ms Jones BA and picked up the turnip which had collided with Ms Jones BA's leg. 'Don't you worry about getting in the way,' he told Ms Jones BA with another rather gummy smile. 'Mr Hewitt said I can take my go again.' Mr Livingstone sometimes took his teeth out and left them in a glass in his bathroom. 'They cost me a fortune,' he once explained. 'I don't want to wear them out.'

'You're a menace!' snarled Ms Jones BA at Mr Livingstone.

'You'll be hearing from my solicitors. You could have broken my leg.'

'I beg your pardon,' interrupted Mrs Caldicot. 'But if you're contemplating legal action I feel I should perhaps point out that I did warn you that Mr Livingstone and Mr Hewitt were playing bowls.'

'No you didn't!' protested Ms Jones BA. She turned to Mr Muller-Hawksmoor for support. 'Did she?'

Mr Muller-Hawksmoor looked at her, looked at Mrs Caldicot and then looked embarrassed. 'Well, actually, I think she did say something of the kind,' he admitted.

Ms Jones BA, gave her ankle another rub and picked up her clipboard. She muttered something inaudible under her breath.

'Where would you like to start?' Mrs Caldicot asked them brightly.

'Oh don't you worry your-little-old-self about us,' said Mr Muller-Hawksmoor, brightening a little. 'You get on with your daily duties. I'm sure you've got lots to do. Floors to sweep, beds to make, lavatories to clean – that sort of thing. We don't want to interfere with the smooth running of your establishment. We'll just wander around and take a few notes. Just pretend we're not here.'

Mrs Caldicot had put up with Mr Caldicot, also a condescending, patronising man, for most of her adult life. Her patience with such people had long since evaporated. She turned away, marched into her office and slammed the door, feeling her cheeks redden with fury. 'You stupid, arrogant, preening, self-satisfied, pea-brained moron,' she said out loud. She was aware that it wasn't the best she could have done, as insults go, but it had passion on its side and it made her feel a little better.

Seconds later someone knocked timidly on the door.

'Yes!' shouted Mrs Caldicot through the closed door. 'Who is it? What do you want?'

The door opened a few inches. 'It's me,' whispered Mrs Roberts nervously poking her head through the gap. 'Have you got someone with you?' she looked around. 'I wondered ... I thought perhaps ... would you like a cup of tea?'

Mrs Caldicot opened the door and let Mrs Roberts in. 'I'm sorry,' she said. She put her arm around Mrs Roberts's waist and gave her a cuddle of apology. 'That man infuriates me,' she explained. 'I could happily throttle him.'

'Have a cup of tea instead,' Mrs Roberts suggested.

'How long do you think I'd get if I throttled him?' Mrs Caldicot asked her friend. 'Do you think Mr Roxdale would bury the body for me? Of course I'd have to throttle Ms Jones BA as well. But that would be a pleasure too.' She thought for a moment and smiled to herself. 'How long would it take Mr Roxdale to dig a hole big enough for the two of them?'

'I'm not sure,' said Mrs Roberts, quite seriously. 'Do you want me to ask him?'

Mrs Caldicot laughed. 'No, Mrs Roberts!' she said.

'OK,' said Mrs Roberts. 'I think that's probably wise anyway,' she added confidentially.

'But I will have a cup of tea,' said Mrs Caldicot. She thought for a moment. 'And a plateful of calorie free Jammy Dodgers,' she added. 'I need cheering up.'

'Shall I offer Mr Muller-Hawksmoor and Ms Jones BA some tea and biscuits?' Mrs Roberts asked.

'Certainly not,' replied Mrs Caldicot. 'They don't need cheering up and if they do we're not going to do it for them. If they want tea they can pop out to a teashop. We've got better things to do than make tea for them.' This undeniably petty moment of vengeance made her feel much better. As Mrs Roberts disappeared and headed for the kitchen she sat down behind her desk and started to open the second post. It was, just like the first post, largely composed of circulars and bills. The circulars she tossed, unopened, into the waste-paper basket. The bills she carefully unfolded and then slid them into the cardboard file where Mr Twist now kept such items. 'You have to take your turn,' she told the invoices as she slid them out of sight. 'No cheating and no queue jumping.'

Mrs Caldicot had just completed this small and unrewarding task, and was waiting patiently for Mrs Roberts's return with tea and Jammy Dodgers, when she heard the unmistakeable booming voice of Mr Muller-Hawksmoor shouting her name.

'Oh no,' she thought, her heart sinking. 'What does he want now?' She leapt up from her chair, shimmied neatly around her desk, opened the door into the hallway and found a red-faced Mr Muller-Hawksmoor standing so close to her that she automatically stepped back a pace or two.

'There is a woman in your lounge who is bound and gagged!' shouted Mr Muller-Hawksmoor, his eyes bulging and his face an unhealthy shade of red.

'Oh, yes, that'll be Mrs Torridge,' explained Mrs Caldicot, calmly.

'You knew?' exploded an incredulous Mr Muller-Hawksmoor. 'You knew about this?'

'Of course,' said Mrs Caldicot. 'It's my responsibility to know what is going on.'

'B...b...but,' stuttered Mr Muller-Hawksmoor, struggling to overcome a rare attack of speechlessness. 'You can't just go around tying up your customers.'

'Oh, I didn't tie her up,' said Mrs Caldicot. 'And she's not a customer. She's a friend.'

'If you didn't tie her up who did?' he roared.

'I think it was Mr Roxdale.'

'And just who is Mr Roxdale?'

'Another guest. He lives here too.'

'He's another of your customers?'

'I do wish you wouldn't use the word 'customer'. It makes me feel as though I'm running an off-licence or a hairdressing salon.'

'What we call him is utterly irrelevant,' said Mr Muller-Hawksmoor.

'I disagree. I think that what we call him is very relevant,' insisted Mrs Caldicot.

'Whatever we call him, the man should clearly be locked up,' said Mr Muller-Hawksmoor firmly. 'He's nothing more than a common pervert.' He shook a bony finger at Mrs Caldicot. 'And you aren't a lot better,' he told her.

Suddenly, from behind Mr Muller-Hawksmoor, there came a blood curdling scream.

The colour drained from Mr Muller-Hawksmoor's face. He tucked his clipboard under his arm and turned towards the source of the cry. 'Good heavens!' he cried. 'What the hell was that?'

'It sounded like Mrs Torridge,' said Mrs Caldicot. 'It came from the lounge.'

'Ye Gods!' said Mr Muller-Hawksmoor. 'It sounded terrifying. We'd better go and see what the hell it was.' He moved out of the way so that Mrs Caldicot could get ahead of him and lead the way. Mrs Caldicot suspected that this was done more through cowardice than any desire to behave like a gentleman.

'It did sound like Mrs Torridge,' said Mrs Caldicot, hurrying across the hall. She spoke over her shoulder. 'But it can't be. She's gagged.'

Mrs Caldicot was right about the scream coming from Mrs Torridge but wrong about her being gagged.

'Just look at what this stupid woman has done!' shouted Mrs Torridge angrily, when she saw Mrs Caldicot.

'What's the matter with her?' whimpered Ms Jones BA, who was cowering on the far side of the room, and appeared to be trying, with very marginal success, to hide behind her clipboard. She was not a big woman. But the clipboard was smaller.

'Oh dear,' said Mrs Caldicot to Ms Jones BA. She shook her head disapprovingly. 'You really shouldn't have done that, dear.'

'But she's tied up!' explained Ms Jones BA, pointing to Mrs Torridge. 'And she was gagged.'

'I'm going to call the police!' said Mr Muller-Hawksmoor, who had brought up the rear and was now standing staring at a scene which he was clearly having some difficulty in believing. He spoke firmly and with authority.

'Don't be silly,' said Mrs Caldicot. 'The police won't want to arrest Ms Jones BA. What she did may have been stupid but she thought she was being helpful.'

Mr Muller-Hawksmoor stared at her open-mouthed. 'Why on earth should the police want to arrest Ms Jones BA?' he demanded. 'She didn't bind and gag this unfortunate woman.' He paused and frowned, clearly thinking hard. 'She was the one who ungagged her!' he announced.

'But Mrs Torridge wanted to be tied and gagged,' Mrs Caldicot pointed out.

Mr Muller-Hawksmoor and Ms Jones BA looked at Mrs Torridge and then at Mrs Caldicot.

'It's a sort of game she plays,' explained Mrs Caldicot. 'It doesn't do anyone any harm.'

'Who are you calling an unfortunate woman?' demanded Mrs Torridge, angrily.

'Shall I put the gag back in, dear?' asked Mrs Merivale, who, disturbed by the noise, had temporarily moved away from the television set.

'Yes, please,' said Mrs Torridge, gratefully. 'I'd nearly got rid of it by myself,' she muttered, almost under her breath. 'That's twice.'

'Now don't exaggerate dear,' said Mrs Merivale, giving her a soothing but at the same time admonitory pat on the shoulder. 'I don't think you'd nearly got that gag out at all.'

'Well I was making progress,' said Mrs Torridge, a little sulkily.

It was the last thing she said for a while. Mrs Merivale picked the now sodden yellow bloomers off Mrs Torridge's lap and stuffed them neatly in Mrs Torridge's mouth.

'Wait!' said Mr Muller-Hawksmoor. 'What on earth is going on here?'

'Mrs Merivale is replacing Mrs Torridge's gag,' explained Mrs Caldicot patiently.

'Do you mean this woman *really* wants to be gagged?' demanded Mr Muller-Hawksmoor.

'Yes,' confirmed Mrs Caldicot.

'Is this a regular occurrence?' demanded Mr Muller-Hawksmoor.

'Oh no,' said Mrs Caldicot. 'It's just for today. At least I think it is. Mrs Torridge think's she's Harriet Houdini.'

'And just who is Harriet Houdini?' demanded Mr Muller-Hawksmoor.

'Harry's sister,' explained Mrs Caldicot. She looked at Mrs Torridge, waiting for her to explain. But Mrs Torridge was gagged and Mrs Merivale was tying the yellow bloomers in place with Mr Roxdale's tie. 'As I understand it Harriet Houdini was rather over-shadowed by her brother but Mrs Torridge believes that she was an impressive escape artist in her own right.'

'Well I've never heard of Harriet Houdini,' snorted Mr Muller-Hawksmoor, rather unwisely forgetting about Ms Jones BA's presence. 'And I don't care who she was or how good at it she may have been,' he added, compounding the error.

'Please remember that women have been oppressed for cen-turies,' Ms Jones BA reminded him. 'My sister Harriet Houdini is simply another example of male chauvinism.'

'Had you ever heard of Harriet Houdini?' demanded Mr Muller-Hawksmoor.

'No,' admitted Ms Jones BA. 'And that's just the point, isn't it?' The relationship between two council employees was deterio-rating rapidly.

'Yesterday she was Queen Elizabeth I,' said Mrs Caldicot, who thought she ought to interfere before the two social workers came to blows. 'We all had to curtsey.'

'I'm not interested in any of this piffle,' snorted Mr Muller-Hawksmoor, unpleasantly. He was, thought Mrs Caldicot, an exceedingly easy man to dislike. She now wished she had not interfered but had allowed the dispute between him and Ms Jones BA to follow its natural course.

'Well, not the men, of course,' added Mrs Caldicot. 'They had to bow.'

'I don't know what sort of establishment you are accustomed to running but now that you're in the retirement home business you simply cannot allow your customers to tie one another up.'

'They don't make a habit of it,' Mrs Caldicot reassured him. 'But I think you will find that, according to articles 93 and 94 of the appropriate international human rights legislation, Mrs Torridge has a perfect right to have herself bound and gagged, if that is what she wants.' She had no idea whether or not this was true. But it sounded convincing and she had learnt enough to real-ise that people who live by the rule book are for ever conscious that they can sometimes die by it too.

Mr Muller-Hawksmoor strode over to Mrs Torridge's chair. 'Did you ask to be tied up and gagged?' he demanded. Mrs Torridge stared up at him, unblinkingly.

'Mrs Torridge has a gag in,' said Ms Jones BA, who had emerged from behind her clipboard.

'I know she's got a gag in!' snapped Mr Muller-Hawksmoor.

'Would you like me to remove the gag?' asked Ms Jones BA.

'I don't think that's a terribly good idea,' said Mrs Caldicot. 'I think Mrs Torridge will be very upset if you do that again.'

Mr Muller-Hawksmoor, turned round and glared at his assistant. 'I don't think it would be a good idea at this stage to remove the gag,' he said, speaking through gritted teeth.

'Would you like me to call the police?' asked Ms Jones BA.

'No, thank you,' said Mr Muller-Hawksmoor.

'If you want to talk to her while she has the gag in place, we will have to create a communications code,' Ms Jones BA pointed out.

Mr Muller-Hawksmoor, turned his head and stared at her. 'Thank you, Ms Jones BA,' he said icily. 'Thank you so much for your help.' He turned back to Mrs Torridge. 'I am going to ask you some very simple questions,' he said. 'Do you understand that?'

Mrs Torridge stared at him.

'Nod if you understand me,' said Mr Muller-Hawksmoor.

Mrs Torridge slowly but firmly nodded her head.

'There you are, Ms Jones BA!' said Mr Muller-Hawksmoor proudly. 'We now have a communications system which will enable us to talk to Mrs Torridge.'

Ms Jones BA said nothing.

'Did you ask to be bound and gagged?' Mr Muller-Hawksmoor asked Mrs Torridge. 'Was it something you voluntarily requested, of your own free will? Or were you tied up and gagged against your will? Is it true that Mr Roxdale was responsible? If so, would you like us to call the police and have Mr Roxdale arrested?'

Confused by this flurry of questions Mrs Torridge said nothing.

'I think you'll have to ask one question at a time, Mr Muller-Hawksmoor,' suggested Ms Jones BA, perhaps unwisely. 'If you keep the questions simple so that she can just nod for 'yes' and shake her head for 'no'...'

'I do realise that, Ms Jones BA,' said Mr Muller-Hawksmoor, speaking to his assistant through teeth now gritted more thoroughly than any icy winter road. 'I'm not a complete fool,' he added.

Mrs Caldicot, who had been watching this bizarre exchange with considerable pleasure, suddenly became aware of someone standing next to her. She turned her head. It was Mrs Roberts.

'I'm sorry to bother you, Mrs Caldicot,' said Mrs Roberts quietly, but just loud enough for Mr Muller-Hawksmoor and Ms Jones BA to overhear. 'But if you can spare a few moments you're needed in your office.'

'Excuse me,' said Mrs Caldicot, turning to Mr Muller-Hawksmoor.

'Of course, of course,' said Mr Muller-Hawksmoor, with an irritated wave of his hand. He had forgotten that Mrs Caldicot was still there. 'You attend to your business.'

Mrs Caldicot followed Mrs Roberts into her office.

'What is it?' asked Mrs Caldicot.

'Can you deal with that?' asked Mrs Roberts, nodding to a nice looking cup of tea and a plateful of Jammy Dodgers on her desk.

Mrs Caldicot beamed at Mrs Roberts. 'Oh, I should think so,' she said. 'Where are yours?'

'In the kitchen,' said Mrs Roberts.

'Well smuggle them in here,' insisted Mrs Caldicot. 'Let's have a little party.'

Chapter Fifty Five

The arrival of Mr Muller-Hawksmoor and Ms Jones BA had not gone unnoticed among the other residents of the Twilight Years Rest Home.

'What do they want?' Mr Livingstone asked Mr Merivale,

who had slipped out of the lounge and, followed faithfully by Miss Nightingale and Mrs Bartholomew, was hurrying around the house warning the others that the enemy was within.

'I don't know,' admitted Mr Merivale.

'They're doing a census,' explained Mr Hewitt. 'They're going to count us all,' he explained. 'I think they're trying to prove that there aren't enough staff members for the number of residents.'

'Are you sure?'

Mr Hewitt nodded. 'I heard him say they'd come to do a census when Mrs Caldicot let them in.'

'I don't want to be counted,' said Mr Livingstone. 'Do you?'

'Certainly not,' replied Mr Hewitt. 'They'll be wanting to tattoo us with numbers next.'

'Do we have to let them count us?'

'I don't think so.'

'Right,' said Mr Livingstone. He closed his eyes and thought for a moment. 'I've got a plan,' he announced proudly.

The others waited.

'We'll just keep moving around,' said Mr Livingstone. 'Running up and down the stairs and hiding in cupboards. That sort of thing.'

The others looked terribly disappointed at this. Running up and down the stairs was not their forte and none of them would have put 'hiding in cupboards' at the top of their lists of favourite things to do on a dull afternoon.

'And we'll add to the confusion by dressing up in different clothes,' continued Mr Livingstone. 'I know what these people are like. We all look the same to them.'

The others recognised the truth in what he said and looked more interested. They liked the idea of dressing up.

'I like that idea very much,' said Miss Nightingale. 'Can I dress up as Florence?'

'Florence who?'

'Florence Nightingale.'

'Of course you can,' said Mr Livingstone. He stopped and thought for a moment. 'Have you got anything suitable to wear?'

'Oh yes,' said Miss Nightingale. 'I've got an old nurse's uniform. I bought it at a car boot sale.'

'Why on earth did you do that, dear?' asked Mrs Merivale, who enjoyed jumble sales but who always managed to resist the temptation to buy things for which she could not immediately think of a practical application. She would buy a potato peeler for ten pence but not a first edition by Charles Dickens for a pound.

'No one else wanted it so I got it for a shilling,' explained Miss Nightingale. 'Well, five of those new pennies.' She looked thoughtful for a moment. 'I've never actually worn it,' she admitted. 'But it looks plenty big enough.'

'I think that's a terrific idea,' said Mr Hewitt. 'If we dress up and run around the house Muller-Hawksmoor and that funny BA woman will think there are more of us than there actually are...'

'Exactly!' said Mr Livingstone, triumphantly; delighted that his idea had received such approbation.

'...but that's not actually a terribly good idea,' continued Mr Merivale. 'If Mr Muller-Hawksmoor thinks that there are more of us than there really are, Mrs Caldicot will get into even more trouble than she would have got into if we hadn't done anything.' The others all looked at him, displaying roughly equal quantities of alarm and puzzlement. Although they loved Mrs Caldicot very much and did not want to do anything which would make things worse for her they didn't yet quite understand just how confusing Mr Muller-Hawksmoor could possibly cause trouble for Mrs Caldicot. 'We've got to convince him that there are enough members of staff for the number of residents,' explained Mr Merivale. 'If we convince him that there are more residents than there really are he will also expect there to be far more nurses than there really are.'

The others thought about this for a while.

'Do you know, I think he's right,' said Miss Nightingale at last. The others nodded their agreement. Mr Merivale, who had been waiting for the result with all the nervousness of a politician on polling night, looked very relieved.

'Of course he's right,' said Mrs Merivale instantly. For her loyalty to her husband always came first.

'Let's go and find your uniform!' Mr Merivale said to Miss Nightingale.

She headed for her room. The rest of the residents hurried after her. Mr Livingstone, not a man to dwell on disappointment, hurried after her with them.

CHAPTER FIFTY SIX

'We're sunk,' said Mrs Caldicot gloomily.

'Why?' asked Mrs Roberts.

'They'll close us down,' said Mrs Caldicot. 'Every residential home is supposed to have the right proportion of staff members to residents. Muller-Hawksmoor will close us down today.' She paused. 'With great glee,' she added.

'But we've got the Merivales doing the cooking and Mr Roxdale doing the gardens,' Mrs Roberts pointed out.

'Yes, but you and I are the only official, full-time paid members of staff,' Mrs Caldicot pointed out. 'As far as the Council is concerned the others don't count.'

'And because of that they'll close us down?'

'Yes.'

'How many more members of staff do we need?'

'One would do,' said Mrs Caldicot. She sighed miserably. 'But where am I going to find someone at such short notice?'

'Do we need somebody now?'

'Now,' agreed Mrs Caldicot. 'We need another nurse on duty while Muller-Hawksmoor and Ms Jones BA are here.'

'Oh dear,' said Mrs Roberts.

'I think that sums it up quite nicely,' agreed Mrs Caldicot. 'They'll close us down,' she said, flatly. 'Without one other member of staff we're in breach of EU regulations.' She took another Jammy Dodger and bit it in two.

Suddenly Mrs Roberts's face brightened up. 'I've got an idea!' she said. 'Why don't I ask Miss Smith to help us out?'

Mrs Caldicot, munching on the first half of her Jammy Dodger, looked up. 'Who's Miss Smith?'

'A friend of mine. She works at the 'Happy Years Retirement Home' round the corner.'

'How on earth can she help?' asked Mrs Caldicot.

'If she comes round we'll have another member of staff, won't we?'

Mrs Caldicot stared at Mrs Roberts. 'Can we do that?' she asked.

'Of course we can. Anyway, she hates bureaucrats too.'

'It's a bit dishonest, isn't it?' said Mrs Caldicot, slightly nervously.

'We're just trying to satisfy their silly rules,' Mrs Roberts pointed out.

Mrs Caldicot swallowed the biscuit she had been chewing, leant across the desk and lowered her voice. 'Do you think it will work?'

'I don't know,' admitted Mrs Roberts. 'But it might. And what have we got to lose? If we don't try they're going to close us down anyway.'

'Ring her,' said Mrs Caldicot firmly. She put the other half of the Jammy Dodger into her mouth. 'Hrink jher!'

Mrs Roberts picked up the telephone.

'Miss Smith, we're in trouble,' she said, moments later. 'Can you help us out?'

There were some sympathetic sounds from the other end of the telephone.

'We're got the inspectors in and we're a nurse short,' Mrs Roberts explained. She listened, smiled, nodded, said 'thank you', put the telephone down and turned to Mrs Caldicot. 'She understood. She says she'll come straight round,' she said. 'She'll be here in five minutes.'

CHAPTER FIFTY SEVEN

The good news was that Miss Nightingale had found her nurse's uniform. The bad news was that it didn't fit her.

'I can't understand it,' she said, as full of woe as a person can be over an outfit which does not fit. The dress wasn't long but it looked as though it had been built for a prop forward. The top half of the dress hung loose in every possible direction and the sleeves were so long that they completely covered her finger tips.

'Maybe we could adjust it,' suggested Miss Nightingale, gloomily looking down at the ill-fitting uniform.

'I don't think so,' said Mrs Merivale sadly. She was standing behind Miss Nightingale and examining the size printed on the label at the back. 'It's an XXXXL,' she announced. 'I think it must have been built for a rugby player.'

In fact she was closer to the truth than she perhaps suspected. The nurse's uniform had, in fact, arrived at the jumble sale where Miss Nightingale had found it from a theatrical costumier who had hired it out to large young gentlemen looking for something saucy to wear at fancy dress parties.

'Who on earth is going to wear it?' asked Mr Livingstone. 'It's miles too big for any of us.'

'Hello, everyone!' said Jenkins, suddenly appearing, as though from nowhere. 'I wondered where you'd all got to!'

CHAPTER FIFTY EIGHT

'I can't wear this!' protested Jenkins, as he was hurried along the landing towards the staircase. For the fifth time he stopped and stared at himself in a mirror.

'Stop admiring yourself!' said Mr Roxdale.

'Men can be so vain,' said Miss Nightingale. 'That's at least ten times he's looked at himself.'

'Give us a twirl!' suggested Mr Merivale, cruelly.

'Actually, I hate to say this,' said Mr Roxdale, who didn't at all. 'But that dress really suits you.' He stood back and rubbed his chin thoughtfully. 'You actually do look very nice.'

And the truth was that the uniform fitted Jenkins very well.

'I'm a respectable editor. I have a position to uphold. I can't be seen like this!' said Jenkins, though he immediately felt so embarrassed at the pomposity of what he had said that he knew that he would have to go through with it.

'I have to admit that if I weren't a happily married man I could quite fancy you,' said Mr Merivale. He turned to Mr Roxdale who was standing next to him. 'Hasn't he got lovely legs?'

'Amazing,' agreed Mr Roxdale, admiringly. 'They do say men have better legs than women.'

Mrs Merivale had lent Jenkins a wig which, she said, she sometimes wore on rather special occasions. Two grapefruit and an appropriate undergarment (loaned by Mrs Merivale) had been used to help fill in the baggy portion of the front of the dress. And Mrs Merivale had done Jenkins's make-up so effectively that when he looked in the mirror he had to touch his chin with his forefinger to reassure himself that he truly was looking in a mirror.

'Ouch!' cried Jenkins. He turned round. 'Who did that?'

'You've got a lovely bottom too,' said Mr Roxdale.

'Well, I'd be grateful if you'd leave it alone,' said Jenkins.

'It was just a playful slap,' said Mr Roxdale. 'I thought you'd be flattered.'

'You are a terrible sexist pig, you know,' complained Jenkins. 'It's men like you who give men a bad name. If you do that again I'll bash you with my handbag.'

'Gosh,' said Mr Roxdale. 'You make more fuss about a little slap on the bottom than a real woman would.'

'You try slapping me on the bottom and see what it gets you!' said Miss Nightingale sternly.

'Why would I want to slap you on the bottom?' demanded Mr Roxdale, genuinely confused by this intervention, not to mention slightly horrified by the very thought of slapping Miss Nightingale on the bottom. He glanced across at the bottom in question and shuddered.

'We'd better get you downstairs and counted,' said Mr Livingstone.

'What's wrong with my bottom?' asked Miss Nightingale, full of indignation. Mr Roxdale tried to melt into the background.

'They'll spot that I'm a fraud in seconds!' protested Jenkins.

'No they won't,' insisted Mr Merivale.

'The minute I open my mouth they'll realise I'm not a woman,' protested Jenkins.

This comment was so obviously accurate that no one said anything for a few moments.

'So, keep your mouth shut,' said Mr Roxdale eventually. 'Don't say anything!' he added.

'But if they're doing a census they're bound to ask me my name,' said Jenkins.

'Try talking like a woman,' said Mr Roxdale. 'Let's see what you sound like.'

'What shall I say?'

'Say your name?'

'My name is Jenkins,' said Jenkins, in a rather bizarre falsetto.

'Not your real name,' said Mr Livingstone, despairingly.

'What name shall I give then?' asked Jenkins.

'Doris,' said Mr Merivale. 'You look like a Doris to me.'

'What the hell does a Doris look like?' demanded Jenkins.

'You,' replied Mr Merivale. 'You're definitely a Doris.'

'Doris what?'

'Day?' suggested Mr Merivale.

'Don't be silly. He doesn't look the slightest bit like Doris Day,' said Mrs Merivale.

'Dolittle,' suggested Miss Nightingale.

'Dolittle?' said Jenkins, puzzled. 'Why Dolittle?'

'Because it goes nicely with Doris.'

Jenkins shook his head. 'I don't like Doris much,' he said, reverting to his true voice. 'But I like Dolittle even less. It reminds me of that daft bloke who talked to animals. It isn't,' he paused, searching for the appropriate word. 'It isn't believable. I want something believable.'

'Night,' suggested Mr Williams. He paused. The enthusiasm

for his suggestion seemed muted. 'Knight,' he said. 'With a 'K'.'

'Doris Knight,' said Jenkins to himself. He repeated the name. 'Actually, I quite like that,' he admitted. 'It sounds quite good.' He tried out the falsetto again. 'Doris Knight. Hmmm. Yes, I like that.'

'He doesn't sound very convincing, does he?' said Miss Nightingale to everyone in general and no one in particular.

'I'll tell them you've got a sore throat,' said Mr Merivale. 'I'll come with you and speak for you.'

'Do you think that will work?' asked Jenkins. He seemed unconvinced.

'It will have to,' said Mr Merivale with a sigh. He led the way. 'Come on, Doris.'

Doris followed him down the stairs.

CHAPTER FIFTY NINE

Ms Jones BA was in the kitchen, checking the cupboards. She and Mr Muller-Hawksmoor had split up so that they could search the house more efficiently.

'Hello there, can I help you?' asked Mr Merivale.

Ms Jones BA, looking slightly embarrassed, shut the door to the cupboard she had been examining. 'We're doing a census,' she explained. 'We're checking the customer-staff ratio.'

'Good heavens!' said Mr Merivale. 'You don't want to waste your time doing that.' He tried to laugh at the thought, though the noise he made sounded more like a drain emptying. 'There are so many members of staff here that we spend our days falling over them.'

'As far as we are aware Mrs Caldicot and Mrs Roberts are the only full-time members of staff,' said Ms Jones BA coldly.

'And there's my wife and myself,' said Mr Merivale.

'You may help out,' said Ms Jones BA coldly. 'But you're registered as customers. You can't be staff as well.'

'Oh.' Mr Merivale sounded disappointed. 'And there's Doris,' he added.

'Doris?' repeated Ms Jones BA frowning. 'Who's Doris?'

'Doris Knight,' said Mr Merivale. 'She's around here somewhere.' He turned round and jumped slightly when he discovered that Doris was standing right behind him.

'There you are. What did I tell you? There are so many staff members in this place that they follow you around all over the place. Can't get a minute's peace and quiet.'

Mr Roxdale, Miss Nightingale, Mr Livingstone and the rest of the residents were lined up behind Doris.

'Your name is Doris?' said Ms Jones BA, consulting her clipboard.

'Yes,' replied Mr Merivale. 'She's Doris.'

'She's not on this list,' said Ms Jones BA.

'She's new,' replied Mr Merivale.

'She can answer for herself, can't she?' said Ms Jones BA.

'She's very shy,' said Mr Merivale. At the very same moment Doris pointed to her throat. 'Sore throat!' she rasped hoarsely in a strange falsetto. 'And she's got a sore throat,' Mr Merivale added, without a moment's hesitation.

Ms Jones BA stared at Doris as though she thought she knew her. 'Haven't we met somewhere before?' she said.

'Oh I expect you've seen her around,' said Mr Merivale. 'She's always rushing around with a duster or a syringe. Polishing here, injecting there.'

'I thought you said she was new?'

'She is. But she's already done a lot of rushing around. Amazing hard worker.'

'Dusters and syringes?' said Ms Jones BA, putting all the emphasis on the second word. 'Polishing and injecting?' Once again the emphasis was on the second word. She glared at Doris searchingly. 'Are you a nurse or a cleaner?'

'She does a bit of both,' said Mr Merivale, quickly. 'We don't have any union demarcation rules here.'

'It's most unusual to hear of nurses doing the dusting,' said Ms Jones BA. 'And it would be illegal for a cleaner to give injections.'

'Oh she's fully qualified,' said Mr Merivale.

'Loads of diplomas,' said Mr Livingstone.

Doris looked down, as though overcome by modesty. His gaze fell upon his own black, size twelve, lace-up brogues. There hadn't been time to find any more suitable footwear. He lifted his eyes quickly.

'I think I'd better ask Mrs Caldicot about Doris,' said Ms Jones BA, marching out of the kitchen.

She was very upset about this new discovery. It didn't look as though Mrs Caldicot was short of staff after all. And if Mrs Caldicot wasn't short of staff she and Mr Muller-Hawksmoor wouldn't be able to close down the retirement home. Unlike Mr Muller-Hawksmoor she had no financial incentive to put Mrs Caldicot out of business. She was doing it for sheer, unadulterated pleasure. She was doing it for fun. She liked her work.

Ms Jones BA was feeling very glum and very aggrieved as she headed up the stairs looking for Mrs Caldicot.

Chapter Sixty

'One of your grapefruit is slipping,' muttered Mr Livingstone to Doris.

Doris looked down. 'Oh damn.' 'He' unbuttoned his dress, slipped a hand inside and began to make the necessary adjustments. 'How on earth do women manage?' he demanded, in a whisper.

'I don't think they ever face quite that problem,' whispered Mr Livingstone to Doris. 'I'm speaking from memory, and memory can sometimes be very misleading, but I don't remember ever coming across a woman who filled her bra with grapefruit.'

'No. I suppose not,' sighed Doris. 'If this goes on much longer I think I'll have breast reduction surgery. I'm sure I can cope with being flat-chested.' His left bosom slipped through his fingers, slid down inside his dress and landed on the floor with something of a thud.

'Damn!' said Doris, forgetting his falsetto, his sore throat and his shyness.

Appropriately, the grapefruit rolled underneath a large chest. It was a large stripped pine chest of drawers, but it was a large chest.

'I'll go and get you another,' said Mr Livingstone. 'We can always get that one back later.'

'There aren't any more,' said Mrs Merivale.

'No more grapefruit?'

'No. We only had two left. Those two.'

'Damn!' said Doris again. 'Then we'll have to get this one back. I can't go around looking lopsided.' He fell to his knees and tried to reach under the chest.

'Take the other one out,' suggested Mr Livingstone, still standing. 'We could say you've had that breast reduction surgery.'

Doris turned his head and glowered up at him. 'Don't be silly,' 'he' snapped. 'This dress needs a bosom. And anyway I'm not going around looking shapeless and flat-chested. I've got my pride, you know.'

'But a moment ago you said...'

'I changed my mind,' insisted Doris, turning back so that he could concentrate on searching for his missing grapefruit. 'Woman's prerogative.' He sat up for a moment and adjusted his remaining, solitary breast which had slipped out of position and was threatening to escape and join its companion in exile. 'If I've got to be a woman I'm certainly not going to be a flat-chested one.'

'I'll help you,' said Mr Livingstone. He walked to the front door, collected an umbrella from a stand, and walked back to where Doris was on his knees. He looked up, slightly alarmed at the sight of the umbrella but Mr Livingstone simply sank to his knees and slid the umbrella around underneath the chest to help locate and retrieve the missing bosom.

'Do you want any help?' asked Mr Merivale.

'No thanks,' said Mr Livingstone, without looking up. 'Don't hang around here. You'll draw attention to us. Go and wait for us in the lounge.' He waved the umbrella around again underneath the chest.

'I think I've found it!' he said. He waved the umbrella around again and dragged out an old slipper.

Chapter Sixty One

Ms Jones BA hadn't found Mrs Caldicot. But, instead, she had found Mr Muller-Hawksmoor. He was wandering disconsolately around the empty bedrooms upstairs. The census wasn't going well. He had heard a lot of noise but had got there minutes after Doris and the rest had all headed back downstairs.

'They've got another nurse,' said Ms Jones BA glumly.

Mr Muller-Hawksmoor stared at her.

'It's true, I'm afraid,' said Ms Jones BA, seeing the disappointment and frustration on Mr Muller-Hawksmoor's face.

'Another nurse? And she works here?'

'So she says. The residents claim she does too.'

'I bet she's a fake,' said Mr Muller-Hawksmoor firmly. 'Someone dressed up as a nurse.' He wasn't going to let his £50,000 windfall blow away this easily.

Suddenly Ms Jones BA snapped her fingers in delight. 'Do you know, you're right!' she said, excitedly. If she had been an entirely different person she might have kissed Mr Muller-Hawksmoor. 'I know where I've seen Doris before!' she said.

'Where?'

'That man who calls around to take Mrs Caldicot out. What's his name?' She struggled for a moment. 'Jenkins! That's his name. I heard someone say he's a journalist.' She looked very pleased with herself. 'I knew I'd seen her somewhere before!' she said.

'Never seen him,' said Mr Muller-Hawksmoor. 'He's Mrs Caldicot's boyfriend, you say?'

'Absolutely. I'm certain.'

'Right!' said Mr Muller-Hawksmoor, tucking his clipboard under his arm and rubbing his hands with glee. 'I'll soon expose this little scam.'

CHAPTER SIXTY TWO

Mr Roxdale, Miss Nightingale, Mr Williams, Mr and Mrs Merivale and the rest of the residents headed for the lounge where they found Mrs Caldicot and Mrs Roberts sitting facing Mrs Torridge offering her encouragement. Miss Smith, Mrs Roberts's friend, wearing a nurse's uniform, sat nearby. She had worked in nursing homes and rest homes for nearly twenty years and thought she'd seen everything. It wasn't the sight of a resident tied up which surprised her, but the sight of a resident who was tied up being encouraged to escape. Normally, in the homes where she had worked, the residents who were tied up were intended to stay that way.

'Come on, Mrs Torridge!' said Mrs Caldicot. 'You're doing brilliantly.'

Mrs Torridge had, by rubbing her mouth against her shoulder managed to free part of the restraint which kept the yellow bloomers in her mouth. As a result of this energetic endeavour Mr Roxdale's tie, the restraint holding the gag in place, had slid down towards her chin. Another half an inch and it would fall down around her neck, loose and irrelevant. At the same time Mrs Torridge had, by bouncing up and down in her chair, succeeded in loosening the ropes which bound her.

'Marvellous!' cried Mrs Roberts, enthusiastically.

The others, seeing that Mrs Torridge was very nearly free, offered her their verbal encouragement.

Suddenly Mr Muller-Hawksmoor burst into the room, followed at some distance, by Ms Jones BA.

'I'm sorry to butt in on what is undoubtedly a very important part of your management responsibilities,' said Mr Muller-Hawksmoor to Mrs Caldicot. 'But I believe that you're trying to pull the wool over our eyes!'

'What on earth do you mean by that?' demanded Mrs Caldicot, with all the indignation of genuine innocence. She stood up, closely followed by Mrs Roberts and her friend the nurse.

'Is that the woman you claim is a staff member?' demanded Mr Muller-Hawksmoor, pointing at Miss Smith.

'She is a member of staff,' said Mrs Caldicot, quite accurately. 'But just not here,' she muttered under her breath. 'She's a fully-qualified nurse,' said Mrs Roberts.

'Ha. That is no woman!' said Mr Muller-Hawksmoor. 'Here is your fraud!' And with that he strode across to Miss Smith.

'No!' cried Ms Jones BA. 'Not that one!' But it was too late. Mr Muller-Hawksmoor had already struck. He dropped his clipboard on the now empty sofa. With his left hand he took a good chunk of Mrs Roberts's friend's hair. And with his right he tore at the front of her uniform. His attempt to remove what he imagined to be a wig was, inevitably, a dismal failure since the hair he had got hold of was firmly attached to Mrs Roberts's friend's head. His lunge at her uniform was far more successful and while Ms Jones BA stood behind him frozen in horror, her arm outstretched in a belated attempt to stop Mr Muller-Hawksmoor, her colleague tore the woman's uniform from the neck to the hem, scattering buttons and badges all over the carpet. 'This nurse is a man!' cried Mr Muller-Hawksmoor. It was quickly apparent that this accusation would receive no points for accuracy.

'Help!' screamed Mrs Roberts's friend, attempting to cover up her semi-nakedness in the time honoured fashion. One hand across her bra and the other across her floral knickers. There could now be no doubt at all that Mrs Roberts's friend was not Jenkins in disguise. Nor could there be doubt that Mr Muller-Hawksmoor's allegation was entirely unjustified and unjustifiable.

'Oh dear me,' said Mr Muller-Hawksmoor. Horrified, he stepped back. 'Oh, golly. I'm so sorry...'

Mrs Roberts's friend was no shrinking violet. She had been in not entirely dissimilar situations before. Indeed, on one occasion, at a doctors' party at the hospital where she had trained, she had found herself in a situation which bore a startling resemblance to this one. But if a man was going to tear off her clothes in public she expected him to, at the very least, ply her with substantial amounts of alcohol and flattery. Mr Muller-Hawksmoor had done neither of these things. Abandoning her modest pose she pulled her right arm back, took a good pace forward and aimed a solid fist at Mr Muller-Hawksmoor's jaw.

Unfortunately, just as her fist shot out Mr Muller-Hawksmoor moved slightly to one side. Ms Jones BA, standing behind him did not move. The nurse's fist landed not on the nose of Mr Muller-Hawksmoor's but on the nose of Ms Jones BA. Ms Jones, although hit only a glancing blow, collapsed as though felled by a boxing ox. When she realised that she had missed her primary target the nurse let fly with her other fist. This time the intended target was the recipient.

Mr Muller-Hawksmoor hit the floor at almost exactly the same moment that Mrs Torridge succeeded in spitting out her gag and freeing herself of the ropes which had bound her. Mrs Torridge was not a woman for whom a grudge was a long-term affair. For her a grudge was something to get rid of in as rapid and as dramatic a fashion as was possible. 'Hoorah!' she shouted. She took two strides to where Ms Jones BA was attempting to sit up, bent down and proceeded to flatten the council employee with a single, effective blow. Ms Jones BA collapsed again and lay sprawled on top of Mr Muller-Hawksmoor's unconscious body. Mrs Torridge, avenged, stood and beamed.

'Well, I do declare,' said Mrs Caldicot, who had watched these events with all the curiosity of a disinterested spectator.

Just then Doris and Mr Livingstone entered the room. Mr Livingstone had succeeded in locating and rescuing Doris's missing grapefruit and the well-rounded citrus fruit, restored to its temporary owner, had been reinstalled in its new home.

'Mrs Caldicot,' said Mr Livingstone, taking advantage of the fact that both Mr Muller-Hawksmoor and Ms Jones BA were no longer taking much interest in the proceedings and stepping over the scattered bodies as though this was something he did every day of his life, 'I think you should meet Doris Knight, your new nurse,' he said.

Mrs Caldicot's reaction was not quite what he, or anyone else in the room, expected.

She burst into laughter. 'So,' she said eventually. 'Would someone like to explain to me why Jenkins is dressed up as a nurse with what looks very much like two grapefruit stuffed down his dress?'

Jenkins stared at her. 'Well damn me,' he said. 'You saw through it.'

'Would anyone like a cup of tea?' Mrs Caldicot asked. There was much murmuring of assent. 'I'll put the kettle on,' she said. She turned to Jenkins. 'Perhaps you'd be kind enough to ring for an ambulance, nurse,' she said.

Chapter Sixty Three

By the time the ambulance arrived both Mr Muller-Hawksmoor and Ms Jones BA had regained consciousness. Ms Jones BA, still sitting on the carpet, turned towards Mrs Caldicot. 'What happened?' she asked.

'You keep still, love,' one of the ambulance men told her. 'We'll have you on a stretcher in just a jiffy.'

'I don't need a stretcher!' snapped Ms Jones BA, turning towards the ambulance man and attempting, unsuccessfully, to struggle to her feet. She turned back to Mrs Caldicot and repeated her question.

'I'm afraid that Mr Muller-Hawksmoor sexually assaulted one of our nurses,' Mrs Caldicot told her. 'He tore off her dress and exposed her. You were helping him. The nurse simply defended herself.'

Ms Jones BA remembered. She would have gone pale, had her natural skin colour allowed such a thing. 'I wasn't helping him,' she said. There was a catch in her voice. 'I was trying to stop him!' she protested, rather weakly.

'I'm afraid that isn't quite how it seemed to the rest of us,' said Mrs Caldicot rather coldly.

'He thought the nurse was a fraud,' said Ms Jones BA. 'I ... er ... we ... thought she was a man I recognised.'

'She wasn't,' pointed out Mrs Caldicot.

'No,' agreed Ms Jones BA. She closed her eyes and shuddered. 'I remember.'

'Come along now, love,' said the ambulance man, trying once again to move Ms Jones BA onto a stretcher which he had arranged on the floor next to her.

'I'm not your 'love'!' snarled Ms Jones BA. The ambulance man recoiled, as though threatened by a snake. Ms Jones BA pushed away his helping hand and stood up. She wobbled for a moment and then sat down on the arm of a nearby easy chair. The ambulance man, looking rather hurt, picked up his stretcher and moved across to his colleague, who was kneeling next to Mr Muller-Hawksmoor.

'What happened?' asked Mr Muller-Hawksmoor, blinking and looking around him. There was a trickle of blood running from his nose and he still had a rather dazed look. He had never been hit before, let alone knocked out.

Ms Jones BA told him. She did not spare him any of the details. Mr Muller-Hawksmoor, being quite capable of going pale went pale. The pallor increased as he gradually realised the full consequences of what he had done.

'Is the nurse going to, er, press charges?' Mr Muller-Hawksmoor asked Mrs Caldicot.

'I don't think so,' replied Mrs Caldicot. 'Can I assume that this visit is now over and that you're happy with our staffing arrangements?'

'Oh absolutely,' said Mr Muller-Hawksmoor, eagerly. 'Very satisfied.' He did not struggle as the ambulancemen moved him onto their stretcher. He turned to Ms Jones BA as they wrapped a blanket around him.

A couple of minutes later the ambulance left, siren squealing, with Mr Muller-Hawksmoor in the back.

Ms Jones BA, having rejected offers of a cup of tea or a bed for an hour or two, drove after the ambulance. She was not a good driver and as her little car jumped and bounced down the rutted drive she had to concentrate hard on what she was doing. She had to concentrate so hard, in fact, that as the car left the driveway she did not notice the three people standing on the pavement nearby selling their last few bunches of flowers.

CHAPTER SIXTY FOUR

The flower selling was going very well.

The arrival of Jenkins, still dressed as Doris, had added the glamour which Mr Roxdale and Mr Williams had been unable to provide, and had provided evidence to support the old adage that you can use sex – even the rather superficial sexual artifice of a middle-aged man and two grapefruit sharing a frock – to sell virtually anything.

Attracted by the grapefruit rather than the middle-aged man cars squealed to a halt by the pavement's edge and Mr Roxdale and Mr Williams sold every freesia, carnation, rose and dahlia in minutes.

'So,' said Mr Roxdale, contemplating several buckets, containing nothing but a few broken green stalks and some slightly grubby water, 'now what shall we do?'

'We could mend the roof,' suggested Mr Williams, without a moment's hesitation. 'That would give Mrs Caldicot a nice surprise.'

'That's a splendid idea,' agreed Mr Roxdale, with a nod of approval. 'Mrs Caldicot would be delighted.'

'She's been trying for weeks to find someone to put those loose slates back,' said Mr Williams.

'Even if she could find someone they'd no doubt charge a fortune,' said Mr Roxdale.

'So we'll do it,' said Mr Williams.

'It can't be all that hard,' said Mr Roxdale.

'I shouldn't think so,' agreed Mr Williams. 'But we'll need a ladder.'

'Can't do it without a ladder,' nodded Mr Roxdale.

'Big ladder,' said Mr Williams. 'Have to be a big ladder.'

'Long way up to the roof,' said Mr Roxdale.

'Long way,' agreed Mr Williams.

Jenkins, still disguised as Doris, feared that mending roofs might prove more demanding than selling flowers. 'Does either of you know anything about mending roofs?' he asked.

'Don't be a wet blanket,' said Mr Williams, sharply.

'It can't be all that difficult,' insisted Mr Roxdale. 'I've known several roofers and they were all complete idiots. I knew one who failed his driving test three times.'

'I know where there's a ladder,' said Mr Williams. 'I saw one round the back. In the shed. Hanging on two nails on the wall.'

'What on earth has failing a driving test got to do with mending roofs?' asked Jenkins.

It was not an entirely unreasonable question but the other two didn't hear him and so they didn't bother to try and answer. They were halfway up the driveway, carrying their empty buckets (they had emptied the water down a nearby drain and stuffed the remaining bits of greenery behind a bush so that they could, as Mr Roxdale put it, 'compost down') and hurrying towards the hut where Mr Williams felt sure he had seen a ladder.

CHAPTER SIXTY FIVE

They found the old wooden ladder and carried it around to the front of the house.

'Gosh,' said Mr Roxdale, looking up. 'They put the roof up very high, didn't they?'

Mr Williams started up the ladder, reached the third rung and stopped. 'I feel dizzy,' he said. 'Hold the ladder. It keeps going round and round.'

'You're only two feet off the ground,' Mr Roxdale told him. 'And I am holding the ladder.'

'I never did have much of a head for heights,' Mr Williams admitted.

'I'll blindfold you,' suggested Mr Roxdale. 'If you can't see anything you'll be fine.'

'What are you going to do when you get up there?' asked Jenkins.

'He's going to mend the roof,' said Mr Roxdale. 'He can either take off the blindfold or else I'll shout instructions.'

'But what's he going to mend the roof with?' asked Jenkins.

Neither of the other two said anything. Mr Williams, still standing on the ladder, turned and looked at Mr Roxdale. Mr Roxdale looked back at him.

'He won't know that until he takes a look around,' said Mr Roxdale. 'If the slates have just slipped then all he needs to do is to climb onto the roof and push them around a bit.'

'I'm going to get out of this dress,' said Jenkins, deciding that things were getting a little too serious for him to be sharing a dress with two grapefruit. He hurried off towards the front door.

As he disappeared Mr Williams turned, clearly startled. 'No one said anything about climbing onto the roof. I don't like this 'all he needs to do is climb onto the roof' stuff. What do you think I am? A cat?' Clearly unhappy, he stepped back down a rung. The wooden rung, which had held his weight when he'd been going up decided that it had had enough and snapped in two.

'That's it,' he said, jumping down onto the ground. 'I've had enough. I'm not going up there again. It was terrifying.'

'Hello, there,' said another voice. 'What are you lot doing?' They all turned. It was Mr Merivale. They explained.

'But we're all a bit nervous,' admitted Mr Williams. 'It's a long way up and the ladder is rotten.'

'You speak for yourself,' said Mr Roxdale. 'I didn't say I was nervous.'

'Then why don't you go up the ladder?' demanded Mr Williams, not unreasonably.

'Someone has got to stay down here and give instructions,' said Mr Roxdale. 'I'm management.'

'Since when?' asked Mr Williams.

'Since we decided to mend the roof,' replied Mr Roxdale.

'I'll go up,' offered Mr Merivale.

'OK!' said Mr Williams and Mr Roxdale simultaneously. 'If you insist,' added Mr Williams.

Gingerly, Mr Merivale tested the bottom rung of the ladder with his foot. It snapped in two. He tested another rung, by putting his weight onto it. That broke too. Now the bottom three rungs were all broken. 'Is this the best ladder you've got?' he asked.

'It's the only one we've got,' replied Mr Williams.

'I really don't think you should go up it,' said Mr Williams. 'I don't think it looks very safe.'

Mr Merivale smiled at him, put his right foot onto the edge of the lowest remaining rung and launched himself upwards. He scampered up the ladder more like a monkey than a man and reached the top in less time than it would have taken any of the others to run the same distance on the flat. Every rung snapped as he ran upwards. As soon as Mr Merivale reached the top of the ladder he clambered onto the roof and Mr Roxdale, down below, was left holding two long thin pieces of wood which were no longer connected to one another.

'He made it!' said Mr Williams.

Mr Roxdale struggled to hold onto the two separated poles but failed. The two side pieces of the former ladder fell sideways and crashed onto the ground.

'That was absolutely amazing!' said Mr Roxdale. He and Mr Williams clapped enthusiastically

'What do I do now I'm up here?' yelled Mr Merivale, peering over the edge of the roof and shouting down. He waited for some response.

But down below Mr Roxdale and Mr Williams had panicked and had rushed into the house to fetch help.

There was a long pause. 'Er ... why did I come up here?' Mr Merivale called. 'Is anyone there? Hello? Hello? Is anyone there?'

CHAPTER SIXTY SIX

There was some dispute about who panicked first.

Mr Williams claimed that it was Mr Roxdale. 'It was definitely Mr Roxdale,' he still claims. 'Mr Roxdale ran into the house and telephoned for the fire brigade.'

'I didn't panic at all,' insisted Mr Roxdale. 'Mr Williams was hysterical. He was convinced that Mr Merivale was going to fall off the roof. I quietly walked into the house and telephoned for the fire brigade before things got completely out of control.'

The fire brigade arrived within ten minutes (a huge, bright red engine and a large number of large men still buttoning up their tunics and stuffing stockinged feet into their boots, as though they had all been disturbed at some extraordinary single sex orgy) but by then it was dark. The residents and staff of the Twilight Years Rest Home were gathering and standing on the lawn looking up at the roof. Jenkins had had time to take off his dress but not time to put on his trousers. He shivered in Doris's underwear.

'I can't see any fire,' said Mr Livingstone, who had left the house with Mr Roxdale to join Mr Williams on the lawn and was now peering up at the house, the roof and the sky, searching in vain for flames or smoke.

Before leaving the house Mr Livingstone had broken the glass on the fire alarm just inside the front door. It was something he had always wanted to do but the fulfilling of this simple ambition had, in the effect, proved to be rather disappointing.

'There's isn't a fire,' said Mr Roxdale. 'Someone is stuck up on the roof.'

'The ladder simply fell apart,' explained Mr Williams.

'Why did he go up there in the first place?' asked Mr Livingstone.

Mr Roxdale explained.

'Who is it?' demanded Mrs Merivale. 'Who's stuck up there?'

Mr Williams looked at her and placed a comforting hand on her arm. 'It's Mr Merivale,' he said.

'My Mr Merivale?' said Mrs Merivale.

'Yes,' admitted Mr Livingstone. 'I'm afraid it is.'

'Oh well he'll be all right,' said Mrs Merivale. 'Who on earth called the fire brigade?' she demanded. Mr Livingstone stared at her and assumed that she was in shock. 'I'll fetch you a blanket and a cup of tea,' he said. 'Would you like some brandy in it or just sugar?'

'What's happened?' demanded Mrs Roberts, looking up at

the front of the house. 'Where's the fire?' On Mrs Caldicot's instructions she had left the house to start a roll call of the residents.

Mr Roxdale explained.

'Who's in charge here?' demanded a stout, round-faced man whose helmet carried a very large badge and an instantly identifiable yellow flash.

'Mrs Caldicot,' said Mrs Roberts. 'She'll be here in a moment,' she began. 'Oh, there she is!' she said, interrupting herself and pointing towards the front door where Mrs Caldicot was following Miss Nightingale and Mrs Peterborough down the steps. Mrs Caldicot was holding Kitty and a torch. Kitty looked very upset at having been moved from her warm place in front of the fire.

'Is everyone out of the building?' demanded the stout man, striding over towards Mrs Caldicot.

'I'm not sure,' replied Mrs Caldicot. She walked towards Mrs Roberts, standing with the residents and asked her the same question. She remembered, too late, that she had forgotten to put the fireguard in front of the fire.

'Everyone except Mr Merivale,' said Mrs Roberts.

'Mr Merivale?' called out Mrs Caldicot. She decided that not having put the guard in front of the fire didn't much matter if the house was already on fire.

'I'm here,' said Mr Merivale from the darkness at the outer edge of the group.

'Everyone is accounted for,' said Mrs Caldicot, feeling a great sense of relief.

'We had a report that there was a man stuck on a roof,' said the chief fire officer.

'Perhaps I can explain,' said Mr Roxdale. 'It was an accident.'

'I rather thought it might have been,' said the chief fire officer, drily. 'Most of our 'men stuck on roofs' incidents are accidents. Where exactly is he and what happened?'

'I'm not sure where he is. We can't see him. But a friend of ours climbed up onto the roof to repair some slipped slates,' explained Mr Roxdale. 'And then the ladder broke.'

The chief fire officer removed his helmet and scratched his head. 'And he's still up there?'

'He must be,' said Mr Roxdale. 'He couldn't have come down because we don't have another ladder.' He lowered his voice and looked around to make sure that no one else was listening before adding, 'And if he had fallen off we'd see the body, wouldn't we?'

The chief fire officer walked over to the fire engine and gave some brief instructions. Moments later the fire engine's huge ladder swung into action, slowly rising up into the sky. A fireman stood on the top rung of the ladder and rose with it. A searchlight attached to the top of the ladder lit up the house roof.

At the back of the crowd Mr Merivale put his arm around his wife. 'Exciting, isn't it?' he said to her. She looked at him. 'I thought it was you up there.'

'Oh no,' he replied. 'I came down. It was cold and I didn't know what I was supposed to be doing up there anyway.'

'That's good,' said Mrs Merivale. 'Would you like me to get you some cake in a minute?'

'That would be nice,' said Mr Merivale. 'And a cup of tea perhaps. Who's up there? Do you know?'

'I dunno,' replied his wife. 'Someone said it was you but I told them they wouldn't need the fire brigade to get you down. How did you get down? Down a drainpipe?'

'No. The guttering and down pipes were all too loose. I just took a few slates off the roof, climbed down into the loft and then came down the stairs,' Mr Merivale told her.

'Best way,' nodded his wife, who after being married to a film stunt man for forty years was accustomed to her husband's acrobatic ways.

Chapter Sixty Seven

'I can't see anyone up here,' shouted the fireman at the top of the ladder. 'But there's a big hole in the roof.'

'That's why we wanted to go up there,' explained Mr

Roxdale to Mrs Caldicot. 'We thought we'd mend the roof for you. As a sort of surprise. Mr Merivale climbed up but the ladder broke.'

'That was very sweet of you,' said Mrs Caldicot. 'But there shouldn't have been a big hole in the roof. There was only a tiny leak.'

'The slates have all been removed very carefully,' said the fireman at the top of the ladder. 'None of them are broken.'

'Very odd,' said the chief fire officer. 'Is the hole big enough for a man to get through?' he shouted back.

'Yes,' came the reply.

'I'm just popping indoors to get some cake and a cup of tea for my husband,' said Mrs Merivale to Mrs Caldicot. 'Shall I make enough for everyone?'

'Would your men like a cup of tea and a piece of cake?' asked Mrs Caldicot.

'Well, that's very nice of you,' agreed the chief fire officer. 'I dare say they wouldn't say no. Would that be home-made cake?'

'It certainly would,' said Mrs Caldicot. 'And Mrs Merivale is a splendid cook.' She turned back to Mrs Merivale. 'Tea and cake for everyone then, please,' she said. 'Do you need some help? I could ask someone to help you if you like.'

'Oh no, don't you worry, Mrs Caldicot' said Mrs Merivale. 'Mr Merivale will give me a hand.' And off she trotted.

It was several seconds before Mrs Caldicot realised exactly what Mrs Merivale had said.

CHAPTER SIXTY EIGHT

The chief fire officer was very understanding.

'Just delighted that everything turned out well,' he said, alternately sipping a mug of Mrs Merivale's tea and munching a large slice of her very best coffee and walnut cake. 'How old did you say that chap was who climbed back through the roof?'

'When I last asked he told me that he was eighty-something,' said Mrs Caldicot. 'Probably.' She didn't like to admit that her residents had now all stopped telling the truth about their ages.

'Amazing,' said the chief fire officer. 'Would you like us to mend that hole in your roof while we're here?' he asked.

'That would be very kind of you,' agreed Mrs Caldicot. 'But I don't want to put you to any trouble...'

'No trouble at all,' the chief fire officer assured her. 'A couple of my blokes do a little roofing in their spare time,' he added. He called one of his men and gave him instructions. The fireman raced up the ladder to the roof and had the slates fixed back in position in minutes.

'Good as new,' he said, when he was back down on the ground. Mrs Merivale handed him a plate containing a large piece of carrot cake, two buttered scones and a slice of treacle tart.

'Well, at least all this added a bit of excitement to your life,' said the chief fire officer, as they prepared to leave. 'I expect it's a bit dull running an old people's home.'

CHAPTER SIXTY NINE

'How much did we make out of selling flowers?' asked Mr Williams, as he and Mr Roxdale had breakfast together the following morning.

'With Doris's help we got up to £112.45,' replied Mr Roxdale. 'That was the takings. But since we didn't have any costs it was also the profits.'

'Not bad. But it's going to take us for ever to raise a decent amount of money,' said Mr Williams.

'And we've sold most of the stuff from my old garden,' said Mr Roxdale with a sigh. 'It'll be months before we have anything else ready to sell.'

'I do wish Mrs Caldicot would accept another couple of photographs,' said Mr Williams, who had, some time before, confided in his friend. 'It would solve a lot of problems.'

'Women can be stubborn sometimes,' said Mr Roxdale. 'It'll probably be pride.'

'Maybe we could think of a way to persuade her to take the money in another way,' said Mr Williams.

They sat for a few moments in silence.

'We're holding a jumble sale soon,' said Mr Roxdale, 'Perhaps you could slip a couple of photographs onto the bric-a-brac stall?'

Mr Williams thought about this. 'They'd probably get sold for 10 pence a piece,' he said, glumly.

'That's true,' agreed Mr Roxdale.

'But maybe there is another way...' said Mr Williams with a big smile.

CHAPTER SEVENTY

It was the day of the jumble sale and fête and, much to everyone's surprise, it wasn't raining. On the contrary, the sky was blue, the clouds were small, white and fluffy and the sun was shining brightly. It was, all things considered, pretty much a perfect day for an outdoor event of any kind.

The event was due to start at 10 am and by 9.30 am all the stalls were stocked and manned. Miss Nightingale and Mrs Peterborough were in charge of the bottle stall, Mrs Torridge was selling hand-coloured paper doilies (each one allegedly painted by Rembrandt's long lost great niece), Mr Livingstone was running a sideshow where visitors could rent three wooden balls for 50p and then throw them at pieces of crockery set out on the shelves of the Welsh dresser borrowed from the kitchen, Mr Williams had organised a competition to guess how many dried peas there were in a jar and the Merivales were running the cake stall (fairy cakes, rock buns, slices of sponge cake all 50p each). Other residents were similarly occupied looking after other stalls. Mr Twist was in charge of collecting and counting the takings. Kitty, who was, as usual, in charge of sleeping was taking a long rest underneath the cake stall. The 'throwing water over the vicar' stall had been abandoned; largely as a result of an acute shortage of vicars.

The first visitors, an elderly couple who were friends of the Merivales, arrived at 10.15 am. They visited the roll a penny stall (and won a bottle of tomato ketchup) and the bottle stall (and won a bottle of brown sauce). They bought two cups of tea, two rock cakes and three paperback books from a stall run by Mr Roxdale. The next visitors, a family of three who had seen the stalls from the road as they had been passing by, arrived at 10.50 am, invested £2.50 in fruitless attempts to win a goldfish and left, grumbling, at 10.58 am.

At 11.03 am Miss Nightingale's niece Daisy arrived on her way to the airport. She kept her taxi waiting and stopped just long enough to win a bottle of pickled eggs and buy a pair of dark green fingerless gloves from Mr Roxdale's jumble stall.

'The residents and I have got a little surprise for you,' said Miss Nightingale, just before her niece rushed off again. She shyly handed Daisy a battered, elderly suitcase. Puzzled, and feeling rather embarrassed to receive a gift when she herself did not have one to give, Daisy accepted the bag, put it down on a nearby stall and tugged at the zip which opened to reveal a mass of small bottles and packets.

'We all collected some pills for you,' explained Miss Nightingale. 'None of them have been used.'

Daisy opened the bag, plunged a hand in and pulled out, at random, several unopened packets of antibiotics and a sealed bottle of painkillers. She was crying with joy and appreciation when she left and gave everyone except Mr Roxdale a kiss and a cuddle. Mr Roxdale, who ran to the end of the line, managed to get kissed and cuddled twice.

'So that's why poor old Dr Bence-Jones spent hours writing out prescriptions,' said Mrs Caldicot.

'Please don't be cross with us,' said Miss Nightingale. 'It was in a good cause.'

'It was in a good cause,' said Mrs Peterborough.

Mrs Caldicot smiled at them both. 'Why on earth should I be cross with you?' she asked them. 'I'm very proud of you all.'

After the excitement of Daisy's visit, the stallholders and jumble salesmen and women had a respite, and yet another opportunity to view one another's wares and prizes, until the next arrival at 11.40 am. The next arrival was Jenkins.

'Are we too early?' the immaculately suited newspaperman asked Mrs Caldicot, who was standing talking to Mrs Roberts.

'No,' replied Mrs Caldicot. 'We're just having something of a lull at the moment.'

'I've brought Samantha Duck-Warmington,' said Jenkins, introducing his companion, a leggy blonde woman who looked about 18 and was wearing gold, high-heeled shoes and a tight fitting gold lamé dress that appeared to have been manufactured out of a piece of material just about large enough to make a hand-kerchief. Her enormous, unrealistically firm breasts appeared to be balanced on a tiny shelf inside the dress. She was dragging behind her a huge aluminium coloured suitcase, the tiny wheels of which did not move well on the lawn.

Mrs Caldicot smiled at the woman but, to her surprise, was conscious that she felt an inexplicable antagonism towards her.

'Samantha reads the weather forecasts on a Welsh Cable Television station programme,' explained Jenkins. 'She was in the area for the weekend and kindly agreed to come along and officially open the fête for you.'

'Oh that's very kind of you, dear,' said Mrs Caldicot to Samantha. She realised, with some surprise, that she disliked Samantha because she was jealous.

'It's a pleasure, I'm sure,' said Samantha, beaming insincerely. 'Can you show me to my dressing room, please?'

'I beg your pardon?'

'My dressing room,' repeated Samantha. 'So that I can change into something more suitable for the photographers.'

Mrs Caldicot was about to point out that the only photographer present was Mr Williams who was, she felt certain, unlikely to have had much experience as a paparazzi photographer, when Mrs Roberts spoke.

'Shall I take Samantha to her dressing room?' she asked. 'I think we decided that your office would be suitable?'

'Oh, thank you, Mrs Roberts,' said Mrs Caldicot, now wondering just what Samantha had in her bag which she felt would be more suitable wear for a jumble sale among geriatrics.

'I'm sorry about Samantha,' said Jenkins, when she and Mrs Roberts had gone. 'I asked our show business department to find someone who was free and willing to come along and open the jumble sale for you.' He shrugged. 'But there must be some big show business event going on somewhere else today. When my reporters rang round all their contacts they found that everyone famous was busy today. Samantha was all they could find.'

'She seems very young,' said Mrs Caldicot.

CHAPTER SEVENTY ONE

It wasn't until 12.55 pm that Mrs Caldicot realised that the day wasn't going to go quite as she had expected.

She and Jenkins were eating crumbly pies, sipping tea from plastic beakers and wondering whether the good weather would hold when a limousine cruised into the driveway. The number of guests had, by now, risen quite considerably and the event no longer looked quite so forlorn. The limousine stopped and most of the residents and guests, including Mrs Caldicot and Jenkins, stopped what they were doing to see who got out of it.

'That man looks like Michael Caine,' said Mrs Caldicot to Jenkins.

'That man is Michael Caine,' said Jenkins.

Mrs Caldicot turned and looked at him.

'One of the reporters must have got lucky,' explained Jenkins. 'I wish they'd telephoned and let me know.'

Mr Caine straightened his jacket, looked around, as though searching for someone he was expecting to see, and smiled generically as people recognised him. Suddenly, there was something of a commotion from near the cake stall and Mrs Merivale, followed closely by her husband, hurried across to greet the film star. The film star put his arm around her and gave her a kiss. She kissed him back. Mr Caine then shook hands warmly with Mr Merivale and punched him playfully on the shoulder.

'They know him,' whispered Mrs Caldicot. 'Mr and Mrs Merivale really do know him!'

'He was one of the stars they said they would invite,' remembered Jenkins. Out of the corner of his eye he noticed that several of the guests had taken out their mobile phones and were excitedly calling friends to tell them who had arrived and what they were missing.

'I don't believe it,' whispered Mrs Caldicot. 'Look,' she added, 'they're bringing him over here.' Moments later Maple Merivale introduced Mr Caine to Mrs Caldicot and Jenkins and Mrs Caldicot and Jenkins to Mr Caine.

'Thank you so much for coming,' Mrs Caldicot managed to croak.

'It's a pleasure,' said Mr Caine, with a beaming smile. 'I'd never turn down an invitation from Maple and Maurice.'

'You, er, all know one another, then?' said Mrs Caldicot.

Mr Caine laughed. 'Know them? I love them both dearly,' he said with evident sincerity. 'I can't remember how many times we've worked together. Maple is a wonderful cook. Film crews all over the world loved her. It broke everyone's heart when she retired. She must have prepared more bacon sandwiches than any woman alive.' He turned to Maurice. 'And Maurice was one of the most amazing stunt men I've ever worked with.' He hesitated then grinned. 'This guy,' he said, 'once won a bet that he could shin up the outside of a building faster than anyone else could get up using the lift or the stairs.' He laughed. Maurice looked embarrassed and modestly lowered his eyes.

'Excuse me, Mr Caine,' said a middle-aged woman in a flowery dress and a straw hat. She thrust a mobile telephone towards his face. 'Would you just say hello to my mother? She's a great fan of yours.'

Unflustered, and with great grace, Mr Caine took the

telephone and spoke to the invisible fan. As he did so a large gleaming green Bentley purred into the driveway and pulled up behind Mr Caine's limousine. The chauffeur got out and opened the back door.

'I don't believe it,' said Mrs Caldicot. 'Look who's getting out. It's Roger Moore!'

CHAPTER SEVENTY TWO

By 2 pm there were seven limousines, Bentleys and Rolls Royces parked in the driveway and Mr Caine and Mr Moore had been joined by (in order of their arrival) Sean Connery, Joan Collins, Peter O'Toole, Pierce Brosnan, Glenda Jackson and Dame Judi Dench. Each one had been invited by the Merivales and each one greeted both Maple and Maurice with kisses, hugs and obvious great delight. The relatively small number of stars who hadn't been able to turn up (in every case because they were filming out of the country) had sent their sincerest apologies and promised that they would be delighted to visit another time.

Not surprisingly, the number of other visitors present on the lawn at the Twilight Years Rest Home had also increased. A generation or two ago the news of such an event would have been spread by word of mouth and limited by the speed at which legs could carry the messengers (and their willingness to leave the scene of all the excitement). Today those present could spread the news in seconds, without moving an inch – simply by pressing a few buttons on their mobile telephones.

The stars mingled easily and willingly, both with one another and with the eager autograph hunters. Cameras flashed incessantly as visitors recorded themselves standing next to their heroes and heroines.

'Excuse me, ma'am, are you Mrs Caldicot?' said a smartly uniformed senior looking policeman.

Mrs Caldicot confirmed her identity.

'I wish you'd given us a little notice of this,' said the police officer, rather sternly. 'I've brought over as many men as I can spare. I hope the local football crowd behaves itself. We've had to bring in most of the chaps from the local ground.' Mrs Caldicot started to explain, realised that she couldn't and so just nodded weakly and said 'Thank you'.

She was saved by the arrival of Samantha who had, at last, managed to complete her change of costume. She was now wearing a silver lamé dress, no more or less revealing than the one in gold, and silver high-heeled shoes. Her still unlikely looking breasts still lay quietly on display, like two pink blancmanges presented for the world's delight.

'Would you like me to perform the opening ceremony now?' Samantha asked Mrs Caldicot, seemingly unaware of the fact that the lawn and those parts of the driveway not occupied by expensive motor cars, were solid with people. The policeman, who had remained standing nearby, studied Samantha carefully until a teenage boy with a cheap camera tried to take a snap of the two together; he then blushed, coughed, looked uncomfortable and hurried away to rescue Mr Brosnan from a cluster of small, overeager boys.

'Er, oh, er, that's very kind of you,' replied Mrs Caldicot. Samantha gave Mrs Caldicot one of her best smiles. 'Oh how sweet!' she said, suddenly spotting Roger Moore talking to Joan Collins. She clapped her hands together like an excited child. 'You've hired some of those lookalikes!'

Samantha stood on an upturned wooden box which Jenkins had found underneath one of the trestle tables, and announced the fête and jumble sale officially open. She seemed blissfully unaware of the fact that no one seemed in the slightest bit interested in her or what she was doing. Jenkins delighted her by taking her photograph with a disposable camera he had bought for five times its cost from a boy of twelve who had spotted a commercial opportunity and bought a bagful of the cameras from the nearest camera shop.

Afterwards the happy weather girl mixed with the guests and posed for photographs with several film stars. Endearingly, she still did not realise that they really were film stars. She believed that she was honouring them by allowing herself to be photographed next to them. 'This will help you get your picture into the papers,' she told a smiling but slightly puzzled Peter O'Toole. 'You look just like him,' whispered the well-meaning weather girl, as she hobbled off to give Michael Caine's career a boost.

CHAPTER SEVENTY THREE

'That was a wonderful day,' said Jenkins.

'It was, wasn't it?' replied Mrs Caldicot.

The two of them stood on the steps and looked out across the lawn. The local publican, aided by two of his barmen, was reclaiming the tables and umbrellas which he had lent. Mr Roxdale and Mr Williams were helping them by offering advice and instructions. Balloons and bunting decorated the trees. One or two visitors still stood around polishing off the final few sandwiches and fancy cakes.

'Mr and Mrs Merivale really came up trumps,' said Jenkins. 'Not since the Oscars have I seen so many stars in one place at the same time.'

'I feel really guilty,' said Mrs Caldicot. 'I didn't think they really knew any of those people.'

'Nor did I,' admitted Jenkins.

'And thank you for bringing along...' Mrs Caldicot paused. 'I'm sorry I've forgotten her name again. The weather forecaster.'

Jenkins laughed and looked down at his feet. 'Samantha,' he said. 'I'm sorry about her. But at least I know now where all the stars were.'

'Sorry? Don't be silly. It was really good of you to bring her,' said Mrs Caldicot. 'She was good fun.'

'Actually she was good fun, wasn't she?' said Jenkins, brightening up. 'Perhaps not in the way she had meant...'

'I heard her tell Joan Collins that she would put in a good

word for her with you,' said Mrs Caldicot.

Jenkins, embarrassed, covered his face with his hands and shook his head. 'What did Miss Collins say?' he asked.

'She thanked Samantha very much and said it was very kind of her,' said Mrs Caldicot.

'I overheard her asking Sean Connery if he had a visiting card that she could give to her agent,' said Jenkins. 'She told him she thought he looked so much like Mr Connery that he ought to be able to get some stand-in work in the movies.'

They both giggled. Jenkins put his arm around Mrs Caldicot.

'She is very beautiful,' said Mrs Caldicot.

'You're more vibrant, more exciting, more dynamic and more beautiful than she ever could be,' said Jenkins.

Mrs Caldicot, embarrassed, looked down at her hands. They were, she could not help noticing, showing rather too many wrinkles and liver spots. She wished Jenkins wouldn't compliment her. She wondered if he meant it. She blinked and bit her lower lip to stop herself crying. For the first time in her life she had found a man who gave her compliments, and who, even more remarkably, seemed to mean them. And now he was going to America.

There was silence for a moment. Jenkins was aware that she was upset. He thought that perhaps his compliment had offended her. He took his arm from around her. 'Was it all a financial success?' he asked.

'Oh yes. The whole day hardly cost us anything,' said Mrs Caldicot.

Jenkins looked at her. 'What do you mean 'It hardly cost us anything'?'

Even in the gloaming it wasn't difficult to see that Mrs Caldicot was blushing.

'Well, we didn't charge people to come in,' confessed Mrs Caldicot. 'And there were so many people here that the stalls didn't do very good business.' She looked at Jenkins. 'Isn't it funny how word gets around? Someone told me that there were half a dozen coaches parked outside in the street. How did all those people hear about it? How did they get here? Where did they come from?'

'You didn't make any money?' said Jenkins.

'No,' admitted Mrs Caldicot. 'At least, I don't think so. The only stall that hasn't finished counting its takings is the 'Guess the Number of Dried Peas in a Bottle' stall and I don't expect they've taken very much. When the people did start coming there were so many that no one could move around to buy anything. I don't think people could get their hands into their pockets or their handbags. Most of the visitors just spent the afternoon ogling the stars and collecting autographs.' She looked up at him. 'Are you cross with me?' she asked anxiously.

He laughed. 'Cross with you? Why should I be cross with you?'

'All that effort...' began Mrs Caldicot. For a moment she looked sad. But the sadness quickly disappeared. 'But people had a good time didn't they?'

'People had a wonderful time,' Jenkins assured her. 'An absolutely brilliant time. You gave everyone a day they will never, ever forget.'

'Actually, even Roger Moore said it was quite a day,' said Mrs Caldicot. She leant closer to Jenkins. 'He wiggled his eyebrow for me,' she whispered.

Jenkins looked at her, slightly askance. 'I didn't realise you were the sort of woman who'd let Roger Moore wiggle an eyebrow at her.'

'He was wearing his glasses,' said Mrs Caldicot.

'Oh, that's all right then,' agreed Jenkins.

'Excuse me, Mrs Caldicot,' said Mrs Roberts, appearing as though by magic by her side. 'There's a telephone call for you.'

Chapter Seventy Four

'It's your son,' said Mrs Roberts, leading Mrs Caldicot to her own office. 'Derek,' she added, just in case Mrs Caldicot had forgotten his name.

'Hello, Derek,' said Mrs Caldicot, picking up the telephone.

'Why didn't you tell us?' Derek demanded, indignantly.

'Hello, Derek. How nice to hear from you. How are you, dear?' said Mrs Caldicot.

'You know that I'm an enormous fan of James Bond. And you had three of them there without telling me.'

'Did we?' said Mrs Caldicot. 'Oh yes, I suppose we did. They just popped round for the jumble sale.'

'I couldn't believe it when I heard it on the television news!'

'Gosh. Was it on the news?'

'It was the lead item!' said Derek.

'Well I never,' said Mrs Caldicot. 'I suppose it must have been a quiet day.'

'Why didn't you tell me?'

'I didn't think you'd want to come,' said Mrs Caldicot. 'You did say that you didn't want to have anything else to do with me.'

'Yes but...'

'Yes but what, dear?'

'Yes, but when I said that I didn't know that you knew Sean Connery, Roger Moore and Pierce Brosnan,' protested Derek.

'What a pity you weren't here,' sighed Mrs Caldicot. 'They were all very nice. Mr Brosnan invited me to go to the studios when they film the next Bond movie.'

There was a sound like someone choking at the other end of the telephone.

'Never mind, dear,' said Mrs Caldicot. 'I'm sure you'll bump into them all at your work.' She paused. 'Would you like a photograph?' she asked sweetly. 'Jenkins took one of me standing next to all three of them. If it comes out would you like me to send you a copy?'

'Thank you,' said Derek who could hardly speak. 'That would be lovely.'

The phone went dead.

'Was everything all right?' asked Mrs Roberts, as Mrs Caldicot put the receiver down.

'Oh yes,' smiled Mrs Caldicot. 'Everything is just fine, thank you Mrs Roberts. Let's go back outside, shall we?'

Chapter Seventy Five

'Everything all right?' asked Jenkins, when Mrs Caldicot reappeared.

'Everything is very fine, thank you,' replied Mrs Caldicot.

'Things out here are going pretty well, too,' Jenkins told her. 'You were wrong about making a loss. Mr Twist has just brought over the final figures.'

'Really?' said Mrs Caldicot, clearly surprised. 'Did we break even?'

'You did a bit better than that,' Jenkins told her. 'Tell her,' he said to Mr Twist.

'We made £24,572.16 profit,' said the accountant.

Mrs Caldicot stared at him. She couldn't think of anything to say.

'Not bad, eh?' said Jenkins.

'But how on earth...'

'It seems that a lot of people were anxious to guess the number of dried peas in a bottle,' Jenkins told her. 'What did it make?' he asked Mr Twist.

Mr Twist consulted the piece of paper he was holding. 'That stall made £24,634.34 profit. Without it there would have been a small loss.'

'But that's ridiculous!' said Mrs Caldicot, astonished. 'I can't believe it. There must be a mistake.'

'There's no mistake,' insisted Jenkins. 'I've seen the cash. There's a lot of it and it's all very real.'

'What was the prize?' asked Mrs Caldicot. She suddenly had a terrible thought. 'We weren't offering a million pound prize were we?'

'Not quite,' said Jenkins. He pulled a piece of crumpled paper out of his jacket pocket. 'The prize was a small Stilton cheese, a box of biscuits and a bottle of gherkins. All three items were donated by Mr Williams and so cost you precisely nothing.'

'Did anyone win? Did anyone guess the right number of peas?'

'Miss Nightingale won,' said Jenkins. 'She doesn't like cheese or gherkins but I gather she was delighted to win. She said it was the first time in her life that she'd ever won anything.'

Suddenly something struck Mrs Caldicot. 'Who was in charge of that stall?' she asked Mr Twist.

'Oh, that was Mr Williams,' replied Mr Twist.

Chapter Seventy Six

'I've got so many worries,' said Jenkins, a few days later, as he and Mrs Caldicot had afternoon tea together in a local hotel, 'that I don't know where to start and I don't know where to stop. I even find myself worrying about the fact that I am worrying too much. And sometimes I actually worry about whether I'm worrying enough about my worries. I worry about whether I'm worrying in the right order. I worry about whether I have lost my sense of perspective. And then I realise that I have totally lost all sense of perspective because all I seem to do is worry. I have lost the ability to differentiate between the trivial and the important.'

'I don't really feel old – I still feel the same as I did when I was twenty – but I do feel tired. Not tired of life, but tired of work and tired of trivial worries that really don't matter. I interviewed a fellow for a job the other day and I nearly didn't give him the job because I thought he was too old to cope with the stresses of the work. Just in time I realised that he was fifteen years younger than I am.'

'I'm sorry ...' began Mrs Caldicot.

'No, please,' said Jenkins. 'Let me finish. Where was I? Oh yes. I'm so overwhelmed with trivia that I no longer have the time to think or create. My life has become a treadmill of worries. Most of them inconsequential. I realised the other day that my life has become so over-crowded that I don't have any room left for new crises. I'm losing the ability to differentiate between the significant and the not so significant. If a tap starts dripping I perceive it as a major problem because I don't have any time left to assess it and deal with it for what it really is. I just worry about it and add it to my ever growing list of worries. The result is that I have become inefficient and ineffective. I work longer hours than ever but get less done.' He sighed and smiled. 'That's it,' he said. 'The bottom line is that I want my life back.'

'I hadn't realised,' said Mrs Caldicot quietly. She felt ashamed of herself. 'You've always seemed so strong. I seem to have just taken your strength for granted...'

Jenkins held up a hand. 'I'm not telling you all this because I'm begging for sympathy,' he told her. 'I'm telling you because as I have been thinking about my life I have come to realise that you are the only part of my life that I really care about. You are the only part of it that is really important. I'm telling you all this because I want you to realise that I have thought long and hard about what I am about to say.'

Mrs Caldicot looked at him and felt her heart beat faster.

'I've said 'no' to the job in America,' he told her. 'And I've handed in my notice. I'm retiring at the end of the month.'

'You're leaving the paper?'

'Yes.'

'And you're not going to America to become an important editor there?'

'No.'

'So, what are you going to do?' she asked in a whisper. She knew what she wanted the answer to be but she hardly dared hope.

'I want to spend the rest of my life with you,' Jenkins told her, and Mrs Caldicot knew at that moment that everything was going to be all right. 'And I know that means taking on all this with you,' he waved a hand to include the Twilight Years Rest Home and its residents. 'I know that this place – and, far more importantly, these people – play a large part in your life. In many ways they are your life. And I very much want to be part of your life. I would like the two of us to share a single future.'

Mrs Caldicot, who now needed windscreen wipers, could hardly see him.

Jenkins put a hand in his waistcoat pocket and took out a

small red leather box. He put the box, unopened, on the table and then, with just a very little creaking, dropped to his knee in front of her. He took her hand and looked up into her eyes.

'Thelma,' he said. 'I love you. You are a very special woman to everyone you meet. But to me you are, and always will be, the most special person in the world. Will you marry me?'

CHAPTER SEVENTY SEVEN

'Yes,' said Mrs Caldicot. 'Of course, I will marry you. I love you too.' She had known this truth so long, and yet kept it so secret, that it was a relief to no longer have to guard it. Gently, she stood up and pulled him to his feet. She held him to her and kissed him on the lips. Then she put her arms around him and held him tight. 'I've loved you for so long,' she told him. 'This is,' she said, 'truly, the happiest, most special moment of my life.'

'Better even than a Knickerbocker Glory?' he asked.

'Oh I don't know about that,' she laughed. But the laughter was so fragile it broke and turned to tears. And when the tears had gone she laughed some more. And then they kissed and held and caressed one another and they knew they would both remember for always the moment when they had told one another the truths they had both so much wanted to hear.

CHAPTER SEVENTY EIGHT

The news that Mrs Caldicot and Jenkins were getting married was greeted with universal enthusiasm by the residents of the Twilight Years Rest Home.

There was only one cloud in the blue sky overhead: the fear that Mr Muller-Hawksmoor and Ms Jones BA would come back and find another reason to shut the home down. The staff and residents tried to convince themselves that they were safe. But they all knew that they weren't.

'They won't dare come back here for a while,' said Mrs Roberts, as they all sat around in the lounge one day. 'Thanks to Miss Smith and Doris their records show that we have the right number of nurses.'

'They'll be back,' said Mrs Caldicot, with quiet, resigned certainty. 'They won't ever give up.' She paused. 'They have time, money and the rules on their side. And one day, one day they'll find something that breaks their rules and then they'll close us down.'

'So what are we going to do?' asked Mrs Roberts.

'We could close down the Twilight Years Rest Home before they do it for us,' said Mr Twist.

Mrs Roberts, horrified, stared at him. 'You aren't serious!'

'Oh yes,' said Mr Twist. 'It seems to me that the Twilight Years Rest Home has all the disadvantages of a registered home and none of the advantages.'

'What do you mean?' asked Mrs Caldicot, bewildered.

'As an officially registered Rest Home we have to abide by all the local authority's regulations,' explained Mr Twist. 'Mr Muller-Hawksmoor and Ms Jones BA can come in more or less whenever they like. And they can close us down in minutes if they find that we've broken one of those rules. It will be no excuse to say that we didn't know about the rule. I've made an assessment of the expenses we've incurred since I've been looking after the accounts and I believe that at least two thirds of our expenses are incurred solely because of rules and regulations which relate to our being a Rest Home.'

Mrs Caldicot and Mrs Roberts looked at one another. They both knew that Mr Twist was right.

'I suspect that we will be getting a visit from Mr Muller-Hawksmoor very shortly,' continued Mr Twist. 'This time he will want to check that all our fire exit instructions are available in a variety of languages approved by the European Union.'

'But everyone here speaks English!' Mrs Caldicot pointed out. Kitty, her ever loving cat, leapt up onto her lap. Mrs Caldicot made a big fuss of her.

'That doesn't matter,' said Mr Twist. 'This is a new EU regulation. It doesn't have to make sense. I found out about this by studying an EU website. There are dozens of similar new regulations being introduced during the next few months.'

'They'll be insisting that we have everything printed in Braille next,' said Mrs Roberts.

'No, I don't think that one is coming in until next year,' said Mr Twist.

'But we simply can't close down,' said Mrs Caldicot. 'That's not an option.'

'There is a way to carry on exactly as we are but without people like Mr Muller-Hawksmoor and Ms Jones BA having any control over us at all,' pointed out Mr Twist.

'What's that?' asked Mrs Caldicot, puzzled.

'The obvious alternative is simply to become a private home,' explained Mr Twist. 'Rest Homes have to be registered because they are run as commercial operations. The residents pay fees and the proprietors try to make a profit. As far as I can see here there isn't anyone regularly paying fees. And there is certainly no proprietor making a profit.'

'So we don't really need to be registered as a Rest Home?' said Mr Williams.

'There's absolutely no advantage to our being registered – but there are plenty of disadvantages,' said Mr Twist.

'But if we weren't registered as a Rest Home could everyone still stay here?' asked Mrs Roberts.

'Of course,' said Mr Twist. 'There is nothing to stop Mrs Caldicot – or Mrs Jenkins as she will become – inviting us all to stay here with her as friends. The house would become a sort of 1960s style commune. We could contribute financially as and when we were able.'

'I always wanted to live in a commune,' said Mr Livingstone beaming. 'But when I wanted to do it before – back in the 1960s – they told me I was too old for it.'

They all stared at Mr Twist. It seemed too simple. 'We could do that?' asked Mrs Caldicot.

'Oh yes,' said Mr Twist. 'And then there would be no need

to spend money on obeying all the Council's silly rules and regulations.'

'We wouldn't have to rebuild the kitchen?'

'No.'

'Or put up fire warnings in all major European languages?'

'Certainly not.'

'We wouldn't have to let Mr Muller-Hawksmoor into the building?'

'Absolutely not.'

Mrs Caldicot, stopped stroking Kitty for a moment. 'How long would it take for us to stop being a Rest Home and start being an ordinary private house – albeit with a lot of people living in it?' Kitty lifted her head and looked at Mrs Caldicot accusingly. Mrs Caldicot resumed the stroking. Kitty went back to sleep.

'I took the liberty of obtaining the necessary forms. We could be deregulated within a fortnight.'

'Can we keep the name and our sign?' asked Mrs Caldicot. 'I've rather like living at the Twilight Years Rest Home.'

'I don't see why not,' said Mr Twist.

'Then let's do it!' said Mrs Caldicot.

It was, thought Mrs Roberts, a pity that Mr Muller-Hawksmoor and Ms Jones BA, sitting in their offices several miles away, could not see the celebrations which followed this announcement. Jenkins took them out to a nearby café where, at Mrs Caldicot's suggestion, they all ordered Knickerbocker Glories.

CHAPTER SEVENTY NINE

'Now that we're not going to need to rebuild the kitchen or spend thousands of pounds complying with silly regulations we don't need all that money you gave us at the fête,' said Mrs Caldicot to Mr Williams, an hour or two later.

Mr Williams looked at her as though he didn't understand what she meant.

'What did you do?' she asked. 'Sell a few photographs and then put the proceeds into the stall receipts?'

Mr Williams sighed. 'Three,' he told her. 'I sold three photographs to a dealer in New York. Then I collected the money from the bank in one pound pieces and five pound notes and Mr Roxdale, Miss Nightingale, Mrs Peterborough and I used it to buy guesses in the 'Guess the Number of Dried Peas in a Bottle' competition. It took us ages.'

'Well it was wonderfully kind of you,' said Mrs Caldicot.

'I had to do it that way,' said Mr Williams. 'You wouldn't just let me do it the easy way – by just giving you a few photographs.'

'It was very generous of you,' repeated Mrs Caldicot. 'But now I don't need the money so you must have it back.'

'I refuse to accept it,' said Mr Williams.

'Then, perhaps we should use it to have the whole place redecorated,' said Mrs Caldicot. 'We could get rid of the old furniture and buy something new.'

'I thought you liked the old stuff,' said Mr Williams.

'I do,' agreed Mrs Caldicot. 'But...'

'Do you know whose wallpaper this is?' asked Mr Williams, waving a hand in the direction of the lounge walls.

Mrs Caldicot looked at him, puzzled. 'Well, it's ours, I think.'

'No, I mean, do you know who designed it?'

'I don't have the foggiest,' said Mrs Caldicot. She thought for a moment. 'It wasn't you, was it?'

Mr Williams laughed. 'No, it wasn't me,' he said. 'Your wallpaper and your curtains were designed by William Morris.'

Mrs Caldicot stared at him. 'Are you sure?'

'Oh, I'm absolutely sure. I once edited a book about Morris. You've got several pieces of William Morris furniture too. There's absolutely no doubt about it. You could, of course, sell the wallpaper and the curtains to a dealer or a collector. But they'd take all these beautiful things away and leave you with nothing but money.'

'I hate to ask the obvious question; but how much is all this stuff worth?' asked Mrs Caldicot.

'I have no idea,' said Mr Williams. 'The place is stuffed with valuable bits and pieces.'

'Hundreds or thousands of pounds?'

'Oh, thousands.'

'Tens of thousands?'

'Hundreds of thousands.'

Mrs Caldicot went pale. 'But it was all just here when we bought the place.'

'The previous owners obviously didn't know what they were selling. Nor, it's clear, did the estate agents.'

'What do you think we should do?'

'Enjoy it,' suggested Mr Williams.

'So we really don't need the money you gave us,' said Mrs Caldicot.

'Ah, but you do,' insisted Mr Williams. He stood up and raised his voice. 'Attention, please, ladies and gentlemen!' Everyone stopped what they were doing and looked at him. 'The fête which Mrs Caldicot organised was enormously successful and ended up with a substantial profit. Now that we don't have to spend all our money on rebuilding a perfectly good kitchen I propose that we have a huge wedding reception for our dear Mrs Caldicot and her groom; and then, while she and Mr Jenkins enjoy their honeymoon, the rest of us can recover from our headaches by taking a month's holiday at the seaside where we will make sandcastles and have daily Knickerbocker Glories.'

This announcement, which came as of much a surprise to Mrs Caldicot as everyone else, was greeted with loud cheering and clapping. There was also some stamping of feet but since the feet involved were mostly arthritic or gouty, largely clad in slippers and were being stamped on carpet this did not add greatly to the volume of noise.

'There you are,' said Mr Williams to Mrs Caldicot. 'Now we do need the money.' He grinned at her.

Mrs Caldicot looked at Jenkins, who was sitting next to her. 'I think he's got you,' Jenkins told his fiancée. 'I suggest that you just give in and gracefully accept defeat.'

'That'll be a first!' said Miss Nightingale.

'That'll be a first!' said Mrs Peterborough.

'If only they knew,' thought Mrs Caldicot, smiling to herself. Only she knew that she had spent most of her life giving in. This, however, was the first occasion on which it had been a real pleasure. 'I think a big wedding reception would be a wonderful idea,' she said.

There were more loud cheers. Taking cover of the noise Mrs Caldicot turned to Jenkins. 'Where shall we go for our honeymoon?'

'I don't care,' he told her. 'Wherever we go will be the most beautiful place on earth.'

She shed a tear.

She had never before believed that people really could cry because they were happy. Now she knew that they could. She had never, in her life, been as happy. She looked down at Kitty who was, it seemed, purring louder than ever.

For a catalogue of Vernon Coleman's books
please write to:

Publishing House
Trinity Place
Barnstaple
Devon EX32 9HJ
England

| Telephone | 01271 328892 |
| Fax | 01271 328768 |

Outside the UK:
| Telephone | +44 1271 328892 |
| Fax | +44 1271 328768 |

Or visit our website:

www.vernoncoleman.com